Look what people are saying about Susan Sleeman's *Agents Under Fire* series…

"*Web of Deceit* is a must read for any fan of suspense."
—*Gail Welborn, Seattle Examiner*

"Seriously! Oh my goodness! Full of suspense from the very beginning! I loved every minute of it! Every character was fully developed, their feelings, their emotions, and their realness totally believable."
—*Julie Graves, My Favorite Pastime Blog*

"Don't bother bringing a beverage to drink while you read because you will forget it is there, the story is that intense. Ms. Sleeman batted a thousand on this one. I highly recommend it."
—*Victor Gentile, TheSuspenseZone.com*

"Susan Sleeman has done it again!! She has got to be one of my top three suspense writers, and *Web of Deceit* just goes to show how well she can write."
—*Charity Lyman, Giveaway Lady Blog*

"A fast-paced, hard-hitting suspense novel that is one of the two or three best I have read in the past two years. Highly recommended."
—*Suspense Author, Donn Taylor*

"This book is unputdownable and will keep you on the edge of your seat! I can't wait to read the next book in the series."
—*Romantic Suspense Author, Elizabeth Goddard*

Also by Susan Sleeman from Bell Bridge Books

Agents Under Fire Series

Web of Deceit (Book 1)

Web of Shadows

Book 2 in the *Agents Under Fire* Series

by

Susan Sleeman

Bell Bridge Books

Bell Bridge Books
PO BOX 300921
Memphis, TN 38130
Print ISBN: 978-1-61194-674-1

Bell Bridge Books is an Imprint of BelleBooks, Inc.

We at BelleBooks enjoy hearing from readers.
Visit our websites
BelleBooks.com
BellBridgeBooks.com
ImaJinnBooks.com

10 9 8 7 6 5 4 3 2 1

Cover design: Deborah Smith
Interior design: Hank Smith
Photo/Art credits:
Woman (manipulated) © Mariematata | Dreamstime.com
Landscape (manipulated)© Joe Klune | Dreamstime.com

:Lswa:01:

Dedication

For my family. Ever supportive. Ever patient. And ever understanding of the crazy life of a writer. Without all of your support, none of my books would see the light of day. Thank you!

Chapter One

WILEY LIKED THE dark—liked the way the cool, silky night settled over Oregon's Columbia River Gorge. Clinging to the rocks. Cloaking him. Hiding him. Letting him slide through the fading light without detection and evade those who would harm him.

But tonight was different.

He wasn't in control. The elements were. The sinking sun all but ensured he'd take a nosedive from the winding path into the yawning crevice. Didn't matter. He'd take the risk.

Breathing deep from the climb, he turned to check on his buddy Kip. Great, the guy was peeved. Huffing and puffing up the trail. Scowling as he planted his hiking pole on the packed dirt.

"Dude," he said, trying to get a full breath. "This's crazy. Even if we get to the cache before dark, we'll never make it down again. We need to turn back before we both break our necks."

Wiley shook his head. "Not an option. Not when we're this close."

"Close?" Kip's voice shot up. "It's still a mile up to Triple Falls. More than that to get back down. It'll take us ninety minutes at least. That's if we find the cache right away." Kip looked at his watch. "The sun sets in forty-five minutes."

Figures Kip would wimp out. He was just like the others. Making Wiley's life difficult. "You can turn back, but I'm going on."

"Man, come on, Fagan. Don't make me feel like a jerk for bailing on you."

"Don't sweat it. I'm good to go alone. You can go back to the car."

"Yeah, right." Kip rolled his eyes behind large glasses. "You can't go alone. That's what all the stranded hikers say after they're rescued and interviewed on TV. Don't become one of them, man."

Wiley ignored Kip's warning. As avid geocachers, they used GPS coordinates to find hidden caches and often hiked over rugged terrain like this. Kip might be a coward, but after a stint in prison, Wiley could handle this or anything else by himself.

"I'm going." He turned to head up the narrow trail flanked with trees on one side, the deep gorge on the other.

"Go ahead, risk our lives for a stupid geocache," Kip muttered from behind.

Seeking to keep his temper in check, Wiley fisted his hands. Didn't work. He'd had enough drama for a lifetime. Not only with Kip's whining and complaining. That was bad enough. But his life in general sucked. Big time. Wasn't his fault if he let off some steam now, was it?

He grabbed Kip's plaid wool jacket that likely came from a thrift-store grab bag and slammed him against a pine tree. "I've told you like a million times, dude. My life sucks. No one will give an ex-con like me a job. People see my scars and cringe. Lila dumped me, and if that's not enough for you, I still have nightmares from prison. So I need some-thing—anything—to get my mind off it. At least until I'm able to pay that loser FBI agent back for getting me the max sentence."

Kip shrugged free. "I get it man, but—"

"Get it?" Wiley's voice screeched through the immense divide, echoing off the steep-walled river canyon and sending birds flapping into the descending darkness. "How could you? Not until you spend two years in prison. Two years of nothing to do. Hearing sounds in the night that you wished to God you hadn't heard. Sights you hadn't seen. Knowing they were coming for you. Always coming."

"I can imagine."

"Oh yeah?" Wiley ran his fingers over the scars crisscrossing and running down his face into the heavy beard he wore to hide some of them. "Do you get how it felt to have a homemade shiv slice through my skin? Slash after slash splitting open my face. Almost bleeding out on the shower floor. Then feeling nearly every inch of my face jerked tight with stitches. Or maybe you get how it felt to see Lila take one look at me and bolt like she'd seen Freddy Krueger." A spray of spit followed his words, but he didn't care. He was on a roll. "You've got a charmed life, man. A good programming job. Money to burn. An apartment. So don't tell me again that you get it." He poked Kip in the chest. "Understand? Never again."

Kip nodded, his long pointy nose resembling a bird's beak as he took a lurching step back.

He was afraid. *Good.* It was a long time coming. Wiley had to pay them back. All of them. He'd wanted to blow up at the dude for weeks. Felt amazing to let it go.

He ran the back of his hand over his mouth. "I don't care if you come with me or not. I'm going on."

He took off at a clip fueled by anger, keeping an ear out for Kip should he decide to stop him from reaching his goal. The steep incline would soon force Wiley to slow down, but he'd do his best to power through it. He heard Kip's footsteps pounding on the packed trail behind him. *Fine.* He'd decided to come along. Honestly, Wiley didn't care anymore. Didn't care about anything except making people pay. Big time. Especially that freakin' FBI agent, Nina Brandt. He would get her when the timing was right. Just like the prison psychiatrist. Fool. Claiming Wiley was paranoid. Putting him on medicine he didn't need, dulling his senses.

They weren't dull now. He ached to do Brandt in, but first he needed to come up with a sound plan that didn't put him back behind bars. Until then, he'd settle for beating everyone else to this prize.

He forced his aching muscles to work harder and picked up speed, passing moss-covered trees and ferns that made the place look like a rain forest. They'd summit at Triple Falls in another mile, then cross a fallen log to the cache.

To the prize.

Motivated, he pressed on hard until he rounded a bend and heard the first sounds of water surging over the basalt rock. He stopped to catch his breath and prepare for the next challenge. He'd often hiked this trail with Lila. Hiked many of the gorge trails with her in their three years together. But he'd seen the last of her three months ago when she'd picked him up from prison on his release day, then dumped him on Kip's doorstep like trash. Maybe Lila needed to pay, too.

Maybe. She deserved it. Like all of them did. Always watching. Waiting to pounce. To do him in.

Huffing loudly, Kip caught up and pointed across the steep ravine. "There're the falls. Now let's find the stinkin' cache and get out of here. It better have been worth it."

Geocaches didn't usually offer anything of value. It wasn't about the prize at the end. Cachers liked the hunt and the challenge of the search. But this one was different. Someone posted it on Hacktivists, a Portland geocache group he and Kip belonged to. The listing promised a prize every computer nerd would love.

Kip held a hand over his eyes to peer into the distance. "I don't like the looks of the log we have to cross. It's wet. That means slippery. I don't recommend doing this, man."

Wiley didn't care. He wanted this cache. Wanted it bad enough to ignore their safety and head into the gorge minutes after he'd seen the post. He hoped others in the group were big babies like Kip and had waited until sunrise before setting out. Wiley would score the cache before they rolled out of bed.

"Don't be such a wuss." Wiley dug out a battery-powered headlamp, turned it on, and snapped the elastic around his head.

"Yeah, why worry, right?" Kip's sarcasm accompanied the curl of his lip. "We'll only fall into the river and take a nosedive into the falls."

Wiley was ready to push the guy over the edge himself, but he shoved his hands in his pockets instead. Kip was the only person who hadn't abandoned Wiley during his prison stay. Plus Kip let Wiley sleep on his couch while Wiley got his life together. He would cut the guy some slack. For now.

"Maybe it's best if you wait on this side," Wiley suggested. "Just in case something *does* happen."

Relief flashed on Kip's face. "You don't have to tell me twice."

Coward.

Wiley marched up to the log and shrugged out of his backpack. His boots felt solid on the fallen log at first, but as he moved out over the water, the tree vibrated with the fury of the raging water below. One false move and he was a goner. He'd plunge sixty-plus feet to his death. He doubled his concentration, tuning out other sounds and watching his feet.

Step. Slide. Step. Slide. Rinse and repeat. Over and over until he reached the far side. He jumped down, his feet firmly planted on the water-soaked ground.

At the weatherworn intersection of two logs, a dark object caught his eye. He hurried over, his heart kicking up higher when he located the waterproof case.

Ooh, ooh, ooh. He found it. The prize. Before anyone else. *Oh, yeah.*

"Got it," he yelled above the gushing water, and dropped to his knees. The frigid spray instantly soaked his jeans. So what? He was pumped. He was the first to open the container. He had to be.

With cold hands made clumsier by gloves, he pried the lid open.

"It's a laptop," he shouted as his heart sank. "I thought it'd be some state-of-the-art hardware, but it's a laptop. I risked my life for a stinkin' laptop." He stood. "It's an ultrabook, but I don't know if I even want it. It's probably broken."

"Hey, bring it anyway," Kip yelled. "You need money. Parts for an ultrabook could fetch a few dollars."

Kip had a point. Ultrathin computers were expensive. Not that

4

Wiley actually needed cash. Anytime he did, he could find a hacking job without trouble. But he could dismantle this one and easily score a few bucks from the parts on eBay.

Okay, so he'd take it.

Rules said he should record the find on the cache log and leave something else behind, but he ignored the log and zipped the computer into his jacket, leaving his arms free to balance on the return trip. Adrenaline fading, he moved with more caution and eyed the river, expecting it to rise up and wash him off. With the way his life had been going lately, it wouldn't surprise him if he did fall. Maybe it wouldn't even be a bad thing.

It would end all of his problems.

But then Agent Brandt would get away with ruining his life. That was unacceptable. She couldn't destroy him, then go on as if she'd simply smashed an irritating mosquito.

Revenge first. Then maybe a dive into the waterfall to end it all. Who knows?

He neared the log's end and took a leap to the spongy moss. He'd beat the odds. Made it. Beat nature. Beat the universe that kept pushing him down. Maybe it was a sign things were starting to look up and he shouldn't be so quick to consider ending it all. Especially when he could still look forward to paying Agent Brandt back in the most heinous way he could think of.

Chapter Two

NINA BRANDT'S cell chimed a text from her nightstand, pulling her from a restless sleep. She fought through hazy brain fog and glanced at the clock. 11:45. Still Sunday night.

Three hours, really? She'd only gotten three hours of sleep. Not quality rest either. Visions of terrorists had her tossing and turning. Not surprising. A local terrorist threat against Bonneville Dam had her and her fellow agents at the Portland FBI on high alert status for two solid days, and she was plum worn out.

She turned over and snuggled deep into sheets soft from many washings. Grandmother Hale's reproving face came to mind. Nina groaned.

Ugh! Drat her Southern roots. She'd never disrespect her grandmother's teachings. She was thirty-two. Self-sufficient. Successful. And one thought of her grandmother repeatedly warning her never to shirk her duties had her swinging her legs over the edge of the bed.

She grabbed her phone, then thumbed to the text from FBI analyst Jae Starling. Nina had left Jae monitoring the internet for terrorist chatter about Bonneville.

Chat room buzzing with activity. Need your approval to continue. Good stuff. I'd hate to let it go.

Activity related to Bonneville? Nina typed, then trudged to the adjoining bathroom for a glass of water before Jae's reply came in.

Could be. We have someone looking to sell data. Info too vague to link to BD, but seller says it's hot. Needs your review.

That meant going into the office. Now.

Nina caught her reflection in the mirror and sighed. She had bags under her eyes as big as Granddad's old steamer trunk back home in Mobile.

A yawn slipped out, and her brain struggled for clarity behind layers of fog. She needed sleep. Needed it badly. She could have Jae call in fellow Cyber Action Team members Becca and Kait, but they were lead agents on the investigation and needed sleep more than Nina did.

Besides, Kait and Becca were good friends. If they found themselves in the same situation, they'd let Nina sleep. They had each other's backs in everything.

Nina poked one of the puffy dark circles and frowned. Tired or not, she was going in.

Keep monitoring. Be there ASAP, she typed, then slogged to the kitchen to start a travel cup of her favorite dark-roasted chicory coffee brewing. She doubted she'd be coming home before her workday started, so she showered and selected a navy suit and long-sleeved white blouse from the perfectly bland agent attire lining one side of her closet. As she dressed, she looked longingly at the other half, filled with bright, bold-colored clothing she saved for her free time.

"Right," she mumbled as she settled her holster on her belt and her FBI shield on the other side. "What's *free time?*"

Grabbing her purse and keys, she stepped outside. The air was chilly and humid as usual for February in Portland. Hazy fog hung at ground level, and a fine mist dampened the air in her pin-drop quiet neighborhood.

As she locked the door, the skin on her neck crawled, sending goosebumps rising up to meet the softness of her collar.

Something was wrong. Someone was watching her.

At least it felt that way. Nothing concrete. Just a gut feeling she'd had for days. After five years in law enforcement, she'd learned to pay attention to it. Even when it made sense only to her. Might be something. Might not. But she wouldn't ignore it.

Swallowing hard, she settled a hand on her sidearm and turned to watch and listen, staying fully alert for anything, anyone that didn't belong. Streetlights filtered through the haze, mixing with fingers of fog creeping along the road, obscuring tires on the many cars parked on her street. An eerie sight, but she found nothing amiss

She turned to search houses that had been built so close together in the twenties that she could almost reach across the driveway without leaving home to borrow a cup of sugar from one of her neighbors for one of her famous Southern desserts.

Nina made one last sweep. The whole street was dark, even Mrs. Johnson's house next door. Her husband of forty years died a few months ago. She'd walked the floors all hours of the night, bless her heart. But lately, she'd finally managed to sleep again.

She blew out a breath. This was ridiculous. She was ridiculous.

What an idiot. Just head to your car.

All the talk of terrorists the last few days had her jumping out of her skin. Reacting like a scared little girl instead of an agent. Her emotions were exacerbated by the fatigue, she supposed.

"Well, get a hold of them, Nina," she warned herself as she unlocked her car door with a beep of her remote.

Too bad Becca and Kait weren't at the office. They'd both help shut down her emotions. Becca in her straightforward way, encouraging Nina to be more disciplined and work toward a goal. Characteristics that made Becca a great team leader. Kait would be direct and decisive, maybe pushy, as she was the team perfectionist and she handled team details. Nina liked to think that she brought empathy to the team, remembering the human side. That, though important to their friendship, often didn't advance the FBI's agenda.

There was nothing worse than an agent thinking with her heart. At least, that's what her supervisor had told her so many times that she'd rather wrestle an Alabama swamp gator than go into the office wearing her emotions on her sleeve. Even if the sleeve was part of a nicely tailored Hugo Boss jacket she'd picked up for a song at Nordstrom Rack.

THE DARKNESS WAS Wiley's friend now. The shadows hid him from Brandt as she walked to her car. He slumped as far down as he could in Kip's junky Honda. He probably shouldn't have come over, but after the disappointment in the geocache, he needed to be within spitting distance of her as he planned how to take her down.

Her car suddenly revved, the roar of her engine exploding through the quiet neighborhood. He heard the car thump out of the driveway. Saw a plume of white smoke drift up. He felt the car move past him. His heart pounded hard, sounding in his ears as he held his breath.

She was only a few feet away.

He wanted to jerk open the door and confront her. Taunt her. Shout out little snippets of what he had in store for her. See her fear.

That would be a mistake. A freaking big one. She would be armed. She'd draw her gun and arrest him.

No! He wasn't going to let her arrest him. Ever!

He needed to be more careful. Expect the unexpected. Like her stepping onto the wide porch of her house in the middle of the night when he thought she'd be sleeping. With the powder-blue color and white trim, the place looked like the home of a nice person. A normal person who didn't arbitrarily target people to make themselves feel better. She'd likely heard he'd been released from prison and was hell bent on arresting him again. Meant he had to be even more careful. First thing in the morning, he'd pick up a GPS tracker for her vehicle. That way he'd know her whereabouts at all times.

He waited for the sound of her engine to disappear into the night. He slid up. Slowly. Inch by inch until he could see out the windows.

All clear. The witch was gone, and now Wiley could begin to set his plan.

THE SEA HAWK skimmed the ocean, winging Lieutenant Quinn Stone and his squad of sixteen men home. The familiar *whump, whump, whump* of rotors sounded overhead as murky sea water rolled below, dark and ominous with the moon hiding under thick clouds.

It was a perfect night. Perfect end to another intense special warfare training. One of hundreds, maybe thousands, of training exercises in Quinn's seven-year career as a SEAL.

Man, he loved this job. Loved the missions and training. Learning new skills and perfecting old ones. Fast-roping. Diving. Tactical ambushes. Raids. You name it. He loved it all.

"We debrief in five," Lieutenant JG Cooper's no-nonsense tone cut through the comms loud and clear. "No messing around. Straight to the vans."

The men didn't listen. They were hyped up on adrenaline. Getting rowdier by the minute.

"I mean it, guys," Coop barked. "Stow it. The longer you ignore my orders, the longer it will take to debrief and get you started on your leave."

The promise of leave was enough to make the guys take it down a notch and gather their equipment. When the helo touched down on a Naval Amphibious Base helipad, they jumped down and made a beeline for the vans waiting to take them to a meeting room.

They dumped their packs in the back and climbed in a van that had seen better days. Quinn hung back, slowly shouldering his pack. He had no plans. No family waiting for him. Just three days of nothing. On his own. And that was the way he wanted it right now.

He dropped to the concrete, his boots landing with a thud. When he cleared the swirling winds under the rotors, heat radiated off the concrete. It was usually cooled by a fresh breeze over the naval base jutting into San Diego Bay, but not today.

The van was hotter still. The air was thick with sweltering heat mixed with body odor from a three-day exercise. Quinn lowered his window and breathed in salt air as they followed the first van down Trident Way. His teammates were still laughing. Some arguing. Nearly brawling. Typical behavior.

Quinn shook his head. Give a bunch of SEALs downtime and they had no problem finding a way to get into trouble. For some reason, he couldn't manage to join in. He wanted to. These were the guys, the men, he lived with—worked with—day after day, in dangerous situations where you learned who to trust, who to count on. But something had changed. He was off-kilter. Had been since recovering from the explosion in Afghanistan and coming back to active duty.

Could be because he hadn't gotten his command back. Coop continued to direct ECHO platoon. It made Quinn mad. Not that Coop wasn't a top-notch commander. He was. As a junior-grade lieutenant, he'd served as Quinn's number two for years, but Quinn had expected to resume his status when he'd returned from medical leave. Two months had passed since then and all Quinn had gotten from his CO were excuses. Lame ones at that.

At their low-slung building, he was first out and headed inside for the debrief before downstaging their equipment. Then he'd take a long ride along the ocean on his Harley and grab a beer and Texas-sized steak before tumbling into bed dog tired.

Inside, large fans hummed in the background, making the hallway cooler. Quinn's CO, Commander Hall, stood beside the door. Tension lingered on his face, and he was engaged in a serious discussion with Coop.

Hall eyed Quinn for a moment. He knew his CO was on campus for the debrief, but the fact that he kept staring at Quinn didn't bode well.

Already on the move, Hall called out, "Stone, a minute."

Quinn had no patience for a conversation with his CO right now. Unless, of course, he was planning to tell Quinn he'd be stepping back into his rightful slot.

A few inches shorter than Quinn's six-foot-two, the steely-eyed officer joined Quinn. "I'm gonna cut right to the chase, Stone. You're a good soldier. One of the best. I've tried to be patient, but this isn't working out. It's time to clue me in on what's going on with you."

Quinn had no idea what Hall was talking about. It wasn't the training exercise. That had gone perfectly. "Not sure I follow, sir."

"You're here, but you're not here." Hall held up a hand. "Don't bother to deny it. I see it. The platoon sees it. You do everything with precision as usual—like a machine—but your heart's not in the game anymore."

"If you mean the injury, sir." Quinn looked at his hand, the pink puckered skin a reminder of the explosion. The fire. The searing burns. "I'm carrying my weight. The exercise came off without a hitch, and I'm ready to take charge the minute Coop is reassigned."

"That's not what I said." Hall paused to lock gazes with Quinn. "You haven't been yourself since you came back. The men deserve better from you."

Ah-ha, the real reason Quinn had been sidelined. They thought he was losing his edge. A bogus reason if you asked him. Which, of course, no one did. He might be a bit out of sorts, but he wasn't a liability.

"The men don't need to worry about their backs," he said firmly. "I got 'em covered."

"Again. Not the point." Hall lifted his cap and ran a hand over thinning hair. "Look. You have a few days of leave coming up. Take the time to think about what I said. Maybe you need to talk to someone. Work it out. There's no shame in that."

Right, like Quinn would sit with a shrink and cry about his boo-boos. The only way he'd do that was if they ordered him to. Which they might well do if he didn't shake this thing off, whatever *it* was. They could force him to choose between the shrink and leaving the team.

Hah! Talk about a foolish idea. He'd never leave the one thing that made sense in his life.

"You hear me, Stone?" Hall asked.

"Roger that, sir," Quinn said, trying to sound enthusiastic.

After Hall stepped off, Quinn joined the other guys in the conference room. They were hanging around the table, staring at him, waiting for him to recount Hall's conversation as they always did after little powwows with the CO. Maybe to tell them he was okay and things could go back to normal. He couldn't do that. Not when he wasn't sure it would.

He dug his cell phone from his pack for a distraction and turned it on. In case of an emergency, Quinn brought his phone when training exercises allowed it, but he didn't like to be distracted, so he always turned it off. After it powered up, he found four missed calls and messages. All from his mother. That was out of character for her.

A hint of apprehension settled in his gut as he played the messages. She urged him to call ASAP. Her tone rose higher with each message, heading quickly out of control. His dad was an Air Force general, so she was used to dealing with life on her own. If she was sounding this freaked out, something major had gone down.

Ty. It has to be Ty.

Quinn's kid brother had recently turned seventeen, and he was doing his best to put himself in the running for the "rebellious kid of the year" award.

Quinn stepped out of the room and dialed. "Mom."

"Thank goodness you called." She sighed out a relieved breath. "It's Ty."

Of course it is.

"What's he done now?" Quinn gritted his teeth as he waited to hear.

"I'd rather not talk about it on the phone." She was always uneasy when discussing Ty's latest screw-up, but there was an extra edge to her voice tonight. "Can you come home? To help figure this out."

"When?"

"As soon as you can get on a plane."

"I take it Dad's not available." Quinn's voice came out all surly, but he didn't care. He no longer tried to hide his disrespect for his father. He might be a top-notch general but he blew it as a family man.

"I didn't call him. Not this time. He'd . . ." She stopped. Not that it mattered if she finished her sentence. Quinn knew what she would have said.

His dad only made things worse. He'd shout orders at Ty as if he was one of his airmen, and Ty's back would go up. Then the kid would escalate his pranks and find another way to make the old man mad. As the older brother, Quinn would step in to repair the damage. At least with their dad out of the loop, Quinn only had to deal with the problem, not with their father's exacerbation of it.

"I'll see what I can do," Quinn offered.

"No, Quinn. This isn't a see-what-you-can-do kind of situation. If you don't come home and fix this, Ty will go . . . he'll . . ." Her voice caught. "He'll go to jail."

"Jail?" Quinn yelled, drawing the attention of the last teammates filing into the room. Stepping down the hall, he lowered his voice. "If you want me to drop everything and come back to Portland, then at least tell me what he's done so I can spend my time on the plane thinking of a solution."

"Can anyone overhear us?"

"No."

Dead silence came through the line for a moment. "He's hacked into the No-Fly List."

"He what?" Quinn shouted before controlling his voice. "The No-Fly List, as in the one that keeps terrorists off airplanes?"

"Yes."

"Why in the world did the little punk do that?" he spat out.

"For a girl."

A girl. "Of all the lame—"

"Think back to your first girlfriends," she interrupted. "You did some pretty lame things, too. You just didn't have the computer skills Ty has."

"No, I actually lived my life instead of hiding behind a computer." She didn't respond.

"I'm sorry, Mom. I try to understand Ty, but I don't get him. Not that it matters." He blew out a breath. "Tell me about the girl."

"It was an online relationship. She lives in Phoenix and wanted him to fly out to take her to prom."

"Let me guess. Dad said no," Quinn said, knowing his father was against all fun.

"Yes." She sighed. "So this other kid from school stepped in as her date, and she dumped Ty. He was mad. He didn't want the other kid to be able to go to the prom, so he put him on the No-Fly list."

One part of Quinn was amazed at his brother's skills. The other part was disgusted at the way he chose to use them. "Where does he come up with these ideas?"

"Doesn't matter now. On top of the hack, his computer's missing. He thinks the kid he put on the No-Fly List took it so he could turn Ty in. If the authorities find out about the hack, he'll likely do time." She lowered her voice. "They could accuse him of being a terrorist." A sob followed her words.

"C'mon, Mom, don't go off the deep end," Quinn soothed. "Ty's not a terrorist, and they won't think he is."

"You don't know that. It's serious business." He heard the tears behind her words.

His heart broke for her. She was a wonderful mother. The best. Tough, strong, independent. Loving. Kind. She didn't deserve this. He'd do whatever he could to fix this situation. But what could he do to keep the kid from being prosecuted for potential federal charges?

He had no clout. "I don't see how I can help, Mom."

"Don't say that," she cried. "You're the only one I know with a federal law enforcement contact who can make this go away."

Law enforcement? He only knew one person who fit the bill—his ex, FBI agent Nina Brandt, and she wouldn't be happy to hear from him. "If you mean Nina, that won't work."

His mom sniffed. "Just come home, Quinn, where we can talk about this face to face and figure something out."

Thankful for his upcoming leave, Quinn glanced at his watch. "I have a debrief. Then I'll hop on the first plane. Might not be until the morning though."

"Thank you, Son. You know I wouldn't ask if I didn't believe it was the best course of action."

"I know, Mom. See you soon." He hung up and headed into the meeting room, already pondering the steps needed to enlist Nina's help.

He couldn't call her. She'd ignore it. Ignore him. When they'd broken up a little over a year ago, it had been messy. Shoot, it was worse than messy. He'd screwed things up big time. And he knew he was the last person she wanted to see. She'd told him as much when he'd helped on a case with her FBI cyber team a few months ago.

So what? He couldn't let that stop him. He'd make sure Nina agreed to see him and let him plead Ty's case. He wouldn't let his kid brother go to jail without doing his best to stop it. And as a SEAL, his best was better than most.

Chapter Three

RESIDUAL ADRENALINE kept Wiley wide awake and jittery. He wanted to be alone with his thoughts, to relive being so close to Brandt. But Kip worked nights and wasn't about to change his schedule for the weekend. He was in the kitchen making popcorn so Wiley stepped to Kip's computer and logged in as administrator on the Hacktivist website to see who was dumb enough to have left the ultrathin computer in a cache.

Wiley had no problem getting in. He'd co-founded the Hacktivists, had set up the website, and served as administrator until ugly old Brandt put him in prison. The group had cut all ties with him and made Kip and another dude co-administrator of the account.

Didn't matter. Wiley had left a backdoor. He always left a backdoor. After his first sign-on when he got out of prison, he'd learned Kip's login and password. Now he used Kip's login for everything. Wiley wouldn't want to violate his parole conditions that banned him from the internet. Right. Like he would ever abide by that.

He located the database containing details for the member who listed the computer cache.

Hamid Ahmadi. Interesting.

Did the computer Wiley found in the cache belong to Hamid? Was he dumb enough to put his own machine in a cache? Wiley thought the kid was smarter than that. He'd met Hamid at a geocache Meetup right before Wiley went to prison. The kid was a computer whiz and like many others in the group, hacked sites for the thrill of it. Maybe the machine Hamid left in the cache held data that Wiley could trade for cash.

He grabbed the computer and pressed the power button. The machine immediately whirred to life and booted up.

"Dude." Kip flashed a look at Wiley. "I figured if someone put that machine in a cache, it had to be toast."

"Me too."

The laptop continued booting but stalled at a Windows password screen. Not something that would stop Wiley. Hacking was his specialty.

The microwave dinged in the background as he dove into cracking the password. Time ceased to exist until he beat the machine.

"Score!" He shot a fist into the air as the user's name popped up.

TylerS. Not Hamid or something similar. Looked like the computer belonged to a guy named Tyler. Made sense, Wiley supposed. Hamid wouldn't put his own pricey computer in a cache. That would just be stupid.

Wiley used Kip's computer to check the Hacktivist site. Yeah, there was another kid named Tyler Stone in the group, but Wiley didn't know him. Maybe the ultrathin was Tyler's computer and Hamid was punking Tyler, so he put Tyler's computer into the cache. Sounded like something a teenager would do. Shoot, sounded like something Wiley would do as a practical joke.

Wiley turned his attention back to the ultrathin. The screen held only two icons. One for Facebook. Another, a Notepad document called "No-Fly List Hack".

No-Fly List hack?

Had Hamid hacked the database holding the names for the No-Fly List? Nah, not a decent kid like Hamid. Or was he? It'd been some time since Wiley talked to the guy. Maybe he'd turned into one of those religious zealots involved with a terrorist group and the cache was a way to move things to others without raising suspicion. But if that were the case, he wouldn't have posted it on Hacktivist where anyone could see it, right?

Or maybe that's why he posted it at night, when no sane person would go looking for it. Could be the way the terrorist cell communicated. If so, the laptop might hold some extremely valuable information.

Wiley opened and perused the file. The hacker had done what all good hackers do. He'd kept a step-by-step record of his invasion into the federal database allowing him to get back into the site at a later date.

Oh, yeah. This's good. Real good.

Adrenaline spiked through Wiley's veins. He might have stumbled onto something serious here.

He checked the document's properties. Discovered it was created on this machine. Now, just who did the machine belong to? Tyler or Hamid?

"You find anything?" Kip set the large bowl of popcorn on the table and dropped into a chair by Wiley.

No way was Wiley telling Kip about the hack. The dude was so clean, he squeaked. He would report the hack to the authorities before

Wiley could determine if and how he could exploit it.

He closed the document. "I'm logging on to Facebook right now to see if I can get any of the owner's details."

"Let me see," Kip said, as he grabbed a handful of popcorn and slid closer.

Wiley shifted to give Kip a view. The account password had been stored on the computer, and Facebook opened, revealing a headshot of a white male, obviously in a teenage rebellious phase, with scraggly long hair and a sullen expression.

"Tyler Stone," Kip muttered.

TylerS. The owner of the computer?

Seemed more likely than Tyler having been the last person to access Facebook on a machine belonging to Hamid. Wiley clicked on the "About" tab.

"Dude, he's only seventeen," Kip said. "A junior at Reynolds High in Troutdale. Why would a kid put a computer in a cache?"

More importantly, which one of the teens had hacked the No-Fly List?

Maybe this Tyler kid was buddies with Hamid and they were in on this together.

"Click on his pictures," Kip encouraged. "I gotta see more about a guy who's dumb enough to give up a pricey computer this way."

Wiley opened the page and scrolled down, watching for any pictures of Hamid. There were plenty of shots of a computer club hanging together, but none including Hamid. So what did that mean? Maybe Hamid hacked the list and was setting this Tyler kid up to take a fall. But Wiley's gut told him the computer belonged to Tyler Stone and he'd done the hack. So why did Hamid have the machine and why put it in the cache?

Kip stabbed a finger at the screen. "Dude, isn't that the FBI chick who put you away?"

Wiley quit scrolling to enlarge the picture. He sucked in a breath and held it while he studied the picture. Tyler Stone peered up at Special Agent Nina Brandt wearing a dress that hugged her curves. On her other side, a tall, tough-looking dude dressed in Navy blues stared at her, his face filled with sappy infatuation.

"Check out the Navy guy," Kip said. "He's got a Trident pinned on his uniform. You know what that means."

"No." Wiley had about as much interest in the military as he had in being Kip's roommate for life.

"Means he's a SEAL, and he's clearly got the hots for her." Kip mocked a lascivious smile totally out of character for his mama's-boy personality. "Too bad she was the one who put you away, or I could get all over hanging a picture of her in my room."

Wiley didn't blame Kip. She had a face and body that most guys would drool over, but she left Wiley cold. Frozen-waterfall-in-the-gorge cold. This poor excuse for a human being flashing an innocent smile had sealed his fate for two long years. Since Wiley had never been arrested before, the judge had hinted at leniency. But no. Brandt had to get all up in his stuff and change the judge's mind. Told him that Wiley would repeat if he didn't have the time to see the errors of his ways.

Nasty chick. Mega nasty. She'd ruined his life. Totally ruined it. Just when he was getting ready to take the world by storm. To make his mark in the hacking community. Achieve notoriety so everyone who was out to get him would know he was as hardcore as they come and couldn't be touched.

"What're the odds that you'd find a computer connected to her?" Kip asked as he took over the mouse to scroll down the feed. "I mean, it looks like a remote connection, but a connection all the same."

Indeed. What *were* the odds? Were the gods finally smiling on him?

He could use this information to his benefit, but how?

He let Kip continue to play creepy stalker dude and sat back to think.

If the document panned out, Wiley had a blueprint for accessing the No-Fly List. Possibilities were endless. Terrorists would pay millions to have a door into that system. Thanks to his prison stint, Wiley knew how to find a buyer. He could use the money to put his life back together. Pay for plastic surgery to erase his scars. Set himself up in style. A big win on its own, but with a little sleight of hand, he could make it look like Brandt orchestrated the hack.

Oh, yeah, perfect. She'd go away for a lot more than two years. Maybe for a lifetime. *A lifetime!*

"Here's another picture of them." Kip paused on a photo showing the trio on a picnic. Brandt smiling again. Her love for the SEAL dude shining on her face. She didn't deserve this happiness. Not when he was still suffering from her abuse.

Time to end it. Check out the hack. Sell it.

Maybe he could use this Tyler kid or the SEAL in the plan, too. She obviously cared about them, meaning Wiley could inflict more pain that way. *No. Wait.* Hamid would be a better choice. His nationality would suggest that Brandt was involved in terrorist activities. She'd never see the light of day. Never.

Wiley would have to get to work on this right now. He couldn't risk authorities discovering the hack before he could act on it. Once they did, eliminating the vulnerability would shoot to the top of their priority list.

A flash of unease cut into his conscience. Could he live with the consequences of putting this list into the hands of terrorists?

He looked at Brandt's smirk again. She'd left him to rot in prison. To be a punching bag for the scum of the earth. Made him crawl in their filth. Day after day for two years. Seven hundred and thirty endless nights of darkness that still sent fear to his heart.

His gut churned, forcing acid up his throat. She had to pay. To bring her down he could—he would—do anything. *Anything!* Even if it meant innocent people died in the process.

"DANG, NINA. YOU look horrible." Fellow agent Becca Lange said as she parked herself in the doorway of Nina's cubicle.

"Thanks a lot," Nina replied, then chuckled.

Nina wouldn't let just anyone get away with telling her that she looked bad, but Becca and Kait were almost family, and family was often brutally honest.

Nina stared at her friend for a moment, barely registering her requisite FBI uniform of a dark suit and simple blouse. Her shoulder-length hair was back in her usual ponytail with highlighted streaks from her daily jogs.

Becca rested her steaming coffee mug on Nina's desk. "What are you still doing here anyway? Our suspects are in custody. You should go home and get some sleep."

"I know, it's just . . ." Nina tapped her computer screen displaying the chat room Jae had brought to her attention. Nina had been monitoring it all morning and while she'd scarfed down a quick sandwich for lunch. "It's this conversation. Even if it didn't lead to the Bonneville arrest, it still bothers me, and I want to keep an eye on it."

"Please. If we didn't go home until we tracked down every non-specific piece of intel like this, we'd never get any sleep." Becca smiled, but the stubborn set to her eyes remained. "If it bothers you, assign one of the analysts to monitor it and get out of here."

Could Nina sleep with this lingering unease? She opened her mouth to discuss it when the phone on her desk rang. She checked caller ID. Building security. "Hold that thought a sec."

"I'm not going anywhere." Becca sipped her coffee and waited. She was a pit bull when she wanted to achieve something. She was legendary for her skills in planning and organizing. And her impatience. Man, she was impatient, often taking over the team when things weren't moving as planned. Nina usually appreciated her friend taking the lead, but today she knew Becca would stand there until Nina went home. Maybe she'd even escort her to the door.

Nina grabbed the phone. "Brandt."

"I know you don't have any visitors on the log, Agent Brandt," the security guard said, his words rushing out, "but I got a guy here to see you."

The last thing Nina needed was to chat with someone who hadn't made an appointment. "Take his name and number. I'll get back to him."

"Um . . . I . . ." Roger paused, his uncertainty out of character. "I don't think it's a good idea to try to brush this guy off. He's made it clear he plans to make a spectacle of himself if you don't come down here. He's a SEAL. I believe him."

SEAL? No . . . really? Not Quinn. It couldn't be him, could it? She'd made it quite clear that she didn't want to see him again. "Please tell me it's not Quinn Stone."

Becca's interest perked up, and she mouthed, "Quinn?"

Nina shrugged.

"It's Stone all right. He says he knows you. His brother, a Tyler Stone, is with him."

Ty? The kid Nina had come to think of as her own little brother during her time with Quinn?

"Can you come down?" Roger still sounded anxious.

Nina didn't blame him. He sat behind secured glass, but most guys knew that SEALs were ultimate fighting warriors—operators, as they liked to be called. It was smart to give them a wide berth. And Quinn was all SEAL.

"I'll be right there, Roger." She hung up, but had no intention of rushing down to the security checkpoint. "It's Quinn. He's trying to push Roger around. And Roger doesn't rattle easily."

Becca eyed Nina. "What's he doing here?"

"No idea." Nina resisted the urge to grab her purse and check her appearance before going downstairs. She had no reason to try to impress Quinn Stone. "Ty's with him."

"Maybe Ty wants to shadow you again," Becca suggested.

Nina thought about the day when Ty trailed her, Becca, and Kaitlyn

Knight, one of the FBI's elite Cyber Action Teams. "He was bored out of his mind the last time. I can't imagine he'd ask to do it again. At least not voluntarily."

"You think Quinn dragged him here?"

"If he did, he wouldn't have given Ty a chance to refuse. No one says no to Quinn."

"Um, Nina," Becca said. "You did. Kind of, anyway. Before you broke up."

"Yeah . . . well . . . I'm much older and wiser than Ty, and I know how to stand my ground." Nina came to her feet, straightened her jacket, and resisted another urge to glance in her mirror.

Could she stand her ground? They'd been a couple for a year and had been totally in love. At least, she'd thought they were. But Quinn's life as a SEAL took him to God knows where, doing God knows what, and she couldn't handle not knowing where he was and if he was all right.

When she told him she couldn't live with the uncertainty anymore and something had to change, he froze and did nothing. Didn't say a word. Just bailed. For her own sanity, she had to break things off. Still, she'd hoped he'd come to his senses. But after a few months passed without any contact, she got the message. Eighteen months had gone by since then, and her only contact with him had been on a case six months ago. He'd hinted at getting back together but nothing had changed in his life, and she wasn't going to put herself in a position to get hurt again.

Becca glanced at her chunky sports watch. "I'm heading over to County to question our suspects. I'll walk you down."

Nina got up from her chair and walked with Becca, her head down in her usual get-to-the-problem-and-solve-it mode. The two of them were about the same height, but Nina had a hard time keeping up. Not only a runner but also an all-around athlete, Becca was solid muscle, and her legs powered her down the hallway at a quick pace. She was the fittest of the three agents on the team. In addition to her daily runs, she also worked out. Not to look good, but to stay healthy, and to give her the stamina to work tirelessly on the job and on behalf of foster kids.

She was a former foster child herself, and she volunteered as a Court Appointed Special Advocate for foster children. She truly wanted to help these kids, but her volunteerism was mostly about trying to make up for her foster sister's disappearance when they were teens. Molly had met the lowlife who was suspected of abducting her in a chat room, and she'd never been found. Becca had introduced Molly to the chat room, so Becca took the blame for Molly's disappearance. Becca couldn't help Molly, so she worked tirelessly on behalf of other children to atone for it. Regardless of how much Nina and Kait attempted to help Becca let go of the guilt, she clung to it, and her never-ending schedule of activities required being in excellent shape.

Nina worked out, too. The job required it. But her idea of healthy was cutting back on the plump biscuits she loved to bake then slather with butter and honey until the mixture ran down the crispy edges.

Biscuits. That would soften the sting of seeing Quinn. Too bad it would take a dozen. Plus a glass of sweet tea to wash them down.

She rounded the corner to the elevator. Her phone rang in the tone she'd assigned to her mother who still lived in Mobile. Nina groaned.

Becca rolled her eyes. She and Kait had heard this ring so many times, they recognized it immediately. "Your mom has the most amazing timing."

"'Amazing' isn't the word I'd use." Nina didn't want to answer, but if she didn't, the calls would keep coming. Endlessly. She pressed *Talk.* "Now's not a good time to talk, Mama. Can I call you back later?"

"Why can't you talk? Is everything okay?" Nina could picture her mother's frown as she sat in her kitchen at the worn Formica countertop with copious burn marks from years of use.

"Everything's fine," Nina soothed, though things were far from fine with Quinn waiting for her. "It's just a work thing. I really need to go."

"What time will you call back?" she demanded.

"I'm not sure. But sometime today."

"You promise?"

Nina stifled a sigh. "I promise."

"I'll wait by the phone."

Nina said goodbye and knew better than to tell her mother to enjoy her day. She hadn't enjoyed a day since Nina's brother Garrett had drowned. As a result, Nina had to deal with these daily phone calls reminding her of the loss. Reminding her that she'd been the one holding Garrett's hand until she could hold no more and he slipped away under the rushing water.

"I have a few minutes." Becca boarded the elevator and stabbed the button. "I could come out with you when you meet Quinn."

Nina joined Becca. "I'm good. I got this."

"You're sure?" Concern lingered on Becca's face.

Nina wanted nothing more than to talk this out with her friends, but she had worked hard to get over Quinn. She had to stand on her own two feet when it came to him. "Just tell Kait to clear her schedule for tonight. After this, you know I'll need a girl's night. If I can stay awake." She laughed.

"Oh, we'll keep you awake. At least, until you tell us what this's all about." Becca grinned and gave Nina's shoulder a quick squeeze as the elevator doors split open. "Just remember to breathe. You never wilted under Quinn's intensity before. Don't let him get to you today."

Becca strode toward the parking garage, and Nina stepped out the front door. The sun had burned off the early morning clouds. She guessed the temperature to be around fifty.

As she crossed the grassy courtyard, she could see Quinn pacing like a captive animal in the small security building located at the main road. She wasn't at all surprised he'd convinced Roger to call her. He had a presence about him, and he could con his way in and out of everywhere and everything. *Everything.* Even a relationship with her, when she knew dating someone who put his life on the line everyday, was the worst choice for her.

She dredged up a plastic smile—the one Grandmother Hale had made Nina practice for hours on end until it came easily to her lips and would remain there, even if someone was yanking out her molars with pliers.

She opened the door. Quinn stood with his back to her. He was built like a tank and dressed in a long-sleeved black T-shirt and khaki tactical pants. His dirty-blond hair was cut military-short on the sides, but was long enough on the top so he could shove his fingers into it, which he often did when he was frustrated. He didn't have to turn for her to remember the cute little cowlick on the side that had made him seem less rugged and more approachable when they'd first met.

He spun. She expected him to head her way, but he stayed put and ran his gaze over her, letting his eyes linger along the way. Her skin prickled under his study, and she felt her resolve slipping. She changed her focus to Ty. He leaned against the window a few feet from Quinn, nervously bouncing his foot while chewing on his lower lip. He wore baggy jeans, ratty sneakers, and a faded T-shirt that Nina suspected he'd slept in or picked up from the floor.

She smiled in earnest. He was exactly what a little brother should be. Sloppy and adorable. The direct opposite of his well-polished sibling. She'd really missed the kid since she split up with Quinn.

Ty suddenly looked up. The side of his mouth curved up in what might have been a smile until Quinn whispered something and Ty's expression morphed into a plea for help.

Quinn turned his attention back to her and took ground-eating strides across the small space. They met at the metal detector. Despite her desire to remain detached, her pulse spiked and her smile started to falter. She channeled Grandmother Hale, forcing her lips to lock in place.

"Sorry for surprising you this way," he said, ending with a tight smile of his own. "But I wasn't sure you'd agree to see me if I called first."

Nina opened her mouth to confirm his supposition, but he held up a hand and stepped even closer, the minty soap he favored invading her space.

"Before you tell me to take a hike, this's about Ty, not me," he whispered. "He's in trouble, Nina. *Big* trouble this time, and I need your help to keep him out of jail."

He needed *her* help. That was rich.

"What's wrong? Can't your precious SEAL team help him?" she snapped, not caring that Roger, still seated behind the glass, could hear.

Ty's shoulders drooped even more. She instantly regretted her outburst. But come on! How was she supposed to react? Quinn had walked out on *her*. Chose his team over a relationship with *her*. He shouldn't be at her office asking for a favor.

Ty took a step toward them, then stopped. Poor kid. He was caught between her and Quinn. He had been for some time. Not knowing what to do. Say. He hadn't done anything to her and didn't deserve this. If Quinn was right, he was in trouble. She couldn't turn her back on him.

She stepped over to him. "Hi, Ty," she said, her smile spreading in genuine warmth now.

His eyes were hidden under messy bangs that should have been cut months ago. "Can you help me, Nina?" His voice quivered, and he wrapped his arms around a waist that hadn't a spare ounce of flesh.

He resembled a wounded waif seeking asylum, and her heart broke. Snap, just like that, all she could think about was settling her arms around him and giving him the hug he so obviously needed. Whispering the same sweet soothing things her grandmother had said when Nina had been in her awkward teen years. Even with Quinn watching her.

Dang. She was in over her head here. Way over her head. She should flee for her own sanity, but her feet remained riveted to the floor. She would help Ty. Had to help him.

Not there, though. Not with Roger straining to hear their conversation. That would be akin to talking in a one-room church while the preacher hailed down fire and brimstone. Not only a sin, but a guaranteed way to ostracize yourself from the community.

Quinn moved closer. "Will you meet with us, Nina?"

"I'll give you a few minutes."

His eyes brightened.

"For Ty," she quickly clarified. "Only for Ty."

Quinn's jaw clenched, the muscles working hard.

"Let's get your passes in order." She gestured at Roger and wished she was on the other side of the ballistic glass with him.

The guard made quick work of registering the pair and confiscating their electronics. Then the three of them headed into the courtyard, Ty first, his shoes slapping lazily on the concrete. Quinn followed, his boots pounding along and echoing through the courtyard. A pair of analysts stepped out from the main building, their gazes following Quinn's every move. Not surprising. He drew attention wherever he went. Especially from women.

He had brown eyes, like her favorite chicory coffee. A wide chin and a face that was all angles and hard lines. Confidence in droves. He was every woman's fantasy of a SEAL. A guy could hardly look like that and not be noticed. Even now. After their disastrous breakup, she wouldn't mind watching him. Watching his fluid, almost musical, movements, with not a spare effort wasted.

Seriously, Nina. Get a grip.

Using her ID, she swiped them into the building, performed the same task inside, and escorted them into a lower level conference room. Quinn halted near the door and rested his shoulder on the wall. He always needed a quick exit. It was his SEAL training, she supposed. Or maybe she didn't know him well enough, and he wanted to be able to get away from everything. Including a commitment to a woman. All women, not just her.

Ty slopped across the room, then dropped into a chair at the table.

She sat next to him and smiled. "It's good to see you again, Ty."

"I'm sorry, Nina. Really sorry." His words came rushing out like flood waters after a hurricane.

"Hey now, hon." She spoke slowly, softly, hoping her drawl would relax him a bit. "Nothing can be as bad as the two of you are making it sound."

"Actually it is." Quinn's eyes were dark and intense. "Ty royally messed up this time. Go ahead, Ty. Tell her what you did."

Ty stared at his hands, and his shoulders sagged.

"It's okay." Nina added an extra dose of honey to her tone. "You can tell me."

"I . . . I . . ." His knee frantically bounced as his gaze shot around the room.

"Spit it out kid, or I'll tell her myself." Quinn's bark made Ty cringe.

Nina patted his hand. "Ignore your big oaf of a brother and take your time, hon."

Ty jerked his hand back and stood to pace, darting about the space like an angry wasp. "I hacked into the database for the No-Fly List."

"What?" Nina's voice shot up before she could consider how it would elevate Ty's anxiety. She took a breath. Started slower, calmer. "Say that again."

"I . . . hacked . . . the . . . No-Fly . . . List," he said slowly, raising his volume with each word, as if she were a senile old lady.

"Don't get smart with her." Quinn took a step toward them.

Ty backed up. Even Nina recoiled at the hard steel of Quinn's voice.

As she gave them time to calm down, she tried to process Ty's announcement. To wrap her brain around the seriousness of the offense. This behavior made no sense. None. Why would an all-American suburban teen hack the No-Fly List?

"Why did you do it, Ty?" she asked softly.

"Because of Ham." He frowned. "He's such a jerk. He had it coming." Ty took a step. Another. Then turned. "He made a date with this girl I was going out with online. She lives in Colorado and had this dance she wanted me to take her to. Of course, Dad said I couldn't go. He won't let me do anything."

"So this Ham stepped in," Nina said before Ty lost focus and started railing on his father, who ruled their household the same way he ruled his airmen.

Ty nodded and swiped at his bangs, giving her the first glimpse of eyes filled with teenage rage. "It's bad enough Ham did it, you know? But he kept bragging about it. Like he was some kind of stud or something. I couldn't let him get away with it. He had to pay for stealing my chick. Saturday was the big date. It took me a few weeks to get into the No-Fly List, but I made it with time to spare. I put him on the list last Thursday. He didn't make the date." A hint of a smile formed.

"Wipe that smirk off your face, kid," Quinn growled as he marched over to Ty. "Or I'll wipe it off myself."

Quinn's posture was military perfect, his hands fisted, his expression deadly intense. She could easily imagine him on one of his covert operations facing down the enemy. But Ty wasn't the enemy. He was a mixed-up kid who needed a brother right now. Not Mr. Tough Guy SEAL.

"Relax." She stepped between the brothers. "I certainly don't condone Ty's actions. He's going to get in some serious trouble, but you've gotta give him credit for his creativity."

"He hasn't told you everything." Quinn crossed his arms.

She turned to Ty and waited for an explanation, but he kept looking at the floor, his lips pressed together.

What could he possibly have done that was worse than hacking into the database to keep this kid from his date? Getting the kid arrested would fit the bill. "You didn't assign Handling Code One to Ham, did you?"

"Nah. I made him a Three."

"Handling code?" Quinn asked.

Nina nodded. "When someone is added to the list, they're assigned one of three codes, so if a law enforcement officer encounters them, they know how to proceed. I can't share the details, but someone with a Code One will be detained. Code Three won't, which means Ham wasn't arrested."

Ty scowled and dropped into a chair. "If I'd known he was gonna steal my computer afterward, I would have made him a Code One."

"He stole your computer? The one you used to hack the database?" Nina asked, and knew they were finally getting to the meat of the problem. A problem that could very well go beyond Quinn and his team's ability to fix it. And that's why he'd sought her out. She was his last resort.

"Yeah," Ty mumbled. "That's the bad part. I basically keep a play-by-play of my hacks in a file so I can get back in if I need to." He hung his head. "Now I don't know where the computer is."

Quinn stepped forward. "Which means—"

"I know what it means," Nina interrupted to stop Quinn from mentioning the horrifying acts terrorists could carry out if they had access to this list. "And it's not something we're talking about."

"You're not going to help me?" Ty's words came out in a strangled cry.

With Quinn's eyes boring through her, letting her see and feel what time spent with him would be like, Nina wanted to say no, but she couldn't deny this terrified boy her help, just because she couldn't handle being in the company of his brother. Plus she couldn't turn her back on her country's need to secure the No-Fly List and keep terrorists off American soil.

"Of course I'll help you, hon," she said to Ty. "But with the FBI's connection to the database, I'd rather we have this chat off campus until I know the full scope of the problem. Too many people to overhear us here."

Quinn shot a questioning look at Ty. "What connection?"

"You didn't tell him about the FBI, Ty?" Nina asked.

Ty shook his head hard, his bangs sliding over his eyes again. "I figured if he knew, he wouldn't ask you to help. You're my only hope. I don't wanna be locked up for the rest of my life."

"More importantly, you don't want to be the cause of another terrorist attack," Quinn added.

Nina frowned at him. "We aren't talking about that."

"Fine." Quinn shoved his hands in his pockets, the muscles in his arms flexing under the tight fabric. "Can you at least explain the FBI connection?"

She nodded. "The TSA enforces the No-Fly List and they're under the Department of Homeland Security. But domestic names on the list are fed from a database managed by a division of the FBI. So this is in my own backyard so to speak, and I'll need to tread lightly if I'm to help Ty."

"But you can help me, right?" Ty's voice broke, and Nina could see he was close to tears. He needed to get out of there. To a more relaxed location. A neutral place where they'd both feel free to discuss the details of his hack.

"Let's go somewhere to talk about that." She tugged him to his feet. His cold, clammy hand didn't surprise her. She gave his fingers a quick squeeze before escorting him down the hall. She could feel Quinn's eyes on her back, but she forced her mind to remain on Ty.

The kid was in trouble just as Quinn had said. Big trouble. Federal trouble. As much as Nina's heart ached to work this out without bringing the incident to her supervisor, as a law enforcement officer, she was required to report any crime she had knowledge of. Plus, she followed procedure. All the time. Deviating from it could cost lives. Garrett's death was proof of that.

She glanced at Ty again, her heart breaking for him. She hated to turn him in, but better Ty served time than letting terrorists modify the No-Fly List and perpetrate another unspeakable tragedy on American soil.

Chapter Four

PRETENDING TO dodge the spitting rain, Wiley tucked his head into his hooded balaclava, as they called it at the store, and stepped out of Kip's car. The hood portion of the balaclava kept him warm, and the fabric fold that could be worn around the neck like a scarf also pulled up over his face to hide his scars. Allowed him to travel freely on Portland's mass transit system without raising an eyebrow. It was a solution when the weather was cold, but that wouldn't be a problem much longer. Not when he got the money for plastic surgery.

He watched the trio of pedestrians strolling toward him. A mom, dad, and young boy. Oblivious to him. Oblivious to his secret. Oblivious to the time slipping by.

C'mon, c'mon, c'mon. Move faster.

He didn't like this. Really didn't like it. The bead of sweat running down his back was proof. He was a hacker. He should be sitting behind a computer. Not loitering on the street waiting for a chance to make his move. He'd hated to go over there in broad daylight. Never had before, but time was of the essence. He had to move his plan forward before Brandt somehow wormed her way out of his clutches. That meant taking chances. Even with all these people around him. People who could be watching. Planning against him.

Relax. You have to relax. They'll pick up on your anxiety.

He stepped closer to the building, giving the family plenty of room. He pretended to stare at his phone so they'd pass by without a thought. They were even with him now, not paying him any attention. Their heads bent forward as the rain picked up and they walked by, talking about their day.

Good. They were who they seemed to be. Strangers, not spies Brandt had sent to watch him. No need to worry.

He waited for them to step away and forced himself to count to one hundred when all he wanted to do was bolt. He checked the street. They'd turned a corner. Finally alone. Blessedly alone.

He eased down the street, past the Diamond Hotel's sagging sign and tired facade. He eyed the area again, then ducked into the alley. A few yards in, he found what he was looking for. He slid into an opening not more than a foot wide running between the hundred-year-old hotel and a dive restaurant that changed owners every year. He sidestepped along the wall. The hotel's rough brick sandpapered against the back of his hoodie, and his shopping bag scraped the restaurant's stucco wall.

Midway, he felt the change in the wall and stopped. Listened. Heard nothing. He took a few more steps. Arched his back. Just in the right spot. He pressed hard, opening a hidden door, the warped wood sliding inward toward his underground space. An earthy scent rose up to greet him as he backed inside. One foot at a time. Careful not to trip and tumble down the rotted wooden steps as he had when he'd first discovered the hidden room five years ago.

What a happy accident it was to literally stumble upon this unknown section of the Shanghai Tunnels. Running from the basements of Portland's downtown hotels and bars to the Willamette River, legend claimed the tunnels were built in the 1800s to move goods from ships docked on the Willamette to basement storage areas. Some say they were used to capture and illegally sell able-bodied men to sea captains in need of crew members, shanghaiing them. Hence the name.

Wiley had found this undiscovered section of the tunnels thanks to a miserable job in the Diamond Hotel's laundry room. His manager, Harold Dabchick had been a real jerk. Always needling Wiley. Out to get him, he was. Telling him to work harder. Faster. Letting others slack off. All the time, keeping Wiley constantly under his scrutiny. Story of his life.

But Wiley showed him one night when it'd been particularly bad, when Wiley had needed to spark up a doobie just to stand Harold's griping and the stench of harsh bleach. Wiley had slipped into the alley and had taken a few hits, but, no. Harold wouldn't give Wiley even a minute to himself and came looking. He would have called the cops, so Wiley moved into the space between the buildings. Harold kept coming. Wiley kept moving. In the middle, he put out his joint on the brick and felt the walls closing in. He panicked. Leaned back. Then, bam. The door swung inward, and he took a header down the stairs into a blast from the past.

He felt certain no one else knew about the space. Not surprising. It was claustrophobic heading down the dead-end passageway nearly a block long. If Wiley hadn't been desperate, he'd never have found it.

Plus mounds of boulders blocked the tunnel leading from his space, keeping others from discovering his room from inside the other tunnels. This was his sanctuary and only his. He'd never shared it with anyone. Not even Lila.

Now he was glad he'd kept it from everyone. It was perfect for his plans.

Closing the door, he shone the light from his cell phone and crossed uneven stone floors to his makeshift office. Years ago, he'd found a ratty old table discarded in a corner, probably from the mid-1800s when this network of catacombs had been constructed.

He dropped his bags on the table next to his state-of-the-art computer. He'd worked a few hacking jobs for his former cellmate, Rodolfo Wheeler, a.k.a. Crash, to make enough money to buy the machine and take care of other needs when he'd gotten out of prison. Another secret he kept from everyone. From the FBI. From Kip. From the hotel where he was stealing Wi-Fi and electricity.

He clicked on the lamp he'd added. Light spilled into cobwebbed corners, illuminating the start of a long tunnel ending in a pile of rubble.

He stepped to his table and sighed, contentment settling over him. He was alone. No one was watching. He was safe here. From everything. He'd desperately craved solitude in prison, but there was always someone there. Yapping like Kip. Demanding and bullying. But here? Here, he was the king. In his lair.

He laughed, his voice ringing through the space not more than seven feet high with pipes and wires running through the ceiling.

Like he needed a lair. When he sold the hack, he'd be set and he didn't plan to inhabit an underground space for long. After years in prison, he wanted wide-open windows and light. Lots and lots of light. With walls surrounding his home. Thick, heavy walls. A fortress to keep him safe from others. That took money, and he needed to get to work.

Before he could pull the items from his shopping bag, his burner phone rang. Only one person had this number. Crash.

Wiley had called Crash to use his vast connections to locate a buyer for the No-Fly hack and arrange an advance, allowing Wiley to put his plan into place. Crash would take a cut of the final sale, but Wiley was willing to share for an expedited sale.

Thankful he'd installed a signal booster so his phone worked in the tunnel, he answered it. "Tell me you have good news."

"The buyer's on board. Get me the screenshots and you've got your fifty-grand advance."

Wiley smiled. It would be simple to log in to the list to take a couple screenshots proving to Crash that Wiley could access the database. "I'll get them to you today."

"Then you'll have your money in the morning."

"Perfect." Wiley disconnected. He needed every penny Crash fronted to pull off this deal.

Time to get *Operation Payback* underway.

He snapped on latex gloves, then rifled through his shopping bags and dug out two prepaid phones. He worked quickly to unpackage them. Once he had access to Brandt's and Hamid's wireless access accounts—to leave an electronic trail from their respective homes—Wiley would register one in Hamid's name and the other in Brandt's. Wiley could use the phones to send texts between Hamid and Brandt, making it look like they were communicating with each other about the hack.

When Wiley was ready for the FBI to arrest Brandt, he'd make sure they located the phones. Once the Feds had them, they'd request call logs, and GPS reports would provide the phone's location from where the texts had originated. So Wiley had to hide one phone at Hamid's house and the other at Brandt's home or near her work. It meant he had to keep tabs on both of them and he would feel like a yo-yo as he went between the locations to send texts to the other person, but great victory required great sacrifice.

He set the phones to charge, then removed a loose brick and retrieved his father's old Colt revolver.

A simple gun, but one that worked. Had worked. Perfectly. On the people who'd made his life miserable. It would work now if needed.

He wasn't going back to prison. Ever.

QUINN CROSSED HIS arms and leaned against the column in the small coffee shop as he waited for their drinks. Despite the comforting aroma of freshly ground coffee beans, acid churned in his stomach as he kept an eye on Nina and Ty in the corner booth.

Nina. The woman he'd loved and lost. Correction: let slip away. Chose to let slip away. To keep at a distance, and still, he couldn't take his eyes off her. Off that fiery red hair, and the temper to go with it when she allowed it to take over her Southern upbringing. A smile no man could get enough of. The soft, sultry accent. And curves. Man, the woman had curves that didn't end. She was the direct opposite of everything he'd ever known. Hard meets soft. And she had this way of walking. It drove him crazy just to watch her move.

She was unique—different from other women he'd met. Women

who threw themselves at SEALs. But Nina? Nah, she wasn't impressed with his SEAL status. She'd made him work hard that first night just to get her to talk to him, hooking him on the spot. They might have parted ways, but each time he saw her, he knew he hadn't managed to wiggle off the hook.

"Hot chocolate, coffee black, and a chai," the barista announced.

Quinn shoved off the wall and grabbed their drinks. He stared at the ugly scars crisscrossing his hand like an intricate spider web. The long hours after the explosion lying in the hospital came flooding back. The pain had been excruciating as they removed the rotting, dead skin from his burns. The team had been deployed for most of his stay, leaving him alone for the first time in years and giving him hours of nothing to do but think. He'd gotten a good look at how empty his life was. Didn't like everything he saw. Especially when it came to Nina.

He started for their booth. She snaked her arm around Ty's back and hugged him close. She would be such a great mother and deserved a family. It was something Quinn wanted, too. If for no other reason than to be the kind of father his dad had failed to be. But that wasn't happening soon. The hours of inactivity in the hospital had made Quinn want to crawl out of skin. Living his life, the adrenaline, the excitement, that was the only way he could breathe. It was the very life that kept Nina and him apart. That hadn't changed.

By the time he reached them, they'd separated and both of them stared up at him. Ty's eyes were terrified. Nina's unreadable.

He passed the hot chocolate to Ty. "Did you bring Nina up to speed on everything?"

Ty shook his head, long bangs flopping over Ty's eyes and making Quinn want to pull out his KA-BAR to chop it off.

"Why not?" He tried not to sound demanding.

Ty shrugged.

Nina cast a pointed look at Quinn. "I thought it'd be a good idea to take a break. To give both of you a chance to calm down before things are said that can't be taken back."

Quinn set the tea in front of her and slid into the booth across from them, making sure his knees didn't connect with hers. "You think it's a good idea to waste time on feelings with the database wide open to terrorists?"

She arched a brow. "A few minutes for a mental health break are always in order. That was something you used to believe in. Or did you just go along with it to humor me when we were together?"

"I still think it's a good idea."

"Just not for me," Ty mumbled.

Quinn shot a look at Ty. "What's that supposed to mean?"

"Whatever I do, you want me to do the opposite."

"That's not true."

Ty rolled his eyes. "Right."

"C'mon, Ty. I want what's best for you. You know that, right?"

"Then why the Dad imitation? I'm your brother, man. Not your kid." He crossed his arms. "I get enough grief from Dad."

Quinn took a breath. Calmed his anger. Why couldn't he be as good with Ty as Nina was? In the year they'd been together, she'd served as a positive force when Ty had rebelled against everyone else. He liked her and listened to her.

Quinn couldn't help him. He could barely keep his temper in check around the undisciplined kid, as today had proven. "You're right, Ty. I'm coming on too strong, but I don't want to see you make mistakes that will ruin your life."

Ty snorted. "Then you can relax 'cause I just did that, didn't I? Big time."

Quinn might want to throttle Ty, but his stomach roiled at the angst in Ty's expression. His little brother was likely headed to jail. At the minimum, juvenile detention. And for once, Quinn couldn't do a thing to help. Nothing. That ate him up inside.

"Let's change our focus to fixing this, okay?" Nina asked as she placed a hand on Ty's. "Start by giving me all the details of this incident. Don't leave anything out."

He pulled his hand free and grabbed his cup. "So like I said, Ham—"

"Is Ham his real name?" Nina interrupted.

"No. It's Hamid. Hamid Ahmadi."

"You didn't tell me he was of Middle Eastern descent." Quinn's voice exploded in an accusation.

Ty jutted out his chin. "He was born in the U.S., so what diff does it make?"

Quinn leaned across the table to thump Ty's forehead. "You know, for being such a genius, you can be oblivious at times. This Ham kid's skin color already has people looking at him funny at the airport, and you put him on a terrorist watch list? Now he might have your computer?" He shook his head and sat back. "Unbelievable, kid. Totally unbelievable."

"Let's forget about that for now," Nina said. "Tell me when the computer was stolen and how you know Hamid took it."

"When he got home from the airport on Saturday, he came to our house demanding to see me. He like goes ballistic on Mom, telling her he knows I'm the only one with enough skills to put him on the list." Ty grinned.

The smug look sent Quinn's irritation rising. He fisted his hands to keep from slamming one on the table.

"When I come downstairs, he says he's gonna get back at me," Ty continued. "'Course I had to tell Mom what I did. I mean, you met her, right? You know no one can hold up under her interrogation."

Nina smiled, and Quinn suspected she was remembering meeting their mom and her intense questioning about Nina's intentions in her relationship with him.

"Can't say her interrogations ever made me smile," Quinn said, trying to lighten the mood a bit.

Nina arched a brow. "Maybe we should send her to talk to Hamid about getting the computer back."

Ty shook his head. "Are you kidding? Not as freaked out as she was."

"I *am* kidding, Ty." Nina flashed a quick smile. "What happened after your mother learned of your hack?"

"She said she would call Q, like she always does."

"She knows I want to help you," Quinn said, trying to make Ty see that they both loved him and wanted the best for him.

Ty shifted into the corner of the booth, defiance building on his face. Quinn knew belligerence would soon follow.

"What happened next?" Nina asked softly, defusing Ty's attitude a bit.

"Q was unavailable, but I figure he'd be hopping on a plane as soon as she got a hold of him." Ty sat up a little taller. "I knew once he got here, that I'd be grounded for life. So, I figure, hey, I'll get in a little fun while I can. You know, hang with the guys one last time."

"The guys?" Nina asked.

"There're three of us who work on computer stuff together. Bryce, me, and Jimmy. Kind of a club, I guess."

"So Hamid isn't a part of your group?"

"Not most of the time. If we're in a public place, Ham cuts in some-times, and we let him hang for a while. You know, instead of making a scene. That's how he found out about my girl." Ty shook his head. "Jerk."

"Did you see Hamid Saturday night?"

"Yeah. We were at a diner where we like to work on our computers. Ham was there, but he didn't try to crash the group. Just glared at us from the door. It was kinda creeping us out so we split. We left our equipment in Bryce's car and . . ." He cut a nervous look at Quinn.

Quinn knew the look. He'd gotten to know it intimately well this last year. Ty was about to tell them he'd done something else Quinn wouldn't approve of.

"We have fake IDs," Ty blurted out. "You know. Made 'em ourselves. Ham doesn't have one. With his Iranian heritage, his ID is scrutinized more, and he couldn't create one that passed inspection. To ditch him, we went to a club he couldn't get into. I had a little too much to drink, so I went to Bryce's house to sleep it off. His parents were out of town. Instead of sleeping, we partied through the weekend until I kinda passed out. Jimmy dropped me off Sunday night, but I left my stuff in Bryce's car. I crashed like right away and didn't know my laptop was missing until Q woke me up."

Quinn shook his head. "Now I know why I had to drag your sorry butt out of bed today."

Ty jutted out his chin. "What? You never touched liquor at my age?"

Quinn had, and he couldn't deny it. "We're talking about you."

"Right. Not Saint Q. The perfect son."

Quinn resisted letting out a sigh of frustration. "I didn't say I was perfect."

"You don't have to. Mom says it enough for everyone."

Quinn opened his mouth to respond, but Nina jumped in. "So when you woke up today, is that when you noticed your computer missing?"

"No, but after I crashed, I kind of forgot about it. Then Q busts into my room and wakes me up. Throws all these questions at me about the hack. When he stopped yelling at me for screwing up, I remembered someone had busted into Bryce's car and stole it. I figure Ham followed us to Bryce's house and swiped it for payback."

"Okay, let's say Hamid does have your machine," Nina said. "Could he use your data to access the No-Fly List?"

Ty tipped his head in thought. "First, he'd have to hack my password and it's a good one."

"Is he a hacker?"

"Yeah, I mean, he has skills. He's done a few hacks that I know of. Nothing like me, but like I said, I left a clear trail to follow so I could go back into the database and take him off the list. But if he got through my password and found that stuff . . ." Ty shrugged. "He could get into the database, I suppose."

"Specifically what do you mean by this trail?" Quinn asked, and he could see Nina wanted the same information.

"Two things. I kept a detailed log in Notepad of each of my steps. As a backup, I used a keystroke logger to record my moves. Not that it mattered." He smirked. "With the big stink Ham made, I left his name on the No-Fly List."

Quinn remembered reading something about these logger programs that record the keys struck on a keyboard. It was often done in a covert manner to catch someone doing something illegal, like cheating on a spouse. They were also used by parents to monitor their kids' computer use. Ty had, of course, found a very inventive use for it and could very well have created a trail that would ensure his jail time.

"So if the computer is found, this log and document could be used as evidence against Ty?" Quinn asked.

Nina nodded.

"You'll get my computer back, right Nina?" Ty's brows furrowed. "I mean, Ham's got to be the one who has it, right?"

"It could have been taken in a random burglary," Nina said. "I'll check to see if other break-ins have been reported in the area. For now let's assume Hamid does have it. Any thoughts on what he'd do with it?"

"Dunno." Ty's eyes narrowed in contemplation. "But I'm sure he'll use it to get me in trouble."

That was one of the things Quinn was concerned about. "Which could mean he'd turn it in to the police to prove you hacked the No-Fly List and make sure you're arrested."

"I doubt it. There's a code between us, ya know? We may not like each other, but we don't rat each other out either. 'Sides, turning it in could make the cops investigate Ham, and his hacks are serious enough to get him arrested."

"What about the break-in?" Nina asked. "Did Bryce call the police about that?"

"Not sure. He wouldn't wanna be tied to what's on my machine either. There's plenty on there to—"

"Enough." Nina held up her hands silencing Ty. "I don't want to know about anything else on your computer unless it relates to the case, or I'll have to report it, too."

Ty's head whipped around. "You're turning me in?

"I'm sorry, Ty. I'm a sworn officer of the law. I have to report it."

"But they'll arrest me." His head drooped.

"It's okay, bud." Quinn tried to sound positive, though the world was closing in on him. "I've already lined up a lawyer for you."

"A lawyer?" Ty's head popped up. "You said Nina would help me. I thought that meant she'd take care of this. Man, oh man. You knew all along that she'd turn me in. How could you?"

Quinn saw the betrayal in Ty's expression, and his gut tightened. He wanted to drag his little brother off somewhere and hide him until all of this could be resolved without it ending in a prison sentence. But Quinn lived his SEAL oath. No matter the consequences.

The words echoed in his head. *I humbly serve as a guardian to my fellow Americans, always ready to defend those who are unable to defend themselves.*

Stopping whoever had the ability to modify the No-Fly List superseded any desire to protect Ty.

"I had to, Ty. It's a matter of national security." Quinn cringed at how much he sounded like their father. Mr. General Sir. The all-American who always put country first and family last. The man with expectations so high that neither Quinn nor Ty could live up to them. The man Quinn didn't want Ty to think he'd become. To let *anyone* think he'd become.

Ty shook his head. "I can't believe you did this to me."

"I'm sorry, Ty." Quinn paused to get Ty's attention, but he wouldn't look at him. "We have no choice but to report this if we don't want another catastrophic attack in our country."

"You had a choice. Me or your precious code of conduct." Ty slid down in his seat and crossed his arms. "Guess I shouldn't be surprised. Not after what you did to Nina. Bailing on her like that."

"Ty," Nina chastised. "Don't blame Quinn for that."

"Why not? It's his fault." Ty glared at Quinn, then turned back to Nina. "I mean, look at you. You're the best. A computer pro and hot, too. What more could a guy want?" A flush of red crept up his face. "If Quinn didn't want to be a mini-dad, then he could have found another job and you'd still be together."

"You couldn't be farther from the truth on who I want to be, bud," Quinn growled, but now wasn't the time to elaborate on his desire to be anything but their father. He focused on Nina. "Tell us what happens now."

"I file an official report, and an arrest warrant will likely be issued for Ty. It would be good if you both came back to the office with me and Ty surrenders without anyone having to hunt him down."

Quinn nodded. "We can do that."

"Easy for you to say," Ty mumbled.

Nina turned to Ty. "You're a juvenile, Ty, and should be treated as such. This is your first offense, and you didn't have malicious intent, other than to get back at Hamid. I'll do everything I can to make the DA see you in a positive light and keep you out of juvie."

"Right," Ty muttered.

Nina's explanation made everything suddenly more real. Made Ty's future seem dire, and Quinn seriously thought he might lose it. Right there, right now. He'd faced risks most men wouldn't stand up under. Yet thinking about his baby brother going to jail might take him under. Quinn couldn't let that happen. Not without doing his best to stop it.

Chapter Five

QUINN STEPPED in front of Nina, blocking her access to her car. Getting her on board was now mission critical. He could do it. He'd never failed before. Never. But then, his mission had never included Nina. The woman who went by the book. Always. Controlled and precise. Step by step, logically following the rules. It was an approach she'd adopted long ago to deal with her mother, and he knew it was something he had little chance of overcoming. But he had to try. That meant not running roughshod over her, but asking for her help.

"Please don't turn Ty in," he said. "Not yet. Give me twenty-four hours to see what I can find out about the computer."

She shook her head and dug out her keys. "If you'll let me get into my car, I'll—"

"Wait, hear me out," he interrupted. "I know you have to report Ty. That's a given. But won't they go easier on him if he has the computer in his possession and can prove no one else has access to the No-Fly List?"

She didn't even take time to consider his request. "I should have already reported it."

"Think of Ty here." Quinn clamped his hands on Ty's shoulders and pulled him into the conversation. "He has his whole life ahead of him. We have such high hopes for him. You did too, once upon a time. This will ruin him. Give me a chance to fix it. I can head right over to Hamid's house. See if he has the computer. It might give Ty a better chance."

"I can't, Quinn." She glanced at Ty, and her resolve seemed to melt a fraction.

"Yes, you can," Quinn rushed on, taking advantage of the crack in her armor. "I'm only talking about a couple of hours at most." He looked at his watch. "Hamid should be getting out of school soon. I'll take Ty home where he'll be under house arrest with Mom, then head straight to Hamid's house."

"What makes you think he'll give the computer to you?" Nina asked, sounding as if she was now actually considering his request.

"I've learned to be quite persuasive on the job." He winked at her.

His wink seemed to irritate her, and she crossed her arms. "I'm sorry, Quinn. I can't let you do this."

"Let him, please." Ty grabbed her arm. "For me. Please, Nina, please. I learned my lesson. I'll never hack anything again. I promise. Please."

Her eyes narrowed. "I don't know."

Ty stepped closer to her, a silent plea in his expression. "It's only an hour or two. And you know if Ham has the computer, Q can make him give it up."

She flashed an uncertain look at Quinn. "If I agree to this, I have to insist on nothing physical with this kid. Don't lay a hand on him. I mean it. Not even a pinkie."

"So you're good with me talking to him, then?" Quinn held his breath, waiting for her answer.

"Fine," she said. "I'll give you enough time to talk to Hamid. Don't do anything but talk. If he has the computer, call me so I can get a warrant to take it into evidence. Don't turn it on. If it *is* on, don't turn if off. In fact, don't touch it. Period. Once I have it in house, we can check the logs to see if anyone accessed it since Ty last did. If no one has, then we'll keep Hamid out of this and maybe the DA will go easy on Ty."

"Thank you," Quinn said. "I should get going. The sooner I get the computer away from Hamid, the better our odds that he hasn't hacked the password."

Nina lifted her chin. "One final thing before you go. I'm already risking my job by letting you do this. I can't further complicate things by allowing Ty to go home."

"What?" Ty squeaked. "Why not?"

"Though we all know your mother will watch your every move, I have to be able to look my supervisor in the eye and tell him that once I learned of the hack, I didn't give you the chance to destroy evidence. Going home or logging on to any computer would let you do that, if you wanted to."

"What do you propose?" Quinn asked.

"Ty needs to stay in sight of an agent at all times. With my connection to your family, it can't be me. I'm not considered impartial. I'll arrange for someone on our team to watch him in a neutral location."

"Who?" Ty asked warily.

"I'm hoping Becca will be free by now."

"She's cool," Ty said. "I wouldn't mind spending time with her."

Web of Shadows

Nina looked at Quinn. "Is there a neighbor who would house Ty and Becca for a few hours?"

"Sure. Mom's made friends with most of the neighbors so someone will do it. And, of course, Mom will be joining them." Quinn clapped his hands. "Let's roll."

She focused on Ty. "I need to talk to Quinn alone for a minute."

"Fine." Ty's shoulders drooped as he schlepped toward Quinn's car. His untied shoes slapped on the sidewalk. Quinn's military training and upbringing made him want to tug up his brother's pants and tie his shoes.

"What is it that you need to tell me?" Quinn asked Nina.

"If you don't find the computer, my supervisor will insist on involving the FBI's National Security Branch," she replied. "You better prepare your family. They'll assume Ty's a terrorist first and a stupid teenager second. They'll sweep down on him faster than flies on honey."

As a SEAL, Quinn was fully aware of the kind of sweep that would be forthcoming. "They'll tear our house apart and detain all of us."

She nodded. "Then you'll be faced with endless rounds of interrogations. Homeland Security could get involved, too. Then, there's the press. They're sure to get wind of the investigation. When they find out you're a SEAL and your dad's a general . . ."

"Our family reputation will be toast. We might have to resign."

"I hope it doesn't go that far and I'll try to contain it." She peered up at him. "I love that kid, you know? I'll do my best for him. But I've never dealt with anything like this before, and I'm not sure I have enough clout at the Bureau to make a difference. But I will try. That's all I can promise."

WILEY MADE SURE the area was clear before climbing from Kip's car and hurrying to the back of Brandt's house. He'd never actually broken into a place before, but his prison buddies had taught him how to do it. Thankfully, Brandt didn't have a security system. After donning latex gloves, taking off his shoes, and keeping his hoodie up so he wouldn't leave behind any DNA evidence, he was inside in a few minutes.

All the blinds were closed so he shone his flashlight into the family room. She had that whole rustic décor thing going on.

She wanted rustic, huh? He'd give her rustic. A dark, dank cell. Like his had been while she'd lived it up in the lap of luxury.

He sat in front of her computer, letting his gloved fingers trail over the keyboard. He could imagine her sitting there at her desk. Her freaky

43

red hair in that bun she'd worn every day of his trial. Or maybe she'd let the curls go, as she had in the picture with the SEAL. Curls like Medusa's snakes.

Perfect comparison.

She was just like Medusa. He could easily believe gazing at her could turn a person to stone.

"Yeah, Medusa." He chuckled. He considered calling her that all the time as he rifled though the mounds of papers on her desktop,

Man, what a slob. She didn't file anything. He kept digging until he found her banking information. He didn't want to share his haul with her, but framing her for the hack meant putting money in her account. He dug a little deeper, went into file drawers where papers stuck up at odd angles. She couldn't even file neatly. What a loser.

He soon found the list of passwords he sought. She'd disguised them, but he knew what he was looking at. He clicked a few keys. The computer screen flashed to life.

"Bingo. Medusa is as dumb as most geeks I've met." They secured their wireless routers, thus protecting themselves from unauthorized electronic access outside their house, but foolishly kept enough data lying around to let anyone who entered their home invade their privacy. He now possessed her banking, wireless router, and computer passwords. He dug out a prepaid cell phone from his pocket and registered it in Brandt's name. Then he sat back to gloat for a moment. It was going to be easy to ruin Brandt's life.

HAMID'S HOUSE SAT on a quiet street in Troutdale, not far from Quinn's parents. The typical suburban tree-lined street held cookie-cutter houses grouped close together with manicured lawns. Mailboxes lined the far side of the road. A green space filled with tall pines and large ferns ran along the other.

It was exactly what Quinn had needed while casing Hamid's house. As a SEAL sniper, he was trained to find dead space to put something between himself and the target. He'd arrived fifteen minutes ago and had selected a secluded spot to observe. He'd seen enough to know no one was home, providing him the opportunity to slip inside to locate the computer before Hamid got home.

Nina wouldn't approve, but what she didn't know . . .

He checked the street one last time, then crossed the road. He carried his father's old briefcase and had dressed in his only suit that he'd found buried in the back of a closet at his parents' house. He hoped he looked like a business professional. He chuckled. It wasn't a look he'd ever needed in his many covert operations.

He rang the doorbell. In the event anyone answered, he'd worked out a spiel about getting the wrong address. But no one did.

After a quick look around, he put gloves on, then slipped lockpicks from his pocket and opened the door. He entered the two-story contemporary home, closing the door behind him and making a quick assessment. Stairwell ahead. Family room to the side. Kitchen adjoining. He tugged his necktie loose and listened to be sure no one was home. The refrigerator hum was the only sound. He eased through the foyer and quickly swept the lower level. A calico cat jumped from a ledge, startling him, but it soon wrapped around his ankles and purred.

He scratched it behind the ears, then crossed to the stairwell. Once upstairs, he checked all the rooms, returning to the one with posters of crazy rock bands on walls painted a dark blue. The sheets were jumbled at the foot of the bed, and clothes were strewn on the floor. Quinn wanted to grab up all the mess and chuck it out the window. Much like he wanted to do in Ty's room.

Instead, he stepped through it and checked the laptop model. It wasn't a match for Ty's. Quinn started sifting through the mess, searching for the machine.

Twenty minutes later, he'd left no location unsearched but hadn't come up with the computer. He sat on the window ledge to think, when he heard the front door open.

A young male's voice drifted up the stairs. "I'm home. Gotta grab something to eat and my computer, then I'll be over."

Quinn stepped behind the door and waited for Hamid to enter the room. Quinn had never interrogated a kid before, giving him a moment's pause.

So what if he was a kid? He was also a thief and possessed information that could clear Ty. Quinn's brother. His flesh and blood. SEALs took care of their family. Of their own.

The lives of my teammates and the success of our mission depend on me.

He'd never leave a teammate in trouble without doing everything he could to fix the problem. Never. That went double for a blood relative.

NINA SWUNG HER car into the employee entrance at work. As she waited for the state-of-the-art gate to open, her decision to let Quinn talk to Hamid plagued her. She hadn't really thought it through, hadn't done a cost-benefit analysis as she'd been taught. Instead, she'd just said yes because of the sorrowful eyes of a teenage boy she cared about.

The gate slid open, and she pulled into the parking garage. She had such a soft spot for Ty. Though her brother had been gone for more than twenty years, she'd often wondered if she'd taken to Ty so quickly to try to fill the void left by Garrett's death. It would explain her hasty decision with Quinn.

Decision, right. She'd just committed career suicide. Or not. It all depended on how Quinn handled the visit to Hamid and the outcome. Right. Like she even needed to question what he'd do. He'd barrel into the house. Scare the kid and threaten him. Then what? Hamid would go running to his mom and dad, and she'd be called up to Assistant Special Agent in Charge Roland Sulyard's office, where he'd scream at her. Put her on probation. Maybe fire her.

She swung into a parking space and turned off the ignition, her mind running over her options. As if her thoughts had called up Sulyard, he strode across the lot and swiped his keycard. Six feet, one-eighty, and bald, he carried himself with as much confidence as Quinn. She visualized the two of them meeting. Quinn defending Ty. Sulyard and Quinn sparring. Eyes flashing, tempers rising. She'd never won an argument with her supervisor, but she could imagine Quinn coming out on top.

He'd often mentioned that passing Basic Underwater Demolitions/SEAL training wasn't about physical strength like everyone thought, but about perseverance. He'd passed BUD/S with flying colors and would easily hold his own against Sulyard.

Of course, that would make Sulyard even angrier, and he'd take her aside to chastise her for letting her heart rule her brain again. Chastise her for letting go. For easing up on the self-discipline she tried to maintain in her life.

She groaned. Why had she agreed to this crazy plan anyway? What had she been thinking?

Nothing, just that she had to help Ty. Maybe help Quinn. Which was unacceptable. If she *had* been thinking and doing her job, she'd at least have accompanied him to Hamid's house. Now she had to get out of there and do some damage control. Her career depended on it.

MISSION ACCOMPLISHED. Wiley had managed to hack Hamid's wireless router, register the second cell phone to Hamid and use it to set up a bank account in Hamid's name, then bagged the phone and hidden in the yard. All carried out, no thanks to the SEAL showing up.

Wiley had heard the car arrive from his location in Hamid Ahmadi's side yard. He'd peeked between fence slats and spotted the SEAL step from his SUV. He'd hightailed it back behind the air conditioner where only a moment ago he'd hidden the cell phone.

Thankfully, Wiley had parked Kip's car a few blocks away and the SEAL had gone straight into the house without searching outside. So Wiley sat for a while. Waiting for the dude to leave. He didn't, and Wiley was growing impatient. He went to the gate, cracked it open, and glanced down the street, the idyllic suburban setting grating at him

Where had he gone wrong? Penniless and homeless, at his age. Even a kid whose parents emigrated from the Middle East had it better than he did. So unfair. It had been that way all his life. But that would end now. He deserved so much more than this kid. It made it all the easier to hide the phone and set the kid up.

Wiley checked the other direction. The SEAL's silver SUV sat a few doors down. It hadn't moved, and there was no other movement on the street, except for the wind rustling leaves. Not even kids playing outside. Not surprising. Their parents were too busy running the rat race in the city, making money and ignoring their kids. Like his parents. Too busy to care. Treating Wiley worse than the dog. Making his life hell. Always punishing him. Blaming him. They'd been out to get him from day one.

Then again, look where that had gotten them. He smiled. Yeah, look what he'd done to them. They got what they'd deserved. Just this week. At least Hamid would be saved from *that*.

He stepped out and resisted whistling as he eased along the side of the house. A quick peek around the corner and he jerked back. He'd taken too long and Hamid was home. Wiley checked again. There was no mistaking the dark hair or the typical sloppy dress. The kid wore baggy jeans, a green T-shirt, and headphones as he set down a backpack then shuffled to the mailbox. His focus was on his feet.

Oblivious. Like most teens. No clue Wiley was there.

Good. He couldn't get caught now.

Wiley soon heard the front door opening. He counted to thirty, then risked another glance around the corner. A big black Chevy Tahoe pulled to the curb behind the silver SUV. The door opened and a woman slid down, planting her feet firmly on the ground while she surveyed the area.

What the . . . ? *Brandt*. No freaking way.

Wiley snapped back.

What was *she* doing there? Did she know about the hack? About the computer? Was she there to bring him down again?

Or was this a coincidence? Hamid seemed to be Tyler Stone's friend, so maybe, by extension, he was a friend of hers, too.

Friends don't put your pricey laptop in a geocache.

Maybe Hamid really was a terrorist. Or more likely, this Tyler kid went running to Brandt about Hamid pilfering his computer. Now the stinkin' FBI agent was there to use her clout to make Hamid's life hell.

It was the exact same way she'd targeted Wiley. She'd had tons of criminals on her radar, but she'd set out to get him. Purposefully. Him and only him. Now she was back again. After him? He knew she would do this. Just not there. Not yet.

He jerked out his gun, held it firmly. Considered pulling the trigger to cut his losses. A simple squeeze of his finger. She'd fall to the ground. There. Now. In front of him. But what about the years of his suffering? Would a quick bullet take away the ache?

His head hurt with the pressure of making so many decisions lately. He squeezed his eyes closed. He needed the pain to go away. A bullet to her head wouldn't do it. He'd have to put up with the pain. Just a bit longer.

Chapter Six

NINA ARRIVED IN time to see Hamid enter the contemporary home with angular roof lines. Quinn's car was there, which meant he was already inside. He'd either broken into the house or Hamid's parents had let him in, making this worse than she'd thought.

She straightened her jacket and hurried across the street as fast as her heels allowed. She found the door standing open a few inches. With the door ajar, she could claim concern for the occupant's safety and enter under exigent circumstances. She bumped it open further with her hip and rested her hand on her gun.

"FBI, anyone home?" she called out. She heard movement upstairs and took a step inside. "Hello. Is anyone here?"

"Up here," Quinn replied but he didn't sound happy about it.

She charged up the stairs, following voices down the hallway to a room with dark walls and posters of heavy metal bands. Dressed in a dark-gray suit and white shirt, Quinn was perched on a window seat. The fabric strained over his biceps, and he tugged on the shirt collar as if it was strangling him.

In the year they dated, she'd never seen him wear anything but his uniform or knit shirts and tactical pants. He clearly wasn't comfortable in the suit. She made a mental note to ask about it later and focused on the teen sitting at a desk.

Dark-skinned with glossy black hair, Hamid—she assumed—held a bag of chips and a Coke. He looked terrified. Not surprising, with Mr. Intensity glaring across the room, but Nina doubted Quinn had touched the kid.

"Hamid?" she asked.

He nodded.

She moved her jacket aside to display her badge. "I'm Special Agent Nina Brandt with the FBI. I'm guessing you already know Quinn."

"We're acquainted," Quinn said, sarcasm liberally coating his words.

"He's Ty's brother. A SEAL." The admiration in Hamid's tone mixed oddly with a shaky voice.

"Are your parents home?" Nina asked.

He shook his head.

"Can you call one of them to come home?"

"Nina, don't." Quinn came to his feet and started to walk toward her. "I need to talk to him first."

She fired a warning look for him to stay put and didn't bother apologizing for changing her mind and ruining his plan. She was there and in charge now. Which meant they'd do things by the book. Quinn stopped his forward advance, but she knew it was a temporary victory. She'd have to continue to monitor and manage his movements.

She faced Hamid again. "I really need to talk to one of your parents."

He chewed on his bottom lip. "My dad's on a business trip in Japan. Mom's at yoga, and she leaves her phone in a locker." He glanced at his watch. "She usually gets home in about an hour. If she doesn't have to make any stops on the way."

Nina handed Hamid her business card. "Send her a text anyway. Tell her I'm here, and I need her to join us as soon as she can."

He set down his snack and took the card. "She'll freak out."

"I'm sorry to do that to her, but this is a matter of national security, and we don't have time to wait for her to come home."

"National security?" He glanced at Quinn. "He said it was about Ty's laptop. I didn't do any . . . oh wait." He slapped his forehead. "This isn't just about the computer. It's about Ty hacking the No-Fly List, isn't it?"

"I didn't say that." Though he was right, Nina wouldn't confirm his suspicions so that Hamid could spread the information around their school.

"You don't have to say it. I know he did it." He twisted his hands together. "This can't be happening. I mean, Ty always leaves a record of his hacks on his computer. If someone logs in to it—could they access . . . ? Oh, they could . . . probably already did. That's why you're here." His knee started bouncing as he took out his phone and sent the text. "This is bad, isn't it? Really bad. Will I be blamed? Of course I will. I'm Muslim. They always blame us."

The poor kid had already seen his share of discrimination in his life, but Nina couldn't focus on that right now. Not when he'd just implied that he'd stolen Ty's computer. But he hadn't admitted to logging in to the computer. He'd made it sound more like he'd given it to someone else, which was worse.

She bent down to make eye contact and calm him down enough to talk rationally. "Sounds like you took Ty's computer."

He nodded, but she needed a verbal confession.

"Did you take Ty's computer?"

"Yeah I took it. Man, oh man. Now I'm in trouble. Big trouble. I just wanted to pay him back, you know?" He stared at Quinn. "You do know what he did, right? Putting me on the No-Fly List?" He shook his head. "My mom was with me. They treated us both like dirt."

"I'm sorry that you were treated unfairly." Quinn crossed the room toward them. "If Ty did what you're claiming, then rest assured, he will be punished."

Hamid backed away from Quinn, but he fired a testy look at him. "He did it all right. Who else would?"

"Regardless of who did it or how it happened, we think it was simply a prank that went wrong," Nina explained and moved to the side to block Hamid's view of Quinn. "Just like we believe taking Ty's computer was a prank, too. You didn't have any malicious intent beyond that." She offered a reassuring smile. "If you haven't logged on to his computer and you hand it over right now, I'll work on your behalf to keep anyone from filing charges."

"I didn't look at it." A sheepish expression claimed his face. "I mean . . . I tried . . . wouldn't you? But I couldn't hack the password."

"Okay, get it for me. Once I review the logs, I'll start sorting out this mess."

Seeming like he might throw up, he rocked in his chair. "I don't have it."

"What do you mean, you don't have it?" Quinn clamped his hands on his waist and eased past Nina. "Where is it?"

Hamid cowered even more. "I hid it." He bit his lip and turned away. "In a geocache."

"You what?" Quinn's voice exploded as he shoved his fingers into his hair. "What in the world is that?"

Nina wished Quinn would take his big, burly body and his need to intimidate out of there. She'd earned the kid's trust, gotten him to relax a bit, and Quinn undid it with one look. She gave him a pointed look that told him to calm down.

He fired back with an "as-if" stare. "I asked what a geocache is."

"It's a treasure hunt of sorts," she said. "Someone hides a treasure, then posts GPS coordinates, as well as clues on a geocaching website, and people search for it."

Quinn pushed past her. "And you put Ty's computer in one of these searches?"

Hamid wrapped his arms around his waist and drew back even more. "It was a last resort. I wanted Ty to pay for what he did to me. At first, I wanted to infect his computer with a virus, but like I said, I couldn't hack his password. That meant I had to go to Plan B. I didn't want to just destroy it. I mean . . . it's a sweet machine and all. But he needed to pay. So I set up the geocache and posted it on Hacktivists. Once it was live for a little while, I planned to email Ty so he could see how long it had been out there, and he'd know others were searching for it, too." The corner of his mouth curled up. "Ty would've totally freaked out."

"And you didn't stop to think about what might happen if someone found it before Ty?" Quinn asked.

"I don't care if they did. It would serve Ty right if he never saw it again."

Quinn fisted his hands. It wasn't hard to see he wanted to knock some sense into Hamid. Nina wanted to do the same thing, but she wouldn't give in to the temptation.

Hamid jutted out his chin. "He deserved it, man. Thanks to him putting me on that list, my whole family is under investigation. I had to hit him where it hurt most. His computer." His eyes suddenly flashed with defiance. "Instead of being so peeved, you could be thankful that I only posted it to our Hacktivist group instead of a public site."

Nina moved closer to Hamid to draw his focus. "Tell me about this Hacktivist group."

He sighed out a breath. The defiance disappeared with it. "Membership is private. You need geocache experience to be part of the group. No novices allowed. Plus you have to either work in the IT field or be recommended by another member who can vouch for your IT skills."

Interesting. "Geocaching and information technology is kind of an odd mix."

"The group was started by some friends in the IT business who loved geocaching. Geeks kind of stick together, if you know what I mean, so they decided to limit the group. We have a forum and hold monthly Meetups where we talk IT and caching. It's really just for fun 'cause . . . well . . . you know. Geeks don't tend to get out much."

Since Nina's world revolved around computer nerds—and she was one of them herself—she understood him well.

"How many members are we talking about?" Quinn asked.

"A thousand. Maybe more now."

"So a thousand or more people could have seen your post?" Quinn took a step closer and planted his feet. "And they could all be out trying to find Ty's computer?"

Hamid nodded. "But I hid it well, and I checked on my way home from school. No one claims to have found it."

"We'll need the coordinates for the search." Nina made sure her tone brooked no argument.

Hamid crossed his arms and scowled.

"Don't mess with me, Hamid," she said, starting to get as testy as Quinn. "I've been nice so far, but if you refuse to give me the information, I'll haul you in for impeding an investigation."

"Fine," he grumbled and swiveled his chair.

"Hold up." She slipped between him and his laptop before he could touch it. Hackers often wrote scripts that ran in the background. With a quick flick of a few keys, the script deleted all files. She doubted Hamid was a malicious hacker who had a script waiting in the wings, but she couldn't take a chance.

She held out her cell. "You can use my phone to access the site."

"Why?"

"Long story." She handed her phone to him before she had to explain that, in addition to the possible script, she would be seizing his computer, and she didn't want him touching it. He could log out of or close windows. Or even shut it down before she could stop him, erasing temporary files that could be essential to their investigation. The FBI forensic tech would unplug the machine, causing it to write all temp files to the hard drive, thus making Hamid's most recent activities available for review as well as documenting them for any legal proceedings.

He tapped the screen on her phone, then handed it back to her. "Here's the cache."

After scanning the page, Nina took out her notepad to jot down the website address along with the geocache title in the event her phone malfunctioned. She was a poster child for the use of technology, but it sometimes failed, and she couldn't risk losing the data.

Next, she located the GPS coordinates for the cache and recited them to Hamid for confirmation.

He nodded.

She recorded them on her notepad, too. After leaving there, she'd use them to retrieve the computer. "Give me the approximate area where the cache is hidden."

"It's in the gorge. At the top of Triple Falls."

Not the falls.

Oh, man. That meant climbing up rugged terrain to where the water plummeted into rapids and moved quickly down the gorge. As much she willed her mind not to, it traveled back twenty-two years to the memory of Garrett tumbling into a rushing river. The sharp current grabbing his small body and ripping his hand out of hers. Tugging him downstream toward the rapids and waterfall. The same kind of setting as Triple Falls.

The thought sent her pulse racing. She hadn't been able to go near water since that day. How was she going to get the computer? She could let Quinn go, she supposed, but this wasn't just about locating Ty's computer. It was evidence gathering, and Quinn had no experience in that area. She had no choice. She couldn't let her fears interfere. She had to go up there. Her country needed her. Ty needed her.

Her hands trembling, she thumbed through the site's membership rules. She had to blink a few times to concentrate, but once she did, she saw that users could only deactivate a cache, not delete it. Hopefully that was enough to hide the cache, so others couldn't go looking for the computer.

"I need you to deactivate your post." She held the phone out to Hamid.

He huffed out a breath, but took her phone and tapped the screen. When he'd finished, she checked the site. After confirming the cache was no longer visible to others, she logged him out.

She squarely met Hamid's gaze. "You are not, under any circumstances, to reactivate this cache. Or post another one like it. If I find out you did, I'll arrest you. Understand?"

"Yes," he said sullenly.

"I also want your login and password for the site."

He crossed his arms.

"I'd give it up, if I were you," Quinn said, his eyes awash with mock terror. "You don't want to mess with her. She's something fierce when she gets mad."

"Okay, geez." Hamid rattled off the information.

Nina jotted it down, then stowed her notebook. "Now, I'll need you to come downstairs with me while we wait for your mother."

"I'll stay here."

"I can't let you use your computer, which I know you'll do if I'm not standing over you."

"It's my computer."

"I realize that, but you broke the law when you took Ty's computer and that puts you in the middle of my investigation. Which means, I'll be getting a warrant to search your house and take this computer into evidence."

"No," he whined. "You can't have it. It doesn't have anything on it that has to do with Ty. I swear it doesn't."

"I'm sorry, Hamid, but you posted the cache from here. That means it's evidence, whether you like it or not."

He crossed his arms. "This wouldn't be happening if my parents weren't from Iran."

"It has nothing to do with your nationality, kid," Quinn said. "It has to do with the fact that you stole a laptop that has sensitive information on it."

His eyes widened. "Did Ty do something else besides hack the No-Fly List?"

Nina slashed a hand across her throat to tell Quinn to button it up. "What Ty did isn't your concern. Your concern is cooperating with me and assuring me that you won't do anything to interfere with our investigation."

"When will I get my computer back?"

"It'll remain in evidence for as long as the case is pending. I'll return it as soon as possible. *If* you cooperate and come with me now."

"Fine, I'll go. But where and for how long?"

"We're just going downstairs to wait for your mom to come home."

A smug look claimed his face. "She'll say you can't take my computer."

"Ha, kid," Quinn said. "When Nina's done talking to your mom, she'll not only gladly hand over your computer, she'll probably ground you for the rest of your life."

Chapter Seven

"HOW COULD YOU let Hamid have such free rein?" Quinn's accusatory tone made Mrs. Ahmadi jerk back.

Nina frowned at Quinn. His outbursts were getting them nowhere with Hamid's mother. Much like Nina's talk with Hamid, Quinn hadn't spoken often, but when he did, the conversation came to a screeching halt. This conversation required a gentle touch. Not the bulldozing of a man who wanted to race ahead without a thought and fix the problem. He was not only delaying her trip to find the cache, he was making the entire situation worse. And she'd had enough of it.

"Can I talk with you by the front door for a minute, Quinn?" She didn't wait for his agreement but headed through the formal living room. When he stopped next to her at the front door, she fired a testy look at him. "This isn't one of your search-and-destroy missions. You're alienating the mother."

"So? I don't need her to like me, I need her to give me answers."

"See that's where you're wrong." Nina tugged him closer to the door so Mrs. Ahmadi didn't overhear them. "She can make a big stink about both of us talking to a minor without her present. Plus bring charges for entering her home uninvited. And before you tell me Hamid let you in, I saw Hamid enter the house and you were already in here."

"Could be." He grinned.

"We need her cooperation." She met his gaze and held it. "So this is how the rest of my questioning is going down. You'll go over to Mrs. Ahmadi to apologize. Then you'll excuse yourself to step outside before you do any more damage. I'll try to convince her that all we want is for the two teens not to pay for what they believed were harmless pranks. Then I'll call Kait to come babysit Hamid like Becca is watching Ty and I'll go get that cache. You got that, or do you need me to repeat myself?" She planted a hand on her hip for emphasis.

His lips curved up in one of his dazzling smiles. That familiar warmth rushed through her body. Heaven help her, she almost returned the smile. Almost, until she remembered she was peeved with him. "You think this is funny?"

"Far from it."

"Then why the smirk?"

"I've only ever gotten to see fun Nina. Never work Nina. She's so forceful and in charge." He moved closer, the foot of space between them now a few inches. "It's kind of hot."

She rolled her eyes and planted her hands on his chest to push him back. "Listen to work Nina and wait outside."

He gave a mock salute, and the side of his mouth tipped up in that same adorable crooked grin that made Nina almost forget how much he'd hurt her.

Thankfully, he had no idea that her stomach was flip-flopping over him. He headed back to the family room and Mrs. Ahmadi. "I'm sorry, ma'am, if I offended you. I simply want what's best for my little brother, the same as you want what's best for your son."

He sounded truly contrite. If Nina didn't know she'd made him apologize, she'd have actually believed it. But then, Quinn was always very good at making her believe him. Even when he'd said that he wanted a future with her. Trouble was, he couldn't be trusted not to change his mind.

"I think it best if I take a break and let the three of you discuss this without me," he added.

Mrs. Ahmadi nodded, and her anger seemed to drop a notch. Quinn exited without another word.

Nina smiled at Mrs. Ahmadi. "Why don't we sit down and discuss this?"

Mrs. Ahmadi sat next to Hamid on a traditional sofa in a vivid blue color. Her hair was covered in a traditional gray hijaab, and she wore basic black slacks paired with a powder-blue tunic. She watched Nina warily.

Keeping her smile in place, Nina settled in a club chair across from the pair. "My first goal here is to recover the laptop, but I also want to make sure Ty and Hamid's lives aren't ruined by this incident. I can only help Hamid with your cooperation."

"I don't know." She bit her lip. "You could be trying to trick me."

"I can see why you might be wary of me, Mrs. Ahmadi, but I'm honestly not trying to trick you. I want to solve our security issue, yes, but I'm also here to help. Hamid and Ty did something stupid because they let their teenage rebelliousness get the best of them. They shouldn't have to pay for it for the rest of their lives."

"Agreed, but how will you help Hamid?"

"The computer theft falls under the jurisdiction of local authorities. But if he's cooperative in recovering the laptop, and he hasn't logged in to the computer, I can make recommendations to the locals not to press charges."

"They will listen to you?"

"Can I guarantee it? No. But my experience says they will likely listen and act accordingly." At least she hoped they would.

"Then what is it you wish to do for which you need my approval?"

"First, I will try to recover the laptop. If Hamid has been truthful and provided the right GPS coordinates, we have a much better chance at finding it."

She faced her son. "Tell me you have told the truth in this matter."

"Geez," he said crossing his arms. "Don't go all frantic on me. I told her the truth."

"We will talk about your disrespect later." She swung her gaze back to Nina. "I hope this attitude he has taken lately won't make him seem uncooperative."

Nina offered a reassuring smile. "As long as I find the cache, his belligerence won't be a factor with me. But I suggest you convince him to lose the attitude before going in front of a judge or talking with other law enforcement officers."

"I can assure you he will be dealt with." She cast a quick glare at Hamid, then looked back at Nina. "What happens now?"

"I'll arrange for one of my colleagues to come over and supervise Hamid. Sort of a house arrest. Effective immediately, he'll need to be restricted from using any device with access to the internet."

"What?" Hamid's voice shot high. "No way. I can't live like that. I mean . . . what will I do?"

"Is this really necessary?" Mrs. Ahmadi asked.

Nina nodded. "I have to be sure he can't access files stored in the cloud or on any websites where he's posted this cache and could make changes. Or even try to remotely delete files from his phone or computer. If we can't do it this way, then I'll have to request a warrant and take him into custody to be sure he doesn't have access."

Mrs. Ahmadi gave a firm nod. "Then that is what we will do."

"But Mother," Hamid cried. "No computer. For how long?"

She clasped her hands together. "Until this woman says you are in the clear. Then, maybe I will continue the policy to keep you out of trouble."

"So what am I gonna do then? You let my stupid heart condition keep me from doing anything and the computer is all I have," he grumbled, and Nina could imagine he'd lodged a similar complaint many times.

"Your father will be the final judge of this." She frowned at her son. "For now, you will listen to me."

He jumped up. "Next, you'll tell me I can't even go to the bathroom alone."

"Don't be disrespectful, Hamid. You're free to use the restroom."

"Then may I go to the restroom?" Sarcasm rang through his words.

"Go, and see that when you return, your attitude is gone, or I will let Agent Brandt arrest you." Mrs. Ahmadi curled her fingers into a fist, then quickly opened it, as if she was afraid she might strike her son.

"Before you go—" Nina held out her hand for Hamid. "I'll take your phone."

He frowned and didn't comply.

"Give Agent Brandt your phone," Mrs. Ahmadi commanded.

He slammed it on Nina's palm and marched out of the room. Nina secured it in a Faraday bag that she'd had Quinn retrieve from her car while they were waiting for Mrs. Ahmadi to arrive.

"What is that bag?"

"It's called a Faraday bag. The mesh provides electromagnetic shielding so wireless transmissions can't be received."

"Meaning, Hamid can't access it," she said, sounding sad. "I don't think he'd try to do that after your warning, but I'm not sure about him anymore. He's recently taken an attitude with authority figures. I often wish we hadn't come to America. In my country, this would not be tolerated."

"Has his behavior changed in any other way?" Nina asked, thinking about his room. The posters, especially those of Marilyn Manson, the dark colors—all traits of a youth who could be heading down a road that led to crime. Or it could be innocent, and he simply liked that kind of music. She couldn't be sure at this point.

"Changed in what way?" his mother clarified.

"Has he become secretive? Withdrawn? Moody?"

"Not secretive, but he is far more moody and withdrawn." She bit her lip while twisting her hands together. "As he said, he has a heart condition that keeps him pretty sedentary, so he's always spent a lot of time alone in his room on the computer. I don't think that has increased, but I don't know. I do know he likes to talk back and buck our rules. This you have witnessed."

"Typical teenage behavior." Nina smiled, though she feared his mother might be sugarcoating things, and Hamid might be involved in something much more serious. Perhaps even getting involved with a terrorist cell? The possibility, slight as it was, urged Nina to get moving.

"If you'll excuse me," she said. "I'll call my associate."

She stepped into the foyer and arranged for Kait to babysit Hamid. After she promised to arrive in less than twenty minutes, Nina went back to the family room to tell Hamid. His mother sat in the same position, her expression a mixture of frustration, but Hamid hadn't returned.

"Where's Hamid?" Nina asked.

"I imagine he's still in the restroom."

"Does he usually take this long?"

"Honestly, I haven't been paying attention, so I don't know."

Nina chastised herself for not escorting the kid to the bathroom. "Is there another computer on this floor?"

"My husband's office, why?"

"I'm guessing Hamid's bucking that authority again," Nina replied and went in search of Hamid.

His mother trailed behind. "I wish I could say he wouldn't do something like that, but I don't know anymore."

Nina found him sitting at a large mahogany desk, his face hidden behind a monitor, his fingers flying across a keyboard.

She marched into the room and jerked his chair back. "What part about 'no computer use' don't you understand, kid?"

He peered at her, no remorse in his look. "Since you took my phone, I wanted to ask if anyone found the computer. And if they had, I wanted to tell them to give it back."

"Not cool, kid, not cool. Thanks to this foolish stunt, I'll not only be taking your computer into evidence, but now I'll seize this one, too. I'm sure your father won't be happy about that."

"She's right," Mrs. Ahmadi's chilled voice came from behind, making Hamid sit up straight. "When your father learns that his computer is gone, in addition to what you've done, you will likely never see a computer again."

If they didn't recover Ty's computer from the cache—God forbid—she'd confiscate all computers in the house anyway. But she didn't tell Hamid that. Better to let him feel the seriousness of his offense.

Mrs. Ahmadi jerked her head at the doorway. "Now into the family room where I will be watching your every move. And don't even think I won't be trailing you to the restroom next time where you will leave the door open."

His mouth dropped open for a moment. "But Mother, I'm sixteen. You can't—"

"I can and I will. Now march."

He slunk along behind his mother. Nina turned her attention to the monitor. Just as Hamid had said, he'd logged on to the Hacktivist site to post an update asking for the return of the computer. He'd said the FBI wanted it and it was a matter of national security.

His message brought home the possibility of someone actually possessing the computer and logging in to the NFL for nefarious reasons. That couldn't happen. Not on her watch. She had to get moving and locate the cache before terrorists were given the freedom to travel in America and all of the country's worst nightmares became reality.

Chapter Eight

QUINN BREATHED deeply until his lungs could hold no more air. He felt free after changing out of that crazy suit. What had he been thinking putting it on? He hadn't worn the stupid thing for years. The way it fit wouldn't have fooled anyone into thinking he was a professional sales-man anyway.

He shrugged into a fleece-lined waterproof jacket and leaned against his car, keeping an eye on Hamid's house. He wished Nina would get out of there. She might be an agent. She might be in a house with just a boy and his fit-to-be-tied mother, but Quinn wasn't comfortable leaving her inside. It was like leaving a teammate behind on a mission. He'd never do that. No SEAL ever had.

A gust of wind pummeled his body and drew his eyes to the over-cast sky. A storm was rolling in from the coast and rain was moving in fast. If Nina didn't get out here soon, they'd get soaked trekking up to the cache and it would be dark. Even so, they'd make the trip. No matter the weather or time of day, Quinn was going up there. In fact, he could go up there now. Without Nina. He'd memorized the GPS coordinates when she'd confirmed them with Hamid and considered taking off without her. Several times. He was a take-action kind of guy. Move ahead and achieve his goal. Nina, on the other hand was a thinker. She'd take her time, plan, then plan again. Maybe a third time.

Quinn recognized the need for planning. Without it, his team would never succeed in their missions, and he followed the plan of action once made. At least, most of the time. But he didn't like the downtime, stand-ing around waiting for the plan to be prepared. Still, he wouldn't leave Nina behind. She knew the sense of urgency in getting to the computer, which meant whatever was going on inside that house right now was more important.

A black SUV rolled slowly down the street, then parked outside Hamid's house. Quinn came to his feet, ready to help Nina if needed. Agent Kaitlyn Knight opened the door. Quinn stood down but prepared himself for her anger. She was not only a fellow teammate, but one of

Nina's best friends. Along with Becca, she made up the trio Quinn often called "the three musketeers".

They didn't like the term, but it fit. They were swashbucklers of the cyber variety, and they lived the motto of "one for all and all for one". He oughta know. When he and Nina split up, Kait and Becca had both given him an earful. Despite the reason for their tongue-lashing, the memory made him smile. He liked strong women who gave as good as they got, and this trio could hold their own with anyone.

He knew he was right when Kait slid out from behind the wheel and glared at him. She was the same height as Nina, but she was leaner, without all of Nina's wonderful curves.

She took a step, then stopped and frowned. "Does Nina know you're here?"

"Good to see you, too, Kait." He didn't bother hiding his sarcasm.

She slammed her car door before planting a hand on her hip. "You didn't answer my question."

"Nina knows I'm here. In fact, she's the one who told me to wait for her. What are *you* doing here?"

"If Nina wants you to know that, she'll tell you." She started for the sidewalk, then turned back. "I get that Ty needs Nina right now, but don't mess with her, Quinn, or you'll answer to me and Becca."

"I don't plan to do anything but get Ty out of this jam. Then I'm headed back to California."

"See that you do." She swept her gaze over him, making him feel like dirt, before she walked to the front door.

The way she'd treated him should tick him off, but he respected her loyalty more. Everyone on his SEAL team would do the same thing in her place. Plus he appreciated the fact that Nina had friends looking out for her best interests. God knows he hadn't done that. If he had, she wouldn't be so upset with him. He'd give anything to go back and fix it. He'd still choose to stay on the team—he could do nothing else—but he'd do a better job of listening to her concerns and make sure they parted amiably.

The door whipped open, and Nina stepped outside. He waited for her to glance at him, but she turned to speak to Kait for a moment. When Kait closed the door, Nina rested her head against the wood.

Quinn's alarm bells clanged. Had something even worse happened inside, or was she tired from the interview? Or maybe she needed to fortify herself before looking at him.

She lifted her head and ran a hand over her hair as she turned. The curls sprang back up as always. Despite the tension, he smiled. She'd never been able to tame the crazy curls. She pulled her hair back for work, but by mid-morning, the curls always sprang free from even the strongest pins.

She lifted her shoulders into a hard line, as if heading into battle, and crossed the street.

"I was surprised to see Kait," he said the moment she stepped close enough.

"I called her to keep an eye on Hamid while I check the cache."

"You mean 'we'."

"'We' what?"

"We check the cache."

She arched a brow. "You may be used to taking charge on the job, but you're a civilian where I'm concerned. And the last thing I need is a civilian tagalong."

"I get that. Honestly, I do." He smiled at her, hoping to disarm her mounting frustration. "I'm not trying to be difficult. I promise."

"But?"

"But it's late. You won't reach the falls until dark. You don't likely have the right equipment. I do. Besides, I'm not letting you go up there alone, so get it out of your pretty little head."

"Letting me?"

"You know what I mean. No one should hike alone at this time of day." He gestured at the darkening clouds. "Especially not with a storm coming."

She planted her hands on her hips. Took a few steps, then turned to stare at him. "I suppose you might be useful to have along."

"Ouch." He mocked receiving a knife to his chest to lighten things up. "Thanks for your vote of confidence."

"Just don't get in my way," she said as if he hadn't spoken. "I'm in charge, and you'll do as I say."

"Sure," he replied, but if things went sideways up there, he had no intention of taking a backseat. "My car is better equipped to handle the road. I should drive."

She frowned at him. "If this is the way you intend let me lead, you might as well stay here."

"Geez, Nina. Lighten up. It's just a suggestion. If you want to take your car, we'll take your car."

"I suppose, it wouldn't hurt to let you drive." Her forehead knotted.

"I need to grab my Go bag and different shoes." She held out her hand. "I'll take your keys."

"My keys?"

"Don't think I don't know that you'll take off without me, the minute my back is turned. So, either walk with me to my car or give me the keys."

"You don't trust me." He was surprised at the pain he heard in his own voice.

"Should I?"

"Yes, of course. Just because we broke up doesn't mean I've changed who I am."

Her eyebrow shot up. "Maybe the Quinn Stone who bails when the going gets tough *is* the real you."

"Come on, Nina." He took a step closer. "You know me and you have to know that's not true. You can trust me."

She kept her hand out, her expression now unreadable.

"Or not," he said, the discomfort from her assessment hitting hard. He knew he'd done a number on her when they'd broken up, but this?

She jutted out her hip at an angle. Her comments still stung, but he loved when she got all hot and bothered like this. Her fiery temper kicked his pulse up.

"Time's a wasting." She wiggled her fingers. "Keys, or I go alone."

He hated to give up the keys. It was like an admission that she couldn't trust him, but she was right. They needed to get moving. He dug them out and slapped them on her palm.

She spun, and despite the need to depart, he watched her walk away. She had this way of swaying her hips that he would never get tired of looking at. Not only him. He'd seen other guys watching her, too.

A jolt of jealousy hit him. They talked six months ago when he'd helped on an FBI investigation and she'd said she wasn't dating anyone, but she could be with someone now. He tried to ignore the unsettled feeling in his gut and moved his E&E bag to the back to free up the front seat.

When he'd stopped home to change into the suit, he'd had no idea he'd be heading into rugged terrain, but he'd grabbed his bag anyway. It was a typical escape-and-evasion bag, smaller and meant for a shorter period of time than this one that he kept at his parents' house. Though Nina would bring her Go bag that all law enforcement officers stowed in their trunks, his was geared more for survival, while hers was for self-protection and first aid.

He settled his stuff, including the confounded suit in the back, then saw her marching toward him. A large tote hung from her shoulder, and a pair of worn sneakers dangled from her fingers. He took the bag, his fingers brushing her shoulder.

She shot him a look as sharp as his KA-BAR. He got it. Loud and clear. She didn't want him touching her. Even by accident.

He signaled his understanding by holding his hand up and taking a step back. She jerked her eyes away before sitting down to change her shoes. He tried not to stare at her long legs, bare to the hem of her skirt riding up her thigh. She may be mad at him for leaving, but he could still feel the chemistry sizzling between them. She had to feel it, too. He suspected that was the real reason she didn't want him to touch her.

She slipped on a sneaker and tied it. "So what happened to the suit?"

"I couldn't take it for another second."

She swiveled her legs inside the car. "Then why wear it to begin with?"

"We have this saying in BUD/S." He climbed behind the wheel, tugged his jacket off, and tossed it in the back for the drive. "To survive training with the least amount of turmoil, you want to become the gray man."

"Gray man." She handed over his keys. "I'm going to go out on a limb here and say that doesn't mean wearing an ill-fitting gray suit."

"You're so on the ball." He laughed and started the engine.

"What does it really mean, then?"

"In BUD/S, it's the instructors' job to push you mentally to the end of your reserves. Over and over again, until you're as tough as you need to be to withstand the rigors of the job. Or they break you, you finally give up, and ring the brass bell of defeat. Then you leave your helmet with all the other quitters' helmets for the entire class to see."

"Sound's humiliating."

He shrugged. "Maybe. But we all know going in that it could happen."

"But not to this mysterious gray man?"

"Exactly. From day one of training, the instructors latch onto soldiers who can't cut muster and ride them unmercifully to get them to quit. No one wants to be *that guy*. You want to do everything so well, so perfectly, that the instructors never notice you. That's the gray man."

"You wore the suit so no one would notice you?" She wrinkled her nose at him. "Not sure you accomplished that, but I can see where a suit is less out of place than your usual attire."

"You're just skeptical because you didn't know the suit was part of my cover. I was a door-to-door salesman." Hoping to lighten the mood, he grinned at her. "Want to hear my pitch?"

After rolling her eyes, a slight smile puckered her lips. "What were you selling?"

"Without a demonstration model, vacuum cleaners were out of the picture. As were encyclopedias, for obvious reasons. So I went for the next best thing."

"Which is?" she said, her smile growing.

"Replacement windows."

"What do you know about that?"

"Besides how to break in to them," he said, winking at her. "Not much, but I can wing it long enough not to blow my cover."

She laughed lightly. Her gaze locked on his again, this time lingering with a far different message. His heart took that funny little tumble only she could cause.

Gone was the animosity between them, mutual interest replacing it for the moment. Pure and simple, she was still attracted to him, as he'd suspected. But he also saw the longing behind her look and instantly sobered. She didn't want an uncomplicated relationship like they'd once had. She still wanted it all. Marriage, a family. A man who wasn't deployed most of the time.

Relationships. Impossible. At least for him. For them. He was the very thing she couldn't tolerate, someone carefree and reckless. He'd always been that way, and he didn't know how to be anything else. Even for her.

Chapter Nine

"DO YOU MIND putting the GPS coordinates into the car's navigational system while I get us on the highway?" Quinn asked, interrupting the awkward silence that had settled around them.

"Sure," Nina replied, though that required her to lean closer to him and only made her more acutely aware of him when she was already fighting being pulled toward him. Physically and emotionally. She wanted to feel nothing. Willed herself to feel nothing. But it was still there.

A simple smile from him and that familiar warmth started firing in her belly. She was helpless to stop it and that made her mad. Not at Quinn, but at herself for forgetting everything she'd learned, the lessons that taught her to stay in charge. Keep control. Not to let things, people, put her at risk.

Once on the road, he casually dropped his hand to the gearshift. She studied the raised scars crawling over his skin. She couldn't take her eyes away and wanted to put a protective hand over his. She imagined the accident that happened nearly a year ago. *Accident, right.* The enemy had tried to blow up his SEAL team. Blow *him* up. The explosion had taken them all down. His arm had been covered with flames. Twisted, torn metal, and concrete rubble had engulfed him.

At least, that's the way she'd imagined it whenever she thought about it. Which she did often, ever since she'd learned of his injury. And then, even though they weren't together, the wondering had started.

Where was he? Was he safe? Injured again? A prisoner?

Some women could handle the uncertainty, but she couldn't. She didn't know why she'd ever thought she could. He wanted excitement. Adventure. He risked his life to prove he wasn't his straight-laced father, who was as much of a control freak as she was. She needed order in her life. Things she could plan. Count on. Not a man who ran into danger at the drop of the hat.

The warmth she'd shared with him froze over.

"Is there something you want to ask me?" he asked, his tone deep and intimidating.

"What?" She looked up.

A scowl turned down his mouth. "You're staring at my scars. If you want to ask about them, then ask."

"I'm sorry, I know it's rude to stare."

He shrugged. "You're no different than everyone else."

No different. Right. Except I was once in love with you.

"People stare all the time," he continued. "Especially when I'm wearing a short-sleeved shirt, which I try not to do in public anymore." He shook his head. "It was a whole lot easier when I had to wear the compression bandages. Covered everything up."

"How . . . ?" She let her voice fall off.

"How, what?"

She wanted to hear about the incident and erase what she'd imagined, but she suspected the reality was far worse. She wasn't prepared to hear details of his pain and suffering. He'd come home injured from whatever war-torn part of the world he'd been sent to, wounded and suffering, and she hadn't been there for him. She hadn't even known about it until a few months ago.

That hurt just as badly. They might not be a couple anymore, but she'd have been there for him if he'd needed her. But he hadn't. As usual. All he needed was his team. Something she'd do well to remember.

The accident was none of her business. He was none of her business. Nothing had changed between them. He still lived on the edge. Still disappeared to parts of the world he couldn't discuss. Still made her pulse race.

Stop it.

"You have a question or not?" he asked, sounding irritated with her.

"No," she replied, her tangled emotions making the word sharper than she intended.

"Okay, then." He lifted his hand to the wheel and gripped it tight.

Silence stretched out between them again, and worry about the upcoming climb took over her thoughts. At least thinking about Quinn had served to keep her fears at bay, but they were overwhelming her now.

Hoping to relax, she rested her head against the soft leather seat, closed her eyes, and listened to a freight train rumbling on the tracks running parallel to the scenic highway. The rhythmic *click-clack, click-clack, click-clack* eased some of her concern and lulled her into a drowsy state.

Her phone blared out her mother's ring tone, ending it all.

"She still call you every day?" Quinn asked.

"Yes, and I put her off this morning, so I need to take this." Forcing herself to sound cheerful, she answered, "Mama."

"You didn't call." The accusation came flying out, and Nina was right back in Mobile, coming home late from school, her mother mad and relieved all at once.

Nina's heart grieved for her mother who'd become so terrified of everything that Nina's dad had walked out on her, on both of them, and her mother could no longer leave the house. She'd tried to let Garrett's death go and move on, bless her heart, but she couldn't do it. Each morning, she lectured Nina about safety before she was allowed to step foot out the door. About stranger danger. About never going anywhere without permission. About never being alone anywhere but at home. To watch her surroundings. Stay alert. Always. Every moment. On and on, she went. Grandmother Hale tried to temper her paranoia, and they often argued.

Nina couldn't wait to escape to college. But even then, her mother's watch continued. Multiple phone calls per day. Calls to the RA and Nina's roommate if Nina didn't answer her phone or return a call within five minutes. Once Nina graduated and started working as a network administrator for a local company, her mother backed off to a daily phone call.

Then the company's network was hacked, and Nina felt even more exposed and vulnerable. The agent she worked with to find the hacker said she should join the FBI to help stop hackers like the one they were looking for from violating other people. She wanted to help, but she worried about the danger in the job. He assured her that those agents mostly sat behind a desk. So she'd gone for it and the day she reported for her first assignment, her mother's calls increased.

Nina eventually got her mother to cut back to daily calls, but each one reminded her of Garrett and how, if she'd only tried harder, he might be alive today.

"Are you sure you're okay?" her mother asked. "Nothing's wrong?"

"Nothing's wrong, Mama."

The female GPS voice announced their destination ahead.

"I have to get back to work. I'll talk to you tomorrow." Nina hung up before her mother had a chance to argue. Garrett's loss fresh in her mind, Nina couldn't bear to think about what was ahead. The falls. The rushing water. She drew in a breath. Blew it out.

"Something wrong with your mother?" Quinn clicked on his blinker.

"No," she said unconvincingly.

"Your expression says otherwise."

"I'm not fond of the wilderness. You know that."

"I knew you had a thing about bugs, but I never saw it give you this deer-in-the-headlights look."

She shrugged. "Guess it's the rain and all."

"Guess, so." His questioning gaze said he wasn't buying her story, but he turned his focus back to the road.

The parking area was more of a turnout on the side of the highway than a lot. He maneuvered the SUV around until he'd backed it into a space. Most people would simply pull in, but military types, along with her fellow law enforcement officers, were trained to be ready to take off at a moment's notice, and that meant backing in for a safer and quicker getaway.

"Place is deserted." He shifted into park. "Not surprising, at this time of day."

"Or this time of year," she added, apprehension knotting her stomach.

As he turned off the engine, he appraised her again. She wouldn't talk about what was bothering her, so she stepped outside. An icy wind whistled across the lot, sending a shiver over her body. She wished she'd thought to bring her winter jacket hanging on the hook by her front door, but she'd have to settle for the lightweight fleece jacket in her Go bag. As she dug it out, Quinn pawed through his duffel on the other side of the car.

"That your only jacket?" he asked.

She nodded.

"You'll be an icicle by the time we reach the falls." He grabbed a fleece-lined waterproof parka and handed it to her. "Wear this."

"I'm not taking your jacket."

"I'm not wearing a skimpy blouse and thin blazer."

At the attitude in his voice, she stared at him. "My blouse isn't skimpy."

"Paper thin, then. And don't bother to deny it. If I looked close enough, I'd be able to see every freckle left from the summer on your chest." He shoved the jacket at her.

She still didn't want to take it, but he was the kind of guy who'd refuse to move until she did. She slipped it on over her blazer. The minty smell from his soap clung to the fabric, taking her back to their past. Back to hugs and snuggles. Back to a place she had no business going.

Focus, Nina.

She grabbed her flashlight, a small first-aid kit, and a backup gun, then shoved them all in the jacket pockets. To that, she added additional ammo. It was overkill, but maybe she was hoping the fire power would protect her from the water. Foolish, she knew, but she needed to feel like she had some sort of protection if she was going to make it up to the falls.

"You planning on finding trouble up there?" he asked, his tone joking.

She looked at him as he shoved his KA-BAR in his belt. "No more than you are."

"Doesn't hurt to be prepared."

"Exactly." Too bad she couldn't find a weapon to protect her heart from him.

She added latex gloves and evidence bags to her stash, then closed her door. He shrugged into his large pack, adjusting the straps on his broad shoulders.

She met him near the trail. "You sure you don't want your jacket?"

"I'm dressed in layers. I'll be fine." He dug out his phone. "I downloaded a geocache app while you were talking with Hamid. Let me get the right screen up, and we'll be good to go."

She should have thought to download the app, but she'd let herself be distracted by the thought of the upcoming waterfall and this man standing next to her.

"At a leisurely pace, it'll take about sixty minutes to reach the falls." He looked up. "It'll be dark soon. We need to step up the pace. I'll take the lead. If I'm moving too fast for you, don't be stubborn and try to keep up. Just tell me to slow down."

He had her in the fitness department. She worked out, but she also sat at a desk most days while he jogged and ran drills to keep his body in top shape. Plus, she was as coordinated as a lumbering elephant. She often managed to hurt herself simply by walking. But she wasn't about to admit that she couldn't keep up with him. She'd reach the falls with him. Of that he could be sure. Even if thoughts of the running water threatened to freeze her in place.

NO. NO. NO. *This couldn't be happening.*

Wiley slammed a fist on the steering wheel of Kip's old beater as he watched Brandt and her SEAL start for the trail. That brat kid, Hamid, had obviously caved and told them where to find the computer. Now the odd couple was searching for the cache, which meant they'd soon be searching for evidence to send Wiley back to prison. She wanted to keep him locked up. Just like his psychiatrist. Wiley should have expected it. Planned for it. Everyone was out to get him. Had always been out to get him.

So what? His psycho psychiatrist wasn't keeping anyone locked up any more. Not since Wiley took care of him a couple of days ago. Payback. Winding it all up nicely. *Check. Check.* His parents. The psychiatrist. After Brandt, he'd be free. Emotionally and physically. She wouldn't lock him up. No one would.

Wiley gripped the steering wheel and thought about this recent development. Brandt would climb to the cache and discover the computer was gone. No biggie, right? Unless Wiley had left something behind that could lead her back to him. After all, he hadn't thought about hiding his tracks when he'd found the cache. Had he done anything that could help her locate him?

He ran through his steps that day. No. At least he didn't think so, but once she discovered the computer was missing, they'd head back to Hamid's house. There, they could find the phone Wiley had hidden. He'd have to retrieve it.

Was there anything else?

Think. Before Medusa snares you in one of her traps.

Thinking of another stint in prison sent panic closing in on him. "Relax. Breathe."

She didn't have anything. She didn't even know the computer was gone, or she wouldn't be heading up the slippery path on a day like this. The calculating agent wouldn't take such a risk unless she expected a big payoff. She didn't like risks. He knew her well, from hours of her relentless interrogations. Then the weeks of his trial. She was orderly. Careful. This was a foolhardy, desperate move. One she'd only take if she knew about the hack. But if she knew, had they already alerted DHS to plug the database vulnerability? Would the hack still work when he got ready to sell it?

"No." He pounded the wheel, his mind whirring faster and faster.

This was not going according to his plan. He had to know more. Assess the risk of continuing. Maybe cut his losses, get the forty grand, and kill the loser agent.

No. That was too rash. He needed to know what she was up to before deciding.

But how? He couldn't follow her up the trail. The pair of them might have already seen his car and could make him. She'd like that. Finding him. Locking him up again.

So what then?

Hamid.

When she didn't find the computer, she'd go back to the kid and the other sniveling agent they'd left in charge. Wiley had plenty of time to get over there, put the GPS tracker on the car, and get in position to see what was going on. Then, with the GPS, he could monitor her location and stay one step ahead of her. And he'd buy another tracker tomorrow for the SEAL's car. Just in case. Wiley could never be too careful.

Chapter Ten

DESPITE THE COLD, Nina's palms were sweating as she followed Quinn onto the trail that wound up and disappeared into thick pines and ferns. The sky was gray and angry as the sun sank toward the horizon. Her heart beat hard and not only from exertion. Garrett died at the end of a day much like this one. When everyone had gotten careless on the rafting trip. When cold rain was setting in, hands were icy cold, and they all wanted to get home.

Maybe if they'd gotten an earlier start that day, things could have been different. Maybe not. One thing was sure. If she'd held on, Garret would be with her and the guilt that ate at her would be gone. Even after the passing of so many years wrangling with God, she couldn't let go of the maybes. Let go of the guilt.

Distracted, she caught her foot on a gnarly root and pitched forward. She hit the ground with an *oomph*. Sharp stones sliced into her bare knees and hands. She bit her lip to keep from crying out and righted herself on a log, but Quinn hadn't missed her fall.

"Let's take a quick break." He stopped and leaned against a tree, his chest barely moving while hers rose and fell as she took big heaving gulps of air. Thankfully, he didn't want to talk, since she couldn't possibly hold a conversation. Maybe he knew that.

Sure he knew that. Nothing escaped his attention. Nothing. He was an operator. Trained in covert tactics that included observing and evading. He was stellar at both. She should know. He'd evaded a commitment to her quite well.

After a few minutes, his gaze ran the length of her body. "Ready to go?"

Barely rested, she nodded. He started off, climbing higher and higher. She suddenly heard the rush of water tumbling off the cliff. Her heartbeat thundered in her ears.

They rounded the corner. She caught sight of the terrifying water on the far side of the gorge. She stopped dead in her tracks. She felt lightheaded. Her vision narrowed, and black spots took over. She fought for breath. Struggled. She bent forward and clamped her hands on her knees.

Calm down. It's just a little water. No one's disappearing in the rush of it. Stick to the inside of the path and you'll be safe.

Quinn turned and jogged back to her. "What's wrong?"

"Nothing," she managed to eek out.

"Bull. You look like you're about to pass out." He guided her to a large stone, then pushed her head between her knees. He squatted next to her. "Breathe, sweetheart. Slowly. Nice and easy." He rubbed gentle circles on her back, the warmth of his fingers helping to calm her racing heart. "That's it. You're doing fine."

She focused on his soothing voice and his touch, cutting through the anxiety. Her vision started to clear, and the ache in her chest loosened. She slowly sat up.

He searched her face. "What was that all about?"

She shrugged.

"You're not afraid of heights are you?"

"No," she said and didn't elaborate. She dug out her water bottle and took a long drink.

He rutted through his pack and pulled out a protein bar. "Eat this."

She felt like a fraud for taking it, but the protein would help her cope with the stress. *If* she could eat it. She took a bite, savoring the fruity flavor, but it still settled like a rock in her stomach.

As Quinn watched her, she continued to eat. She concentrated on the fact that they were near the main viewing area and would soon be able to grab the computer and leave.

Apparently satisfied she would make it, he pulled out his phone again. "Coordinates say the cache is over by the falls. We need to keep going."

Which meant a continued climb upward. Away from the exit. Her pulse threatened to pick up speed again, the panic not far behind.

Stop. You can do this. You're fine. Quinn's here. He'll help you. Everything's fine.

She just needed to get moving and get this over with. She stood. Wobbled a bit, but Quinn steadied her.

Hating that she'd let this irrational fear turn her into a big baby, she jerked her arm free.

He arched a brow. "Maybe you should wait here."

She shook her head. "I've done enough to screw up this investigation already. I can't have you contaminate the evidence. I need to follow protocol for collecting it. And that means, I do the work."

He watched her for a moment. "We'll stick together the rest of the way. I promise not to touch you unless you authorize me to. Do I have your permission to do this?" He smiled and cupped her elbow again.

The warmth of his hand penetrated her jacket as the hard lines and angles of his face softened, warming her heart and easing her fear. She nodded, showing her thankfulness and appreciation in a genuine smile.

His gaze heated up. "And this?" He moved his hand up her arm, his fingers sliding down to her back and drawing her closer.

"Yes," she said knowing she should tell him to back off, but she'd rather fight her attraction to him than her fear of the water.

He peered into her eyes. Time seemed to stand still. The sound of falling water fell away. The drive to recover the computer went with it. Nothing existed but the two of them.

They were close again, with only inches separating them. Emotions welled up inside her. If she stood on her tiptoes, she could kiss him. Wanted to kiss him. Like she had so many times before.

Oh my gosh! She still had feelings for him and they weren't just anger. She stepped back, coming up against a thick tree.

His hand fell away. He said something under his breath, then shook his head. He probably wanted to call her on her two-faced behavior. One minute wanting him to touch her, the next acting like the Snow Queen. Thank goodness he'd be heading back to California after they retrieved the cache.

He peered up at the sky. "The light is fading fast. We need to get going."

And just like that, her fear returned like a runaway freight train.

"C'mon." He headed up the path, periodically glancing at his phone.

In an overlook that jutted out toward the falls, he pointed at a log traversing the rushing water to a small landing littered with more fallen trees "The cache is on the other side. You stay here, and I'll check it out."

"No." She grabbed his arm. "Evidence, remember?"

He frowned. "I don't like the idea of you crossing that log. It's wet and slippery."

She liked the thought of it even less. What if she got halfway out there and the panic came back? She'd freeze above the water. Maybe her legs would give out and she'd tumble into the water, just like Garrett.

No. Stop. Get control.

She'd made it though twenty-two rigorous weeks at Quantico. After that, this was a cakewalk. *That's it.* Think of getting home and baking Grandmother Hale's famous whipped-cream cake with chocolate-fudge frosting.

"I have to do this, Quinn." She rubbed her sweaty palms on her legs, then donned a pair of latex gloves and climbed onto the log. She instantly knew he was right. The wood was worn smooth from the pulsing water, and sections were crumbling. She didn't have a death wish. Under normal circumstances, she wouldn't have crossed, but there was nothing normal about potential terrorists having access to the NFL. Or the kid she loved like a little brother going to prison.

She heard Quinn mount the log behind her and sensed him moving close. Despite her bold declaration of being able to do this, she was thankful for his nearness. She moved slowly, planting her feet carefully. Her foot caught on a crumbling spot. She wobbled and shot out her arms to balance, panic rising up.

A strong arm came around her from behind, steadying her. "Relax, sweetheart. I've got your six."

He was right. He did have her back. He'd always had her back when they'd been together. The agent in her wanted to squirm away, but the woman in her felt safe and protected against the solid wall of his chest.

"Okay?" His breath was warm on her ear.

"Yes."

He released her, and she instantly missed his touch. Because of that, she wanted to rush ahead, but she'd never been a fool. Except for when she'd fallen in love with him.

She carefully crossed the remaining log without incident and jumped down, pulling in deep breaths of air and trying to tune out the sound of water surging near her feet. She could finish this. She simply had to find the box and get going.

"Over there." Quinn pointed ahead in the shadows of a disintegrating log.

She dug out an evidence bag and knelt by the cache.

Quinn hovered above her, shining his flashlight on the container. Her heart thudded. She wasn't sure if it was out of fear for what she might find or because of her precarious position near the falls and the rush of water that sounded like a whirling tornado in her ears. She lifted the lid. Empty. Disappointment spread through her chest.

"We're too late." The same disappointment lingered in Quinn's voice. "So now what?"

She shrugged and glanced around. The surrounding area was a

crime scene now. It was her duty to secure it. But how? Staying there to protect it would be foolish. Especially when no one would come up there during the night. The elements were more of a problem than any person could be. Dusk was settling over them, the skies on the horizon even darker and threatening heavy rain any moment. Rain that could wash away evidence in the immediate area.

She dug out her flashlight from one of the large jacket pockets. "It's going to pour any minute. That doesn't give us much time to search the area for anything that doesn't belong here." She flicked the light on and swung it over the ground covered with moss and leaves.

"I'll give you a few minutes, but then we need to get going before the trail becomes impassible."

She hadn't taken the time to think about their descent, but he was right. Heavy rain would make heading down the trail treacherous, but she had to, at least, be able to tell Sulyard that she'd given the area a cursory inspection.

Quinn shone his flashlight on the other side of the box. "Footprints over here. Male. Might be the person who took the computer."

"The rain will wash them away," she said. "Can you snap a picture with your cell? The techs might be able to learn something from a picture."

She heard him getting out his camera, then saw the flash of light. "What about the box?"

"I'll take it with me for processing."

He swung around to stare at her. "I don't care how independent you are, or how worried you are about evidence contamination, I'm not letting you carry it across the log. You'll be doing well just to make it back on your own."

Despite his demanding nature, her near fall and his surefootedness told her he was far better suited to the task. She handed him a pair of gloves. "You can carry it."

His mouth dropped open, but she ignored it and returned to her work. She painstakingly checked the ground as large drops of rain landed on her back.

Quinn tugged on her arm. "C'mon. Time to go."

With the rain starting, she didn't argue.

He nodded at the log bridge. "You cross first."

"Okay." She eyed him. "As long as you promise not to drop the container to try to save me if I wobble again."

"Unbelievable." He shook his head. "I won't drop the freakin' box.

Now get moving before we're both stuck over here."

She climbed onto the log and felt him mount it right behind her. He couldn't possibly have picked up the box in that time. She carefully glanced over her shoulder. His hands were empty.

"What are you doing?" she cried out. "Don't leave the box."

"You didn't want me to drop it to help you, so I'm coming over with you. Then I'll go back to get it."

"I'll be fine."

"It's not negotiable, Nina." His mouth tightened into a grim line, and she knew better than to keep arguing.

She doubled her effort to take careful steps so he wouldn't need to rescue her again. Once she dropped onto solid ground, he spun and returned for the container. She backed as far away from the water as possible and pressed up against a thick tree to watch him. His grace, his balance was so odd for a man of his size, but she had to admit, she loved seeing him move like this. He grabbed the box, tucked it under his long arm, then looked up to catch her eyes on him. Though dusk was upon them, she could see the gleam of his teeth as he grinned.

She snapped her gaze away and checked for a signal on her phone. No bars. Shoot. Now that she knew the computer was missing, she wanted to bring Sulyard into the investigation as soon as possible. The moment Quinn landed safely, she took off down the trail, running from the sound of the rapids.

"Hey." He grabbed her elbow, jerking her to a stop. "I said we had to hurry, but I didn't mean going fast enough to shoot over the edge."

She was looking up at him as a fat raindrop landed on her cheek.

He gently tugged her hood up. "What's going on, sweetheart? It's not like you to be so reckless."

"We need to get going." She sidestepped his concern and started down the path, this time at a slower, more cautious pace. He stuck close to her, the beam from his flashlight mingling with hers near their feet.

Midway down, the sky let loose, drenching them both. Their lights barely illuminated the slippery clay trail. The rain slowed them down. They walked in silence, but it wasn't the comfortable silences of their past. It was as big and deep as the gorge waiting to swallow her up if she took one wrong step. Thunder rumbled in the distance. One roll. Barely discernable. Though it rained nearly 150 days a year in the Willamette Valley, thunder was a sound rarely heard in the area. Unlike in her home state of Alabama.

"Did you hear that?" She smiled at him and let the unusual incident lighten her mood. "We had one whole thunder."

He'd traveled the globe, so he understood her joke and grinned boyishly at her. The atmosphere around them changed. The remainder of the trip seemed easier, more comfortable. As they trekked the lower half of the tail, the rain slowed to a trickle.

"So what happens now?" Quinn asked, his voice barely above a whisper, as if he didn't really want to hear the answer.

She assessed his mood. A sliver of moonlight darkened the angles of his face. She couldn't make out his expression, but she could see his eyes were narrowed. The last thing she wanted to do was tell him that the time had come to report this to Sulyard.

Quinn slowed and crooked his finger under her chin, lifting her head. "What don't you want to tell me?"

"I'll need to call my supervisor as soon as I can get a signal."

"That's not good then, is it?"

"Not likely."

"Which means Ty will be arrested." The finality in his voice made Nina's heart break.

"Depends on Sulyard, but it's likely." She tried to sound upbeat, but she wouldn't mislead Quinn when the outcome was fairly certain. "If for no other reason than to keep Ty away from computers while we investigate."

"Can you wait to tell Sulyard? We could keep looking for the computer."

"This was our deal, Quinn." She tried not to sound like she didn't care about Ty, but she had to let Quinn know where they stood. "We tried to recover the computer. Now that we can't, I have to report the security breach."

"I know, it's just . . ." He started moving, his feet thumping down the trail with frustration. "He's just a kid, you know?"

She was anxious for Ty and even for this man who'd hurt her so badly. "I wish things could have turned out differently here."

"But you will still try to help Ty, right?"

She studied his pensive expression and debated how to answer. "Of course, I'll try. But considering the way I handled this, it's not likely Sulyard will let me get anywhere near the investigation now."

"What?" He swung his head around to gape at her. "You won't let that happen though, right?"

"I'll do my best, but I warned you when we first met that my personal involvement was problematic here."

He jerked his gaze away as if he was disgusted with her.

She placed a hand on his shoulder and waited for him to look at her again. "I'll try to stay involved. To help Ty any way I can. You know that, right?"

He didn't respond right away, but then glanced at her. "I know you're a good person, Nina. You'll do your best, or I wouldn't have come to you in the first place."

"I hear a 'but' in your voice."

"But if you're removed from the investigation, I won't have any connection to it at all. I have no role in this now, and it's eating me up. With you out of the picture . . ." He shrugged. "Can I at least sit in with Ty when he's questioned?"

"I honestly don't know," she said, hating to give him more bad news. "Since your mother is his legal guardian, she'll be allowed in the room. But it'll be up to Sulyard to decide if you can join in."

A shadow of pain fell across his face. "You'll ask him for me."

"That's not a good idea. He's bound to be upset with me. You're better off asking him yourself or have your mom request it. She can be very persuasive." Nina chuckled, hoping to lighten the mood. It didn't help.

Quinn frowned. "I feel so helpless. I never feel helpless. I don't know what to do about it."

Remembering the day he'd chosen the team over her, she knew exactly how he was feeling right now. "I'll do my best to keep you in the loop on anything I can share."

"I know how you guys work. You won't be able to tell me most of what's going on."

"True, but we don't have a choice." She forced a smile and made sure to keep all sarcasm from her tone. "Besides, I'm sure you need to get back to your team, don't you?"

"I'm not going anywhere until this is resolved."

"They'll let you have time off? Just like that?"

He shrugged. "I'll quit the team if I have to. Nothing's more important than my family."

Especially not me. The thought struck like a knife, but he seemed oblivious to how his comment might affect her. Discouraged, she wound down the last section of the trail and kept checking her cell until she had a clear signal. She dialed Sulyard.

"I have an urgent matter that I need to discuss with you," she said. "I can be at the office in an hour or so."

"Sorry. No can do. I have plans tonight. The wife'll kill me if I don't show up."

"This involves our national security." Sadness for Ty filled her already wounded heart. "Trust me when I say, you'll want to wait for me on this one. Even if your wife doesn't speak to you for a very long time."

Chapter Eleven

QUINN TURNED THE corner to the street lined with older single-story homes. Having never lived in Oregon with his parents, he never really considered the place home. He honestly couldn't believe his father had agreed to put down roots before his retirement. This had to have been his mom's idea, for sure. She'd grown up in Troutdale, and despite the two more years General Sir had to serve in Texas, they'd purchased the house in time for Ty to start high school. They'd done it to give Ty a chance at a normal high school experience.

"Look how well that turned out," Quinn mumbled as he pulled into the driveway of the neighbor's unassuming ranch-style house where Ty was hanging out. The house was of the same style as his parents' home, except it was painted blue instead of the neutral white his father had insisted on.

Nina faced him. "What turned out?"

"What?" Confused for a moment, he shoved the gearshift into park, then realized she'd heard him. "It's nothing worth mentioning."

She stiffened. "I see nothing has changed then."

"What do you mean by that?" he asked, far more testily than he should have.

"I always had to drag everything out of you. Even then, I didn't get much." He opened his mouth to argue her point, but she held up a hand. "I get that you deal with a ton of classified information and you can't share it. But I'm pretty sure this is about Ty and isn't classified."

She was right, of course. She had always been able to read him. When he'd clammed up, she was more than willing to call him on it. It had caused some of their biggest fights. But he was in no mood to have one now over something he could easily share.

"I was thinking about how I'd moved around all my life, yet I still turned out okay. Then my parents buy this house to create a stable life for Ty, and he screws up. Big time."

"It's ironic, I'll give you that."

Ironic and his fault for not being there for Ty. It was likely the reason the kid was in this position. Quinn jerked the keys from the ignition. "We should go in. I'll break the news to Mom then let you fill in the details."

He climbed out and started up the walkway. The downpour had subsided, and droplets shimmered in the landscape lighting. Under the small overhang, he paused with his finger near the doorbell and looked at Nina. "Mom's bound to be upset. You've never seen her that way, and I hope you won't take anything she might say personally. Just know that she really does like you. And I appreciate your offer to bring Ty in instead of having Becca do it."

"I want to make this as easy on Ty as possible. If my being here does that, then I'm glad to help."

"Well, thanks," he said knowing he didn't deserve anything after how he'd treated her. He shouldn't even have come looking for a favor in the first place, but Ty deserved the very best chance to get out of this, and Nina was the very best at her job.

He rang the bell and soon heard footsteps clipping across wood flooring. His mother jerked open the door and her gaze flew to his, seeking relief from her worry. Her expression reminded him a lot of Nina's, when he'd deployed in the past. Relief wasn't something he could give either of them, then or now.

"They'll arrest him, won't they?" His mom clutched the sides of her favorite black sweater and tugged it closed. "I can see it in your eyes."

"I'm sorry, Mom. I did my best."

She patted his arm. "I know you did, son. You always do."

Her understanding made him feel worse.

Her expression a twisted mixture of sadness and anger, she turned her focus on Nina. "Will *she* wait to take him until morning?"

Nina flinched at his mother's hostility, but she didn't back away as many women might. His mother was simply acting like a mama bear protecting her cub, and he felt certain Nina understood that.

"Now, Mom." Quinn rested a hand on her shoulder. "Don't blame Nina for this. Ty is the one who hacked the database. He's responsible for all of it. If anything, you should be thanking Nina. She risked her job to find the computer today. Plus, she could have let Becca take him in, but she's here because it will help Ty accept things better."

"I'm sorry, Mrs. Stone," Nina said sincerely. "If he comes with me for questioning of his own free will, I won't have to get a warrant for his arrest. You will, of course, want to come with him."

She watched Nina carefully. "But he will be arrested?"

"It all depends on how the questioning goes."

Her gaze shot back to Quinn. "You'll be there, too, right?"

Quinn hated to answer, but he had to. "I'll try, but since I'm not one of his legal guardians, I might not be allowed in the room."

She opened her mouth to speak, then closed it and wrapped her arms around her waist.

As fear and defeat emanated from her body, Quinn gave her a hug. She was a strong woman. With the General Sir deployed a good bit of their marriage, she'd had to be. But this? This was too much to handle alone.

Quinn pulled back. "Maybe it's time to ask Dad to come home."

She blew out a breath, then quickly drew in another one, looking like she might hyperventilate. "If you want your dad here, then it's worse than I thought."

Yeah, it is. "I just don't want you to go through this alone."

"You're here. Like you always are when I need you." She pulled her shoulders back and looked at Nina. "So how do you want to handle this?"

"I'll take a few minutes to tell Ty what to expect, then Quinn will drive us all to the FBI."

"Let's get started then. Ty's in the family room with Becca." His mom spun and headed toward the back of the house, her shoulders sagging and making Quinn's gut churn.

Nina stepped up to him and gently squeezed his hand. "She'll get through this."

Quinn still watched his mom. She would get through this, but at what cost?

He couldn't let her handle the interview without him. *Wouldn't* let her handle it without him. He'd insist on sitting by his mother and brother's side, no matter what he had to do to be included in the questioning. Even if it landed him in his own jail cell.

WILEY PLACED THE tracker under Brandt's vehicle and crept down the road. Silently, stealthily, he settled behind a tree in the green space across the road from Hamid's house.

Oh, yeah. He was the man. Moving around right under the FBI's nose. Too bad he couldn't let the world know about it. He'd like nothing better than to claim this hack and add it to his reputation. The notoriety would help make up for his former incarceration, but then Brandt would get off scot-free. That was *so* not happening.

He perched his arms on a branch and put the binoculars to his eyes again. He saw someone walk past the front window. Agent Knight. She was probably guarding Hamid and waiting for Brandt to return to question the kid about the missing computer.

Wiley had some questions of his own. Like, why did Hamid take Tyler's computer in the first place? If he'd wanted it for the hack, he would have kept it instead of giving it away. Maybe he wanted the hack to be discovered to get Tyler in trouble. Or maybe Hamid didn't even know about the hack.

Regardless, the Feds would want the computer. That meant they'd review the Hacktivist database and website stats to see who viewed the geocache listing. Surely, they couldn't be doing that this fast, though. Victor Odell, the Hacktivist database administrator, wouldn't just hand over the records. Vic was a lawyer and would demand a warrant. But eventually, it would happen.

Was that a trail Wiley needed to worry about? It wasn't one that led directly to him. He'd used Kip's login to view the post from Kip's house. But Wiley was living with Kip, which left a trail. A weak one, but a trail nonetheless. Wiley could easily go in and delete the records, delete everything about Kip, but he was a backup administrator and that would raise questions.

The front door suddenly opened, grabbing his attention. Light spilled down the walkway. Knight stepped out, glanced around, then motioned inside. Hamid slunk out the door. An older woman wearing a head covering trailed him, her face pinched and severe, her expression similar to the ones worn by many of Wiley's teachers when he'd failed yet another stupid class. She was likely Hamid's mom.

Knight escorted the pair to her car, settling them both in the back seat. It was the same treatment Wiley had gotten the night of his arrest. Only he'd been cuffed by Brandt. The metal had bitten into his wrists as he'd tried to get comfortable. Each bump in the road had been excruciating.

Knight looked around again before climbing behind the wheel and setting off. Brandt wasn't coming back, obviously. Not now, at least.

With Hamid gone, the phone Wiley had hidden only hours ago was of no value in this location. It had to be hidden wherever Hamid was located for his plan to work. Once Knight's car was out of sight, he raced across the road and grabbed the phone then returned to Kip's car. Wiley ripped off his latex gloves and started the Civic so he could follow Knight. The engine sputtered a few times, then caught, sending a cloud of white smoke out the tailpipe. He stowed his thoughts of the possible connection to Kip on the Hacktivist sight for the moment. He didn't need to worry about that yet. Plenty of others had viewed the cache. It would take the FBI time to work down the list to get to Kip.

If they reached his name before Wiley had completed the sale of the hack, Wiley could always silence Kip before he talked to Brandt. It wasn't the first time he'd had to take such drastic action and likely wouldn't be the last. And that included not only Brandt, but Tyler Stone and his SEAL of a big brother.

"I'LL IGNORE THE fact that the three of you conspired to keep this from me. For now." Sulyard scowled at Nina for a moment, then jerked his gaze to Becca standing next to her, letting it linger before moving to Kait.

None of them displayed even a hint of indecision. Nina couldn't be more proud of her friends. Strong women, both of them. They'd helped her out and took the repercussions like real troopers. Nina could always count on them. Always.

"The only thing saving you are the measures you put in place to isolate the teens," Sulyard continued. "That and we don't have an actual confirmation from the Department of Homeland Security on the breach. Who knows? The Stone kid might be yanking our chain. I'll contact DHS after we conduct our interviews of the teens. If the breach is confirmed, you can each expect repercussions. Am I clear?" He focused on them, one at a time.

"It's my fault," Nina blurted. "Becca and Kait were just trying to help me out."

"Save your breath, Brandt. If they don't have the ability to say no, then they have no business being agents." Sulyard paused, a deep scowl drawing down an already long face. "For now, I need to know about everyone's level of personal involvement in this case."

Nina nodded. "As I mentioned, I dated Tyler Stone's brother. I got to know Tyler then." She held back the fact that she was fond of the kid. "But my interaction with him ended when Quinn and I broke up."

"An amiable breakup?"

Nina hated having this discussion with her supervisor. "Not really, but it won't cloud my objectivity on this case."

Sulyard snorted. "It might balance out your fondness for the kid, but even then, you're such a bleeding heart, I have my doubts that a relationship gone awry will be able to keep that in check."

Nina didn't bother to argue. Everyone knew she believed people were basically good until proven otherwise, and Sulyard held the opposite view.

He turned to the others. "And you two? Any personal connection?"

"I only know Tyler from when he shadowed Nina," Kait said, her emotions well hidden. "But we all know Quinn from when he helped bring Fenton in."

"We're all grateful for Stone's help," Sulyard said. "But we can't let that color our judgment either."

"Oh, don't worry," Kait replied earnestly. "With the mess he made of his relationship with Nina, I can assure you I won't be cutting him any slack."

"Ditto," Becca said.

Once again, her friends had her back. On the job and in her personal life. Nina didn't know what she'd do without them.

Sulyard ran a hand over the smooth skin on his head. "I hate involving any of you in this investigation, but it will obviously to be technology driven, and we'd waste valuable time getting another team assigned here. We'll roll with things for now, but any hint of impropriety on any of your parts, and I'll bench you."

"Thank you, sir," Nina said sincerely.

"Don't be thanking me. You won't have any meaningful role in this investigation, if any part at all, Brandt. Lange and Knight will carry the load. I'll have my eye on you all, so don't make me regret my decision." He checked his watch, then tipped his head at the table. "You have five minutes to get the cache box logged in to evidence and clean yourself up, Brandt. Then we talk to the kid. And I better not have to remind you that I need you to remain impartial."

Nina opened her mouth to tell him she could be impartial, but he spun and strode down the hall, nearly toppling an analyst with his cheek to his phone. Sulyard would run all over Ty, too, and there was nothing Nina could do to stop him.

Chapter Twelve

NINA HAD CHANGED in the last hour, but Quinn didn't know why. Gone was the usual compassionate Nina to be replaced with the evil twin version of work Nina. She was not at all attractive, but a mini-me version of Mr. Tough Guy Sulyard who sat next to her. His suit was pricey, his shirt white and crisp even at the end of the day, and the knot of his tie was tight against his neck. So tight, in fact, that Quinn suspected it was cutting off blood flow and could be the reason for his scowl and general foul mood.

He'd shot questions at Ty like he was firing them from the MP-5 submachine gun Quinn favored. Then he sat back while Nina took over, treating Ty like a complete stranger. She'd promised to help him, yet there she was, being all buddy-buddy with Sulyard.

Quinn didn't like it. Not one bit.

So what had happened in the time it had taken her to bring Sulyard back to the conference room where she'd settled them? More importantly, what did this sudden about-face mean for Ty?

Quinn didn't know, and the more he watched her, the less he understood. She held her body rigid and kept her focus on the table or on Sulyard, never once looking at Quinn. *Fine.* She didn't want him around. He got that, but she had to know how freaked out Ty was. She didn't have to sit there with her shoulders in a hard line, her eyes dark with intensity. This Nina was downright scary, and after his time with the SEALs, there wasn't much that scared him.

He tried to get her attention but she avoided his eyes. *Okay, then.* If she was going to be this way, maybe it was time to call in a lawyer or end this whole thing.

"You've repeatedly asked the same question." He locked gazes with Sulyard. "Ty's answered them the same way each time, so we're done here." Quinn stood. "Grab your jacket, Ty. We're going home."

"About that." Sulyard came to his feet, too. He was three inches or so shorter than Quinn and less muscular, but Quinn knew he'd be a worthy adversary in a fight.

"Ty won't be going home," Sulyard said, then fired a pointed look at Nina. "Wrap this up, then meet us in the war room." He let his gaze sweep around the table, pinning each person with a hard stare before he spun and exited the room.

"Ty has two options." Nina rose, her voice softer now, but she still wasn't the woman Quinn knew. "We can take him into custody where he'll likely spend the night in jail, or you can agree to a night at a hotel supervised by an agent." She glanced at Quinn, then at his mom. "You are both welcome to join him, of course."

"But why can't he come home?" his mom asked.

"As Special Agent Sulyard mentioned, our team will be searching your home for evidence. Though you're legally entitled to be there, I can tell you that sitting through it would be uncomfortable. Besides, putting Ty and the two of you in a neutral environment protects all of you from allegations that could be lodged against you for destroying evidence."

"I see." His mom crossed her arms. She'd always liked Nina, but she was acting like she'd changed her mind. Not likely. It was just anger speaking. After all, if she hadn't changed her opinion of Nina after their break-up, this wouldn't do it.

"We'll go to the hotel, then," she said.

Ty nodded. "I totally agree. But why can't you stay with us instead of another agent?"

"My actions are restricted in this investigation because of my personal involvement with your family." She didn't smile. Didn't give Ty the comforting reassurance he needed, just clenched her hands and took a breath before going on. "Y'all wait here. I'll find the agent who'll be accompanying you, so you can get going."

She hurried from the room as if fleeing from his family and cutting all ties with them. For a moment, Quinn sat stunned. He didn't know what to make of this Nina. She sounded like a robot, not a friend. Not the woman who'd made his blood run hot. He couldn't just sit there and accept her treatment. He needed to know what was going on.

"Stay here," he said to his family, then jogged down the hall after her. "Wait up, Nina."

She slowed, but didn't turn to face him.

He rushed around and stood in front of her. She had no choice but to stop. He waited to speak until she looked at him. "What was with that? All of a sudden, you're acting like we have the plague. I know you're not thrilled to be around me, but you haven't acted this way before with Ty or my mom."

She glanced around, then moved closer. "That was a test. One I passed or Sulyard wouldn't have left me alone with Ty for a second. If I show even a hint of affection for Ty or your family, Sulyard will jerk me off this investigation. And trust me, you still want me on the case to look out for Ty's best interests."

"You're making it sound like the hotel thing is temporary, and he'll still be arrested."

"It's possible."

"So what happens next?"

"Sulyard is calling DHS. We wait to hear back from them."

Quinn wasn't surprised they were contacting the Department of Homeland Security.

"As I mentioned," she continued, "they're in charge of the database, and we need them to confirm the intrusion."

"Why? Ty's admitted to doing it."

"Yes, But there's something we didn't consider before. He could be making up the hack to get attention."

"You're kidding, right? Hamid's name was on the No-Fly List. That wasn't made up."

"But that doesn't mean Ty did it."

"I suppose," he said. "Do you think Ty is lying?"

She shook her head. "I can't imagine Ty risking your wrath for a little attention. Not to mention your father's."

What? Him? "Trust me, I get what you mean about my father, but I don't have that kind of relationship with Ty. He doesn't have to worry about my reaction."

She snorted loudly, then covered her mouth for a moment. "You were sitting at the table in the coffee shop, right? When he compared you to your dad?"

"That was an isolated incident."

"I don't think so." She made strong eye contact. "When I think back over our time together, Ty was always a bit wary of you. I mean, he loves you—that I can see. And even behind his smart-aleck comments about your success, he respects you. I don't see that he has the same feelings for your dad. But otherwise . . ." She shrugged. "Ty really does see you and your dad as the same kind of man."

Was she right? Had Quinn actually managed to alienate his little brother?

He had barked at the kid a lot this last year, hoping tough love would straighten him out. Unfortunately, that hadn't worked so well.

Now here they were. Quinn rubbed his forehead, kneading muscles that threatened a headache.

"Don't look so down." Nina glanced around before giving his other hand a quick squeeze. "The kid loves you. Remember that he's your brother, not a recruit or one of your teammates. Just lighten up a bit in the way you treat him, and you can change this."

The discipline and control he'd learned as a SEAL was so ingrained, it was part of who he was. Like breathing. But he didn't want to be his father. Demanding. Domineering. A real jerk who always got his way, no matter what. Quinn had to try harder not to treat Ty that way. He hoped he could accomplish it, even with all the turmoil surrounding them.

"Will you come find me when the hack is confirmed?" he asked, bringing them back to the real topic. "That way, I'll have a heads up on what's happening next."

"I don't know if I can do that. My job is already on the line." She stared at him.

He could tell she planned to shoot him down, so he rushed on. "If I ever meant anything to you, Nina, you'll promise to keep me informed."

She stepped back as if he'd slapped her. Maybe he had. At least verbally.

"That's a low blow, bringing up our past," she whispered, and even with her hushed tone, he heard how much he'd hurt her

"I know, and I'm sorry," he said softly, then firmed his voice. "But you should know, I'll do whatever I need to do to help Ty. And I mean *whatever* I need to do."

NINA ENTERED THE war room where Sulyard had hastily assembled a large team. He stood at the head of the long table, his brow furrowed with displeasure. He'd removed his suit jacket and rolled the cuffs of his sleeves to his elbows. Nina took it as a sign that they would be working late tonight. Sulyard was talking with agents Ivey and Clarke who also wore dark suits, white shirts and navy ties, looking like Sulyard clones. Both were fit and well-groomed, Ivey blond and Clarke dark-haired, but both wore bored expressions. She'd always thought counterintelligence would be very interesting, but now that she thought about it, anytime she ran into the pair, they seemed blasé.

Becca and Kait sat to Sulyard's right, their heads together as they whispered. Becca blond, Kait brunette, both were dressed in plain suits that were rumpled after a long day. Nina pulled out the chair next to Kait and sat. Analyst Jae Starling was seated on Nina's other side. Kait gave

Nina a clipped nod of acknowledgement, but under the table she squeezed Nina's hand. Kait was the affirmer of the group, always praising and keeping team morale high.

"This is gonna be one heck of a case," Jae Starling whispered

Nina faced the analyst who sat next to her teammates Aaron Durham and Pete Lloyd. Though only in her mid-twenties, Jae was one of the top analysts in the FBI, able to do things that were almost superhuman, and they all cut her slack, which included her dress and appearance. Green-tipped fingernails, skinny jeans, and a lime-green T-shirt didn't usually have a place at the Bureau, but Jae got away with it, as well as a liberal amount of sarcasm.

"We'll need everything you've got on this one," Nina said to Jae.

"Then keep the coffee coming." Jae laughed as she lifted her Mario mug with Self-Rescuing Princess printed in neon blue letters.

On the other side of the table, lead evidence tech Henry Greco sat next to fellow agents Gary Ivey and Erick Clarke who usually worked foreign counterintelligence, a division of the FBI she had little to do with. Nina did interact a lot with Henry in his lab or at crime scenes where he wore protective attire, but today he had on a button-down shirt with a coordinating tie and black pants. His glasses were sliding down his nose, and his gaze was open and eager as usual.

"Now that Brandt has arrived, we can get started." Sulyard's irritation at her tardiness was evident in his tone. "I'm assuming both of our hackers are tucked in with their agents at the hotel."

"Yes, sir," Nina replied pleasantly.

"Then let's proceed." He grabbed a dry-erase marker. "Due to the seriousness of this alleged incident, I'll be taking lead on this investigation. Special Agent in Charge Finley will be providing oversight."

Nina's apprehension skyrocketed. Sulyard never took lead, and Finley never got involved in routine details, which meant it would be even harder to keep Quinn in the loop, as she'd ended up promising. With Sulyard all but shutting down her involvement on the investigation, she'd have to count on status meetings and her teammates to keep her updated.

"Alleged incident?" Jae asked. She scowled at Sulyard. "What kid confesses to something like this if he didn't do it?"

"One seeking attention," Sulyard replied. "That said, after talking to him, I have no reason to believe he's lying. We'll proceed as if the breach occurred until DHS tells us otherwise."

Jae rolled her eyes, drawing Nina's attention to lashes coated in black mascara and eyes ringed with even deeper black eyeliner. "We don't need the bozos over at DHS charging in here on their white horses and taking over this investigation. We can handle it." She leaned back in her chair and crossed her arms.

"It's really premature to worry about that, Jae," Sulyard responded. "But if the breach is confirmed, you should prepare yourself for a joint investigation, which will include not only DHS, but PPB as well."

"Oh, goodie." She shook her head in disgust, her ebony-dyed little pigtails swinging. "I don't mind Portland police, but DHS?"

Sulyard ignored her comment and turned to the whiteboard where he jotted down Tyler Stone and Hamid Ahmadi's names. "We have two separate investigations. Though they intersect with one another, I want two independent investigations." He tapped Ty's name. "We'll investigate the Stone kid for the hacking charge. The Ahmadi boy for computer theft, keeping in mind that both, or neither, of these boys might be involved in a terrorist plot."

Hearing the word "terrorist" mentioned in conjunction with Ty's name made Nina's stomach ache.

"Isn't it stretching a bit to call this an act of terrorism?" Jae asked. "I mean, the kid just hacked into a database to get back at the dweeb who stole his chick. It didn't involve any violence for the purpose of intimidation, coercion, or even ransom."

"Thanks for quoting the definition for us, Jae." Sulyard's sarcasm was legendary, and he'd apparently started getting tired of Jae's questions. "We don't know enough yet to classify it as such. That's why I said these boys *might be* involved in a terrorist plot."

Jae opened her mouth to speak, but Sulyard held up a hand. She crossed her arms and slunk down in her seat. When she didn't get her way, she was known to pout a bit. With her pigtails, she simply looked like a spoiled little girl playing dress-up.

"Let me get into this, Jae," Sulyard said. "I promise to answer all of your questions at the end. I want you to take point on performing a deep background investigation into Hamid and his family. We're looking for the obvious information like family finances, criminal records, etc., but I also want you to search for ties to any known terrorist organizations."

"You think the kid is more involved in this than he's saying?" Jae asked before Nina could ask the same thing.

Sulyard shrugged. "On the surface, he seems to be a typical teen who wanted to get back at his buddy like you said, but his attempt backfired on him. But again, we only have the kid's word to go on. We don't have any proof he put the computer in the box. He could have sold it to a terrorist organization for all we know."

"Then there'll be a money trail. If it exists, you know I'll find it." Jae smirked.

"That you will." Sulyard faced Pete who was extremely shy. His chubby face with a bad case of acne and extra fifty pounds added to his insecurities. "Pete, you have Tyler Stone. Same information."

"Got it," Pete said, likely the most they'd hear from the guy during the meeting.

Sulyard jotted down the assignments on the whiteboard and added the name Bryce Young to the list.

"Let me guess." Aaron's tone was as confident as Jae's. Long and lean with a pointy nose, he sat up straighter, towering over most people in the room. "You have no proof Hamid was ever in possession of the computer, and this Bryce kid might still have it, so I'm checking into his background."

"Again, I don't think these kids are yanking our chains, but let's do our due diligence on all of them." Sulyard let his narrowed gaze travel around the analysts. "I expect a report on all three on my desk by sunup."

The wonder trio glanced at each other and shared a roll of the eyes. If it bothered Sulyard, he chose to ignore it. "See me after the meeting if you think you'll need additional manpower to get this done by morning."

"Oh, you know we'll be asking for help," Jae said, appointing herself their spokesperson, as she often did. Her attitude reminded Nina of Becca, who, in a similar situation, would take the lead, too.

Sulyard faced Becca. "Lange, I want details on the theft from Bryce's car. Reach out to the family when we adjourn. We have no probable cause to sit on this kid, but convince them it's in the kid's best interest to allow us to supervise him at a hotel. If they agree, I'll find an agent for the detail."

"I could help out with that," Nina offered, and earned a glare in response. Sulyard may have benched her, but she'd keep trying to get into the game.

"Isn't that an extreme measure, sir?" Agent Ivey flexed the muscles in his wide jaw, adding to his macho look that garnered him many dates and labeled him as the office player.

"Under normal circumstances, I'd say yes and the resources aren't warranted. But there's nothing normal about this. Not only do we want to prevent the circumstances from escalating, but when this hits the media, we do not want to be accused of not taking the situation seriously enough."

"Gotcha."

Sulyard returned his attention to Becca. "Find out if a police report has been filed for the break-in. If not, I want to know why, and I want to know about it immediately. If so, get a copy of the report and question the detective in charge and review any evidence they've collected."

Nina saw Kait's fingers curl into a fist. After Kait's engagement to Detective Sam Murdock last month, Sulyard was purposely keeping Kait from interacting with the Portland Police Bureau. Nina understood that Kait working with the PPB could be seen as a conflict of interest, but honestly, with Kait's integrity, she wouldn't compromise anything. Plus, her connection to the bureau through Sam would help her succeed in getting information on the break-in far faster than Becca could.

ERT Greco pushed up his glasses and focused on Becca. "Since the police likely thought this was a simple B&E, I doubt the criminalist went beyond fingerprinting. If they even did that. It might be a good idea to request that our team be allowed to process Bryce's car or, at the very least, request PPB to process it again."

"Good thinking, Greco. And that brings me to our next point." Sulyard inked PHYSICAL EVIDENCE on the board. "Knowing it would be too dangerous to send an evidence team to the cache site tonight, Brandt had the foresight to bring the cache container back with her." He faced Greco. "Take the prints you took from Tyler and Hamid tonight and compare them to anything you lift from the box. Brandt also took photos of footprints for your review. Let me know A.S.A.P. if either is a viable lead. We have a Multnomah County deputy securing the trailhead. Make sure your team is at the site before sunup to collect any other evidence."

"We'll be there," Greco said in the somber tone he used at crime scenes.

Nina knew he would be there early and he'd come prepared.

"Okay, let's see." Sulyard clamped a hand on the back of his neck, stared at the board for a moment, and then jotted down WARRANTS. "At this point, I'm not planning to request a warrant for Bryce's house, but of course we'll need one for the car. I'll take care of that, as well as warrants for both Tyler and Hamid's houses."

He set down the marker and looked at Becca. "Once the warrant comes in, I want you to supervise the computer seizure at the Ahmadi house so we know everything is done by the book. You'll also be in charge of analysis." He turned to Kait. "Same goes for you for electronic devices recovered at the Stone house."

"Yes, sir," Kait said.

"Hopefully these searches will provide a direction for the investigation."

"I want to make sure we don't overlook the potential terrorist connection in our research on Hamid," Nina added, ignoring Sulyard's scowl over her stepping in. "He has a heart condition, and his mother restricts his movements. It's not hard to see he resents it and feels isolated. He's recently started bucking authority. So he has a grievance, and he's trying to fill a hole in his life. Couple that with his Muslim background and he's ripe for radicalization by terrorists. I could have the tech people check his computer to see if he's been watching extremist videos, or posting and chatting with other radicals."

"Lange, you take care of that," Sulyard said, without even looking at Nina.

"My financial report will reveal any money given to these organizations," Jae added.

"His mother also mentioned he's been more withdrawn of late, and he clearly has anger issues," Nina added, waiting for Sulyard to jump all over her. When he didn't, she went on. "His mother says he's bucking authority at all turns right now. His room is filled with dark posters, including Marilyn Manson. Though idolizing such dark rock groups is more typical of a teen heading toward an active shooter scenario, like a mall shooting and not involvement in terrorist activities, it led me to question his mother."

"Okay, Lange, you good with following up on this lead?" Sulyard asked Becca.

She nodded, and Nina gritted her teeth before she said something to Sulyard that would totally get her kicked off of the investigation.

"I've never been to Triple Falls, Brandt," he said to Nina. "But I'm guessing there's no video surveillance in the area."

"None," Nina confirmed. "But I'll be glad to double check."

"Okay." He kept his focus on her. "We also need to obtain database information for the Hacktivist group. Since you can't modify this information without leaving a trail, it's safe to have you take point here. Find out the name of the database administrator. Get a list of everyone who viewed the cache posting before it was taken down. Then you can get started working the list."

"It could be a large number," Nina warned.

"Then it'll keep you busy and away from the other areas of the investigation."

Nina resisted the urge to stick out her tongue at him. It was a childish response, she knew, but one she wanted to do, nonetheless.

"One last point," Sulyard said. "In case any of you haven't made the connection, Tyler shadowed Brandt last year. We need to make sure there's not even a hint of favoritism shown to this kid. In fact, I want everyone extra vigilant where he's concerned."

That was just what Nina had been afraid of and all the more reason she needed to try one more time to suggest her help. "I've developed a rapport with the Stone and Ahmadi families. I could serve as the family liaison and keep them up to date on information you'd like disseminated to them, and answer their questions if I can. It would keep them out of your way."

Sulyard stared at Nina, his gaze searching, prying for something before he shrugged. "We'll give it a go for a day. If I find you're helpful and you play by the rules, we'll continue."

"Yes, sir." She couldn't wait to tell Quinn about this small victory.

Sulyard clapped his hands. "Okay, people let's get to it. As of now, we're working around the clock."

The group broke up, and Nina shot to her feet to catch up with Jae. "I hate to add one more thing to your list."

"Hah!" Jae exclaimed. "You agents do it all the time. What do you need?"

"I want you to keep monitoring the chat room from the Bonneville Dam investigation."

Her penciled-in eyebrows rose. "You think it's related to this investigation?"

"Think about it. We have a stolen computer that holds the ability to hack the No-Fly List, and we have chatter about something of value for sale."

"Oh, man, like wow. It could be related, right? I mean this could turn out to be a terrorist plot like 9/11." The words flew from Jae's mouth. "Does Sulyard know about this? If not, why didn't you bring it up in the meeting?"

"Calm down, Jae. It's just a hunch. Nothing more."

"Yeah, but Nina, your hunches are usually right on the mark and this . . . the chance to alter the NFL . . . well that scares the crap out of me."

Nina felt the same way and hoped for once in her career, her hunch didn't pay off.

Chapter Thirteen

ENDORPHINS FLOWING, Becca pounded up to the FBI building and used the heavy metal fence surrounding the property to stretch her hamstrings. Light shone through windows, disappearing in the foggy morning. The sun wouldn't be up for hours, and despite fatigue, the team continued to work. Which was why she needed this run. Needed it badly or she'd fall asleep at her desk.

She concentrated on breathing to return her pulse to her usual resting rate and reviewed her night. As soon as the staff meeting had broken up, she'd headed straight to Bryce's house. It had been the wee hours of the morning, but what better time to find the family home and catch them by surprise. It had worked well to get to the truth, and Becca was all about finding the truth. It was a principle she lived by. She'd had enough lies and deceit growing up and didn't tolerate them in her life.

Not that the Youngs had been deceitful. They'd filed a police report for the break-in and even confirmed it by giving Becca the case number. Plus they'd readily agreed to the supervised hotel stay. She'd quickly gotten them settled with an agent at the hotel, then traveled to Hamid's house and oversaw the electronics seizure.

Now she needed to contact the detectives at PPB to inquire about the investigation and, if the computer techs had completed imaging the drives from the Ahmadis' machines, she'd start reviewing the files.

Her breathing near normal, she headed inside to clean up. In the shower, she ticked off a long To-Do list she'd formulated while running. She couldn't take a step forward until she organized herself. Then her focus would be laser sharp and she wouldn't lose precious time along the way. Despite her misgivings about Quinn, Becca had to be there for Ty. Nina was counting on her, and she wouldn't let her friend down.

After dressing, she went to find Kait. Despite Sulyard's boycott of Kait's connection to PPB, Becca hoped Kait would quickly connect her to the right detective. Becca located Kait staring through the conference room window where Nina sat facing the window, her expression brooding.

Kait's concern for their friend was etched on her face. Becca was surprised Kait wasn't in the room with Nina, offering encouragement as she usually did.

Kait turned, and when she spotted Becca, she frowned. "She's been like that since you left, and I don't know how to help her."

"I'm not sure we really can help her," Becca said, wishing it wasn't true. "Other than to quickly close this investigation and stop Quinn from breathing down her neck."

"She doesn't need this, you know?" Kait shook her head. "Not after she worked so hard to put him out of her life. It's not fair."

"Fair?" Becca said. "If you want to talk about fair, I—"

Kait held up her hands. "I know. I know. No need to lecture me. Life's not fair. I get it, but that doesn't mean we have to dwell on it. I just want her to be happy."

"Like you are, you mean? Disgustingly happy." Becca wrinkled her nose.

Kait smiled, her eyes dreamy. She was obviously thinking about Sam. The far-gone look made Becca grimace. She was all for marriage and family for people like Kait and Nina, but not for herself. No way. Not now. Not in the future. There were so many foster kids depending on her—she needed every available hour to help them. No point in wasting time talking about it.

"Since we confirmed the break-in at Bryce's house, I'll be contacting PPB when the sun comes up," Becca said, moving them on. "Have you heard if Greco has finished Hamid's prints? If the local police managed to lift any prints from Bryce's car, I'm hoping they might belong to Hamid."

Kait's eyes narrowed. "Just got an email from Greco. The photos Quinn took of the shoeprints were a bust, but Hamid's fingerprints matched latents Greco lifted from the cache box."

"So, at the very least, Hamid touched the cache box."

"Right, though it still doesn't tell us if he put the computer inside and placed it at the falls."

"But if PPB found his prints on the car, it will at least tie him to the computer theft."

"If you want, I can expedite things by calling Sam to set up a meeting with the detective in charge of Bryce's case."

"That'll make Sulyard mad."

"So?" Kait said as she winked. "Since when did we let that stop us?"

"Never." Becca chuckled.

The three of them had more education, experience, and training than the other CAT teams across the country, so they often took liberties that would get some agents in trouble, but not them. They didn't flagrantly violate orders, but there were times when a case called for coloring outside the lines. Becca and Kait were fine with that, but Nina often had to be convinced to play along.

Kait shoved away a wisp of hair that had escaped from her clip. "What I'd really like to do is have Sam give the file a thorough read, then take over the case. But his lieutenant is a lot like Sulyard. He sees Sam as having a potential conflict of interest with anything FBI-related. I may be willing to risk my job, but I won't ask the same thing of Sam."

Becca liked Sam. He was a standup guy and she didn't want to get him in trouble either. She just wanted to do her job and do it efficiently. "I'm not sure we need Sam to get involved, other than to find out who handled the investigation."

Kait tipped her head in surprise. "Really? With the way you often run roughshod over people to get things done? It's not likely a detective in charge of a simple B&E is a seasoned detective. I would have thought you'd rather work with someone who has experience and doesn't waste your time."

"Roughshod? Really? I'm not that bad." Becca flipped up her hand. "Wait. Don't say anything. Maybe I am, but in this case, beyond getting the detective's initial report, I doubt I'll need to partner with PPB, so it doesn't really matter."

"You never know what might come up. It would be good to have someone who you can call any time of day." Kait stopped and thought for a moment. "Sam's partner, Connor, is definitely good at his job, and Sam trusts him completely. Plus, he'll be cooperative. I'll call Sam right now and see what they can do to get Connor on the case."

"Now?" Becca checked her watch. "It's not even three. He's got to be sleeping. I need to check in on the computer files first. You could wait an hour or so and give him a little more time to rest. I don't want Sam to get mad at you."

"First off,"—Kait smiled sweetly—"he never gets mad at me. Not often, anyway. Second, once I wake him up, he'll call Connor and direct any anger at him."

"Great." Becca groaned. "That'll make a good start to my working relationship with Connor."

"Don't worry, sweetie," Kait said, squeezing Becca's shoulder. "Connor's a nice guy, and he won't hold it against you. Against Sam, maybe. But not you." Still chuckling, she headed for her cubicle.

Becca hoped her friend was right. Otherwise, she'd need to find a way to persuade Connor into helping, and she wasn't nearly as good at coaxing as Nina or even Kait. No, Becca was more the 'meet on the basketball court, toss some hoops and wager on the outcome so he'd lose and have to help her' type.

Too bad there wasn't a hoop here or at the police station. She'd have a far better chance at success doing that than flirting with a man to get what she wanted.

WILEY SWUNG INTO Kip's covered parking spot and got out. Man, he was glad to get out of that piece of junk Kip called a car. He'd had enough of tailing agents around in the cold. But it had paid off. He'd learned the Feds were putting Hamid up at a hotel near the airport. Wiley had no idea why, but it wouldn't stop him from going forward with his plan. So, he'd hacked the hotel's electronic records to find Hamid's room and hidden the bogus phone in a fire hose nearby, thus allowing Wiley to make any texts he sent from Brandt's phone to Hamid match up with the kid's location.

Yawning, Wiley opened the apartment door and stopped dead in his tracks. The lights were on and music from a video game played in the background. *Crap*. Kip was there.

"Dude." He charged at Wiley the minute he stepped through the door. He was wearing black pants and a threadbare white dress shirt with an equally worn bowtie. He thought he had a professional appearance at work, but he only looked like the immense geek he was. "Why in the world aren't you answering your phone?"

Because it was you, fool. Wiley tugged the balaclava from his face. "Guess it must be on silent. What are you doing home anyway? Shouldn't you be at work?"

"I'm on my break, and I wanted to talk to you." Kip dropped into the beanbag chair by his gaming console.

Wiley needed to grab his things and get over to Brandt's house. He didn't have time to have a heart to heart with Kip. "I'm kinda in a rush. Can this wait?"

"You're in a rush?" Kip arched a brow below mousy-brown hair. "Now, in the middle of the night?"

"Got a chick waiting for me." Wiley offered the lie that could always be counted on to disarm Kip. "So make this fast."

Kip eyed him suspiciously. "Thought you said your scars kept you from getting any chicks."

"Can't get any worth looking at, but . . ." He lifted a shoulder in an offhand shrug. "So what did you want?"

"Did you see the Hacktivist site today?"

"No," Wiley answered, but Kip now had his full attention. "Why?"

"You remember that Hamid kid we met at a Meetup? The one who kept complaining about his heart condition and his mom not letting him do anything?"

"Vaguely," Wiley lied. He lounged on the edge of the sofa so he'd appear bored when he was now dying to know what this was all about.

"Yeah, well he's the one who put the computer in the geocache. Now, he's posted this frantic plea. Says the FBI is searching for the computer and whoever has it needs to return it to him. Says it's a matter of national security. If he doesn't turn it in, he'll go to jail."

Wiley snorted. "Yeah, right. Sounds like he reconsidered and wants it back."

"He seems legit, man."

"There's nothing on the machine related to national security. Trust me. I've spent hours scouring it from top to bottom."

"Even if he's just blowing smoke, you should probably still give it back."

Right, Mr. Goody Two Shoes. "It's mine now. I found it fair and square."

"C'mon, man. Think back to when you were a teenager and all the dumb stuff you did. Wouldn't you have wanted someone to give you a break?"

He'd never been dumb enough to do something like this. "I need the money I'll get for selling it, man."

"Tell you what. I'll buy the machine from you and give it to Hamid."

"Nah, I'm not taking your money," Wiley said, though he'd gladly do just that. He just wouldn't turn over the computer. Ever.

"Don't think of it as my money. Think of it as selling the computer like you planned to do."

"Same diff."

"Look, man. I don't want this kid to go to jail." Kip leaned forward, his eyes narrowing. "Don't make me report this to the FBI."

Wiley resisted curling his fingers in a fist and bashing the idiot's face in. "You'd do that? I thought we were friends."

"I don't want to, but if it keeps the kid out of jail. Yeah, I think so."

"Have you already told Hamid I have it?"

"Nah. I wanted to talk to you first. You'll give it back, won't you?"

"Yeah," Wiley lied as convincingly as he could. "If I can keep using your car, I'll arrange to get it back to him first thing in the morning."

"Sure. Fine. The bus isn't that bad." Kip pushed to his feet. "Hamid's phone number's on the site."

"Okay."

"You'll do this today, right? Like you said?"

Wiley nodded. "As soon as I can meet up with Hamid."

"I meant it about the money. I can afford a coupla grand, no sweat."

Idiot. "Okay. I guess I'll take you up on it, then."

"I can do an electronic transfer today."

Wiley didn't want to leave a trail from Kip to his bank account. "I've been cash only since I got out. That a problem?"

"Nah, I'll stop at the bank on my way home from work, and you'll have it tonight."

"Hey, thanks man."

"What are friends for?" Kip said, a dopey expression accompanying his stupid sentiment.

Wiley nearly gagged. Friends. He didn't have any friends. Never had. Not even as a kid. Not with his parents. They scared everyone off.

Even if they hadn't, people were always out for themselves anyway. Finding Wiley's weaknesses. Exploiting them, then turning on him. He couldn't afford to trust anyone. Kip might be putting a roof over Wiley's head, but if Kip kept pushing this thing about returning Hamid's computer, the dude would find himself six feet under in the blink of an eye.

"GREAT, THANKS, Connor." Becca balanced the phone with her shoulder as she closed files on her computer. "I appreciate your agreeing to see me so quickly. Where do you want to meet?"

"After dragging me out of bed in the middle of the night, the least you can do is buy me breakfast." He yawned, then gave her the name of nearby pancake place. "I'll meet you there in fifteen minutes."

She agreed, though a sugary, processed-flour, greasy restaurant was the last place she would choose to eat.

"You won't be able to miss me," Connor continued. "I'm six-two with reddish brown hair, and I'll be intensely focused on the door so I don't miss you. Oh, and if you still can't manage to find me, I'll wear my PPB windbreaker to make it easy on you." He chuckled.

Right. One of those guys who thought a local cop was superior to a Fed.

Confused, she said goodbye and hung up. Either Kait's description of Connor as being a nice guy was way off base or he was joking. Becca hoped for joking, as an attitude like that could get very tedious if they had to work together.

She stopped on the way out of the building to give Jae a task and still made it to the restaurant on time. Despite the calorie-laden dishes that were oh-so-bad for her, the sweet smell kicked up her appetite. It didn't take her long to spot Connor sitting near the back of the narrow diner with scarred laminate tables and worn vinyl booths. He came to his feet and planted his hands on his waist while bluish-steel eyes stared intensely at her. He wore jeans with a gray polo shirt under the navy windbreaker. Hair that was more red than brown, a square jaw and cleft in his chin, all mixed together nicely, making her stomach flutter.

Surprised at her reaction, she gritted her teeth and started toward him.

"Hey, baby." A sloppy guy with a beer belly seated at the counter grabbed her arm. "No need to take another step. There's plenty of room next to me."

She sensed Connor heading her way, but she held up a hand, stilling him, as she jerked her arm free.

"There's plenty of room in County lockup tonight, too." She fixed her eyes on the lowlife eyeing her up like a treat and slid her blazer back to reveal her gun and badge. "Touch me again and you're gonna see how much room."

His buddy broke up laughing and elbowed him. "Guess she told you."

"Geez. I was just kidding." He scowled at her.

She stared him down until he turned away, then kept both men in view while making her way to Connor's booth.

He was watching her every step, his study less intense now, and the side of his mouth had turned up. "Remind me never to make you mad."

"Connor, I presume," she said choosing to ignore Connor's mega-watt smile, as well as the drunk's come-on.

"Yes, ma'am." His eyes crinkled, the lighthearted look doing even more to unsettle her.

She slid into the booth, taking his seat so she could face the door and keep an eye on the men at the counter. Connor didn't miss her move to claim his territory, but he shrugged and took the other bench, sitting sideways, his back to the wall. Odd. She wasn't used to easygoing men in the law enforcement field, and she found his easy acquiesce interesting.

A dishwater-blond waitress with a stained apron and an expression that said she'd rather be anywhere but there, stopped by to fill Connor's cup. Becca grabbed the other mug on the table and turned it over.

The waitress sloshed it full of thick black sludge. "Know what you want or should I come back?"

"I'll have two slices of whole wheat toast. Butter and honey on the side." Once the waitress was gone, Becca caught Connor watching her, his expression one she couldn't quite read. "What?"

He grabbed his mug. "I was wondering if you were one of those women who don't like to eat in front of men."

"I have no problem eating. I just don't want to eat the over-processed unhealthy stuff they make here."

"Ouch." His grin returned.

"I thought you said you were intense," she said in more of a growl.

"Someone's cranky."

She hadn't been. Not until she started feeling like a teenage girl looking for her next boyfriend instead of an agent meeting with a cop. They were there to work, not socialize and waste time. She wished he'd get more serious.

She turned her attention to a case file lying on the table and flipped it open without asking. "Your detective do a thorough job on Bryce's car?"

"Yes, for what he knew the situation to be at the time—a simple B&E. Guess that's not exactly true, though, is it? Sam says this smash and grab is connected to a much bigger case."

She felt him staring at her. Even after knowing him for all of five minutes, she could easily picture his eyes as he watched her. He was likely waiting for her to provide details of her investigation, but she wasn't about to give out any information beyond what was needed to gain his cooperation. Not only was it a waste of time, but the fewer people who knew the NFL was vulnerable, the better.

She looked up at him, making sure her expression was blank. "Let's leave it at the fact that the computer we're seeking contains information that could cause considerable damage, and we need to recover it before that happens."

"Oka-a-ay. I'll buy that for now." He kept his eyes locked on hers and tapped the folder. "As you can see, everything about the incident looked like a simple burglary."

She returned to the folder, and despite his attention remaining riveted to her, she was able to concentrate and finish reading the report. "There's no mention of any other burglaries in the area. Wouldn't it be natural for your detective to get suspicious of a random break-in and ask more questions?"

"No," he replied, a hint of defensiveness in his tone. "It's not unusual for a computer left in a car to be nabbed, even in the safest of neighborhoods. And honestly, something like this isn't top priority when there are more serious crimes needing our attention." He slipped out of his jacket. His arms were covered in freckles, making him seem like the boy next door, but there was nothing else about his build that made him come off as quite so harmless.

"Besides," he continued after he dropped the jacket on the bench. "He followed protocol. Took a report, called in forensics, and canvassed the neighborhood. What more would you have had him do?"

"Nothing, I suppose." She stared at the file.

He reached out and closed it, brushing a hand over hers. She snapped it back and fired a warning look at him. Received a look of surprise in return.

"You got a thing with men touching you?" he asked. "'Cause I promise I'm not a perv like the guy at the counter."

A perv. Right. Like the guy who took Molly.

Becca looked away, but felt his gaze on her. She suddenly wished Nina or Kait had taken this appointment. Her reaction to Connor baffled her. She didn't have time for men in her life. Each day, each step had to be planned to get the most out of the day and have the greatest impact on life. Sure, she'd been tempted to date before, but then all she had to do was think of Molly and *poof*. It went away. Problem was, it wasn't working right now.

"So, how do we want to handle this?" he asked.

Good. If she couldn't focus on the case, at least he was doing so. She had Sulyard's okay to share the investigation details with Connor if she required his help, but after reviewing the burglary case file, needing his help didn't seem all that likely.

She faced him again, making sure she didn't let a hint of her emotions color her expression or her voice. "I'll get things rolling and get back to you if I need you for anything more."

"Right, like I'm gonna let you get me out of bed, give me some half-baked explanation, then run off without me." He crossed powerful arms, tightening the sleeves over his biceps as he stared at her. "We'll be working together on this every step of the way, Agent Lange. Make no mistake about that. The first time you try to ditch me, there will be consequences."

Becca clamped her lips together. The easygoing guy, the one who didn't seem to have a care in the world, had turned into a barracuda, and dang if that didn't make her heart rate kick up even higher.

Chapter Fourteen

BRANDT'S LIGHTS snapped off. Finally.

Wiley couldn't believe how long it had taken her to get ready for bed. He stripped off his clothes and fell in. That was it. Simple. Women took so much longer.

Women. They were good for only one thing, and he was so repulsed by Brandt, she wasn't even good for that.

He gave her thirty minutes to fall asleep, then moved Kip's car closer to her house. He snapped on a pair of latex gloves and grabbed the cheap laptop he'd bought on Craig's List with a new hard drive installed. Once his mission was complete, he'd plant the machine in her house to cement her involvement in the hack. The computer he found in the cache would go to his buyer.

He'd already turned down the screen brightness to keep from alerting the neighbors, making him squint to locate her wireless network. Since he'd found her password on his earlier visit, it took him only a few seconds to connect to the internet, leaving a trail from her IP address for the FBI to follow later. His next steps would take longer, but he didn't care. His goal was in sight.

He first logged in to the Hacktivist database and deleted Hamid's crazy plea to return the computer. Kip wanted to clear his conscience of this matter. Now he could. Just not the way the mama's boy had expected. As a bonus, Wiley had scored an extra two grand.

Wiley then followed Tyler's document that detailed the hack until the final step. He'd been waiting for this moment ever since he'd discover the hack. He'd wanted to try it out earlier, but forced himself to wait. Each time someone went through this virtual door, they risked the DHS database administrator finding the breach and fixing it. That would be the end of Wiley's good fortune.

He lifted his finger. Held it high. Held his breath. Hit enter. The code scrolled down the screen. White text on black suddenly opened to a beautiful, wonderful, data-entry window that proclaimed "No-Fly List" in big red letters.

Oh, yeah. He was in. He'd freakin' done it. For once in his life, he'd done it. This was the bomb.

"Calm down, man," he warned himself. He still had to finish the job, get out of the database undetected, and then get the pictures to Crash.

He navigated through the screens, clicking *Print Screen* on each one. After reviewing each screenshot, he loaded them onto a flash drive for backup and closed the database. He quickly transferred the pictures to Brandt's bogus phone and texted Hamid to cement the connection between them.

Test finalized. Screenshots attached. Money to follow shortly.

Wiley felt almost giddy and knew he was grinning like a fool. Though no one was out at this time of night, he still tugged up his balaclava before climbing out of the car to hide Brandt's phone by her house. He'd next go to the hotel where Hamid was staying to reply to this text, and her phone had to be placed in the right location so the GPS report that the Feds received would make it look like Hamid had texted her while she was at home.

"Game on, Brandt," he whispered as he stashed it in the dark of night. "Game on."

NINA COULDN'T SLEEP. She'd tried. How she tried, but after an hour, she gave up and dressed for work. Kait and Becca wouldn't be glad to see her. Especially Becca. She'd nagged Nina until she'd agreed to go home to get some rest. She knew they had to be tired, too. But Becca saw this investigation as a way to help Nina, and once Becca started one of her quests to right a wrong, she didn't stop until she saw it through.

Nina stepped to the door and glanced in a mirror. A vision from *Dawn of the Living Dead* stared back at her. Dark circles under tired eyes. Face wan from fatigue. Hair frizzing out.

Distraction. She needed something for Becca to focus on so she wouldn't take one look at Nina and send her back home. Nina grabbed a bright Hermes scarf hanging on a hook by the door. A true Alabama belle, her grandmother always said if one could do nothing about one's minor physical flaws, dress to impress, put on a smile, and no one would notice the imperfection.

Fat lot her grandmother knew about the world Nina worked in. Agents were trained to observe every detail. Sure, they wouldn't miss her scarf, but they would also note the fatigue. Still, old habits died hard, so she quickly knotted the soft silk around her neck and slathered on lipstick before heading to the car.

She hadn't been on the road for more than five minutes before her phone sounded in Kait's ringtone. Anxiety took hold. Kait wouldn't be calling when she thought Nina was sleeping unless it was urgent. Nina pulled to the side of the road to answer.

"What happened to getting some rest?" Kait said, not surprising Nina.

"I tried, but couldn't sleep," Nina replied. "What about you? Are you heading home soon?"

"In a bit. At least to grab a shower and clean clothes." She fell silent for a few moments, raising Nina's concern.

"What's wrong?" Nina asked.

"DHS got back to Sulyard. They confirmed the hack, but haven't traced it to Ty's house yet."

"Oh."

"Oh," Kait mimicked. "That's all you've got."

"I didn't think Ty lied to us and expected this response from DHS." She tried to sound casual when she felt sick to her stomach over the official confirmation that someone—someone with potential terrorist ties—possessed the ability to alter the NFL. "Is Sulyard talking about arresting Ty?"

"Not yet."

"Really, why not?"

"DHS hasn't found the database vulnerability Ty exploited. They asked our team to work with him to see if he can recreate the hack. They hope that will help them fix the vulnerability faster."

Nina couldn't believe this. It was almost too good to be true. "That's very open-minded of them, isn't it? I mean, he could do additional damage."

"They've thought of that and plan to dangle a carrot to motivate him to do the right thing. If he succeeds in finding the vulnerability, they won't file charges for the initial hack."

"Wonderful," Nina said. "I'm assuming they won't let him do this unsupervised."

"No, and Sulyard agrees with them. Ty will work out of our office, and one of us will supervise him every minute he's online."

"I don't suppose Sulyard will allow me to do that."

"Actually, he thought you should. He said since you knew Ty and the kid likes you, that you'd be the best one to work with him."

"Wow. Another surprise." Nina imagined Ty's face when she

shared the good news with him, maybe giving him hope that he would get out of this without serving time. And Quinn would be thrilled, too. She suddenly couldn't wait to see them. "I can run by the hotel and pick him up, if it'll help."

Kait hesitated for a long time before saying, "That'd be good."

"You don't sound like you believe that."

"Are you going there to get Ty or Quinn?"

"Both," Nina answered honestly. "I'm sure Quinn or his mom will accompany Ty to the office."

Silence filled the phone again, and Nina could almost hear her friend's unspoken opinion about Quinn. Kait was fiercely loyal and she took it to heart when any of them had problems. Nina always thought of Kait as the mother of the group. Usually Nina liked it, but not when it came to Quinn.

"This's no big deal, Kait," Nina said. "I'll simply tell them about it and bring Ty in as soon as he can get ready."

"Just be careful, sweetie. I don't want to see you get burned by Quinn again."

Right, be careful. Like Nina even knew how to be careful around Quinn. She never had. She'd dated casually in the past and had never been seriously tempted to start a long-term relationship, but it had been different with Quinn from the start. Maybe Kait was right. Maybe she shouldn't go see him. Maybe. Or not.

She sighed and opened a text to him.

You up? she typed.

Yes, he replied.

Can you meet me in the lobby in 10 minutes?

Yes. Even in texts, his communication was short and to the point.

See you then.

She arrived at the hotel early and stepped through the night dark with heavy clouds. At this time of year, the sun wouldn't come up for another thirty minutes, but the dead of night was starting to slip away. Business men were up and moving, pulling suitcases behind them to a sea of rental cars.

As the automatic doors swished closed behind her, Nina searched the lobby and found Quinn, his back to her, staring out a side window. That was odd. He never put himself in the vulnerable stance of having his back to the door. Never let anyone enter his space without knowing about them and assessing the threat. This thing with Ty must really have him off his game.

She approached. Waited for him to turn. He remained, his feet planted wide, long, slender fingers clamped on the thick column of his neck.

"Quinn," she said softly, trying not to scare him.

He turned slowly, proving he'd known she was there despite his continued focus out the window. His eyes were tired, and sad. Dark, haunted. "I suppose you're here to tell me the hack has been confirmed."

She nodded. "We heard from DHS a little while ago."

He drew in a sharp breath.

"They haven't traced the transmission back to your parents' house yet, but they will."

"So does this mean Ty's reprieve from arrest continues?"

"Yes," she said. "But not for the reason you're thinking. DHS has requested his help."

"Help? How?"

"They want him to try to recreate the hack from his memory to help them locate the vulnerability. They won't file charges if he's successful and his work allows them to plug the vulnerability before anyone else can exploit it."

"Then we shouldn't waste any time. Let's wake him up so he can get to work." His tone was less than enthusiastic.

She watched him, waiting for a smile or a hint of happiness at the good news. "I expected you'd be more excited."

He turned away. This dejected, almost sullen man standing before her was starting to worry her. She'd never seen him this down. He rolled with the punches and took immediate action. He didn't brood.

She took a step closer. "What's wrong, Quinn?"

He didn't look at her. "I really failed the kid, didn't I? I mean, I knew Dad wouldn't be there for him. But I should have been. Then I go and treat him like Dad does and . . ."

"You're not his father." She moved in front of him, forcing him to look at her. "You have a life to live." *A life away from all of us*, she thought, but didn't add.

"Maybe that needs to change."

"What are you saying? You'll quit the team and come back to Portland?" She waited for his reply. The other people in the room fell away; the only sound was her brain churning as she willed him to give her the answer she wanted to hear. The answer that said he'd leave the SEALs.

"I don't know . . . I mean, what would I do? There's nothing like being on the team, but . . ." He paused and seemed to think it over. "Maybe I can do a better job with him long distance . . . you know? Quit hollering at him like Dad does and be there for him. Not wait for Mom to call and tell me he's in trouble before I come for a visit. Just get my butt back here more often."

Her heart squeezed as it always did when it came to this man. She wished she could accept a life with him under those terms, but she couldn't. "Sounds like a good start."

"I hope he can pull off this thing for DHS."

"I'll make sure he gets it done," she answered, though after his comment, her heart wasn't in it anymore.

"Thank you, sweetheart. All of this is possible because of you." He stepped closer, his eyes finally lighting on hers. "You've been there every step of the way. Not only for Ty, but for me, too." He cupped the side of her face.

The warmth of his hand, the tenderness of his touch sent her pulse racing. She should pull away. Especially after his confirmation of his continued intention to remain a SEAL. Instead, she leaned into his palm. *Just for a moment*, she told herself.

"I—" He suddenly dropped his hand. She had no time to lament the loss of his touch as he jerked her to his chest and lifted her tightly into his arms. "Thank you, Nina," he whispered, his breath warm on her skin.

She clung to him, inhaled his rich, masculine scent. Reveled in the beating of his heart and pulse at the base of his neck. She wanted this hug to go on and on. To have that life her mother had warned her never to pursue. To risk it all, put everything out there, and throw caution to the wind.

Oh, man. She was right back in the place they'd been two years ago. She wasn't over him. Far from it. And nothing had changed. Nothing.

Except she was older. But wiser? No. The way she was letting him hold her, she clearly hadn't learned anything. Regretfully, she pressed her palms on his chest.

He lowered her to the floor. His eyes were dark with a mix of longing and sadness. She wanted to slip back into his arms. To kiss him and erase his pain. It was for precisely that reason that she stepped back. One foot, then another for good measure.

"I should be getting back to the office," she managed to say while under his careful watch. "Maybe it would be a good idea if your mom came in with Ty instead of you."

"Maybe." His focus didn't leave her face.

"Have her call me when they get to the office. I'll arrange with security to let them in."

He nodded, his eyes still fixed on her. Questioning eyes. Had the hug led him to believe she wanted something from him? If so, she couldn't let him think that.

"About the hug . . . the way I reacted," she said offhandedly. "I was just letting you know I sympathize with your situation with Ty, nothing more. Don't read anything into it."

"Didn't feel like sympathy to me." He shoved his fingers into his hair. "Look. Since we're stuck together for the unforeseeable future, we should probably talk about what happened between us."

"Everything's pretty clear, Quinn. There's really nothing we need to talk about."

"Yeah, I suppose. But then, I never apologized to you. I mean . . . I shouldn't have gotten so mad and stormed out that day. You deserved more. It was just so unexpected."

"You don't need to apologize. You want one thing. I want another. End of story."

"I figured it was all in the past. You know . . . this thing between us?" He gestured between them. "But it's still there. Isn't it?"

She didn't respond.

"You may not be willing to admit it, but there was nothing friendly about that hug."

"Fine, I'll admit it," she acknowledged grudgingly. "But nothing's changed. I'm not dumb enough to act on it and let you choose the team over me again. Not a second time."

He watched her for a long time. "I guess I'm pretty good at causing pain to the people who are important to me. Maybe I am like my dad after all."

"Quinn, don't. You may have some of his tendencies, but you're nothing like him."

He turned back, thunder in his expression. "If I am, I'll fight it till my dying day."

Seeing the determination in his gaze, she knew any dreams she harbored of them getting together vanished. He had to keep proving he was nothing like his in-control father, which meant he would remain a SEAL.

Chapter Fifteen

BECCA LEANED into Bryce's trunk, catching a whiff of Connor's musky aftershave as he bent over the other side of the Honda Civic. He still wore the PPB windbreaker, but today, he had on black tactical pants and a white shirt that stretched tight across a muscular chest.

He could have done this search without her and frozen her out on anything he found, but he gave her a heads up when he went to search Bryce's car and promised to wait for her to arrive. That gave him big brownie points for sure and told her a lot about him as a person.

For a moment, she forgot their mission and wanted to ask why he was still single. Agents talked about their personal lives at crime scenes all the time. Becca only listened and never joined in. She really didn't want to share her very personal work with foster kids. It just wasn't something to gossip about, and it took up most of her free time. The rest of it she devoted to Kait, Nina, and exercise, so she had little else to discuss.

She rifled through a paper bag finding nothing of value. Just an old pair of sneakers, a ratty windbreaker, and two empty Red Bull cans. They worked through the entire trunk, not leaving an inch uninspected.

Connor backed out and snapped off his gloves. "I'll get forensics to vacuum the truck, but I doubt we'll find anything to prove our boy Bryce is involved in whatever you're working on."

"He could have gotten wind of our investigation and cleaned out anything that implicated him."

"How? You said you had the other boys under wraps. And if everyone on your team is as closed-mouthed as you are, no one would have breathed a word."

She shrugged and looked away.

"Come on, Becca. Stop stonewalling me." His tone said the nice guy had a taken a pause and the irritated cop had replaced him. "Tell me what's going on so I can actually do some good here instead of rummaging through a trunk."

"Inspecting the trunk is of value."

"Sure, but any criminalist can do that." He laid a hand on her arm and eyed her as if waiting for her to jump back.

Surprisingly, she was tempted to step closer, but she shut that down by quickly pulling her arm free. She should step back, maybe walk away, but his sincerity in wanting to help made her tell him about the NFL.

When she finished, he let out a long low whistle and ran a hand over his hair, leaving it rumpled. "You weren't kidding about national security."

"That's why carefully processing this car is important. If the boys are involved and feeding us a line, we need to know now, before it escalates."

"I'll get our best forensics team out here and supervise them to make sure they're thorough."

"Thank you." She smiled her genuine appreciation at him.

He drew in a sharp breath before quickly averting his eyes. She didn't know what she'd done, but whatever it was, he'd reacted almost as if she'd stabbed him with a knife. Or like she had when he'd touched her at the restaurant.

"I'd appreciate getting a look at the surveillance video from Bryce's neighbor once you're able to get a copy from them."

He nodded and when he faced her again, the look was gone. "After I contact the neighbors, I'll get our video technician to retrieve the files. I'll call you as soon as they're in."

"Perfect." She looked around, seeking a reason to stay but found none. "I should head back to the office to process the computers we took into evidence."

"I'd offer my help, but I'm almost as helpless around computers as Sam."

"Wow, I was shocked that Sam was so out of touch, but a second guy our age who's that clueless? Impossible," she teased.

"Hey, watch it. I said *almost*." He laughed, and it was deep, rumbling, and contagious.

She found herself joining in and suddenly wished she didn't have to leave. But she had a job to do. Work came first. It always did.

PLACING THE TRACKER on Brandt's car had paid off. She was at work. If she moved her vehicle at all, Wiley's phone would issue an alert, warning him of any danger. His only real concern right now was a nosy neighbor or the SEAL. Wiley had staked out Mr. Military Big Shot's house last night to plant a tracker on the dude's car, too, but the SEAL hadn't come home. In fact, the whole family was MIA. Wiley suspected the Feds had stashed them away somewhere, too.

Wiley grinned with satisfaction and stared at the FBI building down the street. He'd apparently caused all kinds of inconvenience for so many people. The Ahmadis. The Stones. All the agents working their tails off. They were about to be far more inconvenienced than they could possibly know.

He opened the phone he'd assigned to Brandt and logged in to her bank account. He stared at the screen, his heart racing. The money Crash had transferred sat in her checking account like Crash had promised. A wireless transfer routed through a series of banks, making it untraceable. Forty grand. In one big honkin' deposit that screamed she was up to no good.

Sweet. Wiley had achieved his first big goal. He sat for a few more moments, savoring the victory. Letting the joy slide over him and chase out the chill he'd felt since prison. Ah, yes. Revenge. Such sweetness.

He clicked a few buttons to transfer twenty grand from Brandt's account to the bank account he'd set up for Hamid, then opened a text message.

Check your account. Money's been transferred, Wiley typed and sent it to Hamid to establish even one more link between the pair for the FBI to find.

He stowed the phone in an outside hidey hole, then returned to Kip's car and whistled all the way to the hotel. In the hallway outside Hamid's room, Wiley's steps faltered. A skinny agent escorted Tyler Stone, his beefy brother, and a woman he suspected was their mother toward the elevator.

Toward him.

A rush of adrenaline shot through his veins, and the fear of discovery nearly had him charging to the stairwell and out of the building. His heart thumped wildly, but he checked the placement of his balaclava and got his feet moving again.

Straight toward the agent. Toward the SEAL. Each step was torture, combined with a rush that he couldn't describe. It felt a lot like his days in prison when another inmate was stalking him. Minus the dark. Minus the fear of death.

Here, he was in control and could run anytime he wanted. Anywhere he wanted. But he didn't want to. He liked the feeling. Liked his blood rushing. Relished it actually. He was up for the challenge. It was him against the world. Him against these lame agents. He would make the most of it.

He nodded a greeting at the scrawny agent instead of looking away and raising the guy's suspicions. The agent tipped his head in acknowledgement, the aviator sunglasses on his head blinking a reflection from the overhead light.

Stupid agent. The FBI was supposed to be so tough. So on top of things. But Wiley had been right under Brandt's nose. Now this guy and the muscle-bound SEAL . . . neither of them had bothered to check him out. Their loss.

Wiley's gain. He smirked. Not only did he know Tyler Stone was staying there, too, but Wiley could finally put the GPS tracker on the SEAL's car. Bonus!

Wiley waited for them to round the corner before digging gloves from his pocket and grabbing Hamid's cell phone, then darting into the stairwell.

He opened the message he'd just sent from Brandt's phone to confirm it had come through. His fingers shook, but he wasn't surprised. What a rush this was. He'd do it again in a heartbeat. Maybe he'd been playing it too safe. Maybe he needed to risk a bit more. Enjoy the hunt while taking vengeance. He'd have to think on that.

Text confirmed, he logged in to Hamid's bank account. Wiley knew the money would be in Hamid's account and Wiley didn't need to look. But to make it look as if the brat Hamid really *was* involved in a hacking scheme with Brandt, Wiley checked for the deposit. That's what Hamid would do, if the situation was real. If Wiley wanted the Feds to believe Brandt and Hamid were behind the hack, Wiley needed to leave a digital record to show the account had been accessed by this phone in the location where Hamid was at the time.

It's all about leaving the right breadcrumbs, Wiley thought as the screen unfolded.

Perfect. Twenty grand. Big and bold, the transaction was pending in the kid's account. Just as it was supposed to be. The plan was moving along. Smoothly. Still, he'd drop one more crumb.

He opened a text message to reply to Brandt as Hamid would likely do in this situation. *Money received. Proceed with sale as planned.*

IN THE OFFICE parking garage, Nina shoved her phone into her purse. She'd survived her daily call with her mother, meaning her day could only improve from there. The sun had finally burned through the haze and should have served to brighten her mood, but she couldn't shake the feeling that something was wrong. She hadn't been able to shake it since leaving Quinn at the hotel. Nothing concrete, just that warning from her gut again.

Maybe she was overreacting. Maybe it was just that her life was spiraling out of control since Quinn showed up. Having him around left her feeling like something bad would happen any minute. It was the same way she'd felt nearly every day living at home after her brother had died. She'd battled it hard, though, and as she got older, she found ways keep it in check.

As long as her day was planned, she did fine. And as long as Quinn wasn't in her life, she could manage. He wasn't precise and neat, like she was. He was messy and wild. Danger in a uniform. The person she wished she could be. She had tried to be like him once, but who was she kidding? She needed order in her life. Things she could plan. Count on. Not this.

Shaking her head, she swiped her credentials and stepped inside. At her cubicle, she grabbed her laptop and files, then gathered everything she'd need for Ty and headed for the small conference room. She passed through the bullpen throbbing with the tension of an impending time bomb, ticking down the minutes until a terrorist took action with the NFL. If she hadn't been on edge already, this atmosphere would do it.

She put it out of her mind and set up Ty's computer. She heard voices outside the door and saw Kait escorting Ty, his mother, and Quinn into the room.

Kait hung by the door. "Security called your desk but you weren't there, so I answered and went down to get these guys for you."

"Thanks," Nina said, though she wished Quinn had been left downstairs. Why he was even there? He'd obviously decided to ignore her request. So what else was new?

She wouldn't take it out on Ty. She put on a smile and greeted him. "I have everything set up for you." She gestured at the computer. "Take a seat by the laptop, and we'll get started."

Kait stepped into the room. "You need any help?"

"Not at the moment," Nina said, keeping her voice down. "But I might need you to babysit Ty if I can get the Hacktivist administrator to agree to see me."

"Just let me know." She lowered her voice. "And good luck with Quinn. He's acting kind of grumpy. Not sure why. He was like that when I got downstairs."

Kait departed, and Nina glanced at Quinn. He did look out of sorts, but she wasn't about to investigate the reason and open their own personal can of worms again.

She dug deep for her Southern manners and turned to his mother. Tall and slender, with a pixie haircut, she usually had a bright welcoming smile. Not today. She wore a black shirt topped with a short white jacket over coral slacks and had twined a scarf swirling with all three colors around her neck.

Nina had always admired her sense of style. "Go ahead and take a seat anywhere, Mrs. Stone."

"Didn't we get rid of the Mrs. Stone business a long time ago?" she asked pleasantly. "Is this because of the way I behaved last night? If it is, I'm sorry. I was upset, and took it out on you. Will you forgive me?"

"There's nothing to forgive."

She watched Nina from eyes very much like Quinn's. "Then why the formality all of a sudden?"

Nina glanced at Quinn.

"Oh, I get it," Ellie said. "You think since you two aren't together anymore, that I'd be mad at you." She waved a hand. "If I was mad at every woman who'd been in Quinn's life, I'd have—"

"Mother," Quinn warned.

"What I'm trying to say is, I hope we can still be friends, and you'll keep calling me Ellie."

Nina smiled. "Ellie, it is."

She took Nina's arm and hugged her close, far more resembling the quintessential Southern mother than Nina's mama had ever been.

"Beware," she whispered, "Quinn's a bear this morning."

They shared a knowing look before Ellie went to sit near Ty. Quinn leaned against the wall as usual. Nina felt his gaze on her, but she ignored him and joined Ty.

He scrubbed his palms into his eyes as if trying to wake up. "Thanks, Nina."

"For what?"

"For keeping me out of jail."

"Don't thank me yet, hon. This isn't over. Not by a long shot."

"I know. It's just—" He glanced at Quinn, then stared at the computer.

"Quinn told you to thank me," Nina said softly to keep Quinn from hearing.

Ty nodded. "I appreciate your help. Honest, I do, but . . ."

"But you know this could still end badly for you."

"Yeah."

"So let's make sure it doesn't, okay?" She stabbed a finger at the computer screen. "You're all set up, but I have to warn you, your every move, every keystroke is being tracked. No heading to Facebook, Twitter, or email. And it probably goes without saying, no hacking. Just work. Think you can do that?"

"Sure."

"Good. So get started. One of us will be here if you need anything." She stood.

"Hey, Nina." Ty looked up at her, his gaze sincere. "Thanks. For real this time."

She grinned at him and ruffled his hair. He ducked away, a cute little smirk on his face so reminding her of Quinn when he lightened up. A Quinn she'd seen very little of since his arrival. Probably a good thing. She was having a hard enough time resisting grouchy Quinn, let alone dealing with Mister Irresistible who could simply enter a room and kick up her heart rate.

She stepped out of earshot but kept Ty in view and dialed the Hacktivist's database administrator, Victor Odell. He answered on the third ring. She explained her need to see the database records without giving him too many details about the investigation. "Since this is such an urgent matter, I'd like to pick up a copy of the database files this morning."

"I'm not sharing anything without a warrant," he argued.

Surprised by his instant belligerent response, she took a moment to make sure her voice remained pleasant. "That's not really necessary, is it, Mr. Odell?"

"It's absolutely necessary."

She was getting peeved that he wasn't being the least bit cooperative and wanted to snap back at him. But she knew she'd get more with honey than vinegar, so she slathered her voice with sweetness. "If you require a warrant, I'll be glad to request one and deliver it to you within the hour."

He snorted. "Good luck with that, Agent Brandt. I'm an attorney. I doubt you'll be able to accomplish it so quickly."

Great, an attorney. That meant she would have to do everything by the book or he wouldn't play ball. Not that she'd let it stand in her way.

"Never doubt the power of a motivated agent," Nina replied, putting a bit of vinegar in her voice this time. "Prepare to share your data. I'll be there with my warrant in less than an hour."

Chapter Sixteen

QUINN'D HAD enough of this waiting and watching to last a lifetime. It was as bad as standing QRF. And he'd done plenty of Quick Reaction Force stints. Too many times to count. Get ready for the mission. Suit up. Gear on. Weapons loaded, then wait. Their helo and crew standing by, ready for take off. Could be minutes, days, or hours, leading to a lot of sweating and heavy stress. Exactly like sitting there.

It was made worse by watching Nina and thinking about how hurt she'd sounded at the hotel. He didn't know how he could make it up to her—likely he couldn't—but he wanted to.

"I shouldn't be with Odell long," she said to Kait. "Call if you need me." She headed for the conference room door.

Quinn saw his chance to get out of this room and help Ty at the same time. He intercepted Nina on the way out. "I'd like to go with you."

"No," she said without even a moment's hesitation.

He wanted to demand that he accompany her, but that wouldn't help, so he forced himself to relax. "All this sitting around is making me crazy. I have to do something to help Ty, or I might explode." He ended with the grin that had always disarmed her.

It didn't work. She continued to stare at him with a blank expression.

"Please take him with you," Ty begged. "He's making me jumpy with all his pacing and staring. It's slowing me down."

"Then he should go back to the hotel," Kait said, from across the room.

Quinn fired a testy look at her. "I can't be of any more help sitting over there than I can here. But I might actually be able to do some good with this guy."

Nina stared at the ceiling for a moment. Quinn's focus went to the slender column of her throat, pale and smooth, and remained there.

She looked at him. "You can come along under one condition."

"Name it," he said eagerly.

She lowered her voice. "No mention of us or our past. It's strictly business. And if I ask you to do something, you listen to me."

"Yes, ma'am." He gave a mock salute.

Her eyes narrowed. "I'm not kidding about this, Quinn. Odell's an attorney. If this isn't handled right, you could make things worse for Ty."

"I won't do anything to hurt Ty." *Or you*, he thought, then crossed his heart.

Her scowl deepened and remained in place as they exited the building. Normally, he'd stop to enjoy the fresh air after being cooped up, but Nina shot across the parking garage to her car, and he was afraid she'd take off without him. She'd already opened the driver's door and was climbing in. He hated not being the one to drive, but asking for her keys wouldn't sit well with her, so he settled into the passenger seat.

"So what do you hope this Odell guy will tell us?" he asked after she'd maneuvered out of the garage and onto the main road.

She glanced at him. "Are you sure you want me to tell you? It's kind of technical."

"I may be a military grunt, but I'll try to keep up," he joked.

She rolled her eyes. "You're far from a grunt and you know it."

"So tell me then."

"Okay, you asked for it." She smiled tightly. "But I get carried away when I talk about this stuff, so don't say I didn't warn you."

"I'll manage."

"I have a warrant that gives me access to any record that indicates who viewed Hamid's cache posting on the Hacktivist site. These records will be in a database. What I'd really like is to see the entire database, but due to privacy issues, the judge has limited the warrant to this list." She glanced at Quinn, determination in her expression. "That doesn't mean I won't ask for full access."

Quinn could easily imagine her trying to win Odell over. Using her soft Southern accent to come across as nonthreatening. It had always worked with Quinn. He suspected it worked with most people. "This information on people who viewed the post. I'm assuming it will include how to contact them or it wouldn't be of much use."

"Right. Name. Address. Phone number."

"Do all websites track that much user information? If they do, it seems pretty invasive."

"The Hacktivist site differs from most websites that only collect basic visitor stats. Things like city, state, pages visited, browser, IP address, etc., but nothing specific to actually identify them." She held up a hand. "Before you ask, IP stands for Internet Protocol. Think of it like you might a street address. Your internet service provider tracks your access to the internet by this address. Odell can give us a list of IP addresses that visited the site. We could then track these down to their service providers and get a warrant for the visitors' contact information."

"Could? Isn't that your plan?"

She shook her head. "The Hacktivist site is a membership site and requires visitors to have an account to view it. This account already includes contact information that is approved by the administrator. All logins for registered visitors are recorded in the database along with the pages they view. So I can connect every visit to Hamid's geocache page to an actual user with contact information. This is what my warrant will allow me to obtain from Odell."

"Then the person who took the computer should be on this list. All we have to do is work down the list to find him." Excitement about the lead started building in his gut.

She glanced at him. "*I'll* work the list, Quinn. We have to respect the privacy of these individuals. You can't have any part in contacting them."

We'll see about that. "Okay."

She appraised him. "The gleam in your eye says something different."

"You mentioned wanting full access to the database," he continued. "If this info you're after will give us the computer, why do you want the other stuff?"

"Because records can be changed and altered. For example, if Odell was the one who took the computer, as the administrator, he could delete the record showing that he viewed the page. He'd have to change quite a few files to hide it from me, but if he was knowledgeable enough, he could delete the trail and the report he provides won't include his name."

"I get it. If you could see the actual database, you could find any changes. Seems odd that a judge wouldn't understand that and give you a warrant for all of it."

"He understands it, but he's concerned about privacy issues of the users who have nothing to do with this cache."

"You'd think he would take the seriousness of this situation into consideration and be flexible."

"Odell's an attorney and an activist, so the judge wants to tread lightly at first."

"Lawyers." Quinn shook his head. "I have it so much better on the job. None of this messing around stuff. Just swift and concise action to eliminate the problem."

"That won't fly with Odell." She cast him a warning look. "Promise me you won't even try to bully him."

"I'll do my best," he said. But if the guy messed with Nina, Quinn couldn't be sure he'd let Odell get away with it.

It didn't take long to test Quinn's resolve. Odell was brash and insulting from the moment Nina slapped the warrant into the guy's hand.

Five-ten or so, a string bean with a shiny scalp, the guy sneered at Nina. "So you have a judge in your pocket, do you?"

Nina didn't say a word, but stood with an expectant look on her face. How she managed it, Quinn didn't know. The guy needed a good dressing down. Quinn would gladly deliver it, but he followed Nina's lead instead. It took every ounce of willpower he possessed to simply stand by.

"I'll print your report." Odell sat behind a cluttered desk with an ashtray filled with cigarette butts. His printer soon started spitting out page after page.

"Seems like a long list," Nina said. "How many unique page views occurred?"

"Around three hundred."

"So 300 people viewed the post?"

"That's what I said," Odell snapped.

Quinn's optimism disappeared. With so many names to work through, this could take longer than they thought. By the time they got to the end of the list whoever possessed the computer could have sold it. When the printer stopped, the Ichabod Crane look-alike stood and handed the report to Nina.

"Thank you." She smiled, but Quinn could see it was the fake one her grandmother taught her to use. "I'd love to take a quick peek at the database before we go."

"Don't take me for a fool, Agent Brandt." Odell tapped the warrant that he'd dropped on his desk next to a half-eaten bagel. "If the judge wanted you to see the database, the warrant would specify that. Without a more inclusive warrant, I won't answer questions about the database, much less give you access to it."

Nina didn't react again, but slowly flipped through the report, scanning each page. Quinn didn't know if she was doing it because she needed to review the document, or if she was taking pleasure in wasting Odell's time. That's what Quinn would be doing, along with firing a few choice words at the creep.

She finally looked up, her expression friendly. "I have a few questions for you."

"I said I wouldn't answer them." Odell lit a cigarette and blew the smoke across the desk at her.

She didn't step back or grimace. "I didn't say my questions were about the database, Mr. Odell." The words came out like melting sugar, but Quinn knew her well enough to catch her iron resolve. "I'd like to know your whereabouts for the last few days."

"You what?" He jutted out a very angular jaw. "Where I've been has nothing to do with your investigation."

"See . . . here's the thing." She leaned closer, that fake smile widening and belying the fact that she was going in for the kill. "Without access to the database, that you as the administrator could easily have modified, I don't know if my list is accurate. And you're forcing me to get a warrant to view the actual database. To get that warrant, I'll need to show the judge every place you've been in the last few days where you could log in to the database and modify files."

"I can access it from anywhere with my phone. It'll take forever for me to write out such a detailed list."

"Exactly." Her smile remained in place.

Odell took a long drag on the cigarette and exhaled. "This is harassment. I don't need to comply with it."

"Then I suppose I'll have to figure out who you've talked to and where you've been on my own. You know. Dig and pry. Talk to everyone you've come into contact with. Raise their suspicions about what you might be up to. I'd hate for these people to get the wrong impression. I'd think you would, too." She sat back and crossed her arms. "I can wait while you make the list, or I can get started on turning your life inside out. Your choice."

He eyed Nina and took a step closer.

Quinn didn't like the way he was staring at her. He stepped between them. He expected a reaction from her, but she didn't take her eyes from Odell. "I'm just doing my job, Mr. Odell. Of course, there's a third choice, too. If you don't want to waste your time on compiling the list or want me talking to people, I could look at the database now."

He snatched up a pen and dropped into his chair. "You want a list, you got a list." He perched the cigarette on the ashtray and set to work scribbling on the notepad.

Nina smiled at Quinn. She hadn't needed him along for the ride. She was a first-class operator all on her own. Not that she'd succeeded in seeing the database now, but he knew she'd at least gotten the satisfaction of making this creep jump through hoops. And Quinn got to see her in action. It was something he could remember and smile about on those long, lonely nights downrange.

Chapter Seventeen

BECCA SAT BACK in the FBI's busy computer lab staring at her computer. She'd been glued to the screen for the last few hours, and she took a moment to stretch and look around the room humming with computers and very little chatter.

Kait sat just down the aisle, and as she answered her cell phone, she'd mouthed it was Sam. She was soon caught up in her call, but suddenly spun to look at Becca. Sam was likely bringing her up to speed on Becca's meeting with Connor.

Becca got a little twinge in her chest, and she sat back to wait for Kait to share what Connor had said about her. After their search of the trunk, she hoped he would say good things, but she suspected he'd say she was prickly and standoffish. Likely a little weird, too, from the way she'd jerked her hand back at the restaurant. Maybe he'd even mentioned she didn't seem to like his attention.

Just the opposite was true, though. She liked it all right. Too much.

Kait stowed her phone in her pocket, then got up and came over to Becca. "Glad to hear Connor took over Bryce's burglary investigation for PPB."

Good. He'd stuck to business, which is what she was planning to do. "He's really taking it seriously. He had a forensics team process Bryce's car again, and they've lifted additional prints that we hope will match Hamid's. He's also obtained video from the neighbor's surveillance camera and street cams in the area. I'll take Hamid's prints over to PPB for comparison and take a look at the video while I'm there, too."

"See, I told it was a good idea to include Connor."

Becca wished she could agree on a personal level, but professionally Kait was right, and Connor, though seeming easygoing, had moved forward at warp speed.

Kait rolled her eyes, then stared at Becca's computer screen and frowned. "You're working on the Hacktivist connection? Nina didn't give that up, did she? If she did, she's more down than I thought."

"Relax, Mom," Becca laughed. "She's dealing with the database, but

Jae just told me about an oddity on the site so I was checking it out." Becca displayed Hamid's Hacktivist account. "The post where Hamid mentioned us and asked for the computer back has disappeared. You or Nina didn't authorize a takedown did you?"

Kait shook her head. "Besides following protocol in not altering database records, Nina and I hoped the person who had the machine would see the post and call us." Kait stared at Becca. "Which means someone deleted it. On purpose."

Becca ran through possible scenarios in her mind. "Hamid's been in custody without internet access, so he couldn't have done it. I don't think he would have taken it down anyway. It's in his best interest to locate the computer. Same for Ty. So, who would delete it?"

Kait rested on the edge of the table. "Maybe Bryce or one of Ty's other friends?"

"It's possible I suppose, but except for this post, Ty and Hamid have been incommunicado with the outside world. So, how would these friends know to delete it? Besides, they'd likely need Hamid's login to do it, and I doubt Hamid shared that."

"Could be the database admin," Kait offered. "He has access to everything."

"After what Nina said about Odell's unwillingness to cooperate, it'll take some time to prove that." Becca chewed on her lip as she thought. "What if Hamid is lying to us, and we're working the wrong angle?"

"You mean Hamid being in on a terrorist plot?"

Becca nodded. "There could be others in the Hacktivist group working with him. They could be using this group to communicate. Maybe Hamid's post was a warning to them. That's why it's been deleted."

"I see where you're going, but it doesn't add up with everything else. We have no indication that he's involved with a terrorist cell. Jae hasn't found anything in the Ahmadis' background check to suggest that, either, and you know how thorough she is."

"Did you find anything on the Ahmadi family's computers?"

"No, but that doesn't mean anything. If Hamid's active in a cell, he's probably smart enough not to leave anything behind to implicate himself."

"You're probably right." Becca considered their options going forward. "We should take another run at questioning Hamid and Ty."

"Couldn't hurt, I suppose. With your experience with foster kids, you should take the lead. If any of us could get him to talk, it would be you."

"The only downside I can see in talking to Hamid is that we'll need to ask pointed questions about terrorist activities," Becca said. "His parents could freak out and lawyer up. Instead of moving the case forward, we'll be left with nothing to go on and limited access to the teen." She was silent for a moment. "I guess it's a risk we're going to have to take."

BECCA CLEARED HER throat and waited for Hamid to look at her. She sat across the conference room table from the teen while his mother watched. Surprisingly, Sulyard had agreed that her work with foster kids did make her the best person to connect to the teens. She'd started with Ty and that interview had gone well. He'd been very cooperative, but she'd learned nothing new. Hamid, however, had thus far been a bit surly.

"Look at me, Hamid," she finally said when he didn't respond to her last question. "I'm interested in the post you made to the Hacktivist site from your house. The one you created when you were supposed to be using the bathroom. Tell me about that."

Guilt flashed on his face. "I didn't say anything bad. I promise. Just that you guys were breathing down my neck and asked for the computer back."

"If it was so innocent, why did you delete it?"

He shot a quick look at his mother. "I didn't."

Her eyes narrowed. "Tell the truth, son."

"I am. I didn't delete it. I couldn't. You guys wouldn't let me touch a computer." He huffed a mirthless laugh, then held out his hands and mocked a nervous tremor. "See. I have withdrawal symptoms."

Becca glared at him. "This isn't funny, Hamid."

"Okay, geez. I get it."

"Do you?" Becca leaned forward and gave him a look she used on kids who'd used up all but their last chance. "Do you really get that if we don't resolve this soon, a terrorist attack could happen? In addition to lives lost, you could be charged as an accessory to the crime?"

"Is this true?" The words shot out of Mrs. Ahmadi's mouth as she clutched her chest.

Becca nodded. "Especially if Hamid isn't forthcoming and helpful."

Mrs. Ahmadi grabbed Hamid's wrist. "Do not fool around like this. Tell her everything she needs to know."

His smile faltered and fear filtered into his eyes. She'd finally gotten through to him. He now understood the seriousness of his situation.

"Did you delete the post?" Becca asked again.

"No. I swear."

"Did you ask someone else to do so?"

"No. I haven't talked to anyone."

"Well, the post is gone." Becca rested against the back of the chair, hoping Hamid would think she'd relaxed, when in fact she had no intention of breathing easier until they had the computer back and the culprit behind bars. "So who do you think could have made it go away?"

His gaze darted around the space as if searching for a logical answer. "Maybe someone hacked the database and stole my login information. Someone like Ty."

"Ty hasn't had access to a computer either."

"Then I don't know."

"Anyone else know your login? Like some friends in the Hacktivist group who have the same goals as you."

"I've never shared it with anyone. Never. I promise. And I didn't write it down. My computer hasn't been hacked. I'm sure of that." He drew in a deep breath. "That leaves one person. The administrator for the Hacktivist site. Yeah, it has to be him . . . whoever he is. Or it could even be a she. I don't know. But yeah. It's him. Or her. Ask them."

He made a good point, but Becca wouldn't stop there. "Tell me about your friends, Hamid. Who do you hang with from this group?"

"No one."

Not believing him, Becca raised her brows. "Absolutely no one in this group is your friend?"

"Not really. I mean I talk to them at the Meetups, but that's all."

"What about other groups you're involved with?" she asked, being purposely vague.

"I don't belong to any other groups."

"None?"

"No." He glanced at his mother.

Becca leaned forward. "Hey, I get that having your mom here might make you less likely to tell me everything, but I need you to forget about her and answer my questions truthfully."

"I am telling the truth. I'm not part of any other groups."

"Not online or in person?"

"No. None. I swear."

"What about the members of the Hacktivist group that you just talk to, then? Any of them have radical political views?"

"We don't talk politics, so I don't know."

"No mention of how you can help further the cause of a radical group bent on paying the U.S. back?"

"No," he shouted. "Terrorist. Is that what you're getting at? I'm not one. I don't know any." He looked at his mother. "Mother, please. You have to believe me. I would never do this. You know that, right? You can't let them get away with saying I did. Please. Do something."

She nodded solemnly. "I think it is time we contact an attorney."

Just as Becca had predicted. Unfortunately, the interview had ended too soon and she still wasn't sure if Hamid was lying.

QUINN WATCHED Nina from across the table. In the background, Ty's fingers clicked across his keyboard, but the noise didn't seem to distract her. Her head was bent over the list from Odell, her laptop sitting nearby. Three colors of highlighters were scattered around her work. At her precise and measured movements, Quinn resisted sighing. He wanted to rip that infernal list from her hands, rush out of there to hunt down the suspects, and knock on doors until he found the computer.

Not Nina. She'd created a plan of attack, then had run it by Becca and Kait. Only after that did she divvy up the list for her team to begin calling the Hacktivist members. Then she'd started investigating Hacktivist members she'd deemed high priority. When she'd strike out on one—as she had many times—she placed a neat little checkmark next to the name and moved on.

Quinn would have slashed through them with a thick marker. Nah, he wouldn't even have done that. He would have quickly reviewed the data, made a short list of suspects, and paid them a visit to intimidate them into talking. He'd suggested as much to Nina, but she wouldn't waste a moment going to the wrong location. Instead, she'd waste hours planning it all.

Okay, fine. Maybe both of their approaches wasted time, but at least he wouldn't be sitting here twiddling his thumbs while Ty moved closer and closer to a prison sentence.

The door swung open, and Sulyard stepped into the room. Pressed and starched even after a long day, he headed straight for Nina.

"A word," he said and stepped to the far side of the room.

Her gaze wary, she joined him by the door. Quinn couldn't hear their conversation, so he moved closer to eavesdrop without remorse.

"Been a long day," Sulyard said. "All of you are looking beat."

Odd. Small talk? Or even odder, this guy caring about how they were doing.

"We're good." Nina pulled her shoulders back, and her gaze sharpened.

"It's time to take a break. For everyone. Cut the kid loose for the day. Send everyone home."

Her mouth dropped open, but she quickly recovered. "Why? Ty's still willing to work."

"We run the risk of being accused of enslaving a minor."

She glanced at Ty, a fondness for him evident in the way her eyes softened. "I didn't think of that. I'll send him back to the hotel."

She'd given in far too easily as far as Quinn was concerned. He'd have argued the point because Sulyard's argument made no sense, especially with his mom there. Maybe if they'd brought Ty in without her, but not this way. Sulyard had to know that, too.

Quinn appraised the guy. He clearly had a hidden agenda. Did he have additional information about Ty and didn't want him around as they worked on it? Was an arrest imminent?

"You head home, too." Sulyard's tone was no-nonsense. "Get some rest."

"But, sir," she argued forcefully this time. "No one else is going home."

"No one else has the emotional tie to this case that you have, and emotions take their toll."

Sulyard was right. Emotions did take a toll. But everything Nina had told him about Sulyard said the guy wouldn't do this. Plus Quinn's gut said he wasn't sincere. It sounded more like he was reciting a prepared speech.

"I can keep going," Nina offered.

"Go home, Brandt," he said firmly. "It's not optional."

She nodded, her shoulders sagging a bit.

"Before you even think about taking work home with you, don't. Leave everything as is. I'll have someone else take over."

A guilty expression flashed across Nina's face. She'd been planning to bring her work home. Of course she was. She was dedicated to helping Ty. She'd proven that since Quinn had barreled into her life. His heart warmed at her tender concern for his brother. He had the urge to pull her into his arms and hug her. It was the last thing he should do in that room. The last thing he should do anywhere.

"Are we clear, Brandt?" Sulyard asked.

"Yes," Nina replied.

"I'll send someone in so you can brief them on your progress. Then I want you out of here." Sulyard departed as quickly as he'd arrived.

Nina crossed over to Ty. "I suppose you heard that."

"What?" Ty looked clueless as usual when he was wrapped up in his computer.

Quinn watched as Ty and Nina talked and was jealous of the easiness between them. She accepted him for what he was. A computer nerd. She didn't try to change Ty. Quinn had. Big time. And Ty had pulled away from Quinn, just like Quinn pulled away from his father. Doing things his father couldn't abide. Skydiving. Parasailing. Mountain climbing, skiing. The list was endless. All things he'd first gotten involved in because dear old Dad hated them.

Sure, Quinn liked the activities, but why? Because they were fun, or because they took him as far from his father as possible and proved he hadn't turned into the old man? And what about Ty? He excelled in computers, but did he really like them or was he running, too? Quinn had never asked. He needed to talk to him about it. Start respecting the kid's abilities and do a better job of respecting his choices. He'd try. Starting now.

"Let's head back and take a dip in the pool," he said to Ty. "I'll show you some fun tricks I learned in BUD/S."

"But I'm almost done here," Ty complained. "Just a few more hours and I'll find the right fix. I can feel it."

"Sorry, taking a break isn't a request, bro," Quinn said.

Ty frowned. "I just don't get it. I'm making good progress and stopping now is insane."

Quinn agreed. Nina's expression said she did too. But she was a good soldier. Like he was. Take orders from your superior and act on them. It's what kept the organization ticking along like a well-oiled machine.

Nina planted her fake smile on her face. "It's what ASAC Sulyard wants, Ty, so it's what we'll do."

"C'mon, bud." Quinn rested a hand on Ty's shoulder. "Let's do as they say. I, for one, am dying to get out of this room."

"I should have known you'd follow the company line." Ty shrugged off Quinn's hand and stood.

"Now, son." His mother stepped forward. "Agent Sulyard is doing what he thinks is best. It's our responsibility to honor that."

"Best for who? He offers me this deal, then reneges when I get close. I haven't given them anything yet that will secure the database. That's sure not good for me."

His mother took a deep breath and blew it out slowly before smiling at Nina. "Thank you for giving Ty this chance to clear his name. I'm hoping he can come back tomorrow to finish his work."

"I'm guessing that's Sulyard's plan. That is, if we still need Ty's help by then. I'll ask to make sure and give you a call."

Ty and his mom went to the door.

Quinn didn't move. "Are you going to be all right?"

Nina seemed puzzled. "Why wouldn't I be?"

"Because you don't want to go home. You want to stay right here in the thick of things."

"I'll do as I'm told."

"Don't you find Sulyard's decision kind of odd? I mean, why cut off valuable resources in a critical investigation?"

She scrubbed a hand over her face. "I can't begin to know what he thinks sometimes."

He moved closer so Ty and his mom couldn't hear. "I'm trained to read people like you are. But you're too close to the situation to see the nuances of Sulyard's expressions. He's got an agenda, and it's not to make sure you and Ty get the rest you need. I suggest you talk to Becca and Kait before you leave. See if they can shed some light on the situation."

She seemed to contemplate his statement, then she gave a firm nod. "Thanks for mentioning it."

He wanted to take her hand, but he settled for meeting her gaze and holding it. "We may be butting heads, sweetheart, but I still have your back. You can count on that, no matter what."

Chapter Eighteen

NINA WORKED HER way through the dimly lit parking garage, the space eerily quiet in the dusky night. Unease settled over her like the shadows cloaking the cars.

Stop it. No one was out to hurt her. At least not physically. But she was smart enough to listen to Quinn and see Sulyard had an agenda. One she suspected didn't bode well for her. He clearly wanted her away from the investigation for the remainder of the day. She'd tried to talk to Becca and Kait about it, but they were nowhere to be found. Had Sulyard gone as far as isolating her friends so she couldn't contact them? If so, he'd cut Nina off at the knees. No access to her friends made life so very difficult.

Enough.

They were just busy. Simple as that. She was letting the darkness and gloom of the garage get to her. She shook her head and strode toward her car, the staccato of her heels reverberating through the space.

"I wondered if you were coming." Quinn's deep voice came from the shadows.

She jumped, and her heart clutched. "You scared me."

"Sorry." He was standing at alert, his body ready to react to any danger, the muscles taut, his focus riveted to her. "I didn't think it was a good idea to stand around where everyone could see me waiting for you."

Was his cloak-and-dagger behavior really necessary? Or was he thinking like a SEAL on a covert mission to bring some excitement to a day that anyone could see had bored him to death?

"Why are you waiting for me?" she asked, hoping to find out.

He lifted a powerful shoulder in a shrug. "With everything that's going on, I just wanted to make sure you got home okay."

"I appreciate your thinking of me," she said, as she *was* touched by his consideration. "But don't you think you're overreacting to this whole Sulyard thing? He may be up to something, but the only danger I'm in is falling asleep at the wheel on my way home."

"You can play it down all you want, but my gut says it's a good idea for me to see you home." The tension in his shoulders and neck intensified, making her anxious. "I always listen to my gut."

"Again, I appreciate the concern, but I'm fine."

He moved closer and took her hand. His gaze softened. This tender, yet instinctive response to protect her nearly made her invite him to drive her home. But tomorrow would come, and he would go back to his team. The last thing she needed was to be alone with him at her house.

"I can text you when I get home, if that makes you feel better."

His intensity returned. "You ever get one of those feelings that raises all your senses? The one that warns of imminent danger?"

"Sure. After eighteen years under my Mama's roof, I get them far more than the average person. But I dismiss them just as quickly," she said. She wasn't exactly telling the full truth, though, since she'd just had a similar feeling, and she hadn't blown it off so easily.

"I'm not talking about those vague feelings," he continued, "but the ones that make your senses stand up and take notice. *Those* you don't ignore. I know you don't. I won't either. So, your choice is to invite me along, or I'll tail you. Either way, I'm sticking with you until I know you're safely home."

As much as she was frustrated with him, she respected his tenacity. He really was a good man. Strong. Honorable. The kind of man any woman would be lucky to have in her life. The kind of man she would be lucky to have. If he changed jobs. But he wouldn't. Today proved that. He'd been antsy all day, but now that he was free from the building, and he believed there was an underlying threat, his eyes were bright with excitement. She still suspected he had a subconscious need to believe a threat existed, just to get rid of his boredom.

"If nothing else, you can take pity on me." The corner of his mouth turned up in a lopsided grin. "Mom and Ty are long gone. I don't have a ride."

"MAX is a short walk away," she said, fully intending to let him escort her home but not making it easy for him.

"The train. Are you nuts? You want me to take the train?"

"Sure. Why not? It's a wonderful mode of transportation." She tried to look serious, but felt a smile forming.

He groaned and eyed her. His expression suddenly cleared. "You're messing with me."

She grinned. "That I am."

"You know what happens when you tease me." He locked gazes with her, and his eyes heated up.

One thing she'd always loved about him was that he was such a man's man, the big, strong, tough guy, but he still let her tease him and took it in stride. Even seemed to enjoy it. But it also always led to him needing to physically prove his strength. To touch her. She'd loved that, too. Every minute of it.

So when he stepped closer, she was helpless to resist. She leaned in instead of moving back. He rested a hand on her collarbone, then slid it around the back of her neck drawing her toward him.

Every nerve ending fired. She waited for him to lower his head. For his lips to touch hers. Her breath caught. Her heart thundered in her chest. He bent closer. His breath soft on her cheek. The waiting torture. Agony.

"I want to kiss you," he whispered.

Yes, she wanted to say, but didn't speak.

"But I know that's not what you want, so I'll abide by your wishes." His hand suddenly dropped from her neck, and he stepped away. "Want me to drive?"

Anger surged in her gut. He had to know by her body language that she'd wanted him to kiss her—he'd just wanted to make sure she knew it, too. Well, she did. The feelings were still burning bright. She was in over her head. She should send him packing. Instead, she unlocked the car door and tossed him the keys so he'd turn his focus to driving and keep it off of her.

What are you doing, Nina?

She climbed into the car next to him. His fresh scent already permeated the air. His body was large and in charge. Those amazing hands gripped the wheel, and she could see his muscles moving under the tight fabric of his sleeves.

Stop this now. You're playing with fire.

The warning came through loud and clear. But all she could manage right now was to settle in for the ride and pray she didn't get burned.

WILEY YAWNED AND blinked blurry eyes as he climbed the stairs to Kip's apartment for a quick nap. Two nights without much sleep had him ready to drop. With Brandt on his tail, he couldn't afford to let drowsiness make him careless, so he planned to grab a quick catnap. He pushed open the door. The rich scent of frying bacon made his mouth water and stomach rumble. He didn't remember the last time he'd eaten.

He'd always been able to con Kip out of his food, so he headed straight for the miniscule kitchen. "Smells good."

Kip spun, his fork holding a strip of dripping bacon. "Where have you been?"

"I told you about the chick I was hooking up with," Wiley lied.

Grinning, Kip turned back and slapped the bacon into the pan. Grease crackled and spit into the air. "Well, I'm glad you're here."

"Oh yeah?" Wiley slid onto a bar stool. "Why's that?"

"There's an interesting post on the Hacktivist site by one of Hamid's friends. Mike Newman. You remember him?"

"Yeah, the barely twenty-year-old dude who's pulling down big bucks and living like a king."

Kip nodded. "His post claimed Hamid is desperate to get the computer back and asks for whoever found it to return it."

"Ah, man." Wiley slapped his forehead as he carefully considered his response. "I've been so busy with . . . well, you know." He grinned. "It slipped my mind."

"Dude, I totally get that. If I had a night like yours . . . well, the decision would be a no-brainer. But now that you're on a break, you can get the computer to Hamid, right?"

"Sure," Wiley said, trying to sound sincere as he pondered how, with Hamid locked up by the Feds and probably without internet access, this Mike dude could know the computer hadn't been returned. He could be an FBI snitch or maybe because he couldn't contact Hamid and had seen Hamid's plea disappear, Mike just wanted to be sure the computer was returned. Either way, Wiley had another problem to resolve.

Kip eyed him. "I mean, like, fast. The kid's desperate, man. Call him now. Or I can do it if you need me to."

This guy just never quit. Nag, nag, nag. He was worse than Wiley's parents. Always gnawing at him. After him. Getting into his business. Demanding.

Wiley ground his teeth to keep from spitting out a smart-aleck remark. He imagined his hands around Kip's neck, squeezing until the dude's eyes bugged out. Slowly, painfully losing all oxygen. Struggling. His eyes pleading for release.

"Well, are you going to do it, or do you want me to?" Kip glared at Wiley.

"Sure man, I'll do it," he said. But he was now thinking about killing this lame dude for real.

The guy had just proven his true colors. He'd chosen the little kid who'd lost his computer over Wiley. He felt the Colt tucked into his belt and hidden under his baggy T-shirt. Kip deserved a bullet. Deserved to die. Killing him would solve Wiley's issue with returning the computer. He needed to shut him up. Or Hamid. One of them.

He still needed Kip for housing. At least for the short term, but Hamid? Wiley didn't need him after tonight. As an added bonus, he could frame Brandt for the murder. Double score. She might even get the death sentence. Perfect.

"When will you do it?" Kip nagged.

Wiley fisted his hands. "I'll go now if I can use your car again."

Kip nodded vigorously. "I don't want to see that kid suffer anymore. His mother already puts him through enough because of his heart condition."

Heart condition. Oh yeah.

The kid had complained about having an ICD at one of their meetings. Wiley's father had had one of the original implantable cardioverter defibrillators installed, so Wiley had struck up a conversation with the kid and received far more details than he wanted. But now it would pay off. It was a perfect way to kill the kid and make it look like a computer geek had committed the murder. A geek like Brandt.

Wiley could easily hack the remote bedside monitor/transmitter for the device. He'd messed with the programming on his dad's transmitter to play with the old man. Nothing life threatening. Just a little adjustment to deliver a shock. Wiley could have killed him if he'd kept at it. He should have back then, for all the good his dad had done Wiley. But the doctor had figured out that someone had altered the monitor and that put an end to Wiley's fun.

The memory made him smile. His dad knowing what he'd done. Worried Wiley would do it again, he'd locked up the monitor. For once, the shoe was on the other foot. They'd had to worry about what he was up to. Unfortunately, it kept him from taking care of the old man that way. No matter. Wiley had found a way. He always took care of things, and he'd take care of Hamid, too.

Wiley stood and stifled a smile that found its way to his lips. "I'll let Hamid know about the computer ASAP. It'd be a shame for the kid to keep worrying about it."

The furrow in Kip's brow relaxed, and he set down his fork. "Drain my bacon while I get Mike's phone number, and I might give you some."

Wiley grabbed a plate, then lined it with paper towel. He lifted a few dripping pieces of bacon from the pan and blotted them dry. He selected the crispiest strip and blew on it. Biting into it, he groaned at the savory flavor and crunchy texture. He needed to eat and get out of there. He had no time to waste sleeping now. He had another job to do.

Chapter Nineteen

QUINN PARKED IN front of Nina's small craftsman bungalow with a wide front porch. Blue with white trim and a bright-red door, the property was obviously well loved and welcoming. The craftsman styling said Portland while the white cane-backed rockers spoke to Nina's upbringing. A true reflection of her personality. She was an irresistible mix of Northwest independence and true Southern charm.

She stared at him. "Okay, so now what?"

He turned off the engine. "I'll have a quick look around, then call a cab."

"You know it's not necessary to check my place, right?"

"For you, maybe, but not for me." He wouldn't give her a chance to argue, but climbed out.

She caught up to him on the walkway flanked with neatly trimmed shrubs.

"Nice house," he said as they strolled up the walk.

"Thanks, I like it." She climbed the stairs painted in the gunmetal gray of the Navy's battleships to the porch.

He could easily picture her out there with her sugary sweet tea, a child or two on her lap, humming a soft Southern song she'd learned from her grandmother as she often did while cooking. Problem was, he could picture himself there, too. In their house. Maybe a dog and a few kids. It was something he'd once considered when they were together. Before she'd given him the ultimatum, and he realized he couldn't be that guy. The one who woke up, day after day, in one place.

His life was a mix of foreign countries, nights under the stars, and rugged conditions in all terrains. Sea, air, and land, like the SEAL name implied. Getting in and out quickly without being seen. Gathering intelligence. Destroying targets and effecting rescues. An exciting life. Not the humdrum of suburbia.

If he occasionally wanted more, like this time spent with Nina had him pondering, he simply had to get back to base to remember who he was. That had always taken care of things.

Like it has lately?

It really didn't matter what he wanted, did it? He'd blown it with her, and buying her own house said she'd moved on quite well without him. "I didn't think home ownership was in your plans so soon."

She unlocked the door. "The timing was right. House prices and mortgage rates had come down, so I got a good deal. And I'm so glad I did it. This neighborhood is wonderful."

She was settling in there. Making a home, not picking up and moving to San Diego to be with him, should he ask.

"What if you get transferred?"

"It could happen, but I really like Portland and asked to stay here."

"What are the odds of that happening?"

"If I'm working on the CAT team, they're pretty good."

Yeah, she'd put down roots all right.

He trailed her through a small foyer that led to an open family room/kitchen combination. The space had been completely remodeled, yet it still held built-ins from a bygone era. Her contemporary furniture should seem out of place, but everything went together well.

No surprise. Nina had wonderful taste in clothing. He expected she'd put together a home that was warm and inviting, yet stylish.

She shrugged out of her suit coat, revealing a white blouse perfectly tailored to her shape. "I'm going to have a glass of wine. Would you like a beer after you finish your inspection?"

"A beer sounds great."

"Go ahead and check things out. I'll be in the kitchen."

He felt odd looking through her house without her, but that warning to take care wouldn't leave his gut. He would make sure the place was secure. He checked locks on the windows in the family room, then moved down a hallway to the master bedroom. Her flamboyant touches were everywhere except on the walls, which were painted a neutral gray. The space even smelled like her. Rich, spicy, and sweet all at the same time. She'd once told him her perfume contained amber. He didn't have a clue what amber smelled like, but her scent was smooth and intoxicating.

He performed a security check of the other bedrooms, then swept the bathrooms and went into an office with an antique desk holding a computer monitor. Papers and books were scattered everywhere—stacked on two plump easy chairs, piled on the floor, on the desk, and bookshelves. Her messiness had once irritated his military sense of order. Shoot, he'd still like to clean it up, but it hadn't taken him long to figure out this was her way of rebelling against the tight control her mother had exerted over her life.

He joined her in the kitchen with marble countertops and stainless appliances. She loved to cook big Southern meals and gather her friends around her. Her apartment had been small, but he could easily imagine her hosting large groups in this space.

"Everything okay?" she asked, not looking up from the block of cheese she was slicing.

"It's all good." He sat on a counter stool. "This is an amazing kitchen. Did you remodel or was it done when you bought it?"

"Could you see these hands near any construction tools?" She held them out, her nails perfectly manicured in a deep-red color.

"No," he said, as memories of the softness of her fingers on his face came flooding back. His throat suddenly dry, he swallowed hard and retrieved his own beer from the fridge, then took a long drink.

"As long as you're helping yourself, why don't you pour a glass of wine for me and have some cheese while I get out of these work clothes." She didn't wait for an answer but went through the doorway.

Great. Now he had visions of her changing in the room just down the hall. He took another swig, letting the icy liquid slide down his throat and cool him off. He found a bottle of merlot in the refrigerator and located the wine glasses. Small and large glasses sat gleaming on the shelf. She'd had a large-glass kind of day, so he filled a big one and took their drinks, plus the cheese, to the living room.

He settled on the sofa, feeling right at home. All he needed was a remote for the big TV above the fireplace and he'd be happy to put his feet up on the coffee table and stay for as long as she'd have him. Or until he tired of humdrum living.

Nina came back wearing formfitting yoga pants and a purple T-shirt. She was shrugging into an old green sweater that she burrowed into when she was stressed. Or had burrowed into, before they'd become a real couple. After that, she'd snuggled up next to him whenever she needed soothing.

He took another swig of his beer.

She went to her purse and withdrew a sheaf of papers, then grabbed the wine and sat on the far end of the sofa.

No snuggling tonight. Work Nina had returned.

She pulled her legs under her and took a few sips before setting the glass on the table. "I can't quit thinking about what Sulyard's up to."

Right. Business, as he expected. "I suspect we won't know until he chooses to reveal it."

"With him, that could mean days or even weeks. He might even decide I can't come back to work until this is resolved. So I made copies of the list." She pressed out a crease on the paper. "As soon as I have something to eat, I'll get started on reviewing these names again."

"You're playing with fire here, you know," Quinn warned.

Her head popped up.

"Aw, c'mon, Nina. Why so surprised? You know Sulyard will let you have it when he finds out you have the list."

"*Copy* of the list."

"Technicality. He made it clear he didn't want you doing anything."

"What he doesn't know . . ." She started pulling pins from her hair. The light caught each one as she drew them out until her hair caressed her shoulders. She glanced at her watch. "I suppose your mom and Ty have eaten by now. We could order from a Chinese restaurant that delivers before you go. If you want to, that is."

Surprise darted through him, but not nearly enough to replace the joy he felt at the thought of staying with her for dinner. She returned her attention to the papers sitting in her lap. She was completely oblivious to what he was really hungry for.

"Sounds good," he said and chugged the rest of his beer.

She massaged her scalp. She'd once told him it was often tender after restraining her wild mop of hair all day. He'd like to take over the task. *Not a good idea.*

"Go ahead and order. I'll eat anything." He held up his bottle. "Mind if I have another one?"

"Be my guest," she answered, already reaching for her phone.

He fled the room like he was evading a marauding insurgent group in a third-world country. He set the bottle on the countertop and planted his hands on the cool granite. He really didn't want another beer. The one he had was curdling in his stomach, but he'd had to get away from her to stop these ridiculous urges. Stop them now or walk out the front door and leave her alone, despite his certainty that trouble was brewing.

That he wouldn't do. He'd be staying until he knew, for sure, that everything was okay. He didn't run from trouble. Even if it was the two-legged kind who got his heart racing with a simple look.

OUTSIDE HAMID'S hotel room, Wiley retrieved Hamid's phone and carefully settled it in his tote bag next to Hamid's remote bedside transmitter for his ICD. Remembering his late-night trip to Hamid's house to steal it made Wiley smile. As did the trail he'd left leading to Brandt. He'd easily modified the transmitter to deliver the right jolt, but then . . . oh yes, then . . . he'd used her bogus phone to search for internet instructions on how to kill someone using a transmitter. Simple. Now, when he left this phone for the Feds, they would think she'd committed murder.

A rush of excitement shot through him as he ducked into the vending-machine alcove. He used Brandt's phone to log on to the hotel's computer network and access the fire alarm system. He tapped the screen a few times. Saved the change and voila, the alarm couldn't be silenced without the security company's help.

Showtime.

He pressed the activate button. The speakers instantly wailed, and lights flashed above doors. He stared for a moment, taking in the chaos. His heart beating hard, he grabbed the transmitter and perched his finger over the button. He waited for Hamid to come barreling into the hallway escorted by his FBI goons. Tyler's door flew open. The agent in charge rushed Tyler and his mother toward the stairwell.

Wiley fixed his gaze on Hamid's door. Excited. Waiting.

"C'mon, c'mon, c'mon," Wiley whispered. "Get out here already or Tyler will be long gone and miss the excitement."

The door opened. The burly agent stepped out to scan the hallway. After a quick nod to the other agent, he turned back. "Come on, Mrs. Ahmadi. This is most likely a false alarm, but we need to go."

Hamid's mother, her expression anxious, came to the doorway, looking as if she didn't want to leave.

Wiley waited for Hamid. Yes. Hamid would exit next. Wiley would hit the button, and Hamid would drop.

"I can't go." Mrs. Ahmadi's voice was shrill. "Not now. Not without knowing where my son is."

Hamid gone? What in the world?

The agent planted his feet. "I need you to calm down, ma'am. We'll find Hamid. There's no reason to believe he's in any danger. With your help, we can locate him. I'll bet he just snuck out to visit a friend."

"Hamid isn't very social. He has only one friend. Lance. I don't know his last name or his address. How will we find him?"

"Do they go to school together?"

"Yes."

"Then I'll locate him easy enough. Right now, we need to evacuate." The agent took her arm, urging her forward.

Wiley squeezed into a space beside the machine to hide, his mind spinning. Hamid was in the wind. Not something Wiley counted on. Which meant Plan B. Or C or whatever plan he was on now.

First step was to find the little bugger. His mother believed Lance was Hamid's only friend, but what about Mike, who'd posted on the Hacktivist site? He had to be a friend, too, and Wiley suspected he was the best choice if Hamid was hiding from his mother. Plus Mike knew about the missing computer. That could mean he'd posted because Hamid was with him and asked Mike to post the request.

Wiley let out a sigh of relief. Thanks to the post, Wiley had Mike's contact information and finding Hamid was a mere hiccup to overcome.

Wiley waited for a few more minutes, then took the stairs to the parking lot. Guests stood in pajamas and robes, looking angry. He'd caused this chaos and wanted to enjoy it, but finding Hamid was more important.

Wiley shot over to Brandt's house and typed a text on his phone for Mike. *I have the computer Ham wants. Need to set up a meeting to give it back.*

Mike responded immediately. *Ham's here. He wants you to bring the computer over ASAP.*

"Yes." Wiley shot a fist up. He had Hamid's location, but there was no way Wiley would show up at Mike's house. He also wouldn't reveal where he intended to meet Hamid. That would be just plain stupid. Mike could be the kind of guy who saw himself as a hero and showed up to surprise them.

Sorry, Wiley typed. *No can do without talking to Ham first. Have him call me.*

Wiley sat back to wait for his phone to ring. Time ticked by. Slowly. When it didn't ring, Wiley's concern started mounting. Maybe he'd pushed the punk too hard. Scared him off when he'd asked him to talk. Still, the kid was desperate.

Wiley started counting. *One. Two. Three. Four. Five.*

The ringer pealed. Wiley grinned and held back from answering. He didn't want to seem overly eager.

On the fifth ring, he answered casually. "Yo, Ham."

"Who is this?" Suspicion was rampant in his voice.

"I'd rather not say, you know. On account of not wanting to get involved in this FBI thing you've got going on. I'm a Hacktivist, though. I know you, man. So don't sweat it. Met you at a Meetup a few years back."

"Okay." He still sounded uncertain.

"Look, man. I want to help you out, but I can't get jammed up with your stuff. No way I'm getting caught with the computer. So, if you want it under my terms, fine. If not, I can dispose of it. Like today."

"We can meet," Hamid said hastily. "Can you text a picture of the machine to me so I know you really have it?"

"Don't have it with me, but I can describe it." Wiley rattled off the computer specifications.

"Where do you want to meet?"

That was the exact question Wiley hoped the kid would ask. "How about where you hid the cache? That way, you can be sure it's me, since I'm the only one who knows where the computer was found. Deal?"

"Okay. When?"

Wiley wanted to shout, *Now!* He no longer needed the kid alive and wanted to take care of this bit of business so he could go back to focusing on the hack. But he had to figure out a way to lure Brandt to Hamid's execution, so she could take the fall. It might take some time to pull that off. He'd better wait until tomorrow. It was dicey waiting another day, but then, the kid was hiding out from everyone, and he wouldn't post about the computer again since Wiley admitted to possessing it.

"Can't do it today," he said. "How about tomorrow? Around 4:00."

"Fine."

"Come alone, kid. I'll be watching. If you bring anyone, even this Mike dude, I'm bailing. Got it?"

"Yeah." His rebellious tone bothered Wiley.

"Look, kid, I hear your attitude. If you really want to see this machine again, you best get over whatever's bothering you. 'Cause I spook real easy if you get my drift."

"I got it." He sounded sincere. "I'll come alone and be there at four."

"See that you do. Make sure you're on time. I'm not waiting around." With that warning, Wiley ended the call and wondered if he could trust the kid.

Not that he had a choice.

BECCA HAD VISITED PPB's offices many times, but she'd never been to the Forensic Science Division. Not to their fingerprint area or the media room where she now waited while a very capable technician named Wally loaded video files. He appeared to be in his late fifties. His dark hair was messy, as if he'd run his fingers through it in frustration, which she supposed came with the job. On one computer, he opened traffic-cam videos from down the street from the Youngs' house. On the second one, he loaded surveillance footage from the home across the street from the Youngs. Then he stepped back.

"If you have any questions, just holler." He returned to his computer at the end of a long table.

Becca stepped to the second computer and took a seat on a tall stool, not giving Connor a chance to choose between the two. "I'll review the neighbor's file."

"Guess that leaves me the traffic cams then." He sounded less than happy, which Becca understood. Watching hours of traffic footage could be even more tedious than the job she faced, reviewing the wee hours of the night where there would be little to nothing to see.

She started the video for the night Hamid said he'd stolen the computer from Bryce's car and leaned her elbow on the table. The night of the break-in was dark. No moon. Fortunately, a streetlight sat near the end of the Youngs' driveway, illuminating Bryce's older Toyota parked on the street in front of his house. The video rolled past, and she found herself having a hard time keeping her focus on the screen and not checking on Connor.

She finally gave in and turned, but the lab's door swung open, catching her attention.

The fingerprint tech she'd met when she dropped off Hamid's prints poked his head around the door, then stepped inside and held the door ajar. "We have a match."

Becca paused her video and looked at the lanky guy with hunched shoulders, likely from pouring over prints all day.

"Definite match?" Connor asked.

"Yes. His ridges are clearly the same arch pattern you lifted from the car. As you know, it's a less common fingerprint type but the easiest to identify. I'll get an official report to you by morning, but thought you'd like a heads up." He stepped back and let the door close behind him.

Connor looked at Becca. "So Hamid touched Young's car. That doesn't prove it happened the night of the break-in, though."

Becca gestured at the computer. "Which is why we need to keep watching the videos." She focused on her screen again and settled in. She was getting cross-eyed by the time action appeared on the screen.

"Got something here," she said and sat forward to get a better look at the timestamp.

Connor came to stand behind her, close enough for her to feel his warmth and catch his unique scent again.

Though hyperaware of him standing behind her, she turned her attention to her screen and enlarged the video that revealed a male about the same height and build as Hamid approaching Young's car with a tire iron in his hand. "Could be him, but I'm not positive."

"Too bad he parked his car out of view of the camera."

"Maybe we'll get a better look when he leaves."

The kid rested his hand on the window and peered inside.

"Bingo," Connor said. "That's where we recovered Hamid's print."

The kid stepped back, and turning his face away, he smashed the window. He opened the door and grabbed a computer bag from the back seat then charged down the street.

"Looks like Hamid's telling the truth," Connor said.

Becca nodded, but her phone rang, grabbing her attention.

"I need to take this. It's Kait." Becca paused the video to answer.

Connor returned to his stool.

"Hamid's taken off," Kait said, without a greeting.

"He's what?" Becca's voice shot up, grabbing Connor's attention.

"He vanished, right under Agent Yeager's nose," Kait continued. "He believes Hamid exited via his bedroom window and broke his fall on a canopy. Yeager didn't even know the kid was gone until the fire alarm went off and they had to evacuate."

"There was a fire alarm around the time Hamid took off? Sounds too coincidental to me."

"Uh-huh. That's why I'm calling. Sulyard wants you to head over to the hotel to work the scene. PPB officers have responded to the call, so Sulyard wants you take Connor with you as a liaison."

"Got it." After disconnecting, Becca glanced at Connor. "You up for a road trip?"

"With you?"

"Yes."

"Of course," he answered, without asking where they were going.

She told him about Kait's call, in case he somehow mistook her question and thought this was personal in nature. "I could use your help in smoothing the way."

He stood and gestured at the door. They took his car, and she fielded calls and texts on the drive, giving them no time to talk. In the hotel parking lot, they found guests milling around, three patrol cars, and a fire truck with firefighters loading up to depart. Their chief was talking to a PPB officer.

Connor parked and they went straight to the officer and fire chief, who held his helmet in his hand and had unbuttoned his turnout coat.

Connor introduced Becca to the young officer and the wrinkled and wizened-looking chief.

"Since when does the FBI respond to a fire alarm?" the chief asked, watching her carefully.

"We have reason to believe this could be related to an ongoing investigation," Becca replied.

The chief shook his head. "More likely a kid pulling a prank."

"So it was a false alarm?" Connor asked.

The chief nodded. "A station was pulled on the second floor."

Becca looked at Connor. "Same floor as our rooms."

"Exactly," Connor said. And without another word, they pivoted and matched each other's stride, step for step, as they hurried inside to investigate.

Chapter Twenty

NINA'S DOORBELL rang at six the next morning, startling her upright from her yoga pose. Hamid had disappeared from the hotel last night, and Becca had immediately called to tell Nina about it. She'd spent the night worrying about him and hoped yoga would provide some tranquility before she headed into work. A surprise visitor didn't help.

She peered through the peephole to find Quinn, freshly showered and tapping his foot. She ran a hand over her hair and tugged the door open. "Why are you here?"

"Thought I'd see how you were doing before you went to work." He brushed past her without an invitation. "Any progress on the Hacktivist list?"

"Nothing positive, but I did eliminate a few people." She closed the door to keep the cold out, but remained nearby. Things had gone so well between them last night, making her want more of the same. She couldn't trust herself to keep him at arm's length and had no intention of letting him stay.

"Yoga?" He nodded at her mat on the floor. "Since when did you start doing that?"

"You make it sound like a dirty word."

"I don't have time for all that zen relaxation stuff." He mocked a shiver. "Better to fix your problem instead of trying to find a way to avoid it."

"So that's what you think I'm doing? Avoiding?"

He shrugged.

Her irritation started to rise. "Do you have a purpose for your visit, other than to make me mad?"

"Mad? That little comment made you mad? My ever-patient Southern belle?" He grinned.

His? "Okay, I don't mind being called a belle, but I won't ignore being called *your* anything."

His smile fell, and he ran a hand over his clean-shaven face. "I'm not sure how I put my foot in my mouth so many times in less than five minutes. If I apologize for all of it, can we start over?"

He sounded so contrite that her irritation evaporated. "I'm at fault, too. I'm still frustrated by being sent home yesterday. Not knowing what's really going on is making me grouchy." She took a deep breath. "So why are you here?"

"I wanted to ask if you want Ty to come into the office today. And I thought I'd check to see if Hamid's been found."

"You know about Hamid?"

He nodded. "I ran into Becca last night when I got back to the hotel. She told me about him."

"There's no sign of him yet." She shook her head. "Taking off like that was such as stupid thing for him to do. Now it'll seem like he has something to hide. Maybe make people think he has a terrorist connection. At the very least, the DA will see him as uncooperative and press charges."

"Which might not bode well for Ty. It seems like helping DHS find the vulnerability is even more important for him to do now."

"I don't know if Sulyard still wants Ty to help out, but I'll ask when I get into the office."

The doorbell rang.

Quinn's gaze shot to the door. His eyes were deadly intense. "You expecting company?"

"No. It's probably Becca or Kait with news about Hamid."

"Wouldn't they call or text first?" He lifted the hem of his shirt revealing a holstered gun.

"You're carrying?" she asked.

"The hotel fire alarm has me spooked."

His reaction seemed excessive and made her uneasy as she went to the door to check the peephole for the second time that morning.

"What in the world?" She blinked hard, then blinked again to clear her vision. Her visitor still stood there. She stepped back while her mind ran through the possibilities of why he'd visit her at home.

"Who is it?" Quinn asked.

"Sulyard." She didn't want to let him in, but she doubted he'd go away. If she did let him in, he might see the Hacktivist file she'd spread across her dining table. She ran into the room and started grabbing up her research. The doorbell rang again.

"Help," she said to Quinn. "We need to hide this stuff."

He stacked a pile of papers. "What's he doing here anyway?"

"I don't know, but I don't like it." She inserted the last of the pages into a folder and shoved it all into her tote bag before starting for the door. "Sit down. Turn on the TV. Make it look like we're hanging out."

He eyed her for a second, then pulled her against him and kissed her. Hard and long. Her senses flared to life, and she didn't try to pull away. When he released her, he ruffled her hair messing it up even more.

"What was that for?" she asked, her body filled with conflicting emotions.

"You want it to look like we're hanging out. That's what I'd be doing if I was hanging out with you at six in the morning." He grinned from ear to ear, and she almost forgot Sulyard waited on her porch.

Almost.

She hurried to the door.

"This is a surprise," she said, trying to straighten her hair.

"I imagine it is." He didn't ask to come in, but signaled at someone in his car and pushed past her.

Quinn stepped close to Nina as if she needed protection. Sulyard raised a brow in surprise, then pulled a folded paper from his pocket. Nina didn't have to see the document to know what it was. She'd handled plenty of them in her job.

"A warrant?" she asked, wondering if he was there to serve it or hand it off for her to serve on someone else.

"I'm sorry about this, Brandt." He ground his teeth for a few seconds. "We'll be searching your home."

Nina gasped, her hand flying to her chest before she took a step back. She bumped into Quinn who'd moved even closer. She could feel the heat of his body and knew he was there for her. She was suddenly glad he'd stopped by.

He rested a protective hand on her shoulder. "Before I let any of you take another step, I demand to know what prompted this warrant."

"The No-Fly List was hacked again. Monday. Around three a.m. The transmission was bounced all over, but we finally tracked down the source last night."

There was nothing earth-shaking in his statement, and certainly no reason to search her home in the wee hours of the morning. She needed clarification. "Okay, so you tracked it down. What's that got to do with me and this warrant?"

"Simple." Sulyard firmly met her gaze; the intensity of his focus sent a wave of panic curling over her. "The transmission originated here, Brandt. At your house. During the time you came home to rest. I don't want to think you're involved in hacking the NFL, but I can't argue with the evidence staring me in the face."

QUINN DIDN'T LIKE this. Not one bit. Nina seemed calm, reading, then carefully folding the warrant before looking at Sulyard. She chewed on her lower lip as if uncertain about what to do. She hadn't fought back or stuck up for herself. She'd simply acquiesced to Sulyard's bullying as he fired off directions without a care for her feelings.

Quinn had started to tell Sulyard off, but Nina stopped him. Quinn supposed she was acting like a little mouse because Sulyard was her supervisor and he seemed quite willing to believe she'd hacked the NFL. But she had to be confused. Quinn would be in shock if his CO suddenly thought him capable of being a traitor.

Trying to keep his anger in check, Quinn stepped closer to Sulyard. "You can't possibly think Nina has anything to do with this."

"Can't I?" He stared at Quinn. His face was haughty and smug, the way Nina had often described him in the past. "I know you SEALs like to think you know everything about everything, but you're way out of your league here, buddy."

Quinn's anger flared. He fisted his hands to keep from strangling the man who should be acting far more sensitive to Nina's plight. "The least you could do is treat her with the respect she deserves."

"I'm simply looking at the facts and not letting my relationship with her cloud my judgment." Sulyard cocked an eyebrow.

"Facts, as in more than one? All you've mentioned so far is that the transmission originated here."

"Add that to her connection to your brother, which she's readily admitted. And now it's clear she wasn't exactly truthful about having a relationship with you as well." He paused as if he expected Quinn to deny it, but he'd be lying if he did. They didn't have a relationship, but there was something going on between them. Her response to his kiss a few minutes ago proved that.

"Best case scenario," Sulyard continued. "She's trying to help Tyler by covering something up. Worst case, you two have the computer and are planning to use your little brother's hacking skills as a way to make a quick buck."

"Me?" Quinn's anger went from minor irritation to seeing red in a flash.

Sulyard smirked. "Don't think you're immune to investigation because you're a SEAL. I'm sure you've engaged in plenty of off-book ops, giving you skills needed to pull this off without breaking a sweat."

No one questioned his reputation, his honor, and then stood there looking all self-righteous. Quinn didn't think twice. He slammed his fist into Sulyard's face. The satisfying crunch resounded through the room as Sulyard staggered back.

"Quinn, no." Nina grabbed his arm.

At her touch, some of his anger receded. He lived his creed and didn't often fly off the handle, but *come on*. This was unacceptable. No one got away with accusing him or Nina of being a traitor. He'd never betray his country. Never. And she was the most ethical and honest person he knew. She didn't deserve this treatment. Neither did he.

"You'll regret that." Sulyard cupped his jaw. "The local authorities will be happy to haul you in for assaulting a law enforcement officer."

"Go ahead. Call them," Quinn said calmly, not the least bit worried. "I'll be glad to tell the press all about the missing computer."

Quinn would never follow through on his threat, but the last thing Nina needed right now was for him to be arrested. He had no doubt Sulyard would press charges once the case was resolved and Quinn's threat no longer held any power. He would have to deal with the consequences then, but for now, his full attention remained on Nina.

Sulyard glared at Quinn. For half a second, he didn't think the guy would back down. But another agent poked his head through the door to ask a question and Sulyard started barking orders at his staff.

The men spread out like an army of ants. Quinn didn't recognize them, but by their pitiful gazes directed at Nina and her defensive response, it was clear she did. He could only imagine how much it stung, seeing her coworkers paw through her things.

Wait, things. They'd find the list she'd brought home from work. It was obvious that she'd now have to investigate on her own to clear their names. But she couldn't do that without the file.

"Let me get you a glass of water." He headed for the kitchen. On the way, he confirmed he was alone and grabbed her papers from the bag, then slid them into his waistband and pulled his shirt over the top. He had no idea if he was breaking the law.

An agent stepped into the room. Quinn casually strolled to the kitchen for the water. He returned and offered it to Nina, but she shook her head.

He really didn't like seeing her this way. "Are you required to stay for this?"

"No, but I'm not sure I want to leave them alone in my house." She shuddered.

"Won't it be harder to stay and watch?" he asked softly.

She nodded.

"Then let's give Sulyard a key and get out of here."

Nina gave a clipped nod and crossed over to her supervisor. "I'm leaving." She handed her key to him. "Lock up when you're finished."

He curled the key into his fist. "You're a good agent, Brandt. One of our best. I don't want to think you're involved, but—" He paused and peered at Quinn. "Emotions can make us act out of character. Color our judgment."

"Nothing's coloring my judgment," she said adamantly. "You won't find anything."

"I'm hoping you're right. For your sake. Before you go, I'll need your shield and your weapon. And of course, you're suspended until further notice."

Her shoulders drooped for a brief moment before she pulled them back. Quinn imagined standing before his CO like this. His reputation was everything to him. It was the same for all his teammates. They lived by their creed, striving for excellence. There was no room for unethical behavior in that quest.

Nina retrieved her credentials from her purse and handed them over. "My gun's in the safe in my room. I'll get it." She turned for the hallway, but an agent tromped toward her.

He carried a clear plastic bag holding a laptop. "Found this in the back bedroom closet. In a suitcase."

Nina shot a horrified look at Quinn.

"Odd place to keep your hardware, Brandt." Sulyard took the bag and turned it over to study the bottom of the computer.

"It's not mine," Nina said staring at it. "And before you say this is Ty's missing computer, it's not the right brand."

"Still, it's a machine you obviously wanted to hide."

"I didn't put it there."

"Then who did?"

"I don't have a clue."

"This is your house, isn't it?"

Quinn stepped closer to Sulyard. "Why don't you turn the stupid thing on and do your computer mumbo-jumbo to figure out who it belongs to?"

"Forensic protocol requires us to take it back to the lab to image the drive before we analyze it."

"How long does that take?" Quinn asked.

"Nina?" Sulyard asked.

"Depends on the size of the hard drive," she responded. "A typical drive takes anywhere from two to five hours. If it contains a lot of graphic files, it could take longer. Worst case, though, it'll be done by morning."

"Can't you rush it?" Quinn asked Sulyard.

He shook his head. "I want this information as quickly as you do, but we'll do this by the book. We won't rush a thing."

"He's right," Nina said. "He has to be even more careful with me because I know the protocol and could use my knowledge to skate under their radar."

Quinn faced Nina and lowered his voice. "You think they'll be able to build a case?"

"I don't know, but I'm not hanging around to watch." She spun on her heels and marched toward her bedroom.

"Go with her and keep an eye on her," Sulyard said to his agent.

Quinn heard a hint of regret in Sulyard's voice, but Nina's shoulders stiffened anyway. Her pain radiated all the way across the room. Quinn wanted to help, but there was nothing he could do.

This reminded him of the day of the explosion. His buddy Sully had been trapped. Quinn had been faced with a choice. He could either sit on the sidelines to stay safe or save Sully's life. There was no choice, really. It was simple. Sully came first. So did Nina. He'd fall on a grenade for her without a second thought. Unfortunately, it was looking like he might have to do something that drastic to keep her out of jail.

Chapter Twenty-One

NINA SNATCHED up her purse and headed to the door where Quinn waited for her. The weight of her backup gun in the handbag gave her a bit of confidence. Thankfully, Sulyard could only seize her department-issued weapon. Being unarmed when she now knew someone was setting her up to take the fall for this hack would have added insult to injury.

"Just a minute, Brandt." Sulyard held out his hand. "I'll take your cell phone."

She was so flustered that she'd forgotten the warrant covered all of her electronics. "Can I write down a few phone numbers at least?"

"No."

"Why not?"

"You know the answer. One flick of your finger and you alter the data. I can't allow that to happen."

She scowled at him. He was following protocol, but he didn't have to be a jerk about the way he was handling things. He was her supervisor and should know her well enough to realize she wasn't involved in this.

Tears pricked her eyes again, but she'd rather face a firing squad than cry in front of Sulyard or her fellow agents. She slapped her phone onto his palm. The techs would turn it off or put it in a Faraday bag before she could remotely access it to retrieve her data. She'd seen them disable her router, keeping her from remotely accessing her computer, too. This was the final straw. She felt violated. Exposed. For the first time, she realized how suspects felt when her team invaded their privacy. She vowed to be kinder and gentler in the future.

"I'm sorry, Brandt." Sulyard bagged the phone. "But we have to stay objective about this lead. You'd be doing the same thing if you were me."

"I'd be serving the warrant and taking computers, but you can be sure I'd be far nicer to someone who deserved my respect." She turned and marched to the door, her anger at Sulyard taking over her unease. She stopped and glanced over her shoulder. "Tell me one thing before I go. Was the hack successful? Were records in the NFL altered?"

He arched a brow. He likely thought that if she was the hacker, she'd know the answer. "Not that we know of, but DHS is still investigating."

She turned her back on him and stepped onto the porch. Her porch, in the home that had now lost its value as a sanctuary. She took deep gulps of the crisp air as Quinn closed the door and joined her.

"Let's go before he thinks of something else." He put an arm around her shoulder and led her down the steps.

She should probably object, but the strength of his arm, the way he carried himself with confidence, helped her recover from the shock. She didn't know what she'd have done if he hadn't been there. Defending her honor. Even punching Sulyard. That would come back to bite him, but it was heartwarming to think about him defending her that way.

She reached for the car door.

"Let me," he offered, his fingers warm where they touched her hand.

After she got settled, he jogged around the front of the car, leaving her instantly feeling alone and vulnerable. She didn't like it. Didn't like it one bit. She'd clearly let him back into her life. If the kiss hadn't proven it, this would. Shoot. Maybe he'd never been out. Just lingering under the surface. She thought about the hours and hours she'd worked to get over him, time spent in futility.

How would she ever go back to normal again once he took off? Because he'd go. That she was sure of. No matter how much she hoped he'd stay, he would return to his team. Go back to his adventures, and she'd spend night after night trying to forget him.

He slid behind the wheel. "Where to?"

She hadn't thought beyond escaping the house. Correction, she'd been thinking about him leaving her once this was over. She'd be in a similar situation then, too. Looking for support from those around her. And she knew she'd find it with her friends.

"I'll call Becca or Kait." She reached for her purse, then remembered her phone in Sulyard's hand. The memory nearly had her crying. "Can I use your phone?"

"FYI," he said, a little smirk on his face as he lifted the hem on his shirt and removed the folder holding the Hacktivist list. "This stuff accidently got stuck in my jeans when I went to the kitchen for water."

He was a genius. "Thank goodness you remembered. I could kiss you."

He angled toward her. "Well, come on. I'm not stopping you."

She was tempted. Boy, was she tempted. But the last thing she needed was to willingly go down a path she knew she should avoid. She held out her hand. "Your phone?"

He frowned and dug it from his pocket. "Do you want me to sit here while you call?"

"Are you kidding?" She huffed a sour laugh. "Drive. I don't care where. Just take me as far from here as possible."

WILEY HUNKERED down behind the shrub near Brandt's house and watched her drive away, leaving the FBI team behind. She'd come stumbling out of the house wearing exercise clothes. Her hair was wild and crazy, little curls sticking out in all directions. The SEAL had a protective arm around her as they'd climbed into his car to take off, but not before Wiley caught a look at the sheer terror on Brandt's face.

Priceless, and yet, a problem.

The Feds were there before Wiley wanted them involved. With the FBI goons carrying evidence bags from her home, he knew they'd traced his test hack back to her house. That meant he'd have to change his plan for this morning. An inconvenience, but he refused to let it get him down. Not after seeing Brandt's panic. He'd never let himself hope that he'd actually get to see her team turn on her, but he had.

Oh, yeah. It was almost as good as doing drugs.

He could imagine the scene inside. Her team—the men and women she worked with—pawing through her things. Personal things. Things everyone hides about themselves.

Of course, they'd find the computer, too. But what about the tracker on her car and the phone he'd set up in her name? He'd planned to retrieve the tracker and plant the phone in the house after he completed the hack, but he couldn't very well do that with the Feds crawling all over the place. And yet, the phone was crucial in his plan to tie her to Hamid. All the Feds were focused on was the inside of the house. He could safely grab the tracker and leave the cell in her car, right?

Sure, the Feds might find it odd that she'd left an incriminating phone in her car, but she was shocked when they arrived on her doorstep so they'd think they'd simply caught her by surprise and she didn't have time to hide the phone.

He'd buy another set of phones to finish the job, but first he needed to send one last message before he left the phone behind. He crept behind cars parked on the street until he could retrieve Brandt's phone and slide it from the protective plastic bag he'd used. Fear of discovery had his heart pounding, but it was still a rush, just like it had felt when he'd passed the agent in the hallway. He liked it. But he wasn't dumb enough to linger and get caught.

He opened a text message to Hamid. Fortunately, Wiley had hidden Hamid's bogus cell outside Mike's place for just such a communication.

He typed. *They're on to us. Am regrouping at our usual spot to complete transaction. Should have final payment tomorrow night. Don't use this cell again. Will be getting new ones. Give one to you at the meeting.*

He hit *send.* Watched it disappear. He was close now. So close.

Oh, the rush. Pure ecstasy.

He sat back and watched, waiting as a short, stocky agent who'd come outside returned to the house.

Once the door closed, Wiley duckwalked to her car. Quietly, stealthily as he'd learned to do in prison. Sneak up on your intended victim, let your shiv hit the mark, then get out of there.

The phone was his shiv tonight. Making the final cut. Drawing blood. It was the end for Brandt.

BY THE TIME NINA walked through Becca's front door, she was sick with worry and simply wanted to hash the recent incident out with her friends, then create a plan of action. Unfortunately, Kait and Becca weren't alone. Sam and Connor were seated in the small living room, too.

Kait jumped up and rushed over to greet Nina. "I hope you don't mind that I invited Sam and Connor. I thought they might be able to help us figure this out." She drew Nina into a hug. "You poor thing. I can't imagine what it would feel like to have my home searched."

"It was horrible." Tears pricked Nina's eyes, but she willed them away before pulling from Kait's hug. "I have a new respect for how innocent suspects feel. The guys were pawing through my stuff. My underwear drawer. Could it get any more humiliating?" Despite her best effort, the tears started falling. "I'll never be able to look at them the same way again."

"They'll forget it about it soon enough." Sam joined them, his arm going around Kait's waist and tugging her close.

Nina swiped away her tears and forced out a smile for Sam. "Sounds like you speak from experience."

"I had to toss a coworker's house once."

Kait looked up at him. "You've never shared that story with me."

"Trust me, darlin'," he purred in his smooth Texas drawl. "There are a bunch of stories I haven't told you. By the time we're old and gray and rocking on Nina's porch, you'll know most of them."

Kait arched a brow. "Most?"

He winked. "Some stories no one needs to hear."

Usually Nina loved their banter, but right now she was annoyed that they seemed so carefree when her life was crumbling around her. She was ashamed for thinking that way, since they'd had to work through several difficult issues to be together, but at the moment, Nina couldn't get beyond her own problem.

Quinn seemed to pick up on her discomfort and stepped forward to introduce himself to Sam and Connor.

Becca joined them, eyeing Quinn suspiciously. "What are you doing here, Quinn?"

Nina didn't like Becca's tone. Not after the care Quinn had just taken with her. "He was there for me when Sulyard was being such a bully, so I asked him to join us."

Becca and Kait both raised their eyebrows.

"We should get started," Nina said to distract them.

"Nina, can you help me get some drinks from the kitchen first." Becca sounded more agreeable all of a sudden.

Nina suspected the little side trip had nothing to do with drinks, but she wouldn't make a scene by refusing, so she followed Becca into the tiny galley kitchen.

Becca spun on her. "What are you doing?"

"About what?"

"Quinn, as if you didn't know. I'm not even going to ask why he was at your house this early in the morning. But I can't ignore the way you're letting him get to you again."

Nina shrugged and wished she'd opted not to join Becca. She understood the emotions driving Nina when it came to her causes, but Becca often couldn't comprehend the same relationship needs. "I get that he's been there for you, but this is about Ty. Once he's no longer in trouble, Quinn will take off again."

"I know that." Thinking of him leaving again, coupled with everything else, made her so sad. She bit the inside of her cheek to keep from crying.

"Then why don't you send him on his way. You don't need him. You've got us to help get you out of this mess."

"I beg to differ." Quinn's deep voice came from behind them. "I have skills that none of you possess. After Sulyard's little performance, it's looking like Nina will need every bit of help she can find, or she'll end up behind bars."

Hearing Quinn voice her greatest fear was the last straw. She couldn't hold her tears back any longer, and they flowed like a river over her cheeks.

"Leave us, Becca," Quinn commanded.

"Is that okay with you?" Becca asked.

Nina knew she should listen to Becca and send Quinn packing. Yet, there she was nodding. Becca departed, her surly gaze remaining on Quinn as she passed.

Quinn stepped closer and used a gentle thumb to wipe the tears from Nina's cheek. "I'm sorry, sweetheart. I shouldn't have been so blunt, but I don't want your friends shutting me out."

"Why?" she asked with a sob.

He rested his forehead on hers, his breath warm against her skin. "I can't stand the thought of leaving you right now. Not when you're in so much trouble. I want to help. Please let me." He settled his hands on her hips and pulled her closer, then lifted his head and stared into her eyes.

Her skin tingled in response to the caring she saw there. She could barely breathe with him so close—with his sincere desire to be there for her. She knew he'd be gone tomorrow or the next day, but she wanted him there now.

"Stay." The word came out on a whisper.

He cupped the side of her face, drawing her closer. Then his mouth was on hers, warm and gentle. Nina sensed a moment of pure shock as the tenderness of his lips curled through her. It was a kiss filled with promises, so different than the playful one at her house. She let herself melt into him when she should be backing away, but she felt free for the first time in a long time. Felt the wounds from his abandonment disappear. She threw herself into returning his kiss. Deepening it. Forgetting all about her problems. About his leaving.

"Ahem." Kait's voice came from behind. "We all need to get to work, so we should get started."

Nina tried to push away, but Quinn held firm.

"We'll be right there," he said, his breathing ragged.

Nina heard Kait depart.

Quinn leaned back but kept his hands on her hips. "I want you to know I'm here for you, sweetheart. I'm not going anywhere while you're in trouble."

While you're in trouble. Just like that, his cold reminder of why she shouldn't have let him back into her life sent all her warm feelings packing.

QUINN PUSHED HIS plate across the table. He couldn't eat another bite of Nina's biscuits with gravy, grits, and country ham all washed down with black coffee. Thick, dark, and potent—the way he liked it. After their impromptu meeting, she'd offered to cook breakfast for everyone. Cooking was therapy for her, and he wished the others would have joined him, but they needed to go to work. Still, she'd sent Quinn to the store for groceries, then cooked enough for his whole platoon.

He rubbed his stomach and leaned back. He could get used to spending his early mornings this way. Not at Becca's condo where Nina needed to hang out while Sulyard processed her home, but in Nina's cozy kitchen. It was the first time in months that the unsettled feeling plaguing him had let up, and he didn't feel like he needed to be busy to still his mind. Shoot, it was first time in a good long time that he'd been this comfortable.

Not Nina, though. She kept saying she was going to wolf down an entire pan of biscuits, but she'd picked at the same one for almost twenty minutes as she stared into space. She'd been even more uneasy after the group's brainstorming session—the group had concluded that the person trying to set her up was most likely someone she'd once put away, someone seeking revenge. Nina and Becca would try to get Nina's files so she could search for strong suspects.

She was also worried that the recent hack of the NFL meant a potential terrorist had paid to have his name removed and could be entering the U.S. right now.

That possibility had them all acting kind of skittish.

His phone rang, making her jump.

"Relax," he told her as he glanced at Caller ID. He was glad to see it wasn't his mother calling. After Sulyard had showed up at Nina's house, Quinn had phoned his mother to ask her to call if Ty was arrested. Quinn figured it was only a matter of time before that happened, too.

"Stone," Quinn said to the unknown caller.

"It's Becca. Don't tell Nina I'm calling. I don't want her to know anything about this until you're on the road to meet me."

"Meet you?" Quinn stepped outside where Nina couldn't overhear him. "What's going on?"

"Sulyard's on his way to my place to arrest Nina."

"He what?" Quinn's voice echoed down the quiet street.

"Cool it. I don't want her to know."

"Why in the world not? She has a right to know."

"Sure she does, but what do you think she'll do when she finds out?"

"Stand her ground. Argue with him."

"Exactly. She'd never agree to take off without thinking about it first, but that's just what she needs to do when the evidence against her is so compelling."

"What evidence?"

"I don't have time to explain. Just trust me when I say Sulyard had no problem securing an arrest warrant. She'll be booked if she doesn't leave. If someone she arrested *is* setting her up, she won't be able to review her files from jail to determine who it is."

Thinking about Nina in jail made his gut churn. "You seriously think I can convince her to leave without an explanation?"

"You have to. If you can't sweet talk her, then use your usual strong-arm tactics—pick her up and carry her out of there."

A vision of tossing Nina over his shoulder and hauling her out made him smile.

"Meet me at The Falls restaurant." Becca gave him directions to a place near the Columbia Gorge.

"I'm not so sure meeting near Triple Falls is a good idea."

"I'll explain the reason when we meet. Now go. Get Nina and get going."

Quinn hung up, and Becca's sense of urgency had him on the move toward the door. Doubting they'd return, he grabbed her notebook with the list and put it in a grocery bag. In the kitchen, he turned off the oven and took out the last pan of biscuits.

"Hey." Nina shot him a look. "Those have a few more minutes to go."

"We need to leave."

"What? Why?"

"I have a lead to track down, but I need your help," he lied, hoping she'd forgive him later.

"Was that the phone call you received?"

He nodded. "C'mon. Grab your purse and jacket and let's move."

She slipped her feet into her sneakers and ran a hand over her hair. "Let me freshen up first. I'll be ready in five."

"We don't have five."

She studied him. "What's going on, Quinn?"

"Nothing. Now let's go." He took her arm and steered her toward the front door, grabbing the grocery bag on the way past the table. She tried to shake his hand off, but he held firm and hoped he wasn't bruising her.

"Don't manhandle me." She peered up at him, her disappointment making him regret his straightforward tactic.

He met her gaze. "If I let go, will you leave with me right now? No primping. Just walk out the door."

"Will you tell me what's going on?"

"In the car," he said and got them moving again. He loosened his grip, but didn't fully release her. There was no way he would risk her taking a stance and ending up behind bars.

Chapter Twenty-Two

ARMS CROSSED, NINA sulked in the passenger seat. She hated it when Quinn pushed her around. She'd opened her mouth to say something to him many times, but decided there was no point. She was in the car, and they were heading who knows where, whether she wanted to go or not.

He eventually turned onto the scenic highway, and she pointed at the road sign for the gorge. "So the big secret is we're going back to Triple Falls?"

"No."

"Then why are we out here again?"

"We're meeting Becca."

"Becca? She called you?"

He nodded but didn't elaborate.

"Why didn't she ask to talk to me?"

He didn't respond, just kept his focus on the road.

Nina grabbed his arm and held it until he looked at her. "What are you not telling me, Quinn?"

He glanced at her, his eyes filled with remorse. "Sulyard was on the way to arrest you. Becca didn't want that to happen."

"Arrest me? But how?"

"Becca says he has compelling evidence of your involvement in the hack."

"He can't. I mean, I haven't done anything." Her mind raced over this crazy development, imagining Sulyard getting the warrant for her arrest and having everyone think she was a criminal. She didn't have anything to hide. "We have to go back. Running like this will convince him of my guilt. Turn around. I have to tell him he's making a mistake."

Quinn shook his head. "It'd be a good idea to hear what Becca has to say first. Then if you still want me to take you, I will."

He had a point. If Sulyard's evidence was valid—which she knew it wasn't—she could always turn herself in.

"Fine." She released his arm.

They soon pulled into the parking lot of a restaurant that resembled an old barn with rows of white rocking chairs out front. Nina would normally take time to sit a spell, as her grandmother had always said, but Becca's car was parked out front, and Nina was eager to hear what kind of evidence Sulyard had collected.

Becca met them at the door and grabbed Nina up in a hug, raising Nina's concern to Chernobyl level. Becca wasn't a hugger. If she thought Nina needed one, it wasn't a good sign.

Becca drew back. "Thank goodness, you made it."

Nina eyed her friend. "No thanks to you telling me what was going on."

"Go ahead and vent." Becca took Nina's arm and led her to a table. She heard Quinn following. "I'd do it again in a heartbeat. If I hadn't, you'd be on your way to booking right now. At least this way, you have a chance to weigh your options." A deep frown marred her face. "Not that you have many of them."

"You're scaring me, Bex."

"Let's sit down and review the evidence." Quinn pulled out a chair for Nina, then one for Becca.

"Thanks for helping me out," Becca said to Quinn, as she dropped a folder on the table.

He nodded, but said nothing else and took a seat next to Nina. How far they'd come in only a few hours—from Becca busting Quinn's chops at her apartment to becoming co-conspirators.

Becca opened the folder filled with reports but rested her hand on the first one, preventing Nina from reading it. "You should know before we get started that things are moving quickly on the investigation. When I first called Quinn, Sulyard was erring on the side of caution by taking you in. But Kait called me on the way here and they've uncovered additional information that has him upping his search for you." She turned to Quinn. "FYI, you're also included in the alert Sulyard released."

"Quinn's done nothing," Nina said.

He looked at her. "Neither have you."

"And yet, here we are, with overwhelming evidence pointing to your guilt." Becca slid a report across the table. "The first page holds the details for the most recent breach of the NFL. The second page contains information on the computer found at your house."

Nina scanned the pages.

Her heart lurched, and she pushed the report away to sit in stunned silence.

"What is it?" Quinn asked.

She met his gaze. "The MAC address for the computer found at my house matches the computer used to breach the NFL."

"What's a Mac address?" he asked.

"It stands for Media Access Control," Becca offered. "Basically, a manufacturer assigns a unique number to every device that uses IP to access the internet."

"Okay," Quinn said. "Nina mentioned before that the IP address tells you where the internet was accessed from. But I still don't get how that's related to this MAC address."

"For example," Becca said. "If we each used the restaurant's Wi-Fi to access the internet, there would be three separate entries on the restaurant's wireless router log, because we each have a different MAC address."

A light bulb went off in Quinn's eyes. "So if we went to different websites, the router would record which one of us visited which sites."

"Exactly."

He shot a confused look at Nina. "But that means your wireless network was used, too. Is that even possible? Don't you have some sort of password or something to keep unauthorized people out?"

She nodded. "My network is as secure as it can be. It's virtually impossible for anyone to access the signal without the password, so I haven't a clue how he got in."

Becca sat forward. "You secured it electronically, but how about physically?"

Nina swung her focus to Becca. "I don't follow."

"Obviously, the real hacker entered your house to leave the computer. If you have the password written down for the router, which most of us do, he could have gained access that way."

"Well, there you have it." Nina sighed. "The password's in a folder in my desk. He had to have done some digging. Then again, I've been putting in so many hours at the office, he'd have had plenty of time to look." She shuddered at the thought of this person pawing through her stuff. She thought she'd felt violated when her fellow agents had done so. But this was far worse.

Quinn covered her hand, bringing Becca's brows up. Nina should pull back, but his hand was warm and comforting. She liked the connection, the feel of him, so she let it be. "Not that this isn't damning enough, but you said Sulyard had more."

"He ran a current financial profile on you, Hamid, and Ty. Fortunately, Ty's in the clear, but check this out." Becca dug out another report and tapped an entry on an electronic printout of Nina's bank statement.

"$40,000. In my bank account. For real?" Nina brushed Quinn's hand away and picked up the page. "There's another wire transfer out of my account for $20,000." She looked at Becca. "I'm assuming you know where that money went."

"Hamid's checking account."

Quinn let out a low whistle, making Nina's stomach tighten in a knot. She felt herself hyperventilating, but forced herself to relax and concentrate on the problem. "So, not only is someone trying to set me up for the hack by planting the computer at my house, he's making it look like I'm getting paid for it, too. And working with Hamid. Maybe establishing a terrorist connection."

"Have you tracked the wire transfer into Nina's account?" Quinn asked.

Becca shook her head. "The analysts are working on it."

"Okay," Nina said. "We know I had nothing to do with moving this money. Sulyard should know that as well."

"No offense, sweetheart," Quinn said. "But considering the way he's been treating you, why would you think he'd believe in you?"

"I don't mean believe in me as a person. But all agents have to file an annual financial report with the FBI. It's done to keep us from engaging in this kind of thing. So when I filed my next annual report, the money would be discovered. If I'd really wanted to get away with something like this, I wouldn't use my own bank account. Sulyard would know that."

Becca's frown deepened. "He thinks you're planning to sell the hack and take off with the money long before our annual reports are due."

Nina sat forward. "Does he really think I'd betray my country?"

Becca shrugged. "I honestly never know what the man is thinking, but DHS is all over his case. I'm choosing to believe that's got him worried and he's playing by the book to keep them off his back. I don't think he truly believes you could do this."

"Doesn't matter which it is, though, now does it?" Quinn argued. "The fact is, someone is doing a bang-up job of setting up Nina to take the fall for this hack. And it seems like they're doing the same thing to Hamid. Unless the kid really is part of a terrorist cell."

"I'm not sure he's being straightforward with us," Becca said. "But we still haven't found anything to suggest that he's involved in anything illegal. I suspect he's a victim here as much as Nina is."

Nina tossed the report on the table. "So whoever is doing this is using the money to create a trail, making it look like I'm not only a traitor, but a terrorist as well. I'd like to say there's no way they could accomplish that, but then, I never thought I'd ever see forty grand in my checking account either."

"Why would this person be willing to fork over that kind of cash?" Quinn asked.

"If we're right about it being someone seeking revenge, maybe their plan is for Nina to suffer in jail the way they did," Becca said. "If so, there's no telling what he might do next."

The panic returned. Nina took deep breaths and let them out slowly. "Let's not focus on what he might do. Instead let's review what he's done and see if there's anything that can lead us to him."

"That's my girl." Quinn squeezed her hand. "Keeping a positive attitude will help."

There he went, saying *his* again. She wanted to correct him, but not with Becca present. "Maybe the best thing is for me to head back to town and turn myself in."

"No," Quinn shouted. "I'm not letting you do that."

Like she'd let him stop her. She arched a brow and stared at him.

"I agree with Quinn," Becca hastily added. "You're the only one who can figure out the most likely suspect. You can't review your case files from a cell."

"But I—"

"I get it, Nina." Becca rested a hand on Nina's arm. "This goes against your very nature. You tend to take each day minute by minute. But sometimes you need to take a risk. This is one of those times."

"I don't know." She bit her lip.

"You aren't doing anything wrong, you know." Quinn met her gaze. "It's not like Sulyard showed up on the doorstop and you fled out the back door while he was in pursuit."

"Technically, you're right, I suppose."

"He *is* right," Becca added. "All you have to do is lay low and go through your files. DHS mitigated the database breach, so the list is safe for now. At least, you don't have to worry about that. Kait and I'll keep working from our end. We're sure to figure this out and clear your name, but you've got to do your part and avoid arrest. From this point forward, anyone with a badge is off limits to you, except me and Kait."

"Okay," Nina said, not liking the way her stomach ached. "But if we don't make progress soon, I'll contact Sulyard. And neither one of you is going to stop me."

QUINN HATED THAT Nina was the target of the investigation, and he wanted to get all the details he could from Becca before she left. "Does this mean Sulyard isn't considering other suspects?"

Becca shook her head. "With DHS looking over his shoulder, he's assigning resources to every possible lead."

"Such as?" Quinn's words came out like an accusation, but he didn't care.

"I told you about the new developments, but we're still working older leads." Becca sat up straighter. "Jae's still monitoring the chat room. The chatter has stopped, so she's searching for other discussions. We've completed all the background checks and have started one on Odell. We're also continuing down the list of people who viewed the cache posting."

"I might have made a copy of that list." A sheepish expression crossed Nina's face. "I'm doing some digging on my own."

"I suspected as much." Becca smiled. "Just make sure you don't leak your location. We don't want it getting back to Sulyard."

"I'll make sure that doesn't happen," Quinn said. "You find anything on Odell?"

"He's quite the political activist. He's worked on logging, human rights, legalizing marijuana, that sort of thing, but nothing to suggest he has any terrorist leanings. We're still waiting on warrant approval so we can review the database."

"Still?"

"The judge is being a real stickler. We've had to provide additional details to satisfy him."

Quinn fisted his hands. "I have half a mind to go pay Odell a visit myself."

"That's not a good idea," Becca warned. "When the warrant comes through, you could run into an agent at Odell's office."

"I'm willing to take that risk."

"Well, I'm not." Nina fired an irritated look at him. "Let's give Becca a chance first."

"Fine," he grumbled. "We wait. For now. In the meantime, we need to find a place to stay. We could check into a hotel, but I'd rather find a more secluded location."

"I've already thought of that." Becca dug a key from her pocket and slid it, as well as a piece of paper with directions for an address down the road, to Quinn.

"The cabin is located on the river not far from here, which is why I suggested this place to meet up. It's very private. And because it belongs to Kait's family, there's no way Sulyard will connect it to Nina."

"River?" Nina grimaced.

Quinn had expected a reaction from her when she realized she'd have to stay with him, not the cabin's proximity to the river. He watched her carefully. Her pulse was thrumming at the base of her throat, and she clenched her hands. It was an odd response. Something was going on with her. It troubled him not knowing what it was—it could be important to keeping her safe.

"Sorry, Nina." Becca patted Nina's hands as she clearly understood the problem. "I know it's not ideal, but it's the best I could do on such short notice." Becca moved her focus to Quinn. "With an alert out for your car, you'll want to use other transportation. There's a pickup and an SUV at the cabin. Kait says you're free to use them. The keys are hanging in one of the kitchen cupboards."

She pushed back her chair and stood. "I need to get back before Sulyard starts looking for me. Kait and I are working on gathering your files, Nina. Let's plan to meet back here tonight around nine. I should have them for you then."

"It's not a good idea to call me again and risk leaving a trail," Quinn said. "If your plans change, can you leave a message here for us?"

She nodded. "Okay, that's it, I guess." She turned to Quinn. "I'm sure I don't have to give you pointers on how to fly under the radar."

"I got it from here," he said. And suddenly, he was very thankful that he was a master of covert operations.

Chapter Twenty-Three

THE CAR CRUNCHED over the gravel driveway lined with tall trees blotting out the sun. The deeper they traveled on the winding drive, the darker it grew and the more Nina's palms perspired. She was being silly, she knew. It was just a river. Not *the* river where Garrett had died. She'd managed to keep it together the night they'd searched for the cache, but today, she didn't have a cache to distract her.

They came to a large clearing, and Quinn parked near a three-car garage. She forced herself to get out. From her vantage point, it looked like the cabin was buried in the woods below. She could hear the river rushing along. A shiver worked over her body.

"What's wrong?" Quinn came around the car.

"Nothing." She forced a smile and made herself think of something other than Garrett. She'd likely be there for a few days, so she had to make the best of it. A gust of wind pummeled her body, and she wrapped her arms around her waist. "I hope Kait left a jacket here."

"If not, I'll pick one up when I go back to town for supplies."

"What happened to laying low?"

"We'll need supplies if we're going to be successful at it."

"They why come all the way out here just to turn around and go back?"

He nodded at the garage. "We need to trade cars. Besides, the cops are watching for two people, so it's a good idea if you stay here."

She didn't like his suggestion, but his point was valid. She started for the stairs.

He came up behind her. "I assume you have your gun, just in case."

She nodded. "Though, you have to know, if Sulyard comes looking for me here, I won't shoot him."

"Funny, very funny." He rolled his eyes. "I simply need to know you're protected before I leave you here alone."

"I'm a big girl, Quinn. I've taken care of myself for years without your help. I can do it now, too."

He grimaced, and she could swear she'd honestly hurt his feelings.

"I'm sorry if I sound ungrateful for your help. I'm not." She waited for a response but got none. "We're going to be stuck together out here, so let's try to get along. Okay?"

Seeming as if he wanted to say something but reconsidered, he peered up at the sky. "I want to be back by dark, so let's get you settled."

"Before dark? That's hours away. What kind of supplies do you think we need?"

"Leave that up to me." He took the steps two at a time and disappeared around a bend in the stairs. By the time she reached him, he'd already opened the door to the traditional log cabin with a green metal roof.

They entered into a large A-framed living area. One wall held sliding glass doors leading to a deck overlooking the river. Shadows from tall pines played on the water, making it appear dark and ominous. Another shiver claimed her body.

"Let me get a fire going before I take off," Quinn offered.

She turned her back to the windows and checked the hall closet for a jacket. She found a heavy Oregon Ducks sweatshirt and put it on, catching Kait's fragrance on the fabric. She joined Quinn at the floor-to-ceiling stone fireplace. The kindling was already ablaze, and flames were licking greedily at the logs.

Seeing his hand, she couldn't help but wonder if working with fire bothered him. She suspected it was hard to strike a match after what he'd gone through.

"That should do it." He stood, his expression displaying no wariness around the fire.

Her respect for him grew. He wasn't letting a tragic situation keep him from living life to the fullest, the way she was doing with Garrett's death. Quinn had suffered mightily, but he seemed to have overcome it. Maybe it was time she faced her past, too, and dealt with it once and for all. She glanced at the river flowing rapidly downstream. The same old fears reached up to grab her, and a shiver worked down her body.

"What's going on, Nina?" Quinn stepped in front of her. "And don't say you're cold. You've been spooked since Becca told us about this place. Is it because you're stuck here with me?"

"No."

He tipped her chin up. "Then what is it?"

As much as she didn't want to talk about this, she knew she had to. She'd often accused him of not being willing to share. She'd be a hypocrite if she walked away now. "I'm sure I mentioned my brother Garrett, who died when I was twelve," she tried to sound matter-of-fact, but her voice crackled with emotion.

Quinn nodded.

"He died in a rafting accident. My dad took us against Mom's wishes, and Garrett fell out of the raft in one of the rapids. Dad didn't jump in after him. He just sat there while our guides tried to rescue Garret. I wanted to help, and was able to get a hold on his hand. He was so young. Struggling. I couldn't hold on. It was so horrible. His fingers slipped from mine. I . . . all I could do was watch . . . see the water take Garrett under and . . ." Tears threatened and she couldn't go on.

Quinn took her hand and held it against his heart. A flash of grief passed over his face. "I'm sorry, sweetheart. I know how hard it is to lose someone close to you." He understood. She knew it wasn't because of the loss of a family member, but for the men on his team he'd lost over the years. Men he thought of as family. A family she'd asked him to turn his back on for her.

"So this is about the river, then," he clarified. "It's freaking you out. And at the gorge. You weren't hungry. It was the falls."

She nodded, but didn't trust herself to speak without falling apart.

"Shoot, Nina. Why didn't you say something? I could have gone up there alone. You didn't need to come along."

"Not only could you have gone on your own, but you would have insisted on leaving me behind." She shook her head. "I couldn't let that happen. I had to be there."

His brow shot up.

"What?" she asked.

"You really don't trust me, do you?" He let go of her hand and plunged his fingers into his hair. "I'm not the lowlife you think I am."

"No . . . wait. That had nothing to do with trusting you. I do. At least with this kind of thing. But I had to retrieve the cache for my job. I told you that. To ensure proper protocol."

"You're sure that's all it was?"

She nodded. "I'm not happy about your decision to stay with the team, but I know the kind of man you are. You'd walk through fire . . ."

He winced and flexed his injured hand.

"You did walk through fire for your men. Your country. You're someone everyone can count on—on the job. My belief in that didn't change. You always do the right thing."

"You make me sound like a freakin' saint, but I'm not. I proved that when we split up, didn't I?" He sounded so angry at himself for how he'd handled their breakup.

It was the first time he'd let her see that it had affected him, too, and her heart warmed at the open regret in his voice.

Resolve suddenly claimed his expression, and he stood taller. "I should get going. If it'd be easier for you, you can come along, though I'd rather not risk Sulyard getting wind of my movements and seeing you."

"I'll stay." She tipped her head at a computer on a desk in the corner. "I can search the internet for information on the remaining people on the Hacktivist list. That will keep my mind off the water."

"You're sure?"

She gave a firm nod.

Instead of marching off as she expected, he folded her into a hug. His arms were gentle, allowing her to back away if she wanted, but she didn't want to. Not at all. She sighed and rested her head against his chest. He tightened his arms, a sudden desperate edge in the strength. She listened to the even rhythm of his heart speed up and felt at home.

"I'm sorry for hurting you so badly, sweetheart," he whispered against her hair. "I'd rather go back into that fire than hurt you again. If I could change how I handled things, I would. Trust me. I would."

His plea was sincere, and she believed him. He'd walked out on her because she'd forced him to choose between her and his men. If she hadn't they'd likely still be together.

For the first time, she wondered if she'd asked too much.

A CELL PHONE pealed in the distance, bringing Nina to her feet. The ringing was coming from outside the front door. Had Quinn dropped his phone on the way out, or was someone else out there?

The ringing stopped. She waited, listening, her ear cocked toward the entrance. It started again. She grabbed her gun and advanced toward the door. Slowly. She searched the shadowy surroundings and spotted a cell phone sitting on a table just outside the door.

It wasn't Quinn's phone. She checked the area again before stepping outside. She grabbed it, then darted back inside. The ringing stilled before she could accept the call. She waited, phone in hand. It chimed again.

"Hello," she answered.

"Hello, Agent Brandt. Long time, no see." A male voice slid through the phone.

Nina searched her memory, but came up empty. "Who is this?"

He chuckled. "The only person smart enough to set you up and man enough to make it happen."

The man who was setting her up. She expected him to sound more like Quinn, hard and tough, but his voice didn't hold as much bravado as his words. Maybe that meant he wasn't as smart as he thought, and she could trip him up.

"Set me up for what?" she asked innocently.

"You'd like that, wouldn't you? Me telling you something so you can use it to hunt me down again." He paused, and she didn't know if she should speak or remain silent.

"All you need to know right now is that I have a score to settle with you," he continued. "And there's nothing you can do to stop me."

"That's what you think." She tried to sound sure and confident.

"It's what I know. I also know you'll do exactly as I ask."

"Why would I do that?"

"Because I have Hamid, And unless you come to meet us, I'll be forced to kill him."

No. He couldn't have Hamid, could he? Sure he could.

She sucked in a breath to clear her mind and tried not to let her worry sound in her voice. "How can I be sure you're telling the truth?"

Silence filled the phone for a moment, then it dinged. "Check your texts."

She found the right screen and opened the message. He'd sent a picture of Hamid bound and terrified. She clenched her hand around the phone to keep from yelling at the guy. "If this is really about you paying me back, then let Hamid go. He's done nothing to you, and I know you don't want to go away for murder."

"Hamid is looking very concerned, Agent Brandt," he replied. "Don't disappoint him. We're at Triple Falls. On the trail. You have fifteen minutes to meet us, or Hamid will die. Come alone. Don't tell anyone where you've gone. Bring this phone, but leave any other cell you might have behind."

She didn't want to risk her life this way, but she had no choice. "I'll be there."

"We'll be waiting." He laughed again, before the line went dead.

BRANDT WAS ON her way up the trail. Wiley had been watching the movements of her vehicle on the GPS app on his phone, seeing her come closer and closer to the falls. He also watched the SEAL head into town. Thankfully, Wiley had the foresight to put the tracker on the

SEAL's car allowing him to locate Brandt at her little cabin. Then he placed another two on the other vehicles in the garage before the SEAL took off.

Excitement shot through him as he went to join Hamid where he'd left him, farther up the trail. Wiley had done a superb job of restraining the kid. His hands were bound in front, his ankles hog-tied with the rope circling a tree, and a generous gag filled his mouth.

"I'm back, Hamid." Wiley grabbed the bedside transmitter from under a layer of brush. "I suppose you're wondering what I'm doing with this. The people who make these things have done their best to keep them from delivering a lethal shock, but see . . . here's the thing. I've never met a device that I couldn't alter. In fact, I've reprogrammed one of these babies once before, so yours wasn't very difficult at all."

Hamid moaned and tried to scamper back.

"Hey, man, don't be afraid. I'm sure it'll be quick. I'll give you a few seconds for a prayer if you want. Then we gotta move on. Agent Brandt is on her way."

Wiley sat back on his haunches for a moment while Hamid mumbled through his gag. After a respectable time, Wiley lifted the transmitter again. "Thanks for your help in putting away the scumbag agent, Hamid. Your contribution will never be forgotten."

Hamid planted his heels in the dirt, squirming harder. His eyes were wide with fear.

Wiley felt a moment of hesitation. He'd never killed an innocent kid before. People like his parents were easy. The psychiatrist—even easier. But the kid? Wiley hadn't expected this moment of remorse? But then, sacrifice was necessary if he wanted to achieve his goals. He could do this. He was in control. It felt good. So good.

Powerful.

He pressed the button.

Hamid's eyes widened. His body bucked hard in a deep convulsion. Then his limbs went slack, his eyes fixed and open. Wiley watched for a few moments, waiting, before stepping forward and checking for a pulse. He found none. Good. It was over. Time to call the police. He dialed Hamid's new phone, using the speaker button to keep from touching his face and inadvertently putting his DNA on the phone,

"911. What's your emergency?" the operator asked.

"Help," Wiley whispered with an accent that he hoped mimicked Hamid's. "She's going to kill me. I'm all alone up here. Hiding. You have to stop her."

"Calm down, son. What's your name?"

"Hamid Ahmadi."

"Can you tell me where you are, Hamid?"

"Triple Falls Trail in the gorge."

"Do you know your attacker?"

"Yes. Agent Nina Brandt with the FBI. She's hacking into government databases. She's been trying to pin it on me. Now she's trying to kill me to cover it up. Please hurry. Send someone. I have to go. She's coming."

Wiley hung up and tossed back his head to laugh, but Brandt came to mind, stopping him. She might have climbed high enough by now to hear him. He put the phone in the teen's hand, curling his fingers around it to set his prints.

Perfect. Now for Brandt's new phone. Wiley slid it under Hamid's body where Brandt wouldn't likely find it. The police would. Oh, yeah, they would. Before they went searching for the woman they'd believe it belonged to.

Chapter Twenty-Four

HER HEART LODGED in her throat, Nina climbed the trail. She prayed that Hamid was safe, but she also prayed that her caller hadn't somehow found out about her fear of the river and was planning to use it to get back at her.

They were nearing dusk and the light was fading fast. A cold wind whipped down the trail, biting into the sweatshirt she'd thought was so warm back at the cabin. She hated coming up here at all, and climbing toward the falls under these conditions didn't help. Her heart pounded with each uphill step. At each turn of the trail, she expected someone to jump out at her. Was he hiding? Waiting in the woods, ready to pounce?

She held out her weapon and kept going. Just ahead, she saw something odd, so she eased closer. Then she spotted a leg protruding through the underbrush. Jeans and sneakers, red like the pair Hamid had been wearing.

"Hamid," she called out.

No answer.

"Hamid," she called again as she inched forward. She had a clear view of the body now and confirmed it was Hamid, lying on his back, his hands and ankles tied, his phone in his hand. He was staring blankly into the sky.

She forced herself to remain calm, detached, and observe as an agent would. She saw no blood or any apparent injury. She supposed, with his heart condition, he could have collapsed, but everything about this situation felt wrong. She crept closer, her heartbeat thundering in her ears.

"Please, be okay. Please, be okay," she whispered. But she'd been in the law enforcement game long enough to know he was dead. Still, she had to check to be sure. She knelt next to him, feeling for a pulse. None.

Her stomach threatened to empty right there on the spot. She focused on breathing, calming the roiling waves of nausea. Now what did she do?

Think, Nina, think.

Hamid's body was still warm. He hadn't been dead long. Which meant the killer had to be close by, maybe planning to kill her next. She shot to her feet and took shelter behind the tree.

There was no sign of anyone in the area. Not a sound, save the wind whistling down the trail.

She suspected her adversary had lured her there to make it look like she'd been the one to kill Hamid. He was tightening the noose, and she could easily see herself facing a murder rap, as well as the other charges.

She should call 911. Report the death.

No, wait. They'd arrest her. Then what would she do? She hadn't been able to clear her name for the hack. But murder? She'd never be able to do that from a jail cell.

She stared at Hamid, tears starting to stream down her cheeks. The poor, poor boy. He'd lost his life for what? Revenge? Now she was considering leaving him there.

She had to. She couldn't help him now. He was gone.

The memory of her mother's face the moment she'd heard about Garrett popped into Nina's mind. And her father's reaction had been just as unforgettable. All the grief, the recriminations, the blame. They split up shortly afterward. How would Hamid's parents handle this?

Nina knew their pain. She'd lived their pain. She wanted to go to them, to offer comfort. But she couldn't. She had to think of herself instead. Her grandmother would be shocked at this choice, but Nina was making it.

She was going to do something she never thought she'd do. She'd work her way down to the trailhead. Once she was safely in her car, she'd call 911.

That is, if the creep who'd killed Hamid wasn't lying in wait, planning to take her life, too.

QUINN TURNED ONTO the road leading toward the cabin and glanced at his brother, who was sitting in the passenger seat. Nina would be so peeved when she saw Ty, but Quinn had to pick him up. Quinn couldn't take the chance that Sulyard would use Ty as leverage against Nina or arrest Ty and toss him in juvie.

Sure, going to the hotel was risky. But if Quinn couldn't manage to free Ty without capture by an FBI agent, then he wasn't much of a SEAL.

His phone chimed a text, but he was driving so he glanced at Ty. "Can you read that to me?"

Ty picked up the phone. "It's from Nina."

"Nina." He shot a look at Ty. "What? Where'd she get a cell phone?"

Ty fell silent, his eyes widening. "Oh no, man. No. Not this."

"What is it?"

Ty looked up, his eyes now filling with worry. "She said a man killed Hamid at the gorge."

"How in the world does she know that?" Quinn's mind raced over the possibilities. Over the chance that she might be in danger. "Call her. Now!"

Ty dialed and put the phone on speaker. It rang four times.

"Quinn," she responded, a hitch in her voice.

"Are you okay?" Quinn tried to keep the fear out of his voice.

"Yes."

"How do you know about Hamid?" he demanded.

"A man left this phone outside the cabin, then called it. He told me he had Hamid. To meet them at the gorge or he'd kill Hamid."

"I gave you my number. You should have called me."

"There was no time. He only gave me fifteen minutes. I had to go. I found Hamid's body. I figured this creep was trying to set me up for the murder, so I took off. I'm on my way back to cabin."

Quinn slammed a hand on the wheel. "You can't go back there. This guy knows where it is."

She responded. "I have to get the Hacktivist list."

"He could kill you, too."

"He obviously doesn't want to hurt me, or he could have done it at the gorge."

"You can't know that for sure. Besides, we can get the list from Becca."

"She can't compromise her values that way. It's one thing to provide my old files, but giving me a copy of evidence for an active investigation is another thing altogether."

He wanted to argue, but he understood the ethics agents followed. He lived by his own creed. "Then wait. I'll be there in twenty minutes."

"We'll have nothing to go on if he takes the paperwork. I have my gun, and I'll be careful."

"Wait for me, Nina," Quinn barked, his heart shredding.

"Sorry. I have to do this now more than ever. For Hamid."

The line went dead.

Quinn cursed under his breath and pressed the gas pedal to the floor. He didn't care if the roads were treacherous. He was going to make a twenty-minute drive in ten minutes, no matter what.

NINA SWUNG THE truck into the driveway. She was flying by the seat of her pants. No planning, only one goal in mind—to get in, get what she needed, and get to safety. How had she lost control of her life so quickly? She could barely breathe. If her mother could see her, she'd have a heart attack

"Calm down," she warned herself as she cut the engine and listened. *Big breath in and a slow one out. That's it. Another one and another.*

As her body calmed, she surveyed the area. Not sensing an ambush, she drew her weapon and bolted for the steps. She took them one at a time, quietly inching down, for once not caring that she was heading toward water. She got the key in the lock and swung the door open wide, then took cover.

Sensing no movement inside, she inched forward, left the lights off, and crept through the space, first the kitchen, followed by the great room, then the bedrooms. It took her a long time to clear the place in the dark, but she wouldn't turn on the lights until she was sure she was alone. After searching the last room, her legs went weak with relief, and she was afraid she might crumble. But she couldn't. Not yet. Not until she had the list.

She rested against the door until her strength returned, then went back to the great room. Something clicked in the distance outside. A car door closing quietly? Maybe. Or maybe nothing. She couldn't risk it. Nor could she risk closing the door that she'd left wide open to leave a quick escape route.

She took cover behind a floor-to-ceiling cabinet in the kitchen and held her gun at the ready. She'd never shot anyone. She didn't want to now, but she would if she had to. She had no reason to believe the killer would come back there, but then, just a few days ago, she had no reason to believe her supervisor would show up at her house with plans to arrest her. Or that someone would be framing her for terrorism and murder.

She sucked in a breath and let it out quietly. She heard only crickets chirping. Frogs croaking. The hum of the refrigerator behind her. She was expecting to hear footfalls inching down the stairs, closer and closer. But silence reigned. She shifted to look around the corner. A quick peek, then back to cover.

An arm came down over her chest. She screamed. Her gun flew

from her hand, hitting the floor and skittering out of reach. She elbowed her assailant.

"Nina?" Quinn asked, and she was suddenly released.

The lights cut on, flooding the space. She blinked hard.

Gun in hand, Quinn watched her. His eyes were warrior sharp. The fierce hunter expression left her breathless. He eyed her for a long moment, then set his gun on the counter and crushed her to him, flattening her against his chest. "Are you all right?"

"I'm fine." She sagged against him.

"Why are you in the dark like this?"

"I heard a noise and didn't want to be a sitting duck." She laughed nervously. "Though that's exactly what I ended up being."

"If it had been anyone else but me, you'd have done just fine."

He was right. The average person didn't possess his skills.

He set her away, ran his gaze over her body, then pulled her close again. "Thank God you're okay."

The security of his arms, the strength and absolute power circling her, brought tears to the surface. She tried to stem them, but she kept seeing Hamid's eyes staring into the distance. The life gone from his body. She'd spent her whole life trying hard to keep things on an even keel. To plan and prepare. To take precautions. But what difference did it make?

No matter what she did, how she planned, the steps she took to remain safe, someone could destroy it all in a flash. She'd always hated that Quinn ran out and courted danger, but she wasn't safe either. Her mother had been wrong—Nina couldn't control her environment. Sure, there were things people could do to minimize their risk, but to go to the extremes she had?

Quinn leaned back and pressed the hair from her forehead. "Tell me what happened."

"He killed Hamid." Saying it aloud made her give in to her tears.

He kissed her forehead. "Shh, sweetheart. Don't cry."

"But he's dead. Oh, Quinn, he's really, truly dead. If I'd gotten to him sooner, maybe—"

"So, it's true then?" Ty interrupted from the door. "Ham's dead?"

"Ty? What are you doing here?" She tried to free herself, but Quinn held fast.

"Why don't you wait out on the deck, Ty," Quinn suggested. "I'll sort this out with Nina. Then I'll fill you in on the details."

Nina heard the steel under Quinn's words. Ty must have too, since he stepped outside without arguing. She wanted to stay in the circle of Quinn's arms, but that would only make her want to keep crying. She needed to gain clarity so she could move forward. Nearly choking on the tears clogging her throat, she backed away and grabbed a tissue from the counter. She felt Quinn watching her intently, as if he was trying to decide what to do.

She waited for him to say something. He huffed out a breath. Took in another, blew it out. She wanted to look at him. To see what he was thinking. But if she did, her tears would return in full force.

"Why did you go to the falls in the first place?" he suddenly snapped.

His angry tone made her spin. His jaw was clenched, his hands fisted. Gone was the caring man. A SEAL warrior now stood before her, all hard angles and rage. She had no idea what had changed, but something had.

"Answer me, Nina," he ordered. "Why'd you go?"

"I told you. The caller said he'd kill Hamid. I couldn't let him do that."

"Instead, you'd rather he kill you?" The words shot out of his mouth like an accusation.

"I also told you, he doesn't want to do that. If he did, I wouldn't have made it back from the falls."

"You can't know that." He shoved his hand into his hair. "Geez, Nina. Anyone could see that you would have been trading your life for the kid's. You're an agent, for crying out loud. How can you not recognize that what you did was a dumb move?"

"Dumb?" A bolt of anger shot through her, replacing the grief in a flash. "If I was being dumb, then so are you, every time you rush off to rescue someone."

"But I'm trained for it. You aren't. Big difference."

She glared at him. "I'm trained."

"But not to my level."

"I'm quite competent at my job, Quinn." She clenched her hands. "Make no mistake about that."

"I didn't say you weren't competent, but SEALs aren't just competent. We're outstanding in everything we do or we keep at it until we are. We train to excel, then train some more. But that's what it takes to pull off a rescue without people dying in the process."

"I get that you're the big, bad SEAL, the ultimate fighting machine. And you think that none of us can measure up. You've made that clear in the last few days." She fisted her hands. She was actually glad for the anger—it kept the other emotions at bay. "But I'm a qualified federal agent, and you're acting like all the other men I run into on the job who refuse to take me seriously. Suspects. Cops. Even an agent or two. They take one look at me and dismiss me. I don't take that from them and I won't take it from you. If you can't start respecting my skills, it's time for you to walk out that door and head back to San Diego."

WILEY RESISTED clapping his hands. Things were going just as he'd predicted. He'd followed Brandt back to the cabin and knew she'd have called her big, dumb protector by that time. And anyone with an ounce of brains could predict the SEAL would come running back to the cabin and slip down the steps to make sure she was okay.

Exactly what the SEAL had done. Wiley hadn't expected the goofy kid brother to come along, but even he trotted down the steps and left Wiley to do his thing.

Wiley also guessed that the SEAL was questioning how he'd found them at the cabin. Made sense that he'd search the vehicles and their possessions for hidden GPS trackers. If Wiley wanted to keep tracking them this way, he couldn't let the SEAL find the trackers.

He eased out of the scrub and quickly, but silently slid under the vehicles and removed the little devices, then scampered back to his hiding spot, resisting squealing in glee. After the SEAL came lumbering up the steps to search the vehicles, Wiley would put the trackers in place.

He sat back to wait, his gun in his hand just in case, and enjoyed the thought of besting the SEAL again.

QUINN GRITTED HIS teeth as he checked under the vehicles tracking devices. Finding none, he slammed a fist against the truck's hood.

If not via tracker, how in the world did this creep find them? Quinn was certain they hadn't been followed from the restaurant. Was someone in Kait or Becca's inner circle betraying their confidence or had Hamid's killer somehow recorded the other agents' conversations?

Quinn would discuss it with Becca when he next saw her. Right now, he had to focus on moving them to a new safe house.

He jogged down the stairs and found Nina staring out the window. She spun and met his gaze, anger still lingering in her eyes.

What had he been thinking? She could have died and there he was only moments ago yelling at her. Being mean and ugly when all he wanted to do was draw her close. Confirm she was alive and well by touching her. Get rid of the residual fear from almost losing her.

How could he still be angry? He was a jerk, that's how. He was good and mad and couldn't seem to get a hold of it. He had to before he did or said something else stupid.

With her heated gaze still on him, he started to pace, letting the anger subside with each step. Maybe he was really angry at himself for not having her back. Point blank, he hadn't been there when she'd needed him. Like he hadn't been there the day she'd given him the ultimatum. The day she'd needed him to man up and consider what walking away without a word would do to her. Instead, he'd stormed off in a huff. Then, he'd been too proud to discuss things after he'd cooled down.

Yeah, he was mad at himself, not her.

He stopped. Turning toward her, he met her gaze and tied to convey his sincerity. "I'm sorry if you think I don't respect your skills, sweetheart. I do. I'm just mad at myself for leaving you alone and giving you no choice but to head up to the falls."

"Even if you'd gone with me, Hamid would be dead. That wouldn't change."

"That's not the point."

"Then what is?"

His mind flooded with thoughts of her getting the call. Taking off. Racing to the falls without a thought for her safety, her mind solely on helping Hamid. Putting her life on the line. He couldn't handle it. Just the thought . . .

"You're usually so careful. I don't have to worry about you." He took her hands. They were cold and clammy. "But rushing into danger like you did today? That's not good, sweetheart. Not good at all. Don't you care about what losing you would do to me?"

Her eyes flashed wide in surprise. She jerked her hands free. "That's priceless, Quinn. Totally priceless. Did you forget that you deployed, leaving me feeling this way all the time when we were together? But I do it once and suddenly, you can't handle it?"

Her allegation hit him square in the face. He'd known she'd taken his deployments hard, but had he ever actually taken the time to understand how she felt? Really understand it? No. He'd never had to feel the visceral worry twisting his gut right now. She'd never given him reason to experience it before. He could always count on her need to weigh things. To think them through before acting. While he . . . man . . . he'd never really gotten it. Until now.

"I'm sorry," he said sincerely. "I get it. I didn't before."

She shrugged. "We're not together, so it doesn't matter if you understand."

Oh, it mattered all right. He just didn't know what he could or would do about it.

"What's important right now is figuring out how we're going to handle Hamid's death," she continued. "I can't be certain he was murdered, but with his hands and feet tied, I have to assume someone killed him." She paused and lifted her eyes in thought. "Or maybe Hamid was actually involved in the hacking scheme. Maybe something went wrong in their plan and they killed him."

Quinn shifted his mind back to the problem at hand. "Your team has scoured the kid's life. If he was involved in this, wouldn't they have discovered that by now?"

"Likely, but it's possible they missed something."

"Did you call Becca after you found him?"

"No. I need to think this through, first. I didn't even call 911—the calls are recorded." She shook her head. "What kind of a person does that make me? I left the poor kid lying there and didn't do a thing."

And he'd yelled at her when she was struggling with all of this. *What a jerk!* "We can go somewhere and make an anonymous call from a payphone."

"It looks like Hamid's killer already did. As I was leaving, I saw County cruisers race past me so I doubled back and spotted deputies climbing the trail. I'm guessing the killer hoped they'd find me with the body."

"Thankfully, you got away."

A shiver claimed her body, and Quinn worked hard to resist the urge to hug her. She didn't want him to treat her like a damsel in distress. She also clearly didn't want him to care for her, but he did. Big time. And now that a murder had occurred, protecting her became his primary mission. And he'd never failed on a mission yet.

Chapter Twenty-Five

WILEY IGNORED THE dank air in the tunnel and hovered his finger over Tyler's laptop while Crash watched. As much as Wiley wanted to hit *enter* and show Crash what he could do, he also wanted to savor the moment.

"Get to it already," Crash said, irritation coating his words. "The sooner I confirm the hack, the sooner we both get paid."

Wiley drew in a breath, held it, and hit *send*. Instead of looking at the screen, he watched Crash for his reaction. Wiley saw the screen colors flash in his peripheral vision and waited for Crash to be impressed. To praise Wiley's prowess.

"What the . . . ?" Crash's eyes went cold and hard. He glared at Wiley. "You trying to make me mad?"

Wiley peered at the screen. He felt the color drain from his face.

"Wait, no," he said, already knowing the vulnerability had been patched, but needing to confirm it. "Let me try it again." He started the hack sequence over. Followed every step. Double-checked each one. Hit *enter* again.

FORBIDDEN. The big, bold word flashed on the screen.

"Amateur hour." Crash shot to his feet. "My rep is gonna take a beating for this. No one will do business with me again. I want my forty Gs back. Now!"

"No wait," Wiley begged and hated every minute of it. "I can fix this. It just needs some tweaking."

Crash's steps stilled, suspicion consuming his expression. "Fix it how fast?"

"Tomorrow. Next day, at the latest." The words shot out before Wiley could think about it. If Tyler had managed to hack the database, Wiley could do it, too. But in such a short time? Not likely.

This was all Brandt's fault. She'd worked with Homeland Security to fix the vulnerability. Yes, she was to blame. It was the only answer. Now he had nothing. *Nothing!* As usual. He'd been so close, but others had stepped in, ruining it all. They were coming after him. All of them.

Taunting. Trying to control him. Do him in.

He clamped his hands over his ears. Crash was speaking, but Wiley didn't care. Or maybe Crash had done this. Somehow, he'd gotten his hands on the hack and changed things. Stolen the idea out from under Wiley.

Wiley eyed him. His anger grew hot. White hot. He'd kill him.

He slid his hand into his pocket to grip his gun.

"See here's the thing, Fagan. Seeing this fail has me thinking—who would want to buy a hack like this, when it has the risk of not working in a day or two? And when it failed, wouldn't the buyer come after me? Why should I get involved in this?"

"DHS eliminated this vulnerability because they were told about the hack and knew where to look. When I hack it again, they won't have a clue about the path I took," Wiley promised.

"Makes sense, I suppose. But you better be on the up and up or . . ."

Crash didn't have to finish. In prison, Wiley had seen Crash's payback in action. "I hear you."

"Okay, fine. It's better for my rep to put the buyer off than renege," Crash appraised Wiley. "If I give you a second chance, you're sure you can do this?"

"Yes," Wiley lied, his fingers still caressing the gun.

"Fine." Crash narrowed his eyes. "I'll tell the buyer we'll deliver in forty-eight hours. If they go for it, don't bother getting me down here again unless you can deliver the goods."

"I won't," Wiley said.

Crash climbed the steps and disappeared into the night.

Instead of feeling secure as usual, the space was suddenly a tomb. Wiley felt as if he'd died. Much like the day he'd gone to prison. Sure, he'd already succeeded in ending Brandt's life as an agent. She would do some time for the hack and murder. But he was once again left out in the cold. Hurting. Penniless. On his own, with no one to count on.

He slammed a fist on the table. Tyler's laptop jumped.

"So now what do I do?" He stared at the screen and almost wished he'd never found Tyler's computer. At least that way, he wouldn't know what he'd lost.

"Wait, that's it."

Tyler was the answer. He'd completed the initial hack and knew the steps that hadn't worked for him, which would make him able to work faster this time.

Wiley would find a way to get Tyler out from under the Feds' eyes and bring him to the tunnel to complete the hack. But what if he didn't cooperate?

No problem. Wiley had nothing to lose. *Nothing.* If the little punk didn't go along with him, things would get ugly. Very ugly indeed.

WITH THEIR SAFE house compromised, Quinn remained vigilant as they prepared to depart to a new location he'd arranged with his buddy Oscar. His dad owned a floating home—a houseboat in Quinn's book, but that's not how the people who lived on them thought of them—that he rented out to tourists. Quinn hated to put Nina in such close proximity to water again, but she'd agreed to the houseboat without a blink of her eye.

Quinn crossed the room to Ty. "You can drive the truck. Nina and I'll take the SUV."

"Me, alone?" Ty's voice broke in an adolescent squeak.

Quinn nodded. "It's a good idea to have a fallback vehicle that no one can trace to us. I'll be right behind you. But if you're uncomfortable alone, I'll understand."

He bit his lip. "You need me to do this, right?"

Quinn nodded.

"Then you can count on me."

Quinn clapped his brother's back. "Thanks for stepping up, Ty. I really appreciate it."

His face lit with pride, a wide grin following. "You do this spy stuff all the time, don't you? It's so cool."

The last thing Quinn wanted was for Ty to glorify Quinn's work. He didn't want the kid to follow the family tradition of going into the military. Quinn loved his job, but Ty wasn't built for that kind of life. "Not so cool when someone is gunning for you."

Ty blanched.

"Hey, no one's gunning for us here. We'll be fine." He gestured at Ty's backpack. "Get your things together, okay?"

"K."

To be on the safe side, Quinn had to shift a few things, too. He went to the kitchen counter, loaded a clip in his Mark 23 pistol, holstered it, and dropped extra ammo into a cargo pocket. He set three burner phones on the counter, then started transferring cash and his fake ID to another pocket.

Nina came up beside him and snatched the ID from his hand. "This is what you picked up on your errands? You keep stuff like this sitting around?"

"Doesn't everybody?" He laughed.

"I'm serious, Quinn." She eyed him. "Why would you need something like this?"

"With my job, you never know what to expect. It's better to be prepared than sorry." Though her expression still held questions, he picked up an iPhone and handed it to her. "Before you think I have a closet full of phones, this is the only one I had on hand. I bought the others today."

She rolled her eyes. "Like that makes it any easier to understand the other things."

He shoved another phone in his pocket, then gave one, along with the truck keys, to Ty. "It's fully charged. I've programmed our numbers in, as well as Becca's. Only use it in an emergency. Don't turn on the GPS whatever you do."

"Got it," Ty said, already on checking out the device.

Quinn put his hand over the phone. "You'll have plenty of time to look at it when we get to the houseboat. For now, keep your head up and stay behind me on the stairs."

As they stepped out into the cold evening air, Quinn wanted to give the same warning to Nina, but he knew she'd take offense at him taking charge, so he kept his mouth shut. If they ran into trouble on the road, he could only hope that she'd listen to him, so that none of them met the same fate as Hamid.

BECCA GRITTED HER teeth and stared at the body. At Hamid. The belligerent teen she'd recently interviewed was lying there, lifeless, his body illuminated by the harsh rays from a trio of Klieg lights. His eyes were open, staring and vacant.

Medical examiner Marcie Jensen squatted next to him. They were lucky the short and petite firebrand with hair the same color as Nina's had caught this case. She always went the extra mile on investigations she worked. Multnomah County Sheriff deputies were on the scene, too, but the sheriff had agreed to let Becca and Connor take lead on the investigation.

Marcie suddenly stood and held out a cell phone. "This was under the body."

Connor held the evidence bag with the cell found in Hamid's hand and compared the two. "Same make and model as this one. Want to bet the texts on this phone came from that one?"

"Odds are good you're right." Becca took the phone and thumbed through the device to review the recent texts, then gave Connor the only number that appeared in the log.

"Bingo," he said. "We have a match."

Becca continued to search the phone. "Phone's registered to Nina. Just like the one found at her house."

"With the 911 call claiming she's after the kid and this phone," Connor said. "It's not hard to see someone wants her to take the fall for the murder."

"We have no obvious cause of death, so let's be careful about referring to this as a homicide," Marcie warned Connor.

He scoffed. "The kid was involved in a major investigation and is found dead under suspicious circumstances. And there are two burner phones at the scene. Coincidence? I don't think so."

Marcie frowned. "Something feels off to me, too, but I don't want the parents to think he was murdered if it turns out that he died of natural causes."

Becca went back to the phone and reviewed the internet history. She read the last webpage accessed.

"Oh, no," she said, her blood running cold. She showed the screen to Marcie, then faced Connor. "Someone was searching for how to commit murder with an ICD and make it look like an accident."

Marcie's face paled.

"Okay, I'm in the dark here," Connor said. "Someone care to explain, starting with what ICD stands for?"

"It's an implantable cardioverter defibrillator," Marcie said. "It sits under the skin, near the heart to detect an abnormal heartbeat and deliver an internal shock to regulate it."

"Hamid has one of these?" he asked.

Marcie shrugged. "He has a device implanted near his heart, but I can't tell if it's a pacemaker or an ICD. If it's an ICD, this could very well be our cause of death."

"How does a person kill someone with this?" Connor asked.

"Patients with an ICD usually have bedside monitors/transmitters that collect the data from the device," Marcie explained. "The device then transmits the data to the physician, allowing him to adjust the settings remotely. If Hamid's implant is an ICD, and *if*—this is a really big 'if' in my book—if someone got their hands on his transmitter, they could modify the programming and deliver a fatal shock to his system."

Becca's stomach clenched. "It also says there's never been an actual account of committing murder this way, but it's possible. What do you think, Marcie?"

"I don't know anything about changing the programming, but if it can be changed, the transmitter has the capacity to deliver a life-ending shock." Marcie shook her head. "First, I need to confirm Hamid has an ICD. If so, I'll need to get the device to the manufacturer, who can tell us if the transmitter was altered."

"How long will that take?" Connor asked.

"Could take weeks."

"We don't have that long," Becca grumbled.

"One of you could contact the manufacturer and try to speed things up."

"Once you confirm the ICD, give me the details for the device and I'll take care of it," Becca offered. "In the meantime, I'm headed over to Hamid's house to notify his mother. What should I tell her?"

"*We'll* head over there." Connor gave Becca a pointed look.

"Tell the mother he died of unknown causes, and we'll know more after the autopsy." Marcie looked at Hamid. "You might want to ask if Hamid had an ICD and monitor. I don't think the transmitter can communicate with the device over a long distance, so if the monitor is at his house, it's unlikely he died this way."

"I'll call you after I talk to her." Becca turned to Connor. "Can you make sure your team searches for the monitor when they comb the area?"

He nodded and stepped off.

"I'll get the body to the morgue and get started." A grim expression on her face, Marcie turned back to Hamid.

Becca bagged the phone and waited for Connor to finish talking to his team. She hated being there. Hated seeing Hamid, but she was glad to have Connor's company for the death notification. It was going to be rough.

He soon joined her, a determined look on his face. "Let's get going."

Becca started down the path and heard Connor thumping along behind her. She didn't feel like talking, so she kept her head down. Suspicious deaths like Hamid's were always hard to take, but when the victim was just a teenager with so much of his life ahead of him? That left an ache in Becca's heart. A big one, right next to the lingering sadness she felt for Molly. That kind of grief never disappeared. Becca understood, more than many detectives, the anguish Hamid's mother was about to experience.

Mrs. Ahmadi took it as badly as Becca suspected she would, nearly collapsing on the floor.

Becca helped her to the sofa. "Can I get you a glass of water?"

"No." The word came out in a strangled cry as her gaze darted around the room. "When can I see him? I have to see him."

"We'll arrange it with the medical examiner and let you know as soon as possible," Connor offered.

"Thank you." She wrung her hands together. "I always feared this day would come. He has a heart condition and the ICD worked well, but . . ." She let out a long, shuddering breath. "Look at me, assuming that's how he died when we don't know anything."

"So he had an ICD?" Becca clarified.

Mrs. Ahmadi nodded. "His bedside transmitter could help them determine if his heart failed. I'll get it." She jumped up and rushed from the room before Becca could say a word.

"I was hoping he didn't have an ICD." Connor took a seat across from her. He wore a gloomy expression that matched the emotions churning in Becca's gut.

"Me too," she replied, and they fell silent.

Mrs. Ahmadi barreled back into the room and stood gaping at them. "It's gone. Someone took it. I don't know who . . . where . . . it's missing."

"Calm down, Mrs. Ahmadi." Becca led her back to the sofa and tried to remain calm herself. "Tell me what's missing."

"His monitor. The one that reads his ICD."

Becca glanced at Connor. Grim recognition sat on his face. Someone had likely killed Hamid using his transmitter, but before Becca called Marcie, she needed to confirm the device was missing and hadn't just been moved.

Mrs. Ahmadi started crying and dropped onto the sofa. "In all the craziness, I didn't bring it to the hotel. I should have. How could I forget? I never forget."

"You were too busy worrying about how to help Hamid avoid incarceration." Becca softened her voice. "You couldn't think of everything."

"Now it's gone," Mrs. Ahmadi lamented. "Who would steal such a thing and why?"

Becca hated to question Mrs. Ahmadi when she was so upset, but it had to be done. "Did you notice anything else missing, Mrs. Ahmadi?"

She swiped at tears with the back of her hand. "No. No. I don't think so. But I didn't check that carefully."

"Why don't we walk through the house together and take another look?" Becca suggested.

"Yes. Yes." She shot up and hurried to the stairs.

Connor stood. "I'll see if I can find any sign of a break-in while you're upstairs."

Becca escorted Mrs. Ahmadi through the bedrooms. She searched every corner and even pulled out drawers. If this had been a random burglary, the drawers would have been dumped on the floor. They weren't likely to find anything else missing, but Becca let Mrs. Ahmadi continue as a way to work out some of her grief. When they finally met up with Connor, he shook his head.

Becca's heart fell. They had a theft with no signs of forced entry and only one item missing. Someone wanted the device—and only the device—to kill Hamid with a lethal shock to his heart.

Chapter Twenty-Six

NINA TRIED TO ignore the sensation of the floor swaying under her feet as she disconnected the call to her mother. She was the last person Nina had wanted to contact, but she would have been frantic with worry when Nina didn't answer her phone now sitting in evidence. She stowed the new phone and watched Ty playing video games on his.

A groan of defeat slipped from his mouth.

The poor kid. He'd been through so much these last few days. Though Hamid wasn't Ty's friend, he was still affected by the loss. And here Ty was, hidden away and on the run like a criminal, most likely worried the same thing would happen to him. Nina was starting to think it would be safer for him to have stayed at the hotel.

She stepped over to Quinn. "Can I talk to you a minute? Alone." She didn't wait for an answer but crossed to the far side of the family room, well out of Ty's hearing.

Quinn joined her. "What's up?"

"I'm worried about Ty's safety. With a murderer running loose, I think he's better off under the FBI's protection."

"Are you kidding me?" Steely determination filled his eyes. "Sulyard's on a rampage. He wants to toss you into a cell for hacking the NFL. He'll likely find some lame way to connect it to Ty, too. The kid might never make it out of juvie."

"There's no way Ty could be charged with the hack. He couldn't have done it—he was at the hotel under guard."

"You didn't do the hack or put that computer in your suitcase either, but Sulyard will haul you in without blinking. The same thing could happen with Hamid's murder. I won't let Ty go through that." Quinn's voice rose with each statement, drawing Ty's attention.

"Shh. He can hear you."

Quinn lowered his voice. "I won't let him or you go to prison for something you haven't done."

He had a point. Not about the hack, as Ty had a strong alibi where she didn't, but it was hypocritical for her to stay out of jail so she could clear her name and deny Ty the same opportunity.

Quinn stepped closer, his voice even lower. "I get that Ty might still have to serve time for the initial hack, but I won't let him go to juvie because of something someone else did. Once we sort everything else out, he'll turn himself in. I guarantee that." His voice was like stone. Even if it wasn't, she no longer wanted to argue the point.

The timer dinged in the kitchen. "The chicken should be hot. We'll all feel a lot better once we have something to eat."

"Too bad it's takeout and not your famous fried chicken. That, I could get excited about." He smiled, but even his boyish grin couldn't eliminate her fear of Ty somehow getting hurt.

She returned to the kitchen and found him munching on potato chips, acting like a typical teen in a very atypical situation.

"Sorry, Nina," he mumbled around a mouthful, then swallowed. "I got you into this mess and now you're in trouble, too."

"Don't worry about a thing." She squeezed his shoulder. "You didn't plant the computer at my house, so it's not your fault."

"Crazy unbelievable, isn't it?" He shook his head. "I mean some dude broke in and hid it there. I s'pose you're used to stuff like this, but man . . . I'm sure not."

She wasn't used to anything anywhere near this, but she kept quiet and pulled the pan from the oven. "Chicken's ready."

"Oh, yeah, bring it on." He grinned. "Mom's been watching me like a hawk 24/7. I've only had healthy stuff to eat." He shoved another handful of chips into his mouth.

At his boyish exuberance, Nina's fears disappeared for a moment. She laughed at his easygoing attitude, so different from the day he and Quinn had told her about the hack. This was the kid Nina knew and loved.

A sudden longing to have someone in her life hit her. After her breakup with Quinn, she'd convinced herself that she could forgo having a family. That Becca and Kait plus her mother and Grandmother Hale were enough for her.

But she was wrong. She wanted someone to come home to every night, to legally call her own. Children. The white picket fence and front porch. Maybe a dog. The whole dream.

Quinn stepped past her to wash his hands, and her dream bubble burst. She wanted the dream all right, but she couldn't have it with Quinn. Unfortunately, he was the only man who'd ever appeared in that dream.

WILEY HAD TO GET moving. He crept across the parking lot as quiet as a cat. Step by step. On his toes. Right under the big, bad SEAL's nose.

Hah! The guy thought he was all that. No way. Wiley was the man now. It was time for payback.

If only Wiley could tell Brandt what she had to look forward to. She'd hurl and run screaming. He'd had a rough time in prison, but it was nothing compared to what happened to a law enforcement officer locked up with cons. That was truly hell on earth.

He started down the road, keeping to the shadows. The risk of getting caught had been worth it to remove the GPS trackers so if the SEAL checked again, he would have no idea that Wiley had located their little boat and wouldn't be prepared for what was about to come.

Now all Wiley had to do was wait for his chance to take Tyler. Hopefully, they'd leave the kid alone tonight and Wiley could grab him. If not, he wasn't above creating a diversion to draw Tyler away.

He *would* get the kid. They could bank on that.

QUINN HAD TO END this thing before Ty or Nina got hurt. He glanced at his watch and guessed they had enough time to travel to Portland to talk to the Hacktivist's database administrator and get the other files Nina needed.

He stepped over to the dining table where Nina was working her way down the remaining names on the Hacktivist list. "The time has come to pay Odell another visit. We can do that and still be on time to meet Becca."

Nina eyed him warily. "It's late. We don't even know where to find Odell."

"We could stop by his office. If he's not there, we'll move on to his house."

"What if he's not home?" Nina shook her head. "I still have names on this list to contact. If I stay here, I can keep working. Besides, we don't have his home address."

"I have the address." Quinn smiled. "It was on an envelope on his desk. I grabbed a picture of it when he escorted you to the door. Just in case."

He expected a bit of admiration for his foresight but received a frown instead. "We could still sit out there for hours until he comes home. I can get a lot done while you and Ty try to locate Odell from here."

As much as Quinn respected her methodical approach to life,

sometimes it drove him absolutely batty. Now was one of those times. "How do you propose we do that?"

"Ty can use your computer to hack Odell's cell phone account, where he can track his GPS."

"Isn't that illegal?"

"Yes."

"Couldn't Ty get in trouble for it?"

"Not likely," Ty said joining in, a big grin on his face. "I'd be using your laptop, which, if I know you and all this spy business, can't be tracked back to you. Am I right?"

Quinn nodded, but he still wasn't ready to give in. "How long would it take to locate Odell's GPS?"

Ty shrugged. "I could do it in a few minutes or it might take hours. Depends on the security level of his password, or if he even has the GPS turned on."

Quinn looked at Nina. "That could take even longer than driving over there. Plus, if we have to sit in the car to wait for him, you could work from there. So, let's go."

She shook her head.

Quinn crossed his arms. "I've followed your plan and sat around for days now. It's time for you to give my plan a shot for once."

She chewed on her lip, her stubborn expression melting. "I'll go as long as we leave Ty here. Sulyard could be watching Odell's house, and I won't let Ty get even more involved in this."

"You good with staying here, bud?" Quinn asked.

Ty nodded, not displaying even a hint of anxiety. A moment of concern badgered Quinn, but he'd covered all bases and no one could possibly know they'd moved to the houseboat. As a precaution he'd just checked the truck for trackers, and as long as Ty didn't do anything to give away his location, he should be fine.

He fixed a hard stare on the kid. At a flash of defiance from Ty, Quinn felt like his father the control freak. So what? This wasn't as simple as the things they usually fought about. This was a matter of life and death. "We're meeting Becca at nine. We'll be home after that. No one knows our location, so you're safe. You have my new cell number if you need me. Stay inside. You can keep playing games. Don't make any calls. Or surf the web. Got it?"

Ty nodded, but the defiance remained.

Quinn stepped closer. "I mean it, Ty. This is serious business. If you're reckless, you could lead someone here and put Nina in jeopardy."

"Sheesh. Quit treating me like a baby. I got it already."

"See that you do." Quinn went to the counter to gather the items they might need. Nina joined him.

"We'll take the pickup." He headed for the door. "It's easier to maneuver and has four-wheel drive."

"You planning on doing some off-roading?"

"After the last few days, you never know what we might run into. I plan to be prepared."

QUINN SWUNG THE truck onto Odell's street.

"You should park down the block," Nina said. "In case Sulyard has someone watching the place."

Quinn had already thought of that—it wasn't his first rodeo, after all—but there was no point in mentioning it. After parking, he made a thorough sweep of the area with his binoculars. He'd know an agent if he saw one. Luckily, he didn't see one.

"We're clear." He climbed out and met Nina on the sidewalk. He stayed alert as they walked to an apartment building that needed a good coat of paint and fresh landscaping. The hallway wasn't much better.

At Odell's door, Nina faced him. "I'll do the talking."

"Fine by me." Quinn pounded on the door. "But I'm not leaving here without the database."

She opened her mouth to speak, but Odell answered the door before she could.

He scowled at them, his ever-present cigarette between his fingers. "What are you doing here?"

"We need to talk to you." Quinn pushed past Odell before he could refuse.

"I didn't invite you in."

"I invited myself." Quinn stared down at the slight man. "The sooner you quit complaining, the sooner we'll be out of your hair." Quinn continued to eye the man until he caved and led the way to a small dining area. He dropped onto a chair and flicked his ashes into a nearby ashtray. Nina took the chair next to him. Quinn remained standing, in case he needed to react.

Nina held up a flash drive they'd picked up on the way over. "We're here for the database."

"Then you wasted your time," Odell snapped. "I've already told you that it's not happening without another warrant. And I don't see one in your hand."

"Though I'm not at liberty to discuss our investigation, I can tell you it's related to national security and viewing the database could help us prevent a catastrophic incident."

"Hah!" He sneered at her. "If that's so, you'd have the warrant for the information by now."

Quinn had said he'd let Nina talk, but he didn't like the way Odell was staring at her. Quinn glared at the man. "Don't make me step in and ask for access, or you'll wish you hadn't."

In his periphery, Quinn saw Nina fist her hands. He suspected she was glowering at him, but he wouldn't turn away from Odell to check.

The man seemed to be warring with what to do.

Good. Quinn had the guy on the fence. So he took a step closer. Crossed his arms. Flexed his muscles. Took another step and let his hand drift to his gun. "Now."

"Fine." He swung his gaze back to Nina. "I don't care if you're an agent. The minute you leave here, I'm calling the police to report your abuse."

Quinn had to give Nina credit. She didn't react at all except to say, "Guess you need to do whatever you need to do."

"But you might want to wait a few minutes before making the call." Quinn smirked. "I might decide to turn around and come right back."

"I'll get my computer." Huffing, Odell grabbed a laptop bag hanging on a nearby chair. Once he had the computer running, he sat down. Nina stood behind him to watch. Quinn hung to the side—after all, he had no idea what to look for on the computer, but he sure knew how to keep Nina safe.

"I'm creating administrator access for you." Odell started typing.

"So you can turn around and delete my account the minute we walk out that door?" Nina thumped the guy's shoulder. "I don't think so."

He glared up at her. "So what do you want, exactly?"

She waved the flash drive. "If you'll get up, I'll take over and download two copies of the current database, daily backups, and log files."

His eyes narrowed. "You don't need the backups or the logs."

"You're right," she drawled. "I don't, unless of course, I want to check to see if any records have been deleted."

Odell ground out his cigarette, his thumb mashing the butt flat. "I haven't deleted a thing."

"I guess we'll see about that. Because I'm not leaving here without the backups or logs."

Quinn wanted to step forward and jerk the guy out of his chair, but he shoved his hands in his pockets and stood back to let Nina resolve this.

"Don't worry," she said to Odell. "I know what I'm doing. You can watch my every move."

He stared up at her. "I can do it."

"No," she said, her voice brooking no argument. "I want to be sure I have everything I need."

Odell didn't move.

"You don't want us to have to come back, do you?" Nina gestured at Quinn. "My friend here gets very cranky when he has to waste time. Trust me, you don't want that."

Odell tapped another cigarette from his pack and stood as he lit it. He moved slowly, acting as if he was in charge, but Quinn could see he was mad and frustrated at the same time.

Nina sat. Quinn stepped behind her where he could see what she was doing and still keep an eye on Odell. She clicked on a link called "phpMyAdmin", whatever that was. Quinn wouldn't understand even if he asked, so he didn't bother. She clicked on *Export* and files started downloading to her flash drive. Odell watched her, too, alternately puffing and blowing smoke. She repeated the process, over and over.

Thirty minutes later, she removed the flash drive. She stared at Odell. "Now I'll take that admin access, and we'll get out of your hair."

Odell sat and within a few minutes, he'd given Nina a login and password. She recorded it in a note program on the iPhone Quinn had given her and then confirmed it worked.

"Thanks for your cooperation," she said, stowing the phone. "I suggest you refrain from disabling my access."

"Let me guess," Odell said. "Your friend will come back if I do."

Quinn cocked an eyebrow. "You're a quick study, Odell. Remember what I said about waiting to call the cops. I *will* come back here, and you'll wish I hadn't."

Chapter Twenty-Seven

AT THE RESTAURANT, Nina sat across the table from Quinn and sipped her coffee. She saw Becca step through the door and pause to search the room. She caught sight of them and frowned.

"I don't like the look on Becca's face." Nina watched her friend wind her way though the tables.

"I'm assuming she knows Ty is no longer in their custody," Quinn said. "But do you think she's found out about Hamid's death or our visit to Odell?"

"With the size of her frown, it could be all three." Nina prepared herself for the upcoming conversation.

Becca smiled a wan greeting, then dropped the folders she was carrying onto the table before falling into a chair as if exhausted. "I have some bad news, I'm afraid." She glanced around and leaned closer to Nina. "Hamid's been murdered."

Nina couldn't fake a shocked reaction, nor would she lie to her friend. "I already know. I found the body."

"You what?" Becca exclaimed.

Nina recounted her story, including as much detail as possible. "I'm not proud of taking off and leaving him there, I can assure you."

"That's a tough one." Becca furrowed her forehead. "Under the circumstances, it was the only thing you could do, I suppose."

Nina slid the cell she'd found outside the cabin across the table. "He left this by the door. I looked it over and didn't find anything, but maybe one of the techs will see something I missed. I doubt they'll recover any prints. This guy seems too smart."

"I'll get someone on it the minute I get back to the office. Hopefully, this will lead to our killer."

Memories of the crime scene came flooding back. "Do you know the cause of death?"

Becca nodded. "As you know, Hamid had a heart condition. He had an ICD implanted in his chest. This device detects an abnormal heartbeat and delivers a shock internally to correct it."

"I don't follow," Nina said. "The ICD killed him?"

"Unfortunately, yes." Becca sat back and explained how the murderer had used Hamid's own monitor to kill him.

Quinn cast Becca a skeptical look. "You're certain of this?"

"DHS got a tech from the ICD manufacturer out to the morgue. He read Hamid's implanted device which recorded the shock."

Tears started welling up, and Nina worked hard to keep them in check. "That poor kid. What a horrible way to die. His parents must be sick."

"His mother is," Becca said. "I did the notification call with Connor. It wasn't easy. Especially when Mrs. Ahmadi realized she'd forgotten to take the monitor to the hotel. If she'd remembered, it would have been with her instead of at the house." Becca took a few deep breaths. "She'll spend her life feeling guilty."

Nina knew that grief. She'd lived it since Garrett died. "I wish I could help her."

"The best way to do that is to find the person who killed him," Quinn suggested.

Becca frowned.

"What is it?" Nina asked, sliding forward. "What's wrong?"

"With your computer background, reprogramming the transmitter would be a natural way for you to kill someone."

"There's no natural way for Nina to kill anyone." Quinn squared his shoulders as if ready to do battle. "This transmitter or monitor or whatever you call it. Have you found it?"

Becca shook her head. "Not yet, but a call was made to 911 using a phone we found in Hamid's hand. The caller claimed to be Hamid and said Nina was trying to kill him. So, Sulyard thinks that when he finds Nina, he'll find the monitor."

"Unbelievable." Nina sat back and crossed her arms.

"The killer most likely made that call," Quinn said.

"Yes, but with Hamid dead, we can't do a voice recognition comparison to prove it wasn't Hamid. Sulyard has no choice but to consider Nina a murderer."

"So I'm not only wanted for acts of terrorism, but murder, too." Nina huffed a sour laugh. "There's something I never thought I'd hear come out of my mouth."

"I wish that was all, but there's more." Becca pulled a report from a folder. "Agents recovered a prepaid phone when they searched your car."

Nina shook her head. "The hits just keep on coming."

"I'm sorry, Nina. I wish I had better news."

"This isn't your fault." Nina nodded at the report. "Let me have the rest of it."

Becca tapped the top page. "As you can see, the phone was activated and registered to you on Monday." She turned the page. "Another phone was found under Hamid's body, also registered to you."

"This makes no sense," Quinn said. "You don't register a phone in your name if you plan to kill someone and want to keep things on the QT. It defeats the purpose."

"Agreed." Becca looked at Quinn. "We can see that, because we know Nina's not guilty. But when you add the phone to the other evidence Sulyard has gathered, it makes a compelling case against Nina and a jury might buy into it."

Nina couldn't believe they were talking about a jury evaluating anything related to her, but she agreed with Becca. There was enough circumstantial evidence to cast serious doubt on her innocence. She had to figure this out before that happened. "So what was on the phone?"

Becca turned to another page of her report. "It was used to access your bank account and make the $20,000 transfer to Hamid. Plus there were texts from the last few days going to and from one number only. That phone was also registered on Monday in Hamid's name and he was holding that phone when he died."

"Hamid?" Nina looked up. "He couldn't possibly have sent any texts. He was in custody and didn't have access to a phone."

"The report supports him having a phone in his possession." Becca flipped to the last page. "The analysts cross-referenced cell tower hits to the texts received on the phone registered to you to get a geographical location where the text originated."

Nina scanned the report, her heart sinking. "Texts from Hamid came from the hotel where we put up the teens."

Becca tapped the report. "And check out the texts you supposedly sent. They originated from towers by your house and one near work. The last text occurred yesterday morning."

"Then this creep had to be where you were, watching you all this time." Quinn met Nina's gaze, and she wasn't surprised to see anger flaring in his eyes. "He could've . . ."

"What? Hurt me? Killed me?" She shook her head. "I feel so dumb for not having seen him."

"He didn't want to be seen," Becca said.

Quinn leaned closer to Nina. "Which means he's good at this, and we need to keep our vigilance up. You're not to go anywhere alone from this point forward. Got that. Nowhere."

"Relax," she said. "It's not like I'm planning to ditch you."

"That's good, then," Quinn said, sounding relieved.

"I agree." Becca eyed him. "At least until we find the killer."

Quinn cleared his throat, as if he didn't like her last comment. "So I have to ask. Since the texts originated from the hotel, is there any chance Ty could be involved in this?"

"Hamid and Ty had no interaction at the hotel and we found the phone on Hamid," Becca said. "Still, I suppose we could have missed something."

"I'll talk to Ty as soon as we get back to our safe house."

Becca arched an eyebrow. "Not the cabin?"

"I thought it was best to change locations." Quinn met Becca's gaze. "Is there any way this guy could be learning our location from your people?"

"No," she said quickly.

Quinn held up a hand. "Don't be in such a hurry to dismiss the idea. I checked our vehicles for GPS trackers and found none. So that means he had to have heard about it somewhere."

"Kait and I are the only ones who know the cabin location."

"Did you talk to Kait about it on the phone?"

She nodded.

"Then maybe your phone is compromised."

"Not likely, but I'll turn it off for now and check it when I get back to the office." She picked it up from the table and turned it off. "If for some crazy reason I'm the leak, I don't know your new location so that will be the end of that."

"Back to the investigation," Nina said peering at Becca. "Do you think Hamid really sent the texts?"

"Honestly, no. I doubt he could have gotten his hands on a phone. But we were unable to lift any physical evidence, DNA, or fingerprints from it, so we can't prove that he wasn't the one who sent the texts."

"My gut says he's being set up like Nina," Quinn said.

Becca arched a brow. "How can you be so sure of that?"

"I've seen Ty in action. He's more savvy about electronics than most adults. Hamid's the same. He may be a teenager, but if he planned to do something illegal, he wouldn't be dumb enough to register a phone to himself, any more than Nina would."

"True," Becca said.

"What do these texts sent to my supposed phone say?" Nina asked.

Becca flipped a few more pages to another printout. "The first text from you to Hamid was sent Tuesday at three a.m."

"That's when you guys made me go home to try to sleep and the NFL was hacked." Memories of that night came back, and her throat went dry. "He was outside, then. When I was in the shower. In bed."

Quinn gritted his teeth and settled a hand over hers, but didn't say a word. Nina didn't protest as she read the text aloud. "Test finalized. Screenshots attached. Money to follow shortly."

"Screenshots? What's he talking about?" Quinn asked.

"The NFL." Becca turned the page revealing pictures of the No-Fly List data entry screens. "Check out the date. This isn't Ty's initial hack, but the one done from the computer recovered at your house."

"Okay. So, he hacked the NFL and took screenshots," Quinn said. "Why?"

"Maybe as proof that he has access to the database. That could be what generated the cash we found in your account. Sort of like a down payment or a good faith payment."

"That makes sense," Nina said. "I mean $40,000 is a lot of money. But we all know having unfettered access to the NFL is worth far more."

"At first I believed he was making changes to the database for smaller payments, but check these out." Becca pointed at the next few texts. "The first is from Hamid to Nina on Tuesday morning."

Money received. Proceed with sale as planned.

Then Becca pointed at the last one. "Nina, this last text originated outside your house around the time Sulyard showed up. I think our suspect was sitting there, saw Sulyard arrive, then planted the cell in your car."

"Could be, I suppose." Nina read the last one from her to Hamid sent on Wednesday morning. *They're on to us. Am regrouping at our usual spot to complete transaction. Should have final payment tomorrow night. Don't use this cell again. Will be getting new ones. Give one to you at the meeting.*

"Okay," Nina said, thinking this through. "Was Hamid really involved or was he another patsy to make it look like I'm in cahoots with someone of Middle Eastern descent, bringing in the terrorism angle?"

Becca shrugged. "I know I sound like a broken record, but we still haven't found anything to suggest Hamid was involved, beyond hiding the computer."

"I was thinking," Quinn interjected. "If Hamid didn't send the texts, then the suspect knows about the hotel, too."

"We've considered that possibility, so we've moved Bryce as a precaution." Becca flashed a sharp look at Quinn. "Of course you've taken Ty, so he's not in any danger."

Quinn crossed his arms. "I'm not discussing that, so don't even try."

"What about hotel security videos?" Nina asked, bringing them back to the matter at hand before Quinn and Becca started arguing. "Has anyone reviewed them?"

"We're doing it now."

"I should probably tell you, we met with Odell," Nina confessed as she dug out one of her flash drives. "I made a copy of the database for you. I plan to scour it as soon as we get back to the safe house."

"You know we can't use this."

"Why in the world not?" Quinn demanded.

"Because it was obtained without going through the proper channels and protocols for retrieving data."

"So you'll ignore it because of your confounded rules? With a killer running around?"

Becca stared at him. "I'll be all over it, but I won't be able to show it to anyone else. When we catch this guy, anything I use from this to find him can't be used to bring him up on charges."

Quinn rolled his eyes. "I don't know how you guys work under these conditions."

"I don't know how you do some of the things you do, either." Becca gave him a pointed look before turning to Nina. "Sulyard will freak when he finds out you went to see Odell."

"That's the least of my worries right now. I want to make sure that you don't get in hot water, too."

"On that note—" Quinn slid a phone across the table to Becca. "We both have untraceable cells. I bought one for you, too. I programmed in both of our phone numbers."

Becca clutched the phone like a lifeline. "Perfect."

"Were you able to get my case files?" Nina asked.

"They're in the car."

"Then we'll walk out with you."

Quinn dropped a few bills on the table on the way out to Becca's car. She pulled a file box from her trunk, and Quinn opened the rear door of the pickup's cab. He reached for the box, but Becca ignored him and stepped past him.

After their testy interactions inside, Quinn had to think Becca was ignoring his offer of help to get to him, but Nina knew that wasn't the case. She was one of the most independent people Nina knew, never letting anyone do anything for her.

She hefted the files over the tailgate and suddenly gasped. Still holding the box, she backed away from the truck.

Nina moved closer. "What's wrong?"

"I think we found Hamid's missing monitor."

Chapter Twenty-Eight

NINA AND QUINN boarded the houseboat and found Ty lounging on the deck. Quinn went straight to Ty, partly to ask him if he had a phone at the hotel and partly to do something to keep his mind off the monitor discovery.

Quinn felt Nina standing behind him as he waited for Ty to make eye contact. "Did you have a phone at the hotel? Maybe send a few texts?"

"No," he said. "Why?"

"There were some unusual texts from that location. We're trying to figure who sent them."

Ty narrowed his eyes. "Right, and you thought of me first."

"You have been known to bend the rules, Ty."

"I know, geez." Ty jumped to his feet. "I'm not stupid. I get it. I'm a screw-up. How many times do you need to tell me?"

"I didn't say that." Quinn waited for Ty to calm down a bit. "I need to know the truth."

"I didn't send the texts, so lay off." He huffed and glared at Quinn before stomping off to the other side of the deck.

There was that attitude again. Quinn's frustration flared. He took a step to go after Ty. To let him have it like their father would do, but Nina rested a hand on Quinn's arm, reminding him that this was a perfect time to break that cycle.

He pulled in a deep breath, expanding his lungs to bursting and let it out. Repeated the motion several times. The SEAL creed came to mind.

The ability to control my emotions and my actions, regardless of circumstance, sets me apart from other men.

He had no problem with keeping his cool on the job, but with Sulyard earlier? And with Nina and his family, especially Ty? He hadn't managed it of late. He'd definitely lost it when he and Nina split up. And he'd wanted to strangle Ty so many times. . . . But Quinn was going to do his best to stop that.

He'd focus on the things he loved about Ty. His sense of humor.

His dopey grin. The loving kid who'd somehow lost his way in the last two years. That kid was still in there somewhere. Quinn would find him again.

Nina's hand still rested on his arm. Perhaps she believed he needed to be restrained. She had to be disappointed in him. He turned. Her hand dropped.

Quinn's frustration with Ty dissipated at her soft look of concern. "Sorry you had to see that. I wish I was half as good with Ty as you are. All I do is make him mad."

"Don't be so hard on yourself," she said. "You want to fix his problems. I simply want to let him know he's loved. It's pretty much the main difference in the way men and women react."

He shook his head. "It's more than that."

"Well." Her lips quirked up. "You're also a type-A person who jumps in with both feet before thinking about the best course of action. Guess that applies to your relationships as well."

He sensed a change in her tone. "You're talking about us now."

"Maybe." She stared off into the distance. He could almost see the gears churning in her mind.

"You're right, you know," he said. "About me. I react, then think, when it comes to people I care about. That's what happened when you gave me that ultimatum. I didn't think about it. Just acted." He paused to search for the right words to explain himself. "The team's my family, Nina. It has been for years. We've taken bullets for each other. Unless you've had someone willing to die for you, you can't really understand what it means to end that kind of connection. I couldn't let my team down."

"I appreciate the explanation, but there's really no reason to bring it up again." She sighed and took a step back. "You're not leaving the team, so there's no point."

"Don't be so sure about that," he said, the words flying from his mouth before he thought about it.

Her eyes widened. "Where's that coming from?"

That's exactly what he was wondering. Where *had* it come from?

He looked away. Brought his hand up to shove it into his hair. Feeling the scarred skin tighten, he dropped it and stared at the damage.

She took his hand and traced the scars. Her fingers were soft and tender in areas where his nerves still functioned. "You never did tell me what happened."

He wanted to share with her, but she'd admitted she still worried about his deployments and didn't really didn't need to know the horrific details. "That mission is still classified."

"See, here's the thing, Quinn. You say you want to talk about things. Then you back away, claiming things are classified when you know you can share enough for me to understand. But no. It's all on your terms." She dropped his hand. "You won't even let me see how bad the damage is."

He felt his anger rising. Anger at the situation. Anger at the injury. Anger that he used to be able to control before the explosion.

"You want to see?" He ripped off his shirt to display the scars that ran up his arm and over his shoulder. "There. See? Not a pretty sight."

He waited for her to cringe, but she gently took his wrist in her hands and turned his arm to study it. She ran her fingers over the surface, her touch as light as a butterfly. He'd expected her eyes to fill with pity if she ever saw his burns. It was something he'd gotten plenty of at the hospital. He'd heard the nurses when they didn't know he was listening, talking about how hard it must be to bear the damage when he was in his physical prime. He'd expected Nina to act the same way.

Instead, her eyes burned with compassion. With love. That set his heart beating hard. He wanted to wrap that damaged arm around her back and jerk her into his arms. To kiss her senseless. To beg for her to give him a second chance. To agree to give up everything and be at her side no matter what. But that wouldn't be fair to her. Not when he didn't know if he could follow through.

She looked up at him. "I'm sorry, Quinn. I can only imagine how painful this must have been. I wish I could have been there for you while you were recuperating, helping you work through what happened that day. Whatever *it* was."

He'd wished that too—day after day, while undergoing debridement of his wounds, when he'd lay in bed reliving the explosion. He'd missed her. Missed her goodness. Her smile. Her love. He couldn't have that. Couldn't promise what she needed. But he could at least give her one thing she asked for. He could tell her about that day.

"The building exploded in front of us," he said quietly. "Knocked us all on our butts and punched the air right out of me. Sully was in front of me when it hit. A wall landed on top of him and immediately caught fire. When I could breathe again, I saw him. Trapped. I ripped the rubble off him before his clothes started burning. The flames must have caught my sleeve, but I didn't notice them until after I'd freed Sully. I dropped to the ground, but by then, the damage was done."

"Thank you for telling me." She moved closer, circled her arms around his waist, then laid her head on his chest.

He rested his chin on her soft curls and blew out all the past turmoil between them in a long breath. This felt so good, like he'd finally found that place he'd been searching for. A place to put down roots.

He pulled back, traced the side of her face with his finger, then let his arms fall. "Seeing you again has given me a lot to think about."

"Me, too."

A strong wind pummeled the boat, sending it rocking. A moment of unease darkened her eyes.

"Do you want to go inside to get away from the water?" he asked.

She shrugged. "The more time I spend near it, the better I'm doing." She turned to the river. "It's hard to believe something this beautiful terrifies me."

"I think most people have some irrational fear."

She glanced at him. A shaft of moonlight highlighted her face. She was more beautiful than the river, and he couldn't take his eyes off her. Didn't want to take his eyes off her. Ever. Thinking of losing her again sent his own irrational fear swimming through him.

He jerked his gaze away and slipped his shirt over his head. "I should go see if Ty's okay."

"Want some advice?"

"Sure," he said, though he really wanted to bolt.

"It's natural for you to come across like your dad. He's what you saw, growing up. But forget how he dealt with the two of you. Pretend Ty's one of the guys on the team and talk to him."

"I have things in common with the guys. But Ty? We're nothing alike."

"Yes, you are. He adores you, Quinn. He may not show it because you're always riding him, but if you lighten up, he'll open up. You just have to try it."

She could be right. In fact, she likely was. He'd give it a go. "Okay, then. Wish me luck."

"You're an amazing man." She grabbed his hand and threaded her fingers with his. "But you're way too busy looking for the next adrenaline fix, trying to prove you're not your dad, to even know that about yourself. You're not your dad. You're nothing like him. You care— deeply—and value people. Let Ty see that, and the two of you will be fine."

Her words mimicked his earlier thoughts, and the truth hit him hard. It was time to let this thing with his dad go before he ruined his relationship with his brother. Before he lost a chance at ever repairing things with Nina.

"Thank you for being so wise," he said, then kissed the top of her head.

"Quick, let me write that down so that when we're old and gray, I can remind you that you once said it." She flashed him a cute grin, then went inside.

Old and gray. Together. He liked his addition to her comment. He headed to the other side of the boat and found Ty sprawled out in a lounger.

"Mind if I sit here?" Quinn asked.

Ty's phone was in his hand, as usual. He didn't respond.

Quinn's irritation instantly rose, but he tamped it down and took a seat. "The river's something to see in the moonlight, huh?"

Ty glanced at Quinn, then stared over the water. "Yeah."

"Reminds me of when I'd come home on leave. If Dad was home, we'd all go fishing."

"Yeah."

"We had a lot of fun."

"Yeah.

"Too bad you hate fishing so much or we could do it again. You know, you and me."

"Who says I hate fishing?"

Quinn shot him a look. "I figured that's the reason you stopped coming with us."

He shook his head. "I like fishing okay. Dad stopped asking."

Quinn replayed the past, trying to remember when Ty no longer joined them, or if he'd ever talked about Ty with his father. Quinn couldn't remember a specific conversation. He'd just always had the feeling that Ty didn't do anything other than play with his computers.

"Guess I assumed it." Quinn stared over the river again. "Would you like to do it again after this mess gets cleared up? Just you and me."

"Sure."

"Okay, then, we will," Quinn said, his shoulders lighter than they'd been in years.

WILEY BLENDED INTO the darkness as he crouched next to a small storage shed on the houseboat's deck. They had no idea he was there. Watching. Listening. Smiling over Brandt's crazy fear of the water. *Big baby.* Then there was the big, tough SEAL. Getting all sappy and mushy with his brother.

Wiley almost barfed . . . until a moment of jealousy bit into him. He'd wanted a family connection like this, but got parents who didn't have a feeling bone in their bodies. Actually, they couldn't feel anything now, at all. He smiled grimly. But in the past, when he was younger, it would have been nice. He'd wanted to be loved.

He'd gotten indifference.

He'd be taking this away from Brandt, too. No way the kid or the SEAL would hang around when she was found guilty of Hamid's murder and went away for life.

Ah, yes, he was still on top. Still the victor. *If* he managed to hack the database. Thanks to Brandt, he was now one step closer. She'd shown him where to find Tyler. As soon as the kid was alone, Wiley would snatch the brat out of their safety net.

QUINN HAD DONE it. Broken through Ty's wall with a simple suggestion. Nina smiled and returned to the dining table. She shouldn't have eavesdropped on their conversation, but she cared about them both and wanted them to get along better. Both. Yeah, it was time to admit it. She was still in love with Quinn, and she didn't have a clue what she should do about it. If there even was anything to do.

The pair came back inside and settled into chairs. The air in the room felt lighter.

Quinn pulled out a chessboard. "Want to play, Ty?"

"Sure."

They were both trying so hard. She felt like a proud mother, and her anxieties melted away. She'd avoid thinking about Quinn's earlier hint that he might consider leaving the team and enjoy this moment when her little family was in a good place.

She turned back to the database log files on her computer.

"Good thing Q put a computer in his supplies or you'd be out of luck, Nina," Ty called out. His obvious respect for his brother made her smile widen. Even Quinn grinned.

She clicked on the first log file. An hour later, she located a big red flag.

"Got something here," she announced and clicked on a few screens before sitting back in surprise. "Hamid's deleted post isn't connected to Odell's login, but a guy named Kip Ulrich, who also has administrator rights to the website."

Quinn joined her at the table. "Exactly what does that mean?"

"It means he can make changes to anything and everything. But what's bothering me is that Odell didn't mention a second admin."

"That's odd, isn't it?"

"Very." She scanned Ulrich's record. "He was one of the members who viewed the cache."

Excitement sparked in Quinn's eyes. "You think he's involved, then?"

"Don't get too excited," she warned. "As an administrator, Odell has access to all of the logins and could have used Ulrich's login to make these changes. Or he could have made this guy up so the deletion of the post wasn't tied to him."

"Do we have contact information?"

She nodded.

Quinn shot to his feet. "Then I guess it's time for us to pay this mysterious Kip Ulrich a visit."

Chapter Twenty-Nine

SEVERAL EMPLOYEES sat outside the large office building at Ulrich's workplace. They were eating what Quinn could only assume was lunch for the late shift of workers. An average-size male stood and wound through the tables. He was wearing black pants with suspenders and a short-sleeved white shirt with bowtie. His gaze ran up and down Nina, making Quinn want to deck the squirrely guy.

"I don't like this, Nina," Quinn said. "Ulrich looks all kinds of weasely."

"Well don't let it show. He'll clam up, and we won't get a thing out of him."

"Let me guess. You want to do all the talking."

She glanced at him. "I'm that predictable, am I?"

"Yes, and honestly, I like it. It's something I can count on."

She looked surprised, but Ulrich stepped up to them, drawing her attention.

"Agent Nina Brandt." She shot out her hand.

Quinn suspected it was because she didn't have credentials to display.

Ulrich didn't take her hand. "I know who you are."

Quinn found his combative attitude odd, but Quinn didn't want to give the guy time to request her ID, so he herded them toward a private space to talk.

"Thanks for seeing us at such short notice," Nina said.

"Let me be clear, I'm only doing it for Ham. I like him. If he's in trouble, I'll do anything I can to help." He sat on the edge of a stone bench and planted his hands on his bony knees

Quinn glanced at Nina to see if she noted that Ulrich was talking about Hamid as if he were still alive. Nina gave the briefest of nods in acknowledgement.

"How well do you know Hamid?" She sounded casual as she sat next to Ulrich, but Quinn saw the distress from Hamid's death lingering in her expression.

Ulrich scooted away from her, moving to the far end of the bench. "Not real well, but I was worried about him when he posted about needing his computer back. Thank goodness my roommate and I found it, so I could get it back to him."

"Wait!" The word exploded from Nina's mouth, making Ulrich lurch back. "You found the computer? The one in the cache?"

He nodded, his glasses sliding down his ski-slope nose. "Technically, my roommate found it, but I told him about Ham's post, so he gave the computer back."

"Is that why you deleted the post from the Hacktivist database and tried to erase all record of it?'

"What? No. I didn't delete anything from the database. That's not sound procedure for database management. As a computer professional, you should know that." He eyed her. "I didn't change any files at all. Just looked at Hamid's posts."

"So you only visited the website twice, then?"

He crossed his arms. "That's what I said."

"That's odd. The logs show you accessing the site two additional times. First to view the cache before Hamid took it down, and then a second time when you deleted Hamid's post."

"That wasn't me."

"Someone impersonating you, then?"

He tipped his head in thought. "It has to be Victor. He's the only one who could get my access information. Though, I doubt he would delete a record."

"We'll have a chat with Odell and ask him about that." She paused. "But for now, let's go back to the computer you found. You claim it's been returned to Hamid, but he's been in the FBI's custody for days, and no one has returned the computer to him."

"You're lying to me." He tsked. "Not surprising. I know how you like to lie to get the maximum sentence for people you arrest."

"What in the world are you talking about?"

"C'mon Agent Brandt." He glared at her. "We both know what you did. I see it in my roommate's eyes every day."

Quinn stepped closer to draw the guy's venomous gaze from Nina. "What's your roommate's name?"

"Not like she cares, but it's Wiley. Wiley Fagan."

"Wiley Fagan. Oh." Nina clutched her chest. "Him."

Even in the dark, Quinn could see the color drain from her face. He knew immediately that this guy was someone Nina feared.

THE MIST FROM Wiley's breath lingered in the cold air as he crossed the parking lot to the houseboat. Soft swells of the river lapped against boats. Muted and rhythmic, it allowed his sure and swift movements onto the deck and to the door. His hands were cold from sitting in the car, making him fumble the lockpick, but he soon had the door open. Drawing his gun from his belt, he found Tyler slouched on a sofa, his feet up, and his face in his cell phone. He didn't have a clue Wiley was creeping up on him from behind.

"Time to take off, kid." Wiley waited for Tyler to jump up in surprise.

"You must have the wrong boat." He didn't bother to look up.

His lack of fear made Wiley mad. "Ah, no I don't, Tyler. I'm here for you."

That made the kid shoot his head around, his eyes widening when he saw the gun.

Wiley gestured at the coffee table. "Lay face down on the floor by the table."

"Dude. I don't know you. Why would I do what you want me to do?" Tyler asked, that fear still missing.

The kid was spunky, Wiley would give him that, but he wouldn't put up with it. He jiggled the gun in the kid's face.

"Gee, let's see," Wiley said, coating his words in sarcasm. "Should you do it because I asked so nicely, or because I'm holding a .38 and could blow you away with the jerk of my finger? Your choice. But Tyler,"—Wiley made strong eye contact—"you should know that the last time someone refused to do as I asked, I wasn't afraid to use my gun." He grinned. "I wasn't afraid at all."

ULRICH FIRED AN angry look at Nina. "I'm not surprised at your reaction, after what you did to Wiley. Making sure he went away for the max time. That was harsh."

Nina barely heard him as the details of Fagan's case played like a video in her mind. Acid rose up her throat. He was a ruthless hacker, not feeling any remorse for the people he scammed out of millions of dollars. That man, that barbarian, was in possession of the computer. She had no doubt he'd sell it to the highest bidder.

And this kid next to her thought she was the bad guy. *Unbelievable.*

"I'm not sure what Wiley told you about his case," she said, trying to gentle her voice to disarm Ulrich's anger. "But a group of jurors found him guilty of unethical hacking. He stole credit card numbers and caused irreparable damage to thousands of people. He was given plenty of chances to offer his regret for the pain and loss he caused, but he said nothing. Many of his victims lost everything, and he didn't care. That's why he got the maximum sentence. It wasn't anything I said or did."

"He said you would say something like that."

The acid burned higher. "You told him you were meeting with me?"

"No. But he rants about you all the time. He also said if I ever ran into you, you'd play dumb."

"Look, Ulrich." She wanted nothing more than to tell him his friend had killed Hamid so Ulrich would see Fagan for who he was, but she wouldn't divulge confidential information. "I get that you want to protect your friend. It's an admirable trait. He's lucky to have you. I'm sorry if you think I'm the one who hurt him. But be that as it may, we are dealing with a national security issue here. We need to retrieve that computer. If Fagan still has it, we need to talk to him."

"Good luck." Ulrich crossed his arms. "He won't talk to you."

"Listen up, kid." Quinn stepped in, appearing as irritated as she felt. "Agent Brandt is a lot more patient than I am. Plus, she's bound by rules and ethics that I don't care about right now. My kid brother is in trouble because that computer is missing."

"I know." Ulrich smirked.

Quinn hauled Ulrich to his feet and glowered at the little pipsqueak. "You're going to tell me what you know right now."

Nina waited to act until fear consumed Ulrich's eyes. "Put him down, Quinn."

"Be glad to. As soon as the punk tells me what I want to know."

"All I know is that Wiley saw a picture of the three of you on Facebook. He keeps talking about paying Agent Brandt back, but I don't think he really would."

Quinn let go. Ulrich dropped to the bench like a puppet with severed strings.

"And the computer?" Nina asked.

"I don't know where it is. Honestly, I don't."

"Where can we find Fagan?"

"He hangs out at a coffee shop a lot of the day." Ulrich gave them the name of a nearby place. "When he's not there, he's home or out trying to find a job." Ulrich aimed a testy look at Nina. "I'm sure you know isn't easy for a convicted felon to find one of those."

"In case Fagan isn't home, I'll take the key to your apartment so we can look for the computer," Quinn demanded.

"I don't think that's a good idea." Ulrich bit his lip.

Quinn took a step toward Ulrich, but Nina stepped in. "Give us the key, or we'll have to take you in for questioning. You'll lose time at work. Of course, you'll also have to explain to your boss and co-workers why the FBI is hauling you off in cuffs."

"Fine." He jerked a key from a *Star Wars* key ring. "I get off at 7:00. You better have it back here by then so I can get in."

Nina took the key. "We'll do our very best."

"It's apartment 3C." Ulrich gave them the address, then turned to leave.

Quinn clamped a hand on the guy's shoulder. "You'd better not be calling Fagan to warn him we're coming. Or you'll find yourself arrested for aiding and abetting a criminal."

"I won't call." His voice wasn't much louder than the squeak of a mouse.

"Nice add," Nina said as they walked to the car. "I couldn't have done any better myself."

"Hopefully, I'll do just as well at locating and nabbing this Fagan guy."

QUINN SWUNG THEIR vehicle into Ulrich's apartment complex, and Nina pulled her gun from her ankle holster.

Quinn drew his .45 and chambered a round, then jumped out of the car. He seemed a little too eager to be using his gun, Nina thought. Although it wasn't surprising. He was a soldier, after all. But she wouldn't let him take over the way he had with the other people they'd questioned.

She hurried after him and grabbed his arm. "You're not pushing your way into Fagan's apartment like you did with Odell."

"Now's not the time to hang back." He raised his eyebrow in a challenge. "It's the time to act."

"Think of this as one of your missions. You would create a detailed plan and practice the scenario over and over, right? You don't run in half-cocked."

"When all hell's breaking loose around us, we go in barrels blazing."

"Hell isn't breaking loose here." She sighed. "It's not a matter of life or death. Even if it was, you would have a group of men backing you up. We're a team of two, and we need to work out a strategy first. One needs to take the front of the building. The other, the back, in case Fagan bolts."

"I'll take the front," he insisted. "You the back. Contain if necessary."

She shook her head. "You've got it backwards, pal. I'm already risking my job by not calling Sulyard in to check this out first. If we disturb anything, Fagan could use our mistake to escape charges. I won't let that happen. Which means I need to go in first, so I can be sure protocol is followed. No more Neanderthal man, okay?"

"Neanderthal man. Is that what you think of me?"

"Let's just say you're used to getting your way using intimidation and force if necessary. I'm not saying that's all you are, but that attitude has definitely come out when someone hasn't immediately cooperated with me."

"Okay, fine. I may have a thing about people giving you a hard time." He paused, then added, "Especially men."

"Do you know how crazy that sounds, coming from the man who put me through one of the hardest times in my life?"

He seemed genuinely upset, and she used the distraction to start up the walkway to the low-slung apartment building. She didn't hear him coming after her. At the building entrance, she glanced back and saw him still standing there. She jerked her head toward the back and entered the building. At Fagan's apartment, she pounded on the door. "FBI!"

There was no answer. She knocked and announced herself again. Nothing.

In case he was waiting to ambush her, she stood to the side and opened the door with the key Ulrich provided. The place seemed empty. She surveyed the area, which was lit by a streetlight and the LED on a gaming console.

Keeping her back to the wall, she stepped into the hallway that led to a living room. She swung into an opening on the right. A small kitchen, just big enough for a microwave and refrigerator. No Fagan. Back in the hallway, step by step, she moved to the family room. Quick sweep. To the right. A bedroom and bathroom. Both small. Both vacant. She turned to go back to the door, only to bump into Quinn.

Startled, she jumped back. She hadn't heard him behind her. Not a squeak. Not a whisper. He was in stealth mode again, which scared her as much as it thrilled her.

"So much for watching the back door," she managed to say, even though her heart was thumping wildly.

"I didn't like the idea of you in here alone. Not if Fagan's a killer." He held up his hand. "Before you say I don't respect your skills, I do. I just . . ." He shrugged. "Thinking about anyone laying a hand on you makes me crazy. As does the thought of losing you. Can we leave it at that for now?"

He was right. While they were standing in the middle of Fagan's apartment was not the time to talk about their personal situation. It was the time to search the place and find a lead to help them capture the man who wanted to send her to prison for life.

Chapter Thirty

FOR HOURS, QUINN stood out front of the coffee shop Fagan frequented, watching for the guy. It made Quinn cold and cranky. He'd tried to think about the stakeout as one of his ops where the conditions were often brutal, but with Nina on his mind, he couldn't make the transition.

He'd left her outside Fagan's apartment until Becca could assign someone to watch the place in case Fagan came home. Quinn didn't like leaving her alone. It was more than his concern for her safety. They'd been together a lot in the last few days and he missed her company.

So how are you going to walk away when this is resolved?

The light went out inside the shop, and the baristas locked up before departing. So Fagan was a no-show. Grateful to be on the move instead of lost in his thoughts, he pushed off the tree and booked it down the street to Ulrich's apartment. Nina sat behind the wheel of the SUV, and he dropped into the passenger seat. It wasn't much warmer inside, but at least the wind wasn't cutting through his jacket.

"Perfect timing," she said before he closed the door. "Becca has Fagan's prison file and hopefully we'll find something in there that leads to him. She's on her way over here now with the ERT team to process Fagan's place. She'll text us when she gets close to give us a location where we can meet her. That way I can still keep an eye on the apartment until she gets here and can take off before anyone on the team sees us."

"Sounds like a plan." He settled into the seat.

She peered at him for a long time, searching for something he couldn't decipher. "I know we've had our differences." She sighed, her breath coming out in a cloud of steam. "I've been a bear to be around, but thanks for disregarding that and being here for me."

He rested his hand over hers. "There's nothing I'd like better than to be there for you all the time."

She shot him a puzzled look. "But you can't . . . I mean . . . what are you saying?"

"Honestly." He locked eyes with her. "When it comes to you, I don't know what I mean anymore. Other than you're very important to me and the thought of leaving the team doesn't seem as daunting as it once did."

A look of regret crossed her face, but she didn't speak.

Her phone chimed, and she seemed relieved for the interruption. "It's a text from Becca. We need to go."

It was just as well. He'd laid it all out there for her. He'd never done that before, and she didn't say a word in response. She didn't have to. Her silence said she wasn't ready to give him a second chance. She might never be ready. He was a fool for even contemplating it.

They drove to a nearby restaurant with an all-you-can-eat pizza bar. Quinn's mouth started watering the minute they entered the door. Nina chose a slice of vegetarian pizza, totally out of character for her, but he loaded his plate with slices covered in thick chunks of pepperoni and large mounds of spicy sausage. They sat in a booth across from each other. She grabbed the sugar container and dumped about a pound of it into her iced tea.

"What gives?" He nodded at her plate. "You'd give up your life before going without fried chicken, so I know you're not a vegetarian."

"My stomach's been a bit unsettled since all this started. I thought the grease might upset it." She glanced at his plate. "Guess you're not having a problem with that."

"I've learned to eat pretty much anything when I'm hungry enough."

She frowned, and he suspected she was thinking about his deployments again.

"So tell me more about Fagan," he said to change direction.

She swallowed hard, then took a long drink of the tea.

Nice one. Bring up an even bigger problem.

She set her glass on the table, turned it a few times, then looked at him. "You know those people who can look you in the face and lie to you? You know they're lying, but you can't find anything concrete to prove it?"

"I've seen my share of people like that over the years."

"Well, Fagan was—or I should probably say, *is*—a master at it. Clean cut. Well spoken. An all-American kind of guy on the outside. But he always seemed like he had an evil secret. Like he'd pulled something over on me, you know?"

His mouth full of a pizza, Quinn nodded.

"After we arrested and charged him, I figured his secret was out in the open, but the look never left his face. Even after he was sentenced and on his way to prison, there was still something about him that made me think he'd done something bigger. Something grander that he wanted to brag about, but couldn't."

Quinn didn't like the sound of this guy and hated that he was likely the man who had set Nina up. "Did he ever threaten you?"

"No," she replied, seeming lost in thought. "He just stared at me with that smug expression as he walked out of the courtroom. I never heard from him again and, honestly, I forgot all about him."

The bells above the front door jangled. Quinn shot a look at the entrance, his hand drifting to his weapon. Becca stepped inside and he waved her over.

Hugging a folder to her chest, she hurried across the room and slid in next to Nina. "Fagan's still a no-show. We have a detail watching his place."

The waitress joined them and set a glass of water in front of Becca. "You want the buffet, too?"

Becca shook her head. "Your house salad to go, please."

Quinn remembered Becca was a health-food nut. He tried to eat well for the most part, but didn't live his life by it. Still, he admired her dedication.

"To go?" Nina faced Becca when the waitress departed. "Aren't we going to talk about Fagan?"

"Sorry. Can't," Becca said, her expression unreadable. "Someone tried to hack the NFL again today. I need to get back."

"Tried?" Quinn asked.

"They used the same vulnerability Ty had exploited, but as I mentioned, DHS finished the work Ty started and the NFL is safe for now."

"That's good, then," Nina exclaimed.

Becca didn't respond at first, and Quinn had to wonder what she wasn't telling them. He didn't think Nina could handle any more bad news, but if there was more, they had to hear it if they were to clear Nina's name.

"What aren't you telling us?" Quinn asked.

Becca took her time, slowly resting her hands on the table. Then she looked at Nina. "DHS warned that thanks to Ty's hack, they uncovered additional issues in the database, and a good hacker could find his way around them. They're working overtime to fix the problem."

"So you're saying the person who took Ty's computer might be able to find these vulnerabilities, too," Quinn clarified.

"Unfortunately, yes," Becca said without looking at him, focusing on her hands instead. "Hackers are often very talented. Many of them are better than the legit programmers who coded the site in the first place. They have to be to circumvent security protocols."

Quinn didn't like the fact that the database was still vulnerable, but it seemed there was still something else on Becca's mind. "I'm guessing since DHS fixed the first problem, it means their deal with Ty is off," he asked.

She looked up, meeting his gaze squarely. "I'm sorry, Quinn, but I don't know what's going on with that."

"If they used Ty's work to help fix it, they'll honor the deal, right?" Nina asked.

"We'll do whatever we can to make sure it happens," Becca offered. "Once this is all over, that is."

"Were you able to track the signal of today's hack?" Nina asked.

Becca faced Nina. "We traced it back to the Diamond Hotel in the Old Town area."

"Hotel." Nina's voice rose in excitement. "Maybe that's where Fagan is holed up, and why we didn't find him at the coffee shop or his apartment." She swung her gaze to Quinn. "We should get down there."

Becca shot up a restraining hand. "Sulyard already has a team tearing the place apart. Unfortunately, he still believes you're the one he's searching for. So, if you show up there . . ."

"I'll be arrested, and . . ." Nina's voice fell off, and Quinn could see the desperation settling into her eyes. She was probably thinking about Ulrich's comment on how a law enforcement officer might be treated in prison.

"Don't lose hope, Nina," Becca said. "I'm headed down to the hotel now to meet up with Connor. We can be your eyes and ears and report back to you."

"Thank you," Nina said, but Quinn could tell her heart wasn't in it.

Becca's phone rang. She grabbed it from the holder on her belt. "Speaking of Connor." She answered her phone, then listened for a few moments. "He wants to talk to us on speaker." She pressed a few buttons and set the phone on the table. "Go ahead, Connor."

"Becca asked me to do some digging into Fagan's activities," he said without a greeting. "She wondered if we'd picked him up for anything else since his prison release."

"And did you?" Quinn asked.

"Not for anything official, but he's on our radar. His parents disappeared a few days ago. Neighbors reported it. They said the couple just up and vanished. There's been no sign of them. The detectives who caught the case say things aren't adding up. They suspect Fagan killed them, but they can't prove it yet."

Nina's face paled. "Why do they suspect him?"

"One neighbor says he's got a paranoid disorder with a capital P and has always had a weird relationship with his parents."

Nina shot a look at Becca. "That's odd. We didn't find anything like that when we prosecuted him."

"Neighbors claim the parents were in denial," Connor continued. "They never took Fagan in for treatment, so there aren't any records."

Nina took a deep breath, consciously focusing on her breathing. Quinn thought she was approaching the end of her rope, a place he'd only seen once. When he'd bailed on her. He didn't want her to go there again.

He had to do something to help. "Can we get a copy of the detective's file? Maybe it'll jog something in Nina's mind to help locate him faster."

"Sure," Connor said. "I'll give a copy to Becca when she gets down here."

Becca promised to be there soon and ended the call. "I'm so glad Kait arranged for Connor to work with us. I doubt another detective would be as willing to share."

Quinn detected a note of something other than gratitude in Becca's voice, but he wasn't about to question it when he needed to keep his full focus on helping Nina.

The waitress dropped off Becca's salad and ended their conversation. "You can pay at the register."

"I got this." Nina took the check. "It's the least I can do."

"Thanks." Becca stood, then reached for her salad and shook her head. "Look at me. I'm so distracted I almost forgot." She handed the folder she'd been clutching to Nina. "Fagan's prison file. I haven't had a chance to review it, but after hearing Connor talk about him, it should make for interesting reading." Becca squeezed Nina's shoulder. "Let me know if you need anything else. I'll keep you updated on developments at the hotel."

Nina said goodbye as she pushed her plate away and opened the file. Quinn knew she'd share the pertinent details, so he continued eating. Her lips moved as she read, and she ran her finger down the page, looking studious. And just plain adorable.

"He was a model prisoner." She flipped the page. "Which is odd, because he was denied parole." She fell silent, but her lips kept moving. "Oh, wow. He tried to hang himself shortly after incarceration. That put him in counseling with the facility psychiatrist. He said Fagan was unstable. He hinted at psychosis—a delusional or paranoid disorder—and suggested detainment in a mental health facility until Fagan's release date."

Quinn finished chewing. "Just like Fagan's neighbors mentioned. That means the guy is feeling persecuted and thinks everyone's out to get him."

"So when I arrested him, he took it as a personal attack and thought I'd purposefully targeted him. Like he's doing to me. Now, he wants me to see how awful his life was behind bars by putting me there to get a first-hand taste of it." She shuddered.

Quinn took her hand in his and met her gaze. "I don't like this, sweetheart. This guy is unstable and dangerous. And he's gunning for you."

"Not literally gunning for me."

"I don't care if it's literal or not. He's dangerous. And before we get into a discussion about how qualified you are to handle something like this, just humor my insecurities and promise you will let me protect you."

He waited for her to get mad at him, but she smiled. "I don't think it's necessary, but if it'll make you feel better, you can protect away."

"Honestly?"

She shrugged. "Why not? It's who you are. What you do. I'm tired of fighting it."

"Thank you," he said.

If their theory was right, this guy could have a plan to send her to jail. But even the best-laid plans sometimes went wrong.

And considering this guy was mentally ill, Quinn could easily see things going very, very wrong.

QUINN GOT NINA settled in the SUV, and she immediately pulled out her phone. Quinn couldn't imagine who she was calling, so he asked.

"The prison psychiatrist," she answered as she opened the folder. "Maybe he can tell us more about Fagan."

Quinn cranked the engine. "It's a little late for that, isn't it?"

"I'm sure they have a mental health professional on staff 24/7, so the psychiatrist could be working. If he's not in, I'll leave a message."

As Quinn backed out of the space, she dialed.

"This is Special Agent Nina Brandt," she said pleasantly. "Is Dr. Driscoll in, by any chance?"

Quinn didn't know how she could be so sweet after everything that had happened tonight, but he knew her grandmother had drilled proper manners into Nina. He could now see how valuable those lessons had been.

"What do you mean?" she asked the person on the other end of the line. "I don't understand. How did it happen?" She listened intently.

"I see." She paused. "No. I really needed to talk with him. Thank you." She hung up and stared down at the folder.

"What's going on?"

"The psychiatrist died this week."

Quinn whipped his head around to stare at her. "Murdered?"

"No, they said it was a heart attack."

"But you're thinking Fagan had something to do with it."

"It would be awfully coincidental that both Hamid and the psychiatrist died from a heart issue. I need to tell Becca, so she can give a heads up to the detectives investigating the death of Fagan's parents."

She dialed Becca, and after a quick conversation, Nina hung up and stared out the window for the rest of their trip. Quinn didn't try to engage her in conversation. He figured she needed some time to process the information they'd just learned. Especially the fact that Fagan seemed to have already killed many times.

As Quinn pulled into the houseboat's parking lot, he noted the interior lights were out, leaving the home dark and foreboding.

His hackles rose as he shifted into park. "No lights on. It's not like Ty to go to bed this early. And even if he did, it would be odd for him to turn out the lights. He's usually oblivious to things like that."

Nina swung her gaze to Quinn. "You think Fagan's here?"

He shrugged. "I'd like you to wait in the car while I check the place out. Just to be sure."

"I doubt that Fagan has a clue where we're staying, but go ahead." She didn't sound happy with his decision.

"Be back in a few," he said. "Keep the doors locked, your gun handy, and your head on a swivel."

"Hmm." She tapped her chin. "If only they'd taught me even one of those things at Quantico."

He rolled his eyes and drew his weapon before slipping outside and melding into the darkness. He crept onto the boat, half expecting Fagan to pounce from the shadows, though in reality he doubted the guy was brave enough to face them. He seemed more like a coward who liked to slink through the shadows.

Gun drawn, Quinn entered the house and worked his way around inside, ending with the bedroom assigned to Ty. The bed was made and empty. Maybe he was sleeping on the couch, and Quinn missed seeing him. He backed his way out of the room and turned on lights for a better view. The couch was empty. As were the chairs. He slid open the patio door and flipped on the exterior light. No one sat in the deck chair.

The place was empty, and Quinn's gut cramped down tight. He waved for Nina to join him.

"What's wrong?" she asked the minute she reached him.

"Ty's not here."

"Not here?" She glanced around the deck, her eyes filling with concern. "Check your phone. Maybe he texted you and you missed it."

Quinn dug out his phone. "No messages. What about yours?"

She located her cell in her purse. "Nothing."

Quinn dialed Ty's number. "It goes to voicemail." Quinn left a sternly worded message. "He prefers texts. I'll try that, too." He thumbed in a message as images of Ty in trouble raced through his brain. He waited for the responding text and started pacing. He clamped his fingers around the cool metal of his phone, willing it to ring.

"Don't be so quick to jump to terrible conclusions, Quinn," Nina said soothingly, though her expression belied her words. "He might just be visiting a friend."

"He often does dumb things, but he knows we'd worry about him. Hopefully he'll answer the text."

"Maybe he's more worried that you'll be mad at him for leaving." She held up her cell. "Let me try him."

Quinn watched her type a sweetly worded message and hit send. He went back to pacing. A few minutes passed. No reply. His anxiety rose.

"What about calling your mom or his friends," Nina suggested. "I'm sure Becca will have those numbers in her files from Ty's interview."

"I gave Mom a burner that's safe to use, but I don't want to make her panic yet. Would you mind going inside out of danger and calling the friends?" He shoved his phone into his pocket. "I'll have a look around out here. Maybe he went for a walk."

She squeezed his arm. "I don't want you to think I'm not concerned about Ty, because I am, but it's probably some teenage thing. He'll be back before you know it."

"If that's the case, he would most likely have taken the pickup, but I saw it on the way in. I'll still take that look around." He took off down the gangway, then wandered up and down the shoreline. Checking docks. Boats. Calling out Ty's name. An hour later, he'd covered every possible spot nearby and returned to the houseboat.

"Anything?" Nina peered at him, hope burning in her eyes.

"No. You?" he asked, though as she shook her head, her expression cemented his fears.

Something bad had happened to his little brother.

Chapter Thirty-One

WILEY SHOVED HIS hand into his hair and paced the small tunnel area he'd once thought soothing. Back and forth. Back and forth. His mind racing. How could the Feds have found the hotel? Now, of all times. He hadn't counted on them tracking his failed transmission so quickly.

He stepped over Tyler's bound feet and glared at him. The kid sat on the cold stone floor, his arms shackled to a thick post, duct tape over his mouth, and fear—blessed, wonderful fear—consumed his eyes. That was the only thing keeping Wiley going right now.

He'd finally gotten the kid down there to do the work, but the brat hadn't accomplished much in the last three hours. Wiley had poked and prodded the kid. He'd made a halfhearted effort, but Wiley knew he was stalling. Then the FBI's minions showed up and scoured the hotel for Brandt. He couldn't risk using the Wi-Fi and had to shut the kid down.

Stinkin' Feds. Time ticked down to the deadline, and they had him on hold.

At least it gave Wiley time to figure out how to motivate Tyler to work. He needed something Tyler loved and feared to lose. Wiley could threaten to kill Tyler's brother, but come on. . . . Wiley wasn't stupid. He'd never pit himself against a SEAL, and the kid would laugh in Wiley's face if he suggested it. But what about Brandt? Tyler seemed to like her, and most guys felt good about saving a damsel in distress.

Yeah, sure, that was it. He'd threaten the kid with hurting Brandt. First, he needed to see if the Feds were still there. He could easily slip out front to take a look. It wasn't as if they were searching for *him*.

He checked Tyler's bindings. "I'm taking a little field trip, kid. Don't get into trouble while I'm gone." He laughed on the way to the door, then slid down the passageway.

In the alley, he merged with pedestrians. The unmarked cars that had double-parked out front were gone. Could they have taken off? Maybe his luck was finally improving. He strolled past the hotel, glancing casually in the window, feigning indifference when he wanted to gape at the place and confirm the Feds had departed.

Satisfied they'd left, he stepped into the coffee shop and ordered a latte. He was sure everyone was staring at his scars. He leaned against the wall, his focus on his feet. He listened to the chatter and waited to hear one of the patrons say something about his face. The woman to his right talked about her dog's back surgery. The next table over, a couple discussed the merits of garden composting. Boring.

The barista called the fake name he'd given. He grabbed the drink.

On his way to the door, he heard a man in a hotel kitchen uniform say, "You should've seen it, babe. The FBI was amazing."

Maybe this guy could give Wiley additional information. He took a chair nearby to listen.

"It was exactly like you see on TV," the guy said enthusiastically. "All these agents busting into the place. Demanding this and that. Joe just gave in and let them take over." He paused to listen for a moment. "They were searching for a specific computer that used our wireless network. They checked all the staff phones and tablets. It was cool, but kinda scary at the same time." He stopped talking. "Yeah, I mean, sure you could come down here, but they're long gone. I heard them say that since we have free Wi-Fi in the coffee shop, it coulda been anyone. They asked Joe to monitor the Wi-Fi to watch for the same computer, but he finally stood up to them and said he didn't have time." He glanced as his watch. "Hey, look. I gotta get back to work. I'll call you if anything else happens, but I doubt it."

Wiley watched the guy leave and sipped his latte, enjoying the drink he'd often craved in prison. His phone chimed. Wiley read the text from Crash.

Buyer jittery. Provide access by 6 pm tomorrow or the deal is off.

Six? Was he nuts? He'd promised forty-eight hours!

Wylie was a fool. He'd trusted Crash because they'd formed a bond in prison, but he was like all the others. Out to get Wiley. Lying in wait. Hoping to best him. Like that kid. Sitting in the tunnel, not cooperating.

Wylie's anger flared. Who did these people think they were? He was better than all of them. He wouldn't let them keep him down. Not again.

"BECCA AND CONNOR will put out an alert for Ty," Nina told Quinn, but he didn't stop pacing to respond. His jaw was set, his lips pressed together in a grim line.

She was frazzled from watching his frantic movements. She stepped in front of him. "Pacing won't bring him back here."

"No, but it'll keep me from going insane."

She rested her hand on his arm. "We'll find him soon. With the alert . . ." She let her voice fall off as her phone rang.

Hoping it was Ty, she looked at the screen. "It's Becca."

"Maybe she has news about Ty," Quinn said optimistically.

"Let's hope so." Nina answered but was quickly disappointed. No news yet. Quinn resumed his pacing, his steps faster and more frantic this time. He was a doer, not a thinker. She knew he had to be ready to explode.

"We basically struck out at the hotel," Becca said.

"Didn't you find anything?"

"We confirmed the hack was done with Ty's computer and it originated at the hotel, but we didn't find the computer. The place has a coffee shop with free Wi-Fi, so we suspect the hacker came in off the street, did his business, then left."

"What about security cameras?"

"I'm at the office with Connor. We're reviewing the feed, along with traffic-cam footage. But even if we catch Fagan on camera, it's not likely to lead to his current location."

Quinn's phone chimed, catching Nina's attention.

"Something seems off about this hotel, but I can't put my finger on it," Nina said to Becca while keeping an eye on Quinn as he typed on his phone. "I'll do a little research on the internet and see if I can figure it out." She disconnected.

Quinn typed another message, then crossed over to her, his steps urgent. "The texts are from Ty. He needs me."

"Where is he?" Nina asked, trying to stay calm.

"Back where this all started. Triple Falls."

Nina's radar went off. "Odd place for him to be, isn't it? Especially at this time of night."

"He received a text saying the computer had been left at the cache site. He went to check on it. Only he fell halfway up and is stuck. I can't leave him there."

Nina's bad feeling intensified. "He didn't take the truck, so how'd he get there?"

"He said he got a ride from a friend." Quinn gave her a tight-lipped smile. "Will you be okay here if I go after him?"

She would, but he wasn't thinking clearly, and she needed to stop him from making a mistake. "Are you sure it's a good idea to go? You don't even know if Ty's in control of his phone."

Quinn watched her for a moment. "You think Fagan has Ty and is trying to lure me up there?"

"It's possible. Is there anything you can text back to Ty that only he would know? Even if Fagan is the one texting you, we'll at least know Ty's with him, and you won't be wasting your time."

"There's no time. Besides, I'm going, no matter what."

She grabbed his arm. "Please do this. For me." She hated to beg, but she couldn't let him race into a trap when Fagan might have already killed Ty as he'd done with Hamid. Perhaps in the same spot.

"Fine." Quinn thumbed a message into his phone. "There. Now we wait."

They stood there, their gazes connected, her hand still on his arm. She tried to convey her concern for him—for Ty—in her gaze. He relaxed a fraction until his phone chimed, and his eyes went hard and warrior-like. He looked at the screen. "We're good. It's Ty."

She watched as he tapped another message saying he was on his way. She waited for him to hit *send*, then said, "I'd like to go with you."

He shook his head and clasped her arms. "If there was an alternative to leaving you alone, I'd take it in a heartbeat. But you're safer here than with me."

"I can't let you go alone. You need backup in case something isn't right when you arrive."

His jutted out his strong chin. "I'm not letting you come with me and that's the end of the discussion."

Nina fisted her hands and prepared to do battle. "But I—"

He dipped his head, stealing her words with a quick, emotion-filled kiss.

"Gotta go." He raced for the door, stopping only to retrieve his rifle.

Shocked at his swift departure, she stood for a moment before pulling herself together and charging after him. Dark shadows clung to the stairway, and she had to stop to let her eyes adjust before she started her climb. She heard him gun the engine, and by the time she reached the driveway, all she could see was the red glow of his taillights. She thought to jump in the truck and go after him, but he was a SEAL with a head start. She'd never catch up to him in time. Her heart creased with the same pain she felt each time he deployed. Her only solace was that he wasn't doing battle with unknown forces today. She was certain Quinn could easily subdue Fagan.

To keep her mind occupied, she returned to the houseboat and sat behind the computer where she connected to the internet. She plugged Diamond Hotel into a map program and reviewed businesses and sights listed in the immediate area. Starting near the Portland Saturday Market, she worked her way north, moving past Voodoo Donuts and the Skidmore Fountain, two local landmarks. The Shanghai Tunnels came next. When she'd first moved to Portland, she'd done all the tourist things and the tunnel tour was one of them, though she had to admit, it was a bit schlocky.

The best she could tell, the tunnels ran near the hotel, but what if they ran under it? She remembered from the tour that unexplored sections of the tunnels still existed. Could Fagan have set himself up in one of them to use the hotel's Wi-Fi? Could he even get a signal underground? Questionable, but possible with the right router. But how would he know about the tunnels? He might have worked at the hotel she supposed and discovered it that way. Kip Ulrich might know.

She couldn't call him from her phone. It was still too risky to let anyone know her number. She'd have Becca phone him as they'd done when they contacted Kip the first time.

As Nina pulled out her phone to call Becca, it chimed with a text. She glanced at the screen and saw a text with a picture sent from Ty's phone. She opened it and nearly dropped the phone.

Ty was sitting on a stone floor, his arms shackled to wooden beams, a laptop on his knees. She enlarged the picture. The place resembled the Shanghai Tunnel she'd visited.

The caption read. *Come now. They're going to kill me.*

Her fingers trembling, she typed. *Where are you?*

Diamond Hotel. I need help hacking the NFL again. He said you have thirty minutes to get here or he'll kill me. Come alone and don't tell anyone. Not even Quinn. Please, Nina.

She doubted Ty was the one typing this text.

Then again, it didn't matter, did it?

Ty's life was in danger, and Quinn was a good hour away by now. Exactly what Fagan hoped for when he'd sent Quinn on a wild goose chase, leaving her as the only person who could rescue Ty.

QUINN ARRIVED AT Triple Falls and scouted the area. There weren't any cars in the lot. As suspected, this seemed more and more like an ambush or a bust. But if Fagan was there, Quinn knew how to easily turn the tables on the creep. He was likely sitting up high, maybe with a weapon. The most important thing for Quinn to do was gain the high ground, something he'd learned in land nav training at BUD/S.

Not that it was a revolutionary tactic or anything. All military forces knew that your field of engagement was better viewed from up high. It was a whole lot easier to fight your way downhill than up.

He slung his rifle on his back, dropped a knife in his cargo pocket, then strapped on his night-vision goggles. Gripping his handgun, he slipped into the brush abutting the trail, moving swiftly but silently. In an op like this one, stealth and accuracy were everything. He'd have to slide past Fagan and strike with the speed and precision of a snake.

If Fagan was even up there.

He approached the midway portion of the trail. When he found no one, he kept going, his breath coming in little bursts in the night, rising up as mist over his goggles. The higher he climbed the more he started to believe Ty wasn't there. Not only Ty, but Fagan wasn't either. Which meant only one thing. The creep had wanted to get him away from Nina. Far away.

Quinn picked up speed, moving as fast as he could without disturbing the brush. Time zipped by. It had been forty minutes since he'd stepped onto the trailhead. When he reached the summit, he was alone. And so was Nina. He had to check on her.

He grabbed his phone, silenced for the climb. Found a message from her.

I know where Fagan is. He has Ty. Forcing him to hack the NFL again. Going to meet him. Undercover. Becca will back me up. See you on the other side.

"No," he shouted, his voice reverberating through the trees.

Adrenaline pumping, he raced down the path. He had to get to Nina and Ty before he lost them both.

Chapter Thirty-Two

NINA PARKED THE pickup down the street from the Diamond Hotel. On the twenty-minute drive, she'd weighed her decision to put herself in a tunnel with Fagan and kept coming up with the same decision. The first rule of law enforcement called for her to protect the innocent above all. Ty may have hacked the database, but he was not to blame for this situation. He was just a boy, one without the skills to save himself. But *she* had those skills. Still, she wasn't a fool either. She'd texted Quinn her plan before leaving the houseboat and called Becca for backup. Now she needed to put that plan into action.

On one of the extra burner phones Quinn had bought, she silenced the ringer and dialed Becca. After Nina's earlier call, Becca and Connor had headed for the hotel. Worried about Fagan seeing a police presence, Nina made Becca promise not to tell anyone but Connor about this for now and arrive silently. No sirens. No lights. No official police vehicles at all.

"I'm at the hotel," Nina said after Becca answered.

"Don't do this, Nina." Becca's plea was heartfelt. "It's a trap, and you know it."

Nina wouldn't let Becca sway her. "Ty's life is on the line here. I can help him."

"Fine. But if I can't stop you, then I sure hope you've come up with a plan."

"As much of one as I could put together in Fagan's short time-frame." Nina took a deep breath and launched into the details. "Once we finish this conversation, I'll leave the call connected to you and hide the phone in my bra. I'll put the phone that Fagan texted me on in my pocket, so when he searches me—which I'm assuming he'll do—he'll find that phone and not look any farther. Assuming he doesn't find this one, you'll be able to hear everything that goes on and can work up a rescue plan that won't endanger Ty's life."

"What if the signal isn't strong enough underground?"

"I believe he texted me from the tunnel, so I'm hoping my phone will work."

"And if it doesn't? Or if he finds the phone? You'll be on your own. Then what?"

"Then I'll have to find another way to communicate. We can assume Ty is using the hotel's Wi-Fi to access the internet for the hack. I'll try to get a message to you via the network if I can. Plus I have GPS turned on."

"Yeah, but the clear line of sight GPS needs to work will be interrupted. We'll lose the signal."

"It'll still give you my last location before I go underground. You can narrow things down from there. Were you able to get the blueprints for the hotel?"

"Connor's got someone working with the City on it, but the fact is, these tunnels aren't on most plans. So even if there is one under the hotel, it may not show up. I hope the hotel manager knows something. I'm about five minutes out."

"Sounds good."

Becca blew out a deep breath that carried over the phone. "Have you thought about what happens if you and Ty can't hack the NFL again? Fagan could decide you're both useless and kill you."

"I've thought of that. I raided Quinn's magic bag of tricks and found a mini revolver with an inside-the-waistband holster. I've put it under a visible holster to hide it. I also have an ankle gun. Again, I'm hoping Fagan's inexperienced enough that he'll take the obvious weapons, think he's found my backup, and stop searching."

"Nina, please don't do this."

"Enough, Bex. We can argue this all day, but my time is running out. I have to go. I'm stowing it for a sound check." Nina dropped it deep inside her cleavage and adjusted it so it didn't show. "Okay, stowed. Can you hear me?"

"Yes," Becca's voice came from Nina's chest. Despite the tension, she smiled at the idiocy of the idea.

"Please reconsider," Becca pleaded.

"Don't worry, Bex. We can do this. I'm stepping outside now. Mute your phone so nothing comes through on this end."

"Going silent," Becca said, sounding very reluctant.

A moment of unease stopped Nina, but all she had to do was think of that picture of Ty. She'd do anything for that kid. She shoved her actual phone into her pocket, tossed up a prayer that Fagan wouldn't find the gun and phone, then climbed from the car.

She headed down the street wet from the recent rain. The few pedestrians on the sidewalks had their heads down, their shoulders hunched against the cold whistling wind. Fagan hadn't instructed her to go inside, so she waited in the cold and resisted tapping her foot on the damp concrete. Her back to the building, she watched both sides of the street. She heard the barest of whispers behind her, and started to turn when the barrel of a gun jabbed in her back.

"Don't react." Fagan's voice slithered over her shoulder like a snake, bringing back unsettling memories of him. "Just start walking. To your right. Quickly now. Ty's waiting."

He stepped to her side, his arm coming around her back and tugging her closer, the gun now lodged in the soft flesh of her side. He had a musty smell, the kind that lingered on clothes after storing them for a long time. She had the impulse to disarm him, but she had no idea where he held Ty. She would have to go along with his plan until she did.

At the corner, he pulled her around the building, shoved her down a deserted street and into an alley. He pressed her up against a wall, and she got her first look at his face. She gasped at the copious scars she saw. Anger flared in his eyes, and she immediately regretted her response.

He slammed his forearm against her neck, pummeling her head into the rough brick. The gun came up to her temple, the barrel icy and hard. "Take a good long look. This is your handiwork. Might as well have been you who took the shiv to my face."

She struggled to breathe, but her attention was still on his scars. He was so close, she could see each line. Each scar. Hundreds of them crisscrossing like a road map above his beard that she suspected covered additional damage. The pain he must have experienced. She actually felt sorry for him until she looked in his eyes. Years' worth of anger was stored behind irises the color of darkness.

He pressed closer, his coffee-scented breath fanning over her skin. His arm lifted, allowing air to flow to her lungs again.

Please don't find my phone. Please. Please. Please.

"I . . ." She started to speak to draw his attention, but she didn't know what to say that wouldn't make him angrier, so she kept quiet and peered at him, making sure her horror for what he must have gone through didn't show.

"I thought that'd shut you up." He stepped back, his free hand going to her gun and jerking it out, then shoving it in his waistband. He ran the same hand over her body in cursory sweep, making her gag with revulsion. He slid it down to her ankles. Found the other gun.

A look of superiority lit his face as he pulled it free. "Clasp your hands behind your back."

She did as asked, praying that the awkward position wouldn't reveal the hidden phone. He pulled out thick cable ties and bound her wrists, jerking the heavy plastic tight and cutting into the tender flesh. Next came a long, dingy cloth that he'd rolled and forced into her mouth. It smelled musty like him. Her gag reflex kicked in. Dry heaves plagued her until she got control of it.

He laughed. "This is only the beginning, sweetheart."

He ran his hands over her body again, discovering the phone in her pocket. He dropped it on the ground and crushed it. She expected he'd yell at her it for bringing a phone, but he jerked her by the cable tie and pushed her toward the hotel's back wall. "In the small opening between the buildings, slide in. Face toward the hotel."

The narrow opening ran the full length between the hotel and another building. It wasn't more than two feet wide and was a long space with no end. She wedged her body inside. It closed in around her, and fear for her life kept her from moving. He stepped in, the hoodie and shadows from the wall masking his face, making him seem more threatening.

Was she wrong? Did he want to kill her too and the whole setup was a ruse for making her let her guard down so he could get to her? After all, he'd likely killed Hamid and the psychiatrist. Maybe his parents, too. Or maybe, this was simply the way he accessed his tunnel.

He nudged her forward. "Keep going until I tell you to stop."

She slid. Step after step. Down the wall. Her arms cramped as she moved, the rough brick snagging on her jacket. The faint glow from the streetlight disappeared. Deeper and deeper they went. The space was black, pitch black. She started to regret her decision and thought Becca might have been right. Nina was going to her grave.

"Stop."

She stopped. She felt him hunch his back, heard something groan, then a rush of air swept over them.

Light flooded out of a small doorway.

He ducked and backed in, his gun coming up again. "Okay, step inside. Slowly. No false moves, or I'll turn and kill Tyler."

She entered, and Fagan backed down a set of rickety wooden stairs. She caught sight of Ty across the small space. His eyes, terrified and red as if he'd been crying, met hers in a silent plea for help. Both arms were still shackled by chains to the wall. His feet were bound, and a rag much like hers was wedged in his mouth and circled his head.

"Over there," Fagan said. "Across the room, by the kid."

She stepped down and wished she could offer Ty comforting words.

"Sit," Fagan commanded. "To the kid's left."

She gestured with her hands to show him she couldn't manage to sit without the use of her arms.

"Really?" he said, sounding incredulous. "You expect me to feel sorry for you and keep you from getting a boo-boo? I don't think so." He shoved her to the damp, cold floor.

Pain shot up her back. When she righted herself, she checked out Ty for injuries. She gently nudged him with her shoulder and tried to send him a "hang in there" message with her gaze. Next, she searched the length of the room. A tunnel led off to the side, but a rockslide of large boulders filled it. Worn lumber leaned against the wall across from her. A solid wall of stone stood by the door and behind them. There seemed to be only one exit, and Fagan was guarding it.

"Looking to escape." He waved his gun at her. "Give it up. There's only one way out, and I'm not letting you get to the door." He shoved the gun in his belt and dug out a key. He released Ty's hand closest to her.

Next, he went to a roughly hewn table and withdrew a long knife from a sheath. He came toward her. She scrambled backward, her arms connecting with the wall. Ty reached out for her and pulled her into a protective hold as he whimpered behind his gag.

"Let go of her, Tyler. I'm only going to cut her wrists free."

Ty complied, and Fagan jerked her forward. He yanked the cable tie, the rough edge cutting her arm as he sliced the tie apart. "If I'd thought I'd have two guests, I would have been better prepared. But this will have to do."

He grabbed her left hand and snapped it into the shackle that had held Ty's wrist. "You can thank Ty here for your visit. I was perfectly content setting you up to take the fall for the hack and Hamid's murder. Then DHS fixed the vulnerability and I couldn't sell the hack. But I think Ty can get in again, only the little punk is refusing to work. So, I need you to motivate him."

Her heart soared at his admission of framing her. She hoped Becca was successful in recording the conversation.

He picked up a laptop from the table, removed Ty's gag, and backhanded him. The boy's head snapped back and slammed into the wall. "You will refrain from screaming for help like a little girl while we work on this hack together." He handed the laptop to Ty and lowered his body between them, then pressed his gun against Nina's temple.

"Enough of your time wasting," he said to Ty. "Get on this computer and fix the hack, or I'll kill her."

"But I don't know if I can do it again. At least not before your deadline."

Fagan glared at Ty. "If you don't have a way into the database by then, you both die. Here, where no one will ever find you."

Nina gasped at the finality in his tone, bringing Fagan's attention her way.

He watched her intently, a smile curling his lips behind the thick beard. "Relax and enjoy my little lair. It's about the size of a prison cell. Take the time to get used to it so the transition to a life behind bars will be easier. That is, if Ty does his work and you live long enough to experience it."

Chapter Thirty-Three

QUINN COULDN'T come racing down the road, but he wanted to. Instead, he pulled a hat over his head, shouldered his bag of gear that he'd picked up at the houseboat on the way, and followed Nina's last GPS signal on foot until he reached a hotel named the Diamond. Quinn recognized the hotel's name. The hack Becca investigated had come from there, and Nina's signal registered just beyond the building.

If Nina was there, Fagan was there, too. But if he was, he'd been crafty enough to hide from very capable agents. So how in the world was Quinn to go about finding him?

He sensed someone approaching from behind and spun to find Becca.

"You shouldn't be here." She scowled at him. "Come inside before you ruin our whole operation."

She led him through the coffee shop to a back storage room where an FBI analyst he recognized from his time in the office sat at a table, a laptop in front of her. Jae, Quinn remembered. Connor stood to the side, talking on his phone. Neither looked at him. A cell phone with wires running to the computer lay on the table next to Jae. She and Connor had earpieces in and several more lay on the table.

Quinn grabbed Becca's arm. "This is your whole team? How on earth do you plan to get Nina back with just the three of you?" His voice came out like a frantic child's. He was usually so cool and calculating on his ops. But this was different—this was Nina. *His* Nina.

"Fagan told Nina to come alone. She didn't want a police presence to spook him. So, we're covert for now." Becca picked up an earpiece and handed it to him. "Nina hid her phone. It's connected to us on an open line. We can hear and record everything said in the tunnel."

His mouth dropping open, Quinn stared at Becca for a moment. "A phone? That's your grand plan to communicate with her? Fagan could find it and end the call."

"We would have liked time to set up a more inconspicuous wire and make a better plan, but he gave Nina thirty minutes to comply before he killed Ty. She wouldn't agree to wait and threw out the cell phone idea. She may or may not be in possession of your mini revolver. It depends on how thoroughly Fagan searched her."

He hadn't even noticed it was missing from his bag. "Why didn't you stop her?"

Becca looked mad. "We couldn't get here on time, and you know Nina. She loves your brother. She'd do anything to help him. No one would stand in her way, even you, I dare say."

Quinn suspected Becca was right. Nina had a heart as big as Texas. He couldn't fault her for caring enough to try to save Ty, but now, two people he loved were in danger and he didn't know how to help them. He didn't like the feeling.

Connor disconnected and stepped across the room. He was frowning.

"What's wrong?" Quinn asked.

"Our interest in Fagan made our detectives go back through their records."

"And?" Quinn said, to move the guy along.

"The neighbors said his parents had lived in their house for the last forty years, so the detectives didn't search for other residences. But they found a cabin. They just searched the area." He ran a hand over his hair. "You won't like this, but they located his parents. A bullet through their heads. They'd been brutally tortured first."

"And now Fagan has Nina and Ty," Becca said.

Quinn wasn't going there. "His parents had no one to help them. Ty and Nina have us. We need to get moving."

"Got the building's blueprints, Detective Warren," Jae called out.

Connor moved to the table. Quinn followed, as did Becca. Schematics for the hotel showing a sub-basement level were displayed on the screen.

"That must be the tunnel, since the manager knew nothing about a basement," Connor said.

Jae tapped the wall by the restaurant next door. "Best I can tell, they entered the tunnel here." She moved her finger to the next wall, then ran it along the map. "It leads north. We might be able to access it here."

Connor shook his head. "Fagan said there was only one way out."

"He might be lying to make Nina think she can't escape," Becca offered.

Quinn scanned the diagram, as did everyone else, his mind racing over the possibilities. He'd rescued hostages in impossible situations before. He certainly had the skills to help Nina.

"There's only one way to find out." Quinn didn't wait for anyone's agreement, but took off to check it out.

THE ATMOSPHERE in Fagan's hidey-hole had deteriorated even more. Nina could feel the pressure mounting. Fagan had released Ty's other arm so he could work faster, and the boy was frantically trying to find his way into the database. Time passed. *Tick, tick, tick,* she felt it move as if a clock was sitting next to her. The deadline was fast approaching. Yet, she kept her panic at bay for Ty's sake.

The warmth of the phone against her chest gave her some comfort. If it was emitting heat, her call was still connected to Becca. She really needed to get Fagan to remove her gag so she could provide Becca with details about the space, but when she tried to take it off with her free hand, he'd slapped it down.

His phone chimed from the table, and he got up to check it. With his focus on his phone, she used her free hand to pull her shirt up. Her fingers slipped around the cool grip of the mini revolver. She carefully lifted it from the holster. Inch, by painstaking inch, she withdrew it, then secured it under her leg. She looked up to catch Ty watching her. He opened his mouth to speak. She held a finger up to her mouth to silence him.

"That was my buyer." Fagan glared at Ty. "He's not happy that you haven't finished your job yet. Maybe you need more motivation."

He grabbed the knife from the table and knelt next to Nina. He ran the backside of the cool blade across her throat, then down her cleavage. His cold eyes pinned hers. "If I take your gag off, will you tell him to work harder? Before I have to start cutting you?"

Though she had no intention of pleading with Ty, she nodded.

He sliced through the cloth, the point of the blade pricking her skin, but she didn't cry out. She cleared her throat and swallowed hard, trying to fill her mouth with enough saliva to speak.

"Ty's waiting for your encouragement." With a quick flick of his knife, Fagan sliced the top button from her blouse.

His knife was now only inches from her phone.

"Go back to work, Ty." Nina's words were muffled as her dry lips caught on her teeth.

He continued to stare at her, his eyes wide with shock.

"Now," she yelled so he didn't see whatever sick plan Fagan had cooked up for her.

He turned back to his computer. Nina waited for Fagan to withdraw his knife, but he let the blade rest on her breasts.

"I'll leave this here for motivation for you, Ty." He turned his sick gaze on Ty. "I don't need a reason to want to hurt her, but I will if you give me one."

QUINN HELD HIS breath as he silently climbed through rubble blocking the tunnel leading to Nina. He still wore his earpiece and Fagan's threats came in loud and clear. It didn't take long to realize this entrance was impenetrable and not a means of escape. He heard the faint sounds of voices, which meant he was close enough to deploy his tactical snake camera that he'd looped over his shoulder.

He slowly eased out the cable, winding it through the rocks until he could see inside. He maneuvered the camera around, winding it into the deeper section of the tunnel to find Nina. She sat on the floor next to Fagan. Ty was on Fagan's other side.

Quinn zoomed in the camera and caught his first glimpse of Fagan. He had a thick beard with scars crawling out of it. He must have suffered from whatever had left those marks. Could have made him crazy, Quinn supposed, if he hadn't had mental health problems already. The large hunting knife Fagan had threatened Nina with rested on her chest. Quinn stifled a curse. It was bad enough to hear Fagan's threats, but seeing the knife pressed against her skin twisted Quinn's gut.

If he could get a clear shot through the rubble, he could take Fagan out with one bullet. But not until the creep stood or the round could go right through him and injure Ty. Quinn evaluated the path of the snake. There was no way he was getting his rifle through the rubble.

He moved the camera through the space, searching for another entrance and zooming in on the main door. With the alleyway outside of the door so narrow, Quinn would have to fling open the door and take a quick shot to surprise Fagan. Quinn was a good shot, but he wasn't willing to risk hitting Nina or Ty.

He turned the camera back to them. Panic gripped him.

Think, man. You've trained for like a million hours for a scenario like this. There's got to be something you can do.

Ty raised his arms and yawned. The kid's tiredness didn't bode well for his success on the hack.

"No time for a break, kid," Fagan warned and shifted the knife on Nina's chest. He must have cut her, because a small gasp of pain slipped out.

Quinn gritted his teeth. It was all he could do not to start tossing these boulders out of the way so he could scramble over the heap to get to her.

"I'm sorry," Ty said. "I can't help it. You have any energy drinks? That would help."

"You think this is the Hilton or something?" Fagan moved his knife, slicing open the next button on Nina's blouse. He let the blade trail down her breast, his eyes suddenly going wide. "What?" He scooted around and ripped her blouse open. "You little sneak." He dug out her phone. "Who's listening to us?"

Quinn waited to hear Becca respond on the phone, but she didn't.

Fagan got in Nina's face. "Who's on the other end?" he screamed at top volume and backhanded her.

Nina's head snapped back. Quinn wanted to break through the boulders and tear Fagan apart.

"Give it up, Fagan," Nina said. "The FBI knows all about your little plan to frame me. I'm not going to prison. You are."

"No!" Fagan shot to his feet.

"Yes," she said, wiping a trickle of blood from the corner of her mouth. "They're outside waiting to arrest you. You'll never sell this hack."

Fagan paced, stroking his beard as he moved. He was mumbling, but not saying anything coherent. Back and forth, he stepped in stilted, quick little strides. The guy was quickly losing it. He wished Nina hadn't told him who was listening. If she hadn't, maybe he would stick with the status quo, giving Quinn time to figure out how to safely end this. Fagan dropped the phone on the floor and crushed it under his shoes. The call went dead.

Quinn quickly deployed the flexible mic along the same path as the camera and put on the headset.

"There's no point in keeping you alive now, Brandt," Fagan said. "I wanted you in prison. To know the horror I went through. But thanks to your interference, that won't happen. So, you will die." He looked around the space, then rushed to the corner. He bent down to retrieve something that Quinn couldn't make out.

Quinn swung the camera back to Nina. She was moving around, digging under her leg. Her hand came out holding the mini revolver. *Yes! She's ending this now.*

Fagan stood up, faced Nina and blanched. He dove behind a stack of old boards. Nina fired. The boards toppled, slamming into her arm and sending her shot wide. She recovered, firing again.

Fagan cried out, then grabbed his leg before rolling behind a pile of rubble. "Drop the gun, Brandt, or I will empty my clip into Tyler. Yes, you may shoot me in the process, but I have nothing to lose now and the boy will surely die, too."

Don't do it, Nina. Don't give up your gun. Not yet.

She did nothing for a moment. The seconds ticked by and Quinn could barely breathe. She suddenly leaned foreword and set the revolver on the stone floor, then sent it skittering out into the open.

No!

"That's a good girl." Fagan came up over the table, his weapon trained on Ty. "I think it's time for you to say goodbye, so Tyler can depart with me."

"We still have time. I can finish. Please," Ty begged. "Then you can have your money and not hurt Nina."

"I think not, punk. You're my ticket out of here." Fagan shoved his gun in his waistband, then grabbed a cloth from the table and tied it around his leg wound. "I need to get help before I bleed out."

"What about Nina?" Ty asked in a choked voice.

Fagan smiled. He picked up the item he'd dropped, allowing Quinn to get a good look at it—an oversized pipe wrench covered in rust.

"Since she's so terrified of water . . ." He laughed and slammed the wrench into a large water pipe. The metal groaned and reverberated. He hit it again. And again. An elbow joint finally gave way and water started gushing from the end.

He dropped the wrench and pulled out his gun, a sick smile on his face. "The space will be full of water in a very short time. It's the perfect way for Agent Brandt to die, don't you think?"

No! Quinn stifled the scream, and his heart refused to beat. He scanned the room for electrical outlets. If the water reached one, Nina would be electrocuted. The only one he spotted hung from the ceiling. But he could be missing something.

Wiley jerked Ty up by the arm. "Put the laptop on the table."

Ty did as asked.

Wiley eyed Brandt and tossed a key over his shoulder into the tunnel. "Just in case your friends get lucky and subdue me. I wouldn't want it to be too easy to unlock the shackle." He jabbed the gun in Ty's neck. "Please understand, I am not at all afraid to use my gun."

Quinn hated losing visual on them, but he had no choice if he was going to rescue them both. He dropped his equipment and scrambled down from the rubble to his rifle case.

"What happened?" Becca asked.

As Quinn dug out and checked a cartridge, he recounted the story. "I'll take a stand and when I get a clear shot at Fagan, I'll take it."

"What about Nina?"

"Find a water shutoff. And see if you can get the electricity turned off. Barring that, do nothing. I'm a SEAL, and water is my forte."

Chapter Thirty-Four

"PUT BRANDT'S OTHER hand in the shackle," Wiley instructed. When the kid didn't move, Wiley kicked him. The movement sent Wiley's leg screaming with pain, but he'd come too far to be bested by Brandt again. She would not send him back to prison. He'd rather die.

"Now!"

"No need." Brandt jiggled her already shackled arm. "This one will hold me."

Wiley smiled. "Ah, but if I don't put the other one on, you might be able to rise above the water." Wiley turned to Tyler. "Do it now!"

"Nina?" Ty looked at her.

She turned her body so he could shackle her other wrist. "It's okay, hon. Go ahead. I'll find a way out."

"How?"

"Don't worry. I will."

Tyler reluctantly closed the metal and locked it. "I'm sorry, Nina."

"Don't be. It's not your fault." She smiled up at the boy. "I love you, Ty. Always remember that."

Wiley wanted to gag. It got worse when the kid started crying like a baby.

"I love you, too," the kid said to Brandt.

"Enough of this sob-fest." Wiley grabbed Tyler's arm and shoved him toward the door. He felt Brandt's focus on him as he made his way up the steps. Once Tyler was in the passageway, Wiley glanced over his shoulder and smiled. "Payback's hell, isn't it, Brandt?"

AT FIRST, QUINN started looking for high ground before he got eyes on the target. Maybe a rooftop? But buildings blocked his view of the alley from too high. So, he needed dead space. He'd get his best shot lying down, but that wasn't an option either, with the tight quarters. His next preference was to kneel behind the dumpster and use an old wooden crate for his bipod. He took his position, scooting around until he was naturally aligned with where he expected his target to be, putting him in a relaxed position for a better shot. He focused through his scope and read the wind. He couldn't get exact coordinates until Fagan actually stepped out, but he was close enough that he couldn't miss, even if he had to make last-minute adjustments.

Quinn held his stance. Silence stretched out for unbearable moments. His mind filled with the thought of water rising up to Nina's mouth, and it ripped his heart in two.

Still, he kept his eye on the scope. Zeroing in on the alley. His body motionless. He recounted the steps he'd performed so many times that he'd often gone on autopilot. Today he had the shot of his life. One chance. That was all he had and he wouldn't mess it up.

Ty finally stepped into the alley. Fagan limped behind him.

Quinn sited his scope on Fagan. Dropped his finger to the trigger and waited for a clean shot. Breathing normally, he prepared to pull the trigger on his natural exhale.

Now! his brain screamed. He squeezed the trigger.

Fagan dropped like lead. Ty's face registered shock. Quinn left his rifle and bolted toward Ty.

"Coming in," Connor called from behind.

"Roger that," Quinn shouted, now nearly at Ty's side.

Quinn stopped to give the kid a quick hug then strapped on a head-lamp. "Connor will take care of you. I'm going in for Nina. Pray that I get to her in time."

THE WATER WAS cold. So cold that Nina's teeth chattered as it lapped against her chin. She turned her face up to the ceiling and wished the lights hadn't gone off so she could see. Her neck was sore, but every time she dropped her chin, she choked on a mouthful of water. She had to get higher somehow or it soon wouldn't matter.

She'd tried to get to her knees early on, but her wrists screamed in anguish. She'd stopped and prayed for help. But now? It was looking like no one was coming in time.

She had nothing to lose.

She dragged one leg through the water. She managed to get it beneath her, but water rose over her chin and filled her mouth. She coughed hard, her lungs screaming with effort. Panic followed.

Garrett.

Is this how he'd felt that day? Going under and not being able to come up for air?

Tears joined the moisture on her face. The irony of her life ending the same way wasn't lost on her. She'd lived life so structured, saying no to anything that she thought might be dangerous. Saying no to Quinn. She'd missed out on so much. If she got out of this mess, that would change. She would let go of any guilt she still held about what had happened to Garrett. She'd been a kid. Younger than Ty. And he was no more responsible for leaving her behind than she'd been for not being able to hold on to Garrett's hand. She'd move forward now. Embrace everything. No matter her fear. That included Quinn, if he'd have her. Even if he remained a SEAL.

Water nipped at her chin again, bringing her back to reality.

She twisted her other leg. Got it behind her. But her arms were shackled low, and she gained only an inch or so. Not enough to keep her face above water for long. She strained as high as her legs would allow, pulling at her wrists. The pain was excruciating.

She laid her head back. The water licked at her chin, filling her mouth.

Panic took hold.

She thrashed. Tried to get higher. Her wrists hurt but she kept going. She felt something pop. Stars danced before her eyes, but she'd gained a slight rise. It only lasted a moment.

She took a deep breath. The water covered her mouth, then her nose. Filled her ears. Her lungs soon screamed for air. Burned.

Oh, God, no, please. Help me.

QUINN PLUNGED down the stairs and plowed through cold water that stole his breath for a moment. His headlamp shone on Nina's face, her mouth and nose barely above water. Her eyes were open. Her lips and cheeks bulging, as if she struggled to hold in her air. He'd have to breathe for her.

He cupped the back of her head and tipped it forward to free her ears of water, allowing her to hear him. "We'll do a modified form of buddy breathing. It's like mouth to mouth. Exhale," he commanded roughly to get through her panic.

She released her breath. He took a deep one and pressed his mouth to hers slowly filling it with air. She drew the air into her lungs. Coughed.

"Let it out, and we'll do it again a few more times." They settled into a rhythm, and he felt her calm down. Each time he lifted his head, he searched the shadowy space for anything he could use to help her breathe. He spotted a cup on the table with a rigid plastic straw that was oversized and should work. He held her head with one hand and reached with the other. He jerked the straw free and put it in her mouth. "Get a good seal on it and don't panic. Nice slow breaths in and out."

He heard her pull air in through the straw, then the sweet sound of it hissing out. She was breathing. For now. For another six inches. That meant he had to work fast.

"I have to find the key, sweetheart. Okay?"

She blinked her eyes. He released her, and watched as she slipped down into the water, his heart breaking. He waited to be sure she was still taking in air, then swam to the other side of the room. He took a breath. Dove deep. Searched in the rocks. Found nothing. Kept searching. His lungs were nearly exploding with the need to breathe, but he stayed down. He was a SEAL and had the ability to remain committed despite physical depletion. Anything short of that meant someone could die in battle. Today, it meant Nina would die.

He crawled along the bottom. Inch by inch. His light finally reflected off shiny metal. The key. He grabbed it and shot out of the water. He gulped in air and went back down, making sure not to create a wave that could swamp the top of Nina's straw. He swam the short distance to her, grabbed a shackle and freed one arm. She struggled for the surface, pounding on his back, but he held his ground and released the other hand. She shot up.

He joined her. She was thrashing around. Seeking air. He held her above the water. She clutched his neck, gasping for oxygen. She nearly took him down, but she was far less difficult to control than his swim instructors had been at BUD/S testing, and he stood fast, the water now approaching his chest.

"Shh, sweetheart," he whispered into her ear. "It's over. I have you. You're fine now. Just breathe. Nice and easy."

She slowly relaxed, her eyes clearing and meeting his. "Thank God, you came."

"Hey." He smoothed her hair back. "I've got your six. Remember?"

Her lips tipped in a wobbly smile. He didn't know if she was so tentative because his promise reminded her that he'd once left her and she thought he might again.

He didn't want to leave this time. Didn't want to go back to that awkwardness with the team. To be alone again.

But despite knowing of the terror she'd just gone through, despite almost losing her, he couldn't reconcile remaining an active SEAL and having a family. They didn't go together well. Add in a woman who clearly had a problem with the lifestyle, a woman who couldn't stand to not know where her soldier was or even if he was alive—a woman like Nina—and it became impossible.

But he knew now that he wanted it all. Wanted the family. Wanted Nina.

So leave the team.

It was as simple as that. He'd leave the team.

It was time anyway. He didn't need the excitement in his life anymore. He had nothing to prove. He wasn't his father, and he never would be. Nina helped him see that. He'd have to figure out how to live his life after the team, but he didn't have to wait for that. He knew this was right.

"Marry me," he blurted out. "We'll figure everything else out. The logistics. All of that. I love you, Nina, and I don't want to be without you."

"Yes-s-s," she said, her teeth chattering. "I love you, too." Her eyes suddenly clouded with fear. "Oh, my gosh, I didn't ask about Ty. How's Ty?"

"Fine."

"And Fagan?"

"Not so fine," he answered, figuring she didn't need to know the details.

WITH QUINN HOLDING her, Nina's fear gradually abated and despite the deep cold making her entire body shiver, pain from her wrist nearly stole her breath. "I think I dislocated my wrist. It's hurting something awful."

"Let me see."

With Quinn's arm still around her, she leaned back and floated her hand between them. As soon as she lifted it, pain sliced through it. She groaned and let the water support it again.

Quinn frowned. "I'll splint it. Then we'll get some medical attention. I have to let you go to do that. Can you stand?"

She stepped back on her own. "I'm fine."

He removed his shirt and ripped off the sleeve, then located a small board and secured her wrist. "You okay to walk out of here?"

"I'd better be," she said with a laugh. "Or they'll have to cut a hole in the hotel floor."

"No problem." He grinned. "I'd demolish the whole place if I had to get you to safety." He led her up the steps and they moved down the passageway.

They stepped into the alley buzzing with activity. Connor and Becca stood near what she figured was Fagan's body, now covered with a tarp. Ty sat off to the side, a blanket over his shoulders. He caught sight of them, jumped to his feet, and ran toward them. "Nina, oh, man. Oh, wow. You're okay." He flung himself at her and hugged her hard. She felt his body convulsing with tears.

"Everything's okay now," she soothed.

He pulled back, then took his blanket and tenderly draped it over her shoulders.

Her heart melted at his concern. "Thank you, Ty."

He blushed, then looked at Quinn and punched his shoulder. "You're the man. You did it. You saved us both."

"No biggie." Quinn lifted a shoulder in an offhand shrug.

Ty took an awkward step toward his brother. Then another, his expression tentative.

"Aw, come here." Quinn scooped Ty into a quick hug then released him. It was as if they didn't know what to do next.

Fortunately, Becca and Connor chose that moment to join them. Connor clapped Quinn on the back. "Good job, man. Glad you were here."

"I second that," Becca said, reluctant appreciation in her voice.

"We'll have to cut through some red tape for the shooting," Connor said. "But you'll come out of it okay."

"We'll make sure of it." Becca changed her focus to Nina. "You okay? Looks like you hurt your arm."

"It's nothing, I . . ." Nina let her words drop off as her attention was drawn to the mouth of the alley where Sulyard turned the corner. "Guess you ended up calling him."

"Sorry. When things got ugly, I had to."

"No problem," Nina said. "I'd have done the same thing."

Sulyard stepped up to her. "Glad to see you all made it out okay."

She was surprised at his sentiment, but hid it and waited for him to go on.

"Lange played the recording of Fagan's confession. You're in the clear."

"That's good to hear," Quinn said, sharing a smile with Nina.

"I hope this clears Ty, too," Nina said.

Sulyard nodded. "And thanks to his help, I'm sure DHS will let him off with a stern warning."

"Hear that, bro?" Quinn's smile widened, and he dropped an arm around Ty's shoulders. "You're good to go."

"My hacking days are over." Ty peered at Quinn. "I promise."

"Of course they are. Mom won't let you near a computer until you're ninety." Quinn knuckled Ty's head.

"As much as I'm enjoying this sentimental family moment"— Sulyard's sarcasm was back—"we need to debrief all of you and get this situation buttoned down. Brandt, you'll see the medic first. The rest of you, we have cars waiting."

Quinn eyed Sulyard and fisted his hands. "I'm not leaving Nina."

"Relax, Rambo," Sulyard said, rubbing his jaw. "I'm giving you a pass on the punch you threw the other day, but if you try it again, you're going downtown in handcuffs."

"It that's what it takes," Quinn said, not backing down.

Nina appreciated Quinn's concern, but there was no way she was going to let him get into it with Sulyard when it wasn't necessary. She stepped between them and looked up at Quinn. "This is standard procedure, Quinn. They separate us so we don't talk about what happened and confuse our stories. So go with them, and I'll join you after they check out my wrist."

He didn't move.

"Please," she said. "I want you to do this."

"Fine," he agreed. "But I'm walking you to the ambulance first."

"Fine by me," Sulyard said.

Quinn took her hand and when Nina was seated on the ambulance bumper, he gave her a quick kiss, then faced the medic. "Take good care of my girl."

The "my girl" raised a few eyebrows, but not Nina's. Not this time. Some women might find it possessive, but to her, it said he was no longer afraid to commit.

The medic examined her wrist. Nina hadn't expected him to insist she take a quick trip to the ER, but he warned she could have permanent nerve damage if she didn't see a doctor. That quick trip turned into another one, this time to surgery to repair damaged ligaments and put her wrist back into place. As the anesthesia took hold, her last thoughts were of Quinn. He was going to be mad when he learned he hadn't been there for her again.

She could just see him. Rushing into the hospital demanding to see her.

No matter. She drifted further under the anesthesia. Kissing his anger away would be worth it.

QUINN STOOD OVER Nina's bed. He liked the chance to watch her while she slept, but he sure wasn't happy that he only had the opportunity because she'd been rushed to surgery. He ran a hand over her hair that had dried in tight ringlets. Even in an ugly hospital gown, she was a real beauty, and she was his. Finally.

She stirred, her long lashes blinking a few times before her eyes met his.

"Hey," she said, her Southern accent more pronounced and sexy as could be.

"Hey, yourself." He sat on her bed and took her good hand.

She smiled. "Guess I didn't get to the office, after all."

"No problem. Sulyard debriefed everyone and is standing by in the hallway to talk to you as soon as you're ready."

"He really wants to wrap this up, then."

"That and the guy actually seems worried about you."

"For real?"

"For real. He's been sitting with Becca and Kait. He has your shield and gun to give back to you."

Her brow arched. "Guess that means I'm not fired. I hope Kait and Becca aren't in a heap of trouble either."

"He's pretty much said there will be reprimands in all of your files, but that's the extent of things." Quinn shook his head. "I don't get the guy. He comes across as this real tough guy, and then he lets us all off the hook when he could throw the book at each one of us."

"That reminds me of someone else I know." She pressed her hand on his chest. "A real toughie who didn't want anyone to see he had a heart of gold—until today."

Quinn didn't like her comparing him to Sulyard, but he couldn't argue her point so he laid his hand over hers. "I've been thinking. Aren't proposals supposed to be sealed with a kiss? 'Cause we never got around to that part. Something about a bum wrist getting in the way."

Her lips tipped in a breath-stealing smile, and she lifted her good arm around his neck. "Nothing's in our way now." She drew him closer. "Nothing," she whispered.

Epilogue

SIX MONTHS LATER

The day dawned clear and bright, but Nina couldn't enjoy it. Not yet. She had a final mission to complete. A mission with Quinn.

He took her hand and wound his fingers with hers, her new engagement ring sparkling up at her. "Are you sure you want to do this? There's no rush, you know."

The houseboat swayed under her feet, and for once, she didn't feel a bit of panic. After six months of intense therapy, she was ready to get into the river. Who better to try it with than the man who was to become her husband?

"You don't have to prove anything to anyone." He shook his head. "I had to learn that the hard way, but you don't."

"I'm not trying to prove anything. I simply want to put this behind me."

"Okay." He sounded unsure.

"Hey, don't worry so much. I might have a hard time doing this alone, but you're here." She freed her hand. "Let's do it."

She stepped over to the ladder at the edge of the deck. She put her foot on the top step and felt only a sliver of apprehension. It was hard to believe she'd been so afraid when she'd stayed on this boat with Quinn and Ty.

Of course, today she wore a life jacket and had had several sessions of desensitization therapy using a swimming pool to get to this point. With Quinn watching over her, she stepped down the rungs into the fifty-degree water, shocking her system.

She shivered. Quinn frowned and lunged off the deck, coming up beside her.

"Are you all right?" He treaded water and held her.

She laughed at his over-protective reaction. "I hadn't expected it to be this cold." She squeezed his bicep and grinned. "Relax. Nothing bad is going to happen to me with a SEAL by my side."

"About that." His forehead furrowed, giving her a moment's concern. "You're not actually with a SEAL right now."

"What are you talking about?"

"I left the team."

She punched him in the chest. "Stop kidding me."

"I'm not kidding. I left the team."

"But why? When?"

"Yesterday was my last day. My heart wasn't in it anymore. It hadn't been since the accident."

She'd wished for this day, but now that it arrived, she wondered if she'd forced him into it. "I'm sorry, Quinn. I know how much you loved being on the team. I hope you didn't do this for me."

"Things are different now. I'm ready for the change."

"Honestly?"

He nodded and smiled sincerely.

She gave him a quick hug. "So what are you going to do? Maybe you could train SEALs. You'd be good at that."

"I didn't just leave the team." He met her gaze. "I took a medical discharge."

She pushed back to get a good look at him. "A discharge. You left the Navy? Completely? But you're a soldier. Now what will you do?"

"How would you feel about me joining the Multnomah County River Patrol? They tell me I meet the qualifications."

"Are you kidding? You'd move here, to Portland? Work here?"

"Be married to you here," he added with a smile.

"Yes, especially the last bit." She frowned. "But is that really what you want to do? After all you've done and seen, it would seem so tame. I know those guys have to wear several hats because of funding, which means you'd likely have to spend a good bit of time on patrol. If it's not really what you want to do, I could move anywhere you found a job. It might take some time, but I—"

"Shh." He pressed his finger against her lips. "Though I appreciate your willingness to sacrifice your job, there's no need. I honestly want to be here in Portland. To be around for Ty and my mom. And I want a job that doesn't take me away from you. So this is a perfect fit, as far as I can see."

"You're certain you'll like the river patrol?" she asked, wanting to make sure he wouldn't some day come to resent her for this decision.

"Water. Boats that go fast. Diving in dangerous situations." His eyes sparkled with mischief. "What's not to like?"

"Exactly," she said and kissed his forehead. His cheek. The tip of his nose. She pushed off from him, swimming in the strong current, then turned with an impish grin of her own and splashed water at him. "What's not to like?"

The End

Acknowledgements

Additional thanks to:

My super agent Chip MacGregor whose book-publishing knowledge knows no bounds. Without you, this series wouldn't have become a reality, and your ongoing support in bringing my books to market and steering my writing career is priceless.

The very generous Ron Norris who gives of his time and knowledge in police and military procedures, weaponry details, and information technology. As a retired police officer with the LaVerne Police Department and a Certified Information Security Professional, your experience and knowledge are invaluable. You go above and beyond and I can't thank you enough! Any errors in or liberties taken with the technical details Ron so patiently explained to me are all my doing.

And last but not least, to the Portland FBI agents and staff for sharing your knowledge and expertise at the Citizen's Academy. I am forever grateful for the opportunity to learn more about what you do and how you do it. I am in awe of your skills, dedication, and willingness to put others before yourselves.

About the Author

Susan Sleeman is a best-selling author of clean read and inspirational romantic suspense books. Awards include *Thread of Suspicion*—2013 Romantic Times Reviewers Choice Best Book Award, and *No Way Out* and *The Christmas Witness*, Daphne du Maurier Award for Excellence finalists.

Susan grew up in a small Wisconsin town where she spent her summers reading Nancy Drew and developing a love of mystery and suspense books. Today, she channels this enthusiasm into writing novels and hosting the popular internet website TheSuspenseZone.com.

Susan currently lives in Oregon, but she and her husband have had the pleasure of living in nine states. They have two beautiful daughters, a very special son-in-law, and an adorable grandson.

To learn more about Susan stop by any of these locations on the web.

Website: susansleeman.com

facebook.com/SusanSleemanBooks

twitter.com/SusanSleeman

Made in the USA
Middletown, DE
29 October 2017